Set the World on Fire

The Complete Duet

By: E. Molgaard

Table of Contents

THE SET THE WORLD ON FIRE DUET BOOK ONE

Ignite
THE FIRE

E. MOLGAARD

Ignite the Fire

The Set the World on Fire Duet
Book One

By: E. Molgaard

Note to Readers

This is a reverse harem romance which means the female main character has more than one love interest and she doesn't choose between them. There are dark themes in this book that can be triggering such as kidnapping, abuse, threats of rape, rape, child abuse, torture, and murder. Please feel free to message me directly if you have any concerns or questions.

About the Book

My name is Riona Murphy and I'm the daughter of the Captain of the Murphy Clan. As a mafia princess, I'm forced to have two faces. The fake innocent princess that everyone sees and the real ruthless killer that lurks in the dark.

At least that's the case until my best friend, Aisling, was taken. Now my mask is down and my daggers are clean. No one is going to stop me from tearing this city apart to find her.

My only problem, or should I say three problems, are the gorgeous Italians that have sworn to help me find her. With each day I spend with them, I find myself being pulled in by Enzo's sweet charm, Matteo's pure sex appeal, and Dante's dark stares.

When I let them into my bed, it was supposed to be just fun. Temporary.

I definitely wasn't supposed to fall for them. Now I'm caught between two families. Pulling toward one while being pulled by the other.
Who will win? Me or my Captain?

Prologue

Riona

Tonight is the annual Murphy Gala. A night that all allies and enemies within the top crime families in New York come together without any violence. Really, it's a night to show everyone how powerful you are and we, the Murphys, are at the top. Which means my perfect princess face needs to be on point. I set my curling iron down, taking in the loose curls that fall across my shoulders, with my neutral makeup, showing off my pale skin, and making me look like an Irish Barbie.

God, I hate when I have to become this persona my father created. The innocent Irish princess that is perfect with a shy smile.

It makes me look weak. And that's not me at all. I'm more of a straight hair, dark makeup and dark, skin-tight clothes kind of girl, with a fiery attitude and a lust for bloody justice. But I can't be me. Why? Nobody looks twice at a quiet, pure princess in my world, so their lips are always loose. And as the daughter to the head of the Murphy Clan, my power is knowledge. I collect everyone's secrets.

I start braiding my deep red waves in a loose side braid, finalizing my good girl look. "Riona."

"Yes, Father?" Through the mirror I watch my father, Lorcan Murphy, in his all-black tux that highlights his salt and pepper hair. For being almost 60 years old, his hair is the only thing that shows his age.

He walks into my bathroom and stands behind me. "You look very *pretty*." I narrow my eyes at him because he knows I hate being called pretty. It's so condescending when he says it. "I have a job tonight for you."

My green eyes connect with his identical ones in the mirror, and our father-daughter relationship immediately turns to business. "There's supposed to be no violence tonight."

His smirk from when he called me pretty disappears into a fierce glare. There is no talking him out of this. "It's my party. I can do whatever I want. Are you telling me you won't do it?"

"No. Who's the mark?" My power might be knowledge, but it's not my only one.

"Carl O'Brien. He's a traitor and a snitch. I don't want another day to come where he's breathing." Lorcan requires two things from everyone. Loyalty and keeping your mouth shut. You fail at one, you die. Carl failed at both.

I turn around, facing him, and lean back on the counter. "You want it done quietly?"

My father smiles at me with so much pride. "I knew you'd be the one for this."

"I'm your only assassin." Oh yeah. I'm my father's assassin. Secret assassin. Nobody knows outside the family. Hence the princess cover. "Do you want him going down here or a delayed death?"

"Here. But near the end."

"Yes, sir."

He gives me a nod and heads out of my bathroom. "Finish up getting ready and get what you need, then meet your brother and me in my office."

I give him a nod. "I'll be there in 15 minutes."

Wrapping a tie around the end of my braid, I head into my closet. My closet has two sides. One side is filled with my true style: leather pants, ripped skinny jeans, crop tops, low cut tops, and short dresses. The other side is for my fake identity. It's filled with evening gowns and conservative blouses and jeans.

Removing my robe, I grab tonight's emerald green evening gown, my signature color, off the hanger and step into it, pulling it up my body. I zip it up, stopping halfway up my back, and hooking the top at the back of my neck, completing the high neckline, A-line gown. The dress has a silk underlay with the top layer covered in lace flowers. Looking at myself in my full-length mirror, I place a sweet smile across my face, completing the image. I really do look like a princess, a Disney princess ready to find her prince. I chuckle to myself at that thought. I won't be finding any princes tonight.

Turning away from the mirror, a genuine smile comes across my face as I open a secret door in the back of my closet, revealing all my favorite weapons. Now these are the things that complete me. The first thing I grab are my favorite daggers and I strap them to my thigh. You always need to be prepared in this world. Then I pull open a drawer with my deadly jewelry to pick my green emerald ring that has a hidden needle in it. With careful hands, I let two drops of my choice of poison fall onto the needle and flip the stone over it before sliding it on my finger. My 15 minutes are coming to an end, so I step into my heels and leave my closet.

Stepping out of my room, I come face-to-face with my bodyguard, Steve. I don't really need him, but father insists, since it helps keep the princess image and that is what Steve thinks I am. He has no idea of my secret exit from the house for my more deadly missions. "Hi, Steve."

"Evening, Miss Murphy." He smiles brightly as he stands from leaning against the wall and straightens his black suit jacket. "You look beautiful."

I give him a strained smile as I look him over. He's always well put together, his auburn hair cut close, his face clean shaven, and not a wrinkle on his suit. He dresses perfectly for his job to blend in and be forgotten. "Thank you."

We both head down the hall toward my father's office. "Tonight you can hang back. Watch from afar." In order to get what needs to be done tonight I can't have a shadow.

"I'm supposed to protect you." There's concern in his eyes, but it's not needed.

"Tonight there's peace. There's no danger. Please stand in the corner. If I need you, I'll let you know. Plus, how am I going to be approached when I have a handsome man shadowing me all night?" I sweeten my smile so he'll believe my lie and he'll give me space.

"Of course, Miss. I'll keep an eye on you from a distance."

"Thank you, Steve." We stop outside my father's office door. "You can go to the party now. I'm walking in with my father and brother."

Steve gives me a nod and walks away. I give the door a single knock before pushing it open and walking in. My father and brother, Killian, are both sitting on the leather couch with a glass of whiskey in their hands. "You look beautiful, Riona. And I mean that."

"Thank you, Father."

"Yes, your princess face is fully in place." Killian mocks my fake appearance because he knows how much I hate it. "One day you'll be able to walk into these parties like the badass that you are."

"Yeah right. That's never going to happen. If anything is going to change, it'll be me walking in with my husband because father has sold me off for an alliance," I joke.

My father sets his drink down and stands up. "Well at least you know that's a possibility." He straightens his tux as he walks toward me. "But no matter who you marry, you'll always be a Murphy. Now let's go make our entrance. Show everyone how strong we are." Killian stands from the couch and straightens his tux. He looks just like our father, with his dark hair styled back and stern face in place. I loop my arm through my father's and Killian walks shoulder to shoulder with him on his other side as we head into our annual party.

My role as princess has been in full force tonight. I've smiled and spoken to all our guests. I've danced with all our allies and the sons of the other families in attendance. But my true mission for tonight hasn't had a chance to be planned out yet.

I'm currently dancing with Ivan Volkov's, the head of the Bratva, son, Maxim, and he is really driving me crazy. I've danced with him several times tonight and all he can talk about is how awesome he is at everything. And I mean everything. His not-so-subtle hints that he'd rock my world are absolutely disgusting and laughable. The word on the street is that he has a tiny cock and only lasts seconds inside a woman.

Finally, the song ends and I step out of his hold, but he quickly grabs my wrist, stopping me from leaving. "Where are you going? I'm not done dancing with you."

"I'm sorry, but I'm done dancing with you." His grip tightens to almost painful, and I hold back everything in me so I don't kill him for touching me like this. Instead, I have to play weak. Tears pool in my eyes as I blink at him timidly when I'm actually picturing his tall, lanky body hanging upside down and slitting his throat so his blood can stain his bleach blonde hair. "You're hurting me."

I try to pull away again but when I step back, I bump into someone. Turning, I find the one person I've been looking for all night. Carl O'Brien. He smiles down at me and then eyes Maxim's hold on my wrist. "May I have this dance?"

Maxim lets go of my wrist, storming off, and I smile up at the seventy-year-old man with gray hair and large belly. "Thank you."

He takes my hand, holding it in his and sets his other on my waist. I rotate my ring around as I place my hand on his shoulder. Looking past him, I see Steve making his way over. Our eyes lock, and I give him a head shake telling him to step back. Following orders, he stops walking toward me and heads for the wall. With Steve handled, I focus on dancing with Carl. "Are you having fun at the party?"

"Yes. Especially now. I've never had the pleasure of dancing with the princess at any of the others."

I fake being bashful by dropping my eyes and giving him a coy smile. "I'm not special."

"That isn't true." Carl tightens his hold on me and moves us in a quick circle, giving me the perfect opportunity. I fake a joyous laugh and trip over his feet as I scrape his skin with the poisonous needle.

"Oh my. I'm so sorry. The adrenaline from earlier must be draining me. I should probably go sit down." I act like I'm dizzy as Carl holds me like he's truly concerned for me.

"Absolutely. Let me help you."

"Oh no..."

Steve shows up at that moment. "I'll help her."

I give him a small nod and turn to Carl. "Thank you for the dance, Mr. O'Brien."

I step away from him and head to my father's sitting area with Steve hovering by my side, making sure people move out of my way. When we get to the couch, I give my father a subtle nod telling him it's done and sit down next to him. "Are you done dancing for the night, Riona?"

"Yes. It is quite exhausting." A server comes by with a tray of champagne and I grab a glass.

His eyes scan over the crowd. "Find any suitable suitors."

"Not the Bratva, Maxim. He grabbed my wrist when I wanted to stop dancing with him." I lean in closer to him. "Can I please poison him too?"

He chuckles. "Not tonight, Riona. But if he ever touches you again, kill him."

"Thank you, Father." We've always bonded over my darker side.

"Do you have enough energy to dance with your loving father?"

"Of course." I smile at him.

He stands, reaching his hand out and I happily take it. My father walks me to the dance floor, and we step into a familiar hold and start gliding across the floor. I've always loved dancing with him. It's the only time I can truly let my walls down because he's the only man to 100% have my back. My father twirls me in a circle and I let out a giggle. "What a beautiful sound. You should definitely laugh more often."

"This world is too dark for laughter."

"Your mother and I used to laugh all the time. When you find your person, you'll find the joy in laughing." The mention of my mother makes my heart hurt. She died fifteen years ago from an attack. Her and my father's second, Drew, were murdered trying to protect me, Killian, and his daughter, Aisling. They locked us in a room and ran, trying to draw our enemies away from us. They were forced into oncoming traffic and hit an 18-wheeler head on.

"One day. Maybe."

All of a sudden, a scream fills the room and all heads turn toward it. A lady I don't know is kneeling down next to Carl, who is on the floor, clutching his chest. "Someone call 911!" someone else yells.

My father's men all file into the room surrounding the body and I stand on the edge of the circle as Carl's son moves next to his father's body and tries to help him, but it's too late. Everyone watches as Carl O'Brien takes his last breath and moments later the EMTs come running into our ballroom and try to restart his heart. They won't be able to though.

People quickly start to disperse as the EMTs roll Carl's body onto a stretcher. Killian appears next to me as father tries to comfort Carl's family. "I guess the party's over."

Chapter One

Riona

"Riona!"

"Aisling!"

I can't help the smile that forms on my face as my best friend, my soul sister, calls out for me. "Where is that fine ass I've missed so much?"

I look over my shoulder as she steps into my closet, looking fantastic with her wavy strawberry blonde hair falling over her shoulders, her face void of makeup, showing off her freckles, and wearing a blue summer dress. Aisling and I grew up together, and after her mother died when she was an infant and her father died with my mom, my father took her in and raised her. "You're in the wrong room if you're looking for the Murphy ass you've been missing."

Lust fills her blue eyes as she thinks of my brother. While I had my best friend growing up, my brother had his lover, soulmate, and future wife. They've been together for as long as I can remember and they're disgustingly cute together. "I'll see his ass later and it'll be naked along with the rest of him."

I scrunch up my face, grossed out. "You know you can't talk about my brother to me like that."

She chuckles and nods her head toward the knife I'm cleaning. "As your new attorney, I can't be a witness to this if you're cleaning off blood from someone you killed."

I look down at the knife and smile at my reflection on the blade. "It's not. Just my training partners. It was a small scratch. But it did bleed a lot." I give her a wicked grin as I set down the knife.

"So bad. How do you keep your training partners when you almost kill them?"

"I pay them well. And if they left, I'd have to actually kill them."

I walk over to her and give her a hug. "I've missed you, Ash. Congratulations on finishing law school. Sorry we couldn't be there for the ceremony."

"I skipped the ceremony because a very handsome brother of yours gave me a surprise visit." That explains where Killian disappeared to a couple of days ago.

"I'm sure he gave you more than one surprise."

She closes her eyes like she's reliving it. "Oh yes. All night long."

"Okay." I throw my cleaning cloth at her. "That is as much as I can take. Are you ready for a girls' night of celebrating?"

"Hell yeah. I need to get drunk. And so do you. Killian has said you aren't getting out as much."

I shrug my shoulders. "I've been busy."

"Well, you need to chill out. Killing takes a part of your soul. I don't want it to consume you."

I look away from her concerned face. "I know. Father is keeping something from me and every time I try to bring it up, he tells me to know my place like I'm not a part of this clan. Ever since the gala, he calls on me less and less. I'm getting bloodthirsty and killing slimeballs is the only thing that helps."

"Then we're going to let loose tonight and use your other favorite outlet." She gives me a wicked grin, telling me she's going to get me into trouble.

"Don't let Killian hear you say that."

"Oh please. A little jealousy won't kill him. Plus, I'll just be dancing. You're the one that needs to get laid." She turns to the side of my closet that holds my favorite outfits and runs her hands over the dresses that hide nothing. "Now let's find something that'll make all the men tonight beg at your feet."

Aisling holds up her shot. "To you finding a fine ass man tonight."

"To you finally stepping over to the dark side." I tap my shot to hers and, in sync, we tap the glasses to the bar and then take them.

"We grew up on the dark side."

"True. Now you get to dirty your hands by bending the law."

The bartender drops off two more shots and points to two guys down the bar. They raise their shots to us with hunger in their eyes. These two are a good start to the night. "Oh, tonight's going to be fun."

We both take the shots and then make our way to the middle of the dance floor. Within seconds, I lose myself in the music and the bodies surrounding us. I really did need a night where I can get out of my head for a while. Not be a mafia princess or assassin. Just a 23-year-old having a good time with her best friend.

I place both of my hands on Aisling shoulders as our bodies dance together. "Ohh... someone's finally onboard with having some sexy fun."

"Are you going to stop me?"

"Never. Wild Riona is one of my favorites." She looks over my shoulder with an excited smile. "It looks like your first contestant is stepping up now. Let's see if he is your lucky winner tonight." I roll my eyes at her acting like this is a game show.

"Hello, beautiful ladies! Can I be the meat to your sandwich?"

"No." Aisling and I both say at the same time while I let him see how grossed out I am by his pickup line.

"Fucking bitches." He glares at us before walking away.

"Contestant number one has been eliminated." We both crack up laughing.

"Hopefully there are better options than that. If not, you're going to warm my bed tonight."

I pull her into a swaying hug, and she pushes me off. "You wish."

We both chuckle but movement along the wall near the VIP area has my smile falling as I watch Maxim Volkov walk past the security guard that is holding the rope open for him and his guys. God, I hope he doesn't see me tonight. I can't deal with him. Ever since the gala, he's been coming on strong, constantly making passes at me.

Aisling looks around trying to figure out what caught my attention. "What is it? Do you see contestant two?"

"No, I see an entitled Russian asshole."

She rolls her eyes as she finds him in the crowd. "Ignore him. We're not mafia tonight so mafia problems don't exist." The song changes to something with a deep bass and I pull Aisling to me, and we dance in slow seductive movements. "I wish Killian could dance like this. It would be great foreplay."

33

"Oh please. It'd be the fastest foreplay ever. He'd pull you into a dark corner within seconds." They're the cute high school sweethearts that are all over each other every second of the day, even if they gross out the people around them. Specifically me.

A cute boy-next-door-looking guy moves his way over to us with his eyes on Aisling. "It looks like you have your first contestant."

Aisling looks over to the guy just as he reaches us. "Hi. Do you mind if I join you?"

"I'm actually taken." Aisling holds up her hand, showing her engagement ring Killian gave her last summer.

The cute blonde holds up his hand showing a wedding band. "Me too." He nods behind us and we both turn to see a muscular man standing on the edge of the dance floor at the railing. He smiles with a nod while raising his glass, giving his silent permission.

"Okay." Aisling shrugs her shoulders and takes the blonde's outreached hand.

I step back from them, pointing toward the bar. "I'm going to get us some drinks." Aisling gives me a nod and I turn away from her.

I have to move through what feels like hundreds of people to get to the edge of the dance floor, but once I do, I'm greeted with a massive crowd surrounding the large bar. Well, this is going to take forever. Walking the length of the bar, I try to find an opening. I'm just about to give up and head back to the dance floor when two guys walk away, leaving a small opening. I quickly slide into the spot before it disappears and lean on the bar top. Standing up on my toes, I look up and down the bar for the bartender.

"It's going to be awhile." I turn toward the deep voice, wondering if he was talking to me, and my breath catches at the tall dirty blonde hair and brown eyed man that is standing just inches away from me.

My skin tingles at his closeness and I fight myself not to lean into him. "Why do you say that?"

He leans on the bar next to me, brushing his arm against mine. A shiver runs through me as he leans across me to point to one of the bartenders. "That guy has only been working that end of the bar because of all the girls giggling over him." He points to the other end of the bar. "She hasn't left that end because she's talking to that guy."

Seeing exactly what he means, I lean back and take in this mystery guy that has me wondering if Aisling could be right about the trouble I could get into. "Well shouldn't there be a third bartender?"

"You'd think." A hint of disappointment flashes in his eyes like he's filing my comment away.

"How long have you been standing here?"

He looks down at his watch. "A couple minutes."

I move closer to him as I lean on the bar with my hip. "So how do we get our drinks?"

"I have an idea." A wicked sexy smile forms on his face.

I think I'd agree to anything right now. "Okay?"

"*You* need to get his attention." Or we could be taking advantage of the open bar top.

"Why me?"

His eyes roam up and down my body and I wish I was wearing a dress instead of this romper. Easier access for whatever he wants to do to me. "Because he won't be able to turn away from someone as beautiful as you."

My cheeks flush picturing what he could do to me out here in the open. I shake my head, wiping that thought away and focus on him and his plan. "How do you expect me to do that?"

"Make him think you're interested."

"Like this." I step closer to him, placing my hand on his chest. I feel his chest expand as I rise up on my toes and skim my lips up his neck.

His hand goes to my hip, fisting my romper and pulling me closer. "I'm not sure you'll be able to get this close to him."

I chuckle. "Good, it's not him I want to touch."

I pull away, standing flat on my feet, and turn back toward the bar. My Mystery Man doesn't remove his hand from my body, as he steps behind, pressing his body to mine so I can feel everything. I take a breath, forcing myself to watch the bartender, and not melt into the stranger behind me, as he finishes up a drink order. Before he could take another, I let out a whistle as I lean the top half of my body across the bar top, making sure my breasts look like they're about to fall out.

His head turns my way and I give him a little finger wave with a sexy come to me smile. "Hook, line…" The bartenders' eyes go directly to my breasts, and he gives me a cocky smirk before swaggering over to me. "And sinker."

My Mystery Man whispers into my ear, "You're a goddess, Beauty."

I bite my bottom lip to stop a moan from escaping. The bartender thinks it's for him and I play it up by running my finger along the edge of my romper down my chest, in between my breasts, to where my deep V stops. The bartender stops in front of me with his eyes zeroed in on my breasts. "What can I get you, dollface?" Ugh. Really. I have to fight myself not to scrunch up my face in disgust. "I'll take three gin and tonics and..." I look to my Mystery Man.

"Three Eagle Rares."

I cock my head to the side with a sweet smile. "You heard him."

The bartender isn't even fazed by my Mystery Man. He tries to show off by mixing my drinks and pouring the three bourbons but I'm not really paying attention to him. My attention is on the man behind me as I wait for his next touch. The bartender sets down our drinks and leans toward me. "What are you doing after this, cutie?" I lose my smile instantly and glare at him. Why don't guys realize that word is demeaning? I'm not a little girl or a puppy.

So I don't blow up on the bartender; I just turn away from him and walk away. But I do hear my Mystery Man say, "Not you, man."

I chuckle as I look over my shoulder to my Mystery Man. He smirks at me as he raises one of his bourbons.

Looking away from him, I move through the crowd back to Aisling. She smiles at me as I break through the crowd. "What took so long?"

I smile at her, excited to see how this night will end. "I might've found a true contestant."

"Oh my god! Where?" I look back to the bar, ready to point him out, but he's nowhere to be seen.

Chapter Two

Riona

"Here is the next round." Mike, Simon's big buff husband, walks over with four drinks. With my previous drink long gone, I could really use this one.

"Are you finally done watching?" Simon steps up to his man, taking two drinks from him and handing them to us.

They don't break eye contact as they instantly start dancing in sync with each other. "You know I love watching you."

Mike slams his mouth to Simon's. Oh shit. I look at Aisling and she is fanning herself. "That's hot." She looks at me. "Do you think I could get Killian to make out with a guy?"

I crack up laughing. "No. I don't."

Aisling pouts for a second then shrugs her shoulders. "I probably wouldn't like it. I'd get jealous."

I shake my head at her and take a sip of my new drink. Closing my eyes, I try to lose myself in the music and enjoy being normal. Feeling eyes on me, I reopen them and scan the crowd, hoping it's my Mystery Man because I haven't seen him again.

Instead, my eyes connect to another tall and handsome man with dark features as he makes his way toward me. As he approaches, I run my eyes over him, taking in his gray slacks and white button-up with his sleeves rolled up and the top few buttons undone. God, he is sexy. And sexy in a different way than Mystery Man. Mystery Man had his light touches and sexy smirk. This guy is steaming hot, in-your-face, sex appeal.

Mr. Sex Appeal approaches our group and Aisling looks him up and down as the guy smiles down at me and extends his hand out. Aisling smiles at me from ear to ear as she gives me a thumbs up and mouths 'contestant two'.

I slide my hand into his and he pulls me into his body. We move together instantly and all I want to do is run my hands all over him. So that's what I do. Looking up at him, I watch his face as I run my hands up his arms, over his shoulders, and down his chest. He is all muscle. He also isn't shy about touching me either. His eyes flare with desire at my touch and as his hands run down my sides and rest just above my ass. "Do you know how beautiful you are?"

My body heats at his question because there is something about it that is about more than my looks. Mr. Sex Appeal takes one of my hands in his and turns me so my back is to his chest and our conjoined hands are across my stomach, holding me to him.

His scruff rubs against the edge of my ear as he whispers, "All these people can't keep their eyes off you. But they can't touch. They all want to bow at your feet, Princess." For the first time ever, someone calling me princess sends a shiver of desire through me.

I squeeze his hand as I melt into him, feeling how hard his muscles are. And I do mean *all of him*. I grind against his hardening length and he curses next to my ear. "God. You make me want to say fuck it."

"So, say it. What's so wrong with going after what you want?"

He growls next to my ear before kissing the spot right behind it. "So many things." He unlinks our fingers. "Thanks for the dance, Princess."

His body moves away from mine and when I turn to look for him, he's gone. How did he disappear so fast?

I stand there looking through the crowd of people dancing to hopefully see his retreating body.

"Hey. Where did contestant two go?"

"I don't know." How have I let two gorgeous men vanish on me?

I look back to Aisling and she's looking down at her phone. "Killian is here. He wants me to meet him outside."

"Go. I'm going to head to the bathroom." I point behind me to the back corner. "Meet you back here?"

She nods and we go in separate directions. I start my way through the dancing crowd for the second time tonight. Right as I get to the edge of the crowd, a guy bumps into my shoulder, knocking me off balance a little, but he grabs my hand to steady me. Looking up at him, my breath catches at the sight of his bright blue eyes that contrast against the dark shadow over his face. But before I can say anything, he turns away and the crowd swallows him.

I shake my head, snapping myself out of another strange encounter with a sexy mysterious man. I'm heading in the direction of the bathroom again when I realize there is something in my hand. A piece of paper. I slowly open it and a shiver of worry runs through me.

Maxim is coming for you.

Looking up from the paper, I do a quick spin, looking for Maxim or the guy who gave me the note. I can't find either of them and for the first time tonight I wish I had my weapons. At least Killian is here now. I just need to go to the bathroom and get back to them because he is definitely carrying.

The bathroom is surprisingly empty when I push the door in. So empty that I do a double check to make sure there isn't a sign on the door stating out of order. With the door empty of a sign, I take the blessing and choose the biggest stall. One thing I hate about rompers is that you have to completely undress to go to the bathroom. And since I can't wear a bra or panties with this outfit, I have to get completely naked.

I quickly go to the bathroom and redress because I'm feeling vulnerable right now. The state of undress, the quiet, the threat of Maxim is making me want to get around people again. Just as I get my romper back into place, the bathroom door opens, letting in the sound of the club and then silence fills the room as the door closes again. A cold chill runs through my body at the sound of boots walking toward me. Black boots appear under my door stall and I take a few steps back because I know they aren't going to wait for me to open the door and I don't want to be incapacitated by the door.

"Hello, Princess." Disgust rolls through me at the Russian accent.

"Maxim." He must feel the hatred in my voice because he kicks the stall door in.

"I don't have to hurt you, Princess. Come with me willingly, be my wife, and I won't have to force the decision on you." His almost black eyes rake over me as he runs his fingers through his blonde hair, a creepy smile on his face.

God, he's an idiot. "What, you're going to rape me to get me to say yes? I'm not a virgin. I don't have to marry the man I choose to sleep with."

He takes a step closer to me as he undresses me with his eyes. "Would it be rape if you enjoyed it in the end?" Yes. Yes, it would.

"If you have to force women into sex then the answer is yes. Plus, would I enjoy it?" I hold up my pinky. "I bet your pinky dick can't make any women come."

Maxim storms to me, pushing me up against the wall with his hand around my neck. "Why can't you see that with you being the Clan princess and me being the Bratva prince that us together could give me so much power."

"I'm never giving my power to anyone. Especially you."

I take that moment to hit his hand away from my neck and throw my other fist into Maxim's face. He takes a couple steps back, shaking off my punch and the shock on his face feels great. He has no idea who he's messing with. Not taking a second to breathe, I continue to go at him. He's not down yet, so I'm not leaving.

Maxim recovers faster than I thought and while I go for another face shot, he takes a swing at my ribs. There is a crunch of bone when our fists connect and my breath is knocked out of me as I stumble back, hoping the crunch wasn't my ribs. His hit had more power than I expected for a tall, skinny man that has never worked for anything in his life. Looking up at Maxim, I see him holding his nose as blood runs down his face. Good, I broke his nose. Tears start pooling in his eyes and I bet he's never broken his nose before. Such a pansy prince. He wants all this power, but he's never worked for it.

Pride washes through me and I charge at him again with one last punch, knocking him out. Standing over his unconscious body, it takes everything in me not to kill him. Instead, I bend down next to him with disgust. "Next time I see you, I'll kill you."

Leaving him on the floor, I head for the sink. As I wash my hands, I look at myself in the mirror, making sure I don't look rattled. After drying my hands, I situate my romper and hair and leave Maxim for someone to find. Not caring who I piss off, I push my way through the dance floor to where our group is. When I finally get to Mike and Simon, I instantly look for Aisling and Killian, but they aren't there. "Where's Aisling?" I ask Simon.

He shrugs his shoulders. "She hasn't come back since going to find her man."

Dread instantly sinks in my stomach. Something isn't right. Pulling out my phone, I hit her name as I make my way to the front of the club. Aisling's phone just rings without her voicemail picking up and I hang up and call again as I step outside. Looking left and right, I try to spot them. They better not be fucking in his car. When she doesn't answer, I hang up and start calling out her name as I walk down the sidewalk.

Clicking my brother's contact, I curse silently because something isn't right. Killian answers on the second ring. "I know. I'm late. I'm just around the corner."

"You mean you're not here? Aisling isn't with you?" I turn in a circle looking for her.

"What are you talking about? No, Aisling isn't with me."

"Killian. You texted that you were here like ten minutes ago. She came out to meet you."

Worry fills his voice. "I haven't texted her since before you left."

45

"Killian, get here now." I hang up on him and yell out for Aisling. I try her phone again, but this time I hear her phone's ringtone. "Aisling?" I run toward the sound of her ringtone. At the edge of the alley, a car comes to a screeching stop next to me and I brace myself for a fight, but then Killian steps out of the driver's seat.

"Have you found her?"

I shake my head frantically. "Her phone was ringing down the alley." Killian pulls a gun from behind his back, and I point at it. "You got one for me?"

Killian hands me a gun as we meet in front of his car. His headlights light up the alley as we walk down it with our guns in front of us. Aisling's ringtone echoes throughout the alley. With each step we take down the alley, my stomach sinks further. There is no way Aisling would willingly go into a dark alley by herself. "Killian."

"I know. I've already called Father."

We find her phone behind the third dumpster, with her clutch, but Aisling isn't here. "Fuck," Killian yells out and punches the side of the dumpster. "You were supposed to stay together, Riona. Why weren't you with her?"

"She was coming to get you. Don't blame me. I was being attacked by the Bratva asshole in the bathroom."

"Kids, that's enough." Killian and I shut our mouths instantly at the sound of our father's voice. We both turn to him, and he looks me over. "What happened? Briefly."

"Aisling received a text from Killian saying he was here and to meet him outside. She left to meet him while I went to the bathroom. Maxim attacked me in there. After I knocked him out, I went back to where we were supposed to meet and they weren't there. I came out here to find her, while trying to call. When I didn't reach her, I tried Killian." No need to say anything else. Aisling isn't here.

"Okay, I'll handle this and Maxim. Go home, Riona."

What? I'm not going. I can find her. "But..."

"Go home," he orders with a glare, telling me to not question him right now. Bowing my head, I walk out of the alley, past my father's men, to the waiting Mercedes with Steve holding the back door open. "Miss Murphy."

"Steve." I give him a nod and slide into the backseat.

I hate being dismissed but at least once I get home, I can start my search for Aisling. I'll burn this city to the ground to find her and I know Killian will be at my side.

Chapter Three

Riona

"Riona, we're back." Killian walks up behind me, looking over me as I try to find something. "Find anything yet?"

"I've hacked the security feed of the club and surrounding streets. I've watched her get taken so many times now. I can't tell who took her."

I look up at my brother and the sadness in our eyes match. "Do you want to see?"

"Not now. Father wants to see you. We also have company."

"Company that requires me to change?" He knows I'm asking if I need to put on my princess face.

"No."

I follow my brother out of my room and toward my father's office. "I'm following where the car that took her went. I lost it within a one block radius downtown. I'm now going to backtrack for smaller cameras. There's a parking garage there."

When we reach my father's door, I grab his hand pulling him to a stop. "I'm going to find her."

"If anyone can, it's you. I'm worried what state she'll be in when we do find her." As he looks at me, I can tell he's tormented by the thoughts of what they could be doing to her. Women in our lives are never not touched when taken. I know this better than anyone. I push down all memories of my past because I need to be strong right now, for Aisling.

I knock once before opening the door. "Father..." I stop dead in my tracks. Standing across from my father is Mystery Man, Mr. Sex Appeal, and the guy who gave me the note. What the fuck? "Why are they here?"

"Riona, meet the Russo brothers."

I look at them with suspicion. It's too convenient that they were at the club and are here right now. "Italian mob." Mr. Sex Appeal gives me a smirk, next to Note Guy, with Mystery Man standing on the other side. I fix my stare on them before turning my back on them to face my father. "Why are they here?"

He leans against the front of his desk with his arms crossed. "You're going with them."

What? There's no way I heard him right? He can't be shipping me off. "I'm what?"

"You were attacked tonight and the pending threat on your life just tripled. They'll protect you."

I'm so confused. "Threat? What fucking threat?"

"Ever since you killed Carl O'Brien, someone has been happily letting me know how much they want to kill you."

"How could you not tell me there was a credible threat against me? I went out unprotected tonight with Aisling. And those men…" I point to the brothers behind me, "were there tonight; how do you know they aren't a part of this?"

He's looking at me with no emotions, even though my life is in danger and Aisling, the girl he raised, has been taken. "You were in their club. And I asked them to keep an eye on you."

Oh yeah. Just an eye. I look over my shoulder at Mr. Sex Appeal, remembering his hands on me hours ago. "If they were watching, why didn't they stop this?"

"They were instructed to watch you."

Realization sets in and I step away from my father. "How could you leave her unprotected?"

Killian steps up to our father, getting in his face, making him stand to his full height to glare down at his son. "You didn't, right? Tell Riona you didn't leave my fiancée unprotected without telling me."

He looks past Killian like he's not there, giving me a stern look. "Riona, you're my daughter, my family."

"Aisling is family." For the first time in my life, I don't recognize the man standing in front of me.

Killian clenches his hand into a fist and I quickly grab it. He looks at me and I shake my head once at him. He can't punch the head of our clan, especially in front of others, even if it's deserved. He'd be punished brutally. Killian jerks his hand out of mine and storms out of the room.

Looking back to my father, I shake my head. "You could've asked one of them to watch her."

Irritation flashes in his eyes that we're still on this subject. "Have you forgotten you were attacked tonight as well?"

I cross my arms over my chest. "And I handled it without them. I can protect myself. I don't need them for that."

"You will go with them." His order rings through the office before he takes a calm breath. "You can't stay here, because you're compromised here. Someone told them you'd be at that club and it had to come from within. While I figure out who, I need you off the grid. Go with them and search for Aisling."

"Fine. I'll go, but what about my other clients?" My father knows I'm talking about the hired hits I have lined up.

"I'm not stopping you. Take one of them with you. You're not to be out alone and don't bring attention to yourself."

I turn from my father and look at the three men that caught my attention with a stone face. "I'll be back down in a minute. I just need to pack a few things."

I head for the door, but my father has one last thing to say, "Your exit has been locked down and is guarded."

Shit, my escape plan from my hidden tunnel was just ruined. "Be down in thirty."

I leave the room and run upstairs to my room. Killian is sitting at my desk, watching the footage of Aisling being taken. "I should've been there. He told me you'd both be protected. I could kill him for sacrificing her." He looks back at me with fire in his eyes.

"Killian, you can't." I walk over to him and place my hands on the back of my chair, watching the footage. "Our family needs to be whole for this."

"How can we be whole without her?"

"We aren't, but we can't be at odds as well."

"Lorcan is causing the cracks. I will never forgive him for this."

"I'm going to find her and every injury she has, we'll inflict on him for his betrayal."

Killian gives me a wicked smile. "I like that idea." He reaches into his pocket and pulls out his phone. "My phone was hacked to send those texts." With two hands, he breaks the phone in half. "Don't contact me on this line. I'll send you my new number later." Killian stands and gives me a hug. "I love you, Ri. Stay safe."

"Love you too, Kill."

Killian leaves me to pack and the first thing I pack are my weapons. All of them. Then I pack up my computer, clothes, and every other essential. My thirty minutes pass too quickly, but when there is a knock on the door, I know my time is up. Steve walks into the room and I give him a smile as I zip up my third bag. "Your father says times up." I give him a nod and he moves to my bed to grab my bags.

"Thank you, Steve."

"Of course, Miss Murphy." I follow Steve down the stairs where I see the three Italians waiting for me and I take the opportunity to really look at them. The Note Guy was the only one I didn't get a good look at in the club, so I take my time going down the stairs, soaking up every inch of him. He stands slightly taller than the other two, with a hint of authority about him and, with his dark hair and short beard, it's almost like a shadow is across his face, his crystal blue eyes being the only light. But his eyes aren't bright with emotions; instead, they show his disinterest and impatience.

My Mystery Man stands to his right, looking completely opposite to his charming self a couple of hours ago. Now his lighter features are closed off, like tonight's flirting never happened.

Mr. Sex Appeal is even bigger than I remember as he stands with his arms crossed over his chest, showing off his muscular upper body, but it's his brown eyes that hold my attention as he smirks at me, taking in my leggings and oversized t-shirt I changed into. He steps forward, taking the bags from Steve, and the other two flank me as we head out the door. I guess my father isn't saying bye. As we approach their black sedan, we stop outside the backseat.

"Sorry Beauty, but you can't know where we're going."
Before I even get a chance to comprehend what he means, someone
pushes a needle into my neck and my vision fills with black spots.

Chapter Four

Riona

Where am I? Why do I feel like I'm floating? I slowly try to peel my eyes open, but they will barely move and everything that I can see is blurry. "Don't fight it, Riona." That voice sounds familiar. I feel like I'm falling and my stomach does a flip until I land on a nice fluffy cloud. Oh, this is so soft. I snuggle into the softness. "Sleep, Beauty. You'll feel better in a few hours." A blanket of warmth covers my body as I fall into a deep sleep.

"Riona!" Aisling screaming my name in fear jolts me out of my sleep and I sit up, breathing heavily. I cover my face with my hands, trying to calm myself from the terror coursing through my body. When my heart rate finally settles, I drop my hands from my face and I realize I'm not in my bed. Looking around, I'm in a room I don't recognize. I see my bags sitting off to the side and the faces of the Russo brothers pop into my head.

I must be in their house, but the question is, how did I get here? We were outside their SUV, and I was going to climb in when...

They fucking drugged me.

I throw the covers off of me and walk to my weapons bag. How dare they? I'm going to show them who they're messing with. With two daggers in my hand and my gun tucked into the back of my leggings, I storm out of the room.

I might be stuck with them, but I'll teach them they aren't my handlers. No one takes my choices away. Their voices fill their hallway in a soft mumble that leads me straight to their kitchen. Like the fiery redhead that I am, I storm into the room. "Which one of you drugged me?"

They all stand there in a muted shock as I glare at each of them and open and close my fists. Mr. Sex Appeal is the first to break from his shock. "Princess, you can't know where we are." He steps forward timidly, and my hand instinctively opens, hovering over my daggers. They're all eyeing me with intense focus as they see I'm armed.

"Which one of you drugged me?" I say again, enunciating each word.

Note Guy crosses his arms, looking annoyed, like I'm a toddler acting out. "Would you have rather us put a bag over your head?"

"I'd be okay with you knocking me out with a punch to the face rather than being drugged. Now answer me." I look at Mystery Man because I recognize his voice from the fog.

"I did." With our eyes connected, he tells me what I assumed.

I relax my shoulders and bring my hands in front of me as I look him over as he leans against a wall. Perfect. "That's what I thought. I just needed confirmation." Within the next two seconds, I throw both my daggers at him and pull out my gun, aiming it at the other two as they draw their guns.

Watching the other two in my peripheral, I walk to Mystery Man, eyeing where the daggers stick into the wall right at his shoulder and lower torso, attaching his shirt to the wall. It's too bad I didn't nick him, but I didn't actually want to hurt him. When I'm standing right in front of him, I scan my eyes over his face as I tuck my gun away. His eyes don't leave my face, even when I hear his brothers move behind me. "Don't ever drug me again."

Mystery Man nods. "I promise." I'm not sure what he sees in my eyes, but his have sympathy in them. "I'm sorry."

I pull the daggers from the wall and tuck them in my leg pocket. "He's forgiven that easily?" Mr. Sex Appeal asks, looking between the two of us.

A wicked grin crosses my face. "Not quite." Mystery Man goes stiff again right before I punch him in the gut. I smile down at him as he's hunched over trying to catch his breath. "Now he's forgiven."

I turn my back to him and give the other two a sweet smile. Note Guy, which I might change to Stinkface because he is always scowling, glares at me but Mr. Sex Appeal looks me up and down like I'm his new toy. "Why not punch him in the face?"

"I didn't want to mess up Mystery Man's face."

"Mystery Man?" the man himself asks.

I shrug my shoulders. "It seems to fit you. And you didn't give me your name."

"What's my name?" Mr. Sex Appeal looks amused that I have nicknames for them.

"Mr. Sex Appeal." Or contestant two, per Aisling.

"That's right, babe." He looks me up and down. I give him a 'really' look. "What about this asshole?" He hits Stinkface on the chest.

"Originally it was Note Guy, but recently it's changed to Stinkface." Both Mr. Sex Appeal and Mystery Man crack up laughing and I can't hide my smile as the grumpy asshole continues to glare at me like he's hoping I'd drop dead.

"Oh, come now, Dante." Dante is his name. It suits him. "It's funny. Don't be jealous. I'm the only sexy one."

"I never said that. You just project sexual desire." I point to Mystery Man. "And any woman would find mystery within a man sexy." He gives me a smirk. Looking at Stinkface, I cock my head to the side. "Even a dark glare can be sexy. If it's attached to a good personality." But I'm not here to explore them. I'm here for Aisling.

I walk past them to the island where they have their laptops out and papers spread out about Aisling. "How far have you gotten? All I was able to get done before being called down to my father's office was getting the club security cameras and street cameras. I track the car to this one-block stretch." I circle my finger over the area on the map. "I figure they went into the parking garage to change cars."

Mystery Man steps up next to me, looking down at the map. "You're right. We got that far as well. Killian and some guys went to this parking garage and found an abandoned van."

"So, we're back to square one?" My shoulders sag at that thought.

"Not quite. Based on the threat, Aisling has to be with the O'Brien's or the Bratva." Mr. Sex Appeal stands across the island from me.

"Let me go get my laptop. I need to check on some of my feelers I sent out to my contacts."

"What kind of contacts does a princess have?" Dante spits out as a taunt.

"Political. International. Black market. Criminal. To name a few."

He looks at me, skeptical. "How do you have those kinds of contacts?"

He's really starting to irritate me. "Because I'm not just a pretty princess. It's just an act. My father likes to keep his deadliest weapon a secret."

"How so?" Mystery Man leans on the island next to me.

I grab a pen and flip a paper over and quickly draw out R-I-O-N-A where the letters overlap, forming my signature M.

"No shit." Mr. Sex Appeal breathes out. He looks up at me with so much desire. "Marry me?"

I chuckle. "I don't know your name; how can I marry you?"

"Matteo Russo. But you can call me anything you want. Marry me?"

I shake my head at him, secretly loving his silly personality. "Just because you can draw the M doesn't mean you're the assassin." But of course, Stinkface has to ruin the moment.

I glare at him. "Well, Stinkface, I could give you all the names of my kills or you can just come with me. My father said I could keep my clients, so I have a kill planned in a couple of days." His eyes narrow at me in irritation as I say his nickname.

"Mafia related?" Mystery Man asks.

"No. I was hired for this one." I look away from Dante, softening my expression as I look at Mystery Man. "It's actually multiple kills. A stepfather and his friends raped his stepdaughter. Her mother hired me. They have a poker night coming up."

"You're taking money for killing a rapist?" Dante criticizes.

"No, I'm hired with favors. Even favors I never plan on collecting. But after last night, I do plan to collect on this one. The mother is a Trauma Surgeon. With whatever Aisling is going through, she's probably going to need a doctor."

"You don't already have a doctor on payroll?" He's going to make this stay long and hard.

"Of course I do, but he's a man and I can bet everything I have that she's not going to want to be touched by any man for a while."

I stare off with Dante until Mystery Man speaks, "I'll go with you." He then knocks my shoulder with his. "My name is Enzo."

"I'm going too," Matteo announces. "I'm not going to let Enzo swoop in on my future wife."

I shake my head at them with a smile on my face. Living here with these two might not be too bad. Maybe even a little fun. Contestant one and two are still on the board.

I head up to my room to get my laptop. I need to find Aisling, and soon. The sound of her screaming my name earlier felt real and I can't stand this awful feeling that they're torturing her.

Chapter Five

Riona

    I walk into a dark cold room and a shiver runs through me as I take in the cement walls with no windows. This place doesn't have happy memories. Why am I here? A small movement catches my eye to my right, and I focus on a woman standing against the wall in nothing but her bra and panties. Her arms are stretched out to her sides, locked there by chains, and her head hangs low with her hair hanging down around her face. Is that me? I take slow quiet steps toward her. "Hello?"

    The girl's head snaps up as she groans and her features become clearer. Looking at her face, I see her right eye is swollen and her lip is busted, but I recognize her immediately. Aisling? I run

*toward her, trying to unlock the chains, but my hands go right
through them. "Aisling. Help me."*

*I look at her, but she's looking past me and a whimper
escapes her. "Hello Aisling." A man walks up to her with a knife in
his hand. "It's time for a new game."*

*He skims the knife across her belly, and I try the chains
again. "Nooo." Please don't cut her.*

*When my hands still won't wrap around the chains, I go for
the guy. Trying to shove him away, but nothing happens. "Little One,
I'm going to carve you with our mark. A mark that should have been
branded on you when you were born. But you're a Murphy instead,
so it'll instead scar your body so you'll always remember our time
together."*

*"No. Don't touch her." I swing my fist at his face, but it does
nothing.*

*I reach for Aisling, this time trying to block her, but I'm
pulled away by an invisible rope. I scream her name as Aisling
screams out in horror and pain.*

I shoot up in bed, breathing hard in panic, gripping the sheets
and looking around. "Riona." The sound of my name has me turning
toward it and I see Enzo sitting on the edge of my bed. I'm
unknowingly squeezing his hand; he squeezes back, and a feeling of
warmth runs up my arm. "Riona. It was just a dream. You're safe."

I look back up to Enzo and tears fill my eyes. "It didn't feel
like a dream. It feels like I was there with her. I could feel her pain."
I let go of the sheet I was gripping and lift my shirt expecting to see

cuts. But there aren't any. Tears form as I think of the pain she's going through and Enzo pulls me to him, wrapping his arms around me and letting me cry into his bare chest. "I can't lose her. I need to find her. I can't take another minute knowing they're hurting her."

He runs his hand down my back. "We will find her. She's probably sitting in a room untouched."

I look up at him and I realize we're laying down in bed. "Have you ever had a connection so strong that you can feel them without being near them?"

He shakes his hand no. "Like twins?"

"Something like that. Aisling and I call each other our soul sister because we can sense each other. It's not all the time and it's mostly when the other is scared or in pain. We first realized it when I was thirteen and she was fourteen." It's normally just a feeling. I've never seen her like I was there before. "Earlier, when I woke up from the drugs, it was to her screaming my name, and now the dream. I'm not sure if what I saw is real, but I do know they're hurting her."

I look up at him and he runs his thumb across my cheeks, wiping away my tears. "Do you want to tell me about the dream?"

I shake my head, looking past him, staring at the black headboard, remembering the screams. "Not right now." Looking back at him, I say, "Maybe in the morning."

He nods in understanding and kisses my forehead. "Go back to sleep, Beauty."

I snuggle into him, loving the sound of his heartbeat. "You're staying, right?"

He wraps his arms tighter around me and takes a relaxing breath. "I'm not going anywhere."

Enzo's heartbeat lolls me back to sleep but before I drift off, I wish for Aisling to get some sleep too.

I can't stop looking at him. Enzo looks so peaceful and handsome sleeping. I woke up a couple of minutes ago, surprised that he stayed and that I'm still curled against his side. I don't normally sleep next to anyone but last night it was what I needed. I'm not sure what it is about him, but he calms me. And I think that's the reason I haven't gotten up yet. Looking down at his bare chest, I run my finger in circles and swirls across his skin. Enzo takes a deep breath making his chest expand and I look up at his face, seeing he's awake. "Good morning."

"Morning." I remove my hand from his chest, but he grabs it, laying it back on his chest.

"You don't have to stop." He removes his hand from on top of mine and I start drawing on his chest again. "How did you sleep the rest of the night?"

"Good. You're a great pillow." He chuckles. "How did you sleep?"

"I slept great. I had a beautiful woman wrapped around me."
I can't believe I'm blushing right now. "Did you have any more
dreams or … connections?"

I look at him, confused, because most people brush me off
about Aisling and I's link. "You believe me?"

He shrugs his shoulders like why wouldn't I. "Were you
lying?"

"No. My father and friends just brush it off as my
imagination. Only Aisling and Killian actually believe it."

"I believe it. I saw how upset you were and that is real. How
about you tell me about the dream? Maybe it'll give us a clue." He
runs his fingers through my hair.

I nod and tell him every detail about the dream. The entire
time, Enzo comforts me by running his fingers through my hair and
moving his other hand slowly up and down my back. When I'm
finished, I can't look at him as my mind remembers her screams.

He places his finger under my chin, lifting it until I look him
in the eyes. "I hope that wasn't real because if it was, it sounds awful.
But if it is, then we learned she's being held in a basement and
maybe the mark he was going to give her might lead to who has her.
We'll need to look into her parents' history."

A smile spreads across my face as he breaks down the
information from my dream that we can try to use. "Why are you
smiling at me?"

"Because you're taking me seriously and actually care."

He looks surprised. "Of course I care, Beauty. We all care. We know how important it is to find her as quickly as possible."

He runs his fingers along the edge of my face and down the side of my neck. It's such a simple gesture but it sends this buzz through my body. I look down to his lips and back up to his eyes, fighting myself not to kiss him. "Why do you call me Beauty?"

He shifts his body so we're laying face to face. This really isn't helping me resist kissing him. "Because you're beautiful. But mostly because you're a princess that doesn't cower at a beast. You accept him."

I really like that answer. "Are you my Beast?"

He gives me a wicked smile. "I'm definitely not Prince Charming."

Not being able to hold his stare, I look to my hand and watch it as I run it over his chest and down his arm. "I wouldn't peg you as a Disney fan."

"We all have our things that give us a break from our world. Your turn." I look back up to his face. "Why Mystery Man?"

"You were calculating when we met but not in a creepy way. It was like you were taking in everything at once and finding a way to get the best results. Plus..." I raise my hand and run my fingers over his lips. "Your smirk told me you have a lot of secrets."

I look in his eyes and I see the appreciation of my assessment and the desire. A desire that I know is matched in mine. The next second, our lips meet together in a wild, desperate kiss. The feeling of his lips on mine makes my whole body tingle with need. I run my fingers through his hair and grab on, holding his face to mine as I deepen the kiss.

Enzo's hands wrap around my lower back, and he pulls me up against him so I can feel all of him. A moan escapes me as I hook my leg over his hip and grind against his hard length. His hands slip to my ass, holding me at the perfect angle for pleasure. My core sparks in the best way and I wish we weren't wearing any clothes. He breaks our kiss to kiss down my neck and chest while pushing one of my tank's straps down my arm, exposing the top of my breast. Yes, please take it off.

But before he can fully expose my breast, my bedroom door opens. "Good morning. I brought..." Matteo doesn't finish his sentence as Enzo and I scramble to cover me.

"What the fuck, man. Heard of knocking?" Enzo glares at his brother.

"You had a sleepover without me." Matteo, not even caring what Enzo said, comes marching into the room, setting a coffee mug on the bedside table and climbing into bed behind me. His arm wraps around my stomach, pulling me against his body and slightly away from Enzo. "If you needed to snuggle, you should have come to get me. I'm much better at it. Plus, I bring coffee."

I look back over my shoulder, giving him a playful grin as I run my hand over Enzo's exposed chest. "I don't know. Enzo is shirtless."

"Well shit, Princess. If you like that, I'd snuggle naked with you." Not being able to hold back my laughter anymore, I bury my face into Enzo's shoulder and let it out.

Both of their holds on me tighten and for the first time I realize I'm lying in bed with two gorgeous men that are practically strangers and they're holding me intimately. And it doesn't feel weird. I lift my head from Enzo's shoulder and look up at his smiling face. I guess he's not upset that his brother interrupted us. Not removing my leg from around Enzo, I lean back into Matteo to look at his face and he looks perfectly happy where he is. "So Princess, do you like to snuggle while sleeping?"

"Not normally, but I'm not complaining about last night." Enzo squeezes my thigh and I move my hips against him.

"Well, I call dibs for tonight."

I'd be okay with that, but I have a busy night. "I'm not going to sleep much tonight."

He runs his nose along my neck and whispers in my ear, "If that's what you want, I'll happily keep you up all night."

I groan, wanting what he's implying but I know I can't. "Not what I meant. I don't sleep very much before a kill. Tonight, I need to go through the man's house, set up cameras, make sure no one innocent is in the house, and start my plan."

"We'll come with you." Enzo runs his hand up my leg and just barely under the edge of my sleep shorts.

I want to tell them I don't need them there, but I know it'll be no use. They're coming. But I'm not mad about it. I actually like being around them. I turn over on the bed, brushing my body against both of them before sitting up and straddling Matteo as I grab the coffee. "This is for me, right?"

He nods up at me, running his hands up my legs, but before he gets to my hips, I move off him and sit in between them, facing them. They both sit up as well and lean against the headboard. "So, what are we doing today?"

"I thought we'd look into the details we discussed." I give Enzo a smile, hoping he doesn't mention the dream, because I'm not sure if I could handle it if Matteo thought it was silly.

I nod. "Okay. I also have a guy that's working on getting the footage of the parking garage. I want to track the cars that leave."

"Well, I'm going to the club. I've got some business to handle since I have to hire new bartenders." Matteo gives me a knowing look, telling me they're hiring because I mentioned they needed a third the night at the club.

I take a sip of the coffee, trying to hide my curiosity. "Where's Dante?"

"He's out searching for Maxim. He wasn't in the bathroom when we went to collect him the other night. He's been silent ever since."

A fiery anger boils inside me at the mention of Maxim. I can't wait to get my hands on him. A flash of all the things I want to do to him has a spark of thrill run through me.

Enzo brings me from my deadly thoughts as he leans forward and takes my coffee, bringing it to his lips and taking a drink. I stare at him in shock as he smirks and hands me the cup back. "I'm going to make breakfast." He leans forward and presses a kiss to my lips, shocking me further as he walks out of the room.

"Hold up." I look back to Matteo, hoping he's not mad about the kiss. "We're kissing now." I smile at his excitement. "Him and I are, apparently."

"Come here, Princess, I need my lips on you now." He hooks his fingers beckoning me.

I lean forward and he captures my lips with his, kissing the hell out of me. When we pull back from each other, I'm dizzy and tingly. Oh, these guys are definitely going to be trouble for me.

Chapter Six

Riona

"Ugh I can't look at these screens anymore. I feel like my eyes are crossing." I lean back from the computer screens and my back muscles scream in protest. "I feel like I'm looking for a needle in a city-block-wide haystack."

Enzo lifts his head from his laptop. "Haven't found anything?"

I shake my head no. "I've only looked into the cars that left after the van went in. I still need to check cars that left right before Killian showed up. I'm thinking they either left right after switching cars or waited until right before Killian got there. If Father was right that someone in his group gave info about what club we were at, then that person could've notified them when Killian was coming."

"That's brilliant." He gives me an encouraging smile.

"Thanks." My cheeks heat and I can't believe I'm blushing right now. "How about you?"

He shrugs with slight disappointment. "Nothing much yet. Only that her mom has to be the connection, but the problem is I can't find anything about her prior to her marrying Drew. It's like she was a ghost before then. No birth records. No school records. No DMV records. No criminal records. No court records. Nothing."

I look at him confused. "How is that possible?"

He shakes his head like it's a mystery. "I don't know but whoever wiped her did a great job."

"What's the first record you have?" I move over to him looking at his screen.

"Their marriage certificate." He clicks on a tab and the certificate pulls up.

I point to the screen. "Look, it lists her as only Anna. No last name."

"I noticed that too. Do you want to know my theory?" He looks up at me.

I nod. "Please."

"I think either her family disowned her or she left them because she loved Drew. And since he was highly ranked next to your father, they had her past destroyed. To protect her family." His eyes stay on my face, watching for my reaction.

It still doesn't all fit. "That would mean they were outside our world. How does her family now connect to it?"

He let out a heavy sigh. "I don't know."

I think over everything he just said. "We need to talk to my father. He's the only one that can possibly give us information." But that means I need to speak to him. We still haven't spoken since that night and I'm not ready to forgive him for not protecting Aisling.

I pick up my phone ready to call my father, but Enzo places his hand over mine. "You don't have to call him. I know things aren't good between you two."

I shake my head and slide my hand out from under his. "I need to do this for Aisling. He has to know something right? They went to high school together."

Enzo gives me a hopeful nod and I press on the call button. I take a deep breath and hold it as the ringing sounds out. With each passing ring, my heart sinks and the air slowly leaves my lungs. My father has never not answered my call. He's even answered during a shootout once.

I have to fight back tears and force myself to breathe as my father's voicemail picks up. "Hi Father. We're doing research into Aisling's parents' past, and I wanted your help. Please call me back." The call ends and I look up at Enzo and the sadness in his eyes makes me mad. I'm not someone who wants to be pitied.

I clench my phone in my hand, wanting to throw it. "I can't believe he didn't fucking answer me. It's his fault she's in this mess. The least he could do is answer."

"He's probably in a meeting." Enzo tries and fails to calm me.

"He's not and I'm going to find him." I turn on my heels and walk away. I hear Enzo push back his chair as I leave the dining room, our makeshift work area, and head to the front door. Right as I reach for the handle, the door opens, making me step back so it doesn't hit me and I collide with Enzo.

Dante steps in through the front door in wrinkly clothes and a tired expression. "Where do you think you're going?"

"To find my father. He needs to answer some questions." I try to walk by him, but he wraps his arm around my center, pulling me away from the door and kicking it shut.

"You're not going anywhere." I'm not in the mood for him right now.

"I'm not your prisoner. Watch me." I swing my elbow back against his ribs and quickly turn, taking a swing at his face but he easily blocks it.

He chuckles with a wicked grin on his face. "Do you really think you can take me?"

Fuming, I clench my hands into fists. "Hell yeah, I can. Do you think you can take a hit from a girl?" Not waiting for his answer, I throw a punch right at his face again but that was a mistake. Instead of making contact with his cheek, he catches my wrist midair and pulls me toward him, throwing me off balance. He takes advantage of that and bends down, throwing me across his shoulder and standing. I rage against his back, screaming threats at him as he carries me to god knows where.

We enter a dark room at the back of the house that I haven't explored yet and Dante throws me down on the ground. But instead of a hard surface, my back hits padded floor mats. The lights flick on that second and I take in the massive gym space, complete with a boxing ring. After taking in the room, I focus back on Dante and Enzo. Enzo is standing in the doorway with an amused smile on his face and Dante is standing over me, looking more pissed than me.

He throws something down at me and when I catch it, I see they're boxing gloves. "You want to fight me because you're having a temper tantrum? Fine. But we aren't going to hurt ourselves doing it."

I throw the gloves down and push off the ground, standing up. Pissed, I glare at him, closing the distance between us. "Don't talk to me like I'm a child."

"Not a child. Just a spoiled princess." A low growl tumbles through me as I tighten my fist to the point my nails dig into my palm. A hand softly wrapping around my fist has me jerking away. I relax when I see Enzo there with the gloves I left on the floor. Dante disappears from my mind as I allow Enzo to put the gloves on and lace them up.

The calmness he surrounds me with is nice but not what I want. I just can't make myself move away from him. "You're ruining my vibe. Being all calm and helpful. Angry is how I like to fight."

"Oh, I think Dante will piss you off plenty." He holds my wrists together when he finishes and leans closer. "He leaves himself open after he punches with his left," he whispers into my ear before

76

kissing my cheek. I give him a nod, letting him know I heard him and he taps my gloves and steps back.

We both look at Dante who has taken off his shoes and shirt and is standing outside the ring. I run my eyes over his exposed chest and abs, and he is sexy as hell standing there in just jeans. "Take a picture, it'll last longer."

I bring my eyes up to his face and give him a cheeky grin. "Enzo, do you mind grabbing my phone and taking a picture for me?"

Enzo chuckles, reaching into my leggings' pocket and pulling out my phone. "I'll hold onto this." He smacks my ass. "Now go kick his ass."

I wink at Enzo as I walk to the ring. "Oh, I plan to." Dante holds the ropes open for me and I climb in, with him following right behind me. We meet face-to-face in the middle like we're about to fight for the championship belt. "Are there any rules?"

"No hitting the face."

I nod. "No serious injuries."

He nods and holds his gloves out in front of him. "Everything else goes?"

"Yep." I give him a wicked grin and bump my gloves to his. He just gave me free rein because while I've been trained in boxing, I prefer a combination of jiu-jitsu and Krav Maga. It allows me to use my whole body instead of just my fists.

We both raise our gloves in a defensive position as we move around the ring. This time I'm not throwing the first punch. I need to see how he moves before I strike. Dante throws a lazy punch at me that I easily duck and he quickly throws a left punch at my ribs. I block it, seeing the opening that Enzo mentioned. "What did your daddy do that pissed you off so much?"

"None of your business." I step forward, testing his movement, and he steps back.

"Aww, did he pull your allowance?" He throws another weak punch that grazes my shoulder.

I tilt my head side to side, acting like my neck is tight. "I haven't taken money from my father since I was eighteen."

"Did he yell at you? Ground you?" He throws two more punches for each question.

"Fuck you." I throw my first punch in anger at him patronizing me. My right hook misses its target as he jumps back.

"Oh, that hit a sore spot. Which is it? Did he yell at you again? Tell you that you're more important than Aisling, again?" He throws a left hook and I take the opening, throwing a punch into his ribs, and then I hook my right leg behind his and force him back so we're both falling to the ground. Using the momentum, I throw punches at his sides until he yells my name.

I stop punching, breathing hard and I realize I've been screaming the whole time. Looking up from his abdomen to his face, for the first time I don't see the stern glare. Instead, he looks at me concerned. "What is it?"

"He didn't answer my call. And before you make fun about that, he's never missed one of my calls. And this call was an important one that could help find Aisling." I take a deep breath and slump my shoulders.

He sits up on his elbows. "What did you need from him?"

"Information about Aisling's mother." I move off Dante and stand up and he sits up fully.

"About the mark from your dream?" I stare down at him, shocked that he asks without a hint of teasing. "Enzo texted me about it earlier." He stands up as well and I look back at Enzo who is leaning on the ropes. He shrugs his shoulders like it's to be expected that he told him.

"Riona." I look back at Dante. "He'll call."

I nod weakly because I'm not sure he will. He walks over to the ropes and opens them for me. "How about we go back to the dining room and you can show me what you've been working on today while Enzo has been looking into her parents?"

I climb through the ropes and pull on the laces of my gloves with my teeth. Enzo walks to me to help get mine off and then we head out of the gym to the dining room. When we get there, we find Matteo with three pizza boxes open and already one slice from each box is gone. He looks at us as we walk in. "Ahh, there you are. I brought pizza for dinner."

Enzo walks over to him and grabs a slice. "We were in the gym; you mustn't have looked too hard for us."

He shrugs his shoulders. "I was hungry."

We all grab a slice and while we eat, I show Dante the footage of the parking garage and my plan to track the cars coming out. After we're all done eating, Dante goes to bed since he was out all day and night looking for Maxim, while I go over my plan for tonight with Enzo and Matteo.

Chapter Seven

Riona

"Can I take this stupid blindfold off now?" We left ten minutes ago to get everything set up for tomorrow night and the guys insisted that I wear a blindfold. I'm not sure why. I've tracked all our turns and I'm pretty sure I could find the house if I had to.

"Yeah, you can take it off." I untie the blindfold and my eyes instantly connect to Enzo's in the rearview mirror. He gives me a smile before looking ahead to the road. I watch through the window as we drive through the Upper East Side and into the Bronx. We eventually drive past the house I'm breaking into tonight and I'm happy to see the house is dark, with only one car in the driveway. "Drive two streets over and park."

When Enzo parks, I pull my hood on and open the door. "Thanks. I won't be more than thirty minutes."

"Oh no. That's not how this works," Matteo protests as he and Enzo open their doors as well.

"We're going with you." Enzo stands in front of me as he closes his door in all black. How they're dressed should've told me they weren't waiting in the car.

"I don't need any help. Plus, three people make more noise than one."

"We're quiet," Enzo says confidently.

"Oh, so you've broken into someone's house and snuck around while they were inside?" I look at him, skeptical. He's definitely more of an IT, behind-the-scenes type of guy, instead of doing the actual dirty work.

"A time or two," Matteo says right behind me, making me jump a little bit. He gives me a cocky smile and I playfully hit his chest.

"Okay. Let's go." With all of us dressed in complete black, we move through the shadows back toward Raymond Swartz's house. We're quiet as we stand next to each other across the street from my mark's house and everything around us is silent. I feel like even a bird chirping would set off some type of alarm, so I whisper. "I don't need you following me around in there, so while I'm setting up my devices and getting the dining room set up, will you check the rest of the house?"

They both nod. "Raymond is in the house currently so don't wake him. I just need to know that no one else is in the house. That there will be no collateral damage."

Enzo turns on my right to face us. "Who do you think will be in there?"

I shrug my shoulders. "Hopefully no one but I want to make sure he hasn't tricked another mother and daughter or somehow kidnapped or lured an innocent kid in his house. He's a disgusting man and only his friends and him need to die tomorrow."

Matteo has fire burning in his eyes from the hate he has for Raymond. I told them the awful things he's done when we were planning and they're happy to help eliminate him. "We'll look through the rest of the house."

"Great. Can one of you lift me up for a second?" I turn toward the building next to us. "I need to attach this camera..."

Matteo quickly places his arm around my waist and pulls me against him. "I got you." I chuckle at his eagerness and at the glare Enzo is giving him. "Don't pout. You got to sleep with her last night." The next thing I know, I'm sitting on Matteo's shoulder. "Where do you want the camera?"

"Rain gutter." I point to the specific one and when I reach up to attach the mini wireless camera, four hands touch my body, giving me support, and those four hands don't leave my body until my feet touch the ground again. "Thanks. Let's go around back. I need to put up another camera and we can go in through the back."

After making sure the street is empty, we head around the back of the house. Enzo unlocks the backdoor as I place a camera on the tree in the backyard, facing the backdoor. I walk up behind Matteo and Enzo just as he opens the door. The three of us walk into the house silently and they split off, clearing the small bungalow as I head straight down the hallway to the kitchen and dining room.

Dr. Gibbons said her ex-husband would come back to his old bungalow every Thursday to play poker with his five buddies at this very dining room table. This is also the house where they raped fifteen-year-old Tiffany when she went to bed during a poker night as her mother was in an emergency surgery.

I'm so disgusted by this house. I can't wait to see it burn down tomorrow. Getting to work, I quietly pull out the gas oven to cut the gas line, making sure it's not a clean cut. I had the gas line shut off earlier so I could cut the line without the house filling with smelly gas. I can't have Raymond knowing something is wrong. Instead, the cut line will make the fire department think it was a freak accident when really, I'm going to blow up this house with them in it.

I push the oven back against the wall and I make my way over to the table and pull out a microphone. Turning it on, I slide my AirPods into my ears and tap the microphone, making sure it works. With it working, I connect it to the bottom of the table and pocket my AirPods.

Matteo walks into the kitchen and gives me a thumbs up. I smile at him and point to the top of the cabinets. Matteo gives me a smile as he walks over to me. A second later I'm on his shoulder for the second time tonight and he walks to where I pointed, allowing me to attach the final camera. When I'm finished, I point to the dining chest next to the table. Matteo walks me over to it as Enzo walks into the kitchen, giving us a thumbs up as well. Good. With everything clear, I set up my gas device.

This device will release an odorless gas at my activation and after an hour of the gas being released, a spark will ignite, blowing everything up. When everything is set, Matteo sets me back down on the ground and we quietly make it back through the house and out the back door, locking it. We don't speak until we're back at the car. "Let me just turn on the cameras."

Pulling out my phone, I pull the app up that the microphone and cameras are linked to. All three camera images pull up and I smile as everything is coming together.

"All good. Let's go." We climb into the car and Enzo starts driving down the road. "So how did the rest of the house look?"

Matteo looks back at me from the passenger seat. "The rooms were all completely empty except for his room which just had him in the bed."

"I took the basement and it's a scary scene." Enzo takes a hand off the steering wheel and pulls out his phone. Pulling up his photos, he hands me the phone. "It was empty, but this is what was down there."

I slide through the photos of dog cages, a workbench with leather cuffs attached to it, a wooden cross on the wall with more cuffs, and a table filled with knives, whips, clamps, large dildos, and other extreme sex toys. "This is disgusting."

I pass the phone to Matteo and he growls at the images. "I'm so glad these men are dying tomorrow. The horror that has been experienced down there makes me sick."

"I can't wait to watch it all burn." Enzo takes back his phone. We're quiet as our rage boils from the despicable men that are dying tomorrow. They should have been killed long ago.

"Hey Riona." I look at Matteo, who is turned, looking at me with hesitation.

"Huh?" Why does he look nervous?

"Can you put the blindfold on again?"

Oh, come on. "Really?"

"I'm sorry, but yes."

I grab the blindfold from the seat and tie it on securely. "Why do I have to wear this again?"

Enzo answers. "We don't like people knowing where we live. We have a lot of enemies and them not knowing where we let our guards down is something we take very seriously."

"But I'm at your house. I'm in your sanctuary."

"It's a first for us. I guess that makes you pretty special." I want to roll my eyes at Matteo's answer but instead I can't help my smile.

I truly don't know how to even act with all his continuous flirting. He makes me feel more seen than anyone has ever done before. "You've really got to stop flattering a girl or she might think you have ulterior motives."

"Oh, I definitely do." I can picture his wickedly cocky smile. "Several actually. Isn't that right Enzo?"

"I can think of a few." His soothing deep voice has my body warming.

"Care to share? I need some entertainment until we get to the house. Maybe we can have some fun with them." Oh, I'm definitely getting myself into trouble.

Even though I can't see anything, I can feel their eyes running over my body. "I'm hoping you'd throw your knives at me like you did Enzo. It was so hot watching it, but I want to experience it."

That wasn't what I thought he was going to say. "I can definitely do that."

"Naked?" There you go. I can picture us both naked with him standing in front of me. Maybe that wouldn't be safe. I'd definitely be distracted.

"How about in lingerie instead?"

"Hell yeah. But I get to pick your lingerie."

I chuckle. "What about you, Enzo?"

"I definitely have dirtier motives that I'd love to whisper into your ear as your body is pressed against mine, but my PG motive is you showing me how you got through the club's firewall to access the cameras. And I wouldn't stop you from sitting in my lap only wearing lingerie while doing it."

I shift in my seat, thinking about Enzo's hands on me as I bend over his desk. "Oh, that was easy. I can give you something better. How about I install my firewall instead?"

The car accelerates faster and I chuckle as I lean my head back thinking about the different lingerie sets I packed. I didn't pack much because I definitely didn't think I'd like these guys, but while I'm linked with them, there is nothing wrong with having fun with them.

A hand runs up the inside of my thigh, stopping mid-thigh with a light squeeze, bringing me back to the present. "We're here." I feel the car slow to a stop as I remove the blindfold. I run my eyes from the hand on my thigh up the arm to Matteo's smiling face. "Come on, Princess. We have plans to get to." He gives my thigh another squeeze before removing his hand and climbing out of the car. I give Enzo a wink as I slide across the backseat to the door where Matteo stands.

When I open the door Matteo quickly grabs me from the seat and slings me over his shoulder. He smacks my ass as he carries me inside. "You better have packed some sexy pieces."

"Anything I put on my body is sexy." I smack his ass.

"True." As we step inside and head upstairs, I look up to see if Enzo is following and the dirty smile that is across his face as he walks behind us has me tingling in anticipation.

Chapter Eight

Matteo

"Fuck me," I say under my breath as I adjust myself in my jeans as Riona walks out of her bathroom in black heels with black stockings that run up her amazing legs to her thighs where the stockings connect to a black lace garter belt and black lace cheeky panties. But what really takes my breath away is her full breasts, barely covered in a lace bra. God, I need to buy her some more lingerie and demand that she only wears them while in this house.

She walks over to me with confidence as she pulls her dark red hair down from her messy bun. "How do I look? Do I meet all your fantasies?"

"Oh, you have no idea. You were born to only wear lingerie. Every man's wet dream." I want to reach out and run my hands all over her curves.

"Wait until you see me naked." Well damn.

"Okay." Let's do that now.

She chuckles. "Where'd Enzo go?"

I wave my hand toward her door, not looking away from her. "He went to change and get our training room ready."

"Training room?" She tilts her head to the side probably wondering where that is, but she hasn't explored half the house yet.

"Come on. I'll show you." I stand up from the bed and hold out my hand.

"One second." She turns from me and I finally get a view of that fine ass on full display. I really need to check myself before I come in my pants like a virgin. "I need to grab a robe and my knives."

I don't want her to cover up. "No robe and you can use our knives."

"Yes to the robe." She steps into her closet quickly and steps out covering her body in a dark green silk robe. "I'm not walking around your house basically naked."

"Why not? It's just us. Enzo is about to see you anyway."

"And Dante isn't. He doesn't want to see me like this."

I crack up laughing. "Yes, he does. He'd probably kill both Enzo and myself to get you like this alone."

"Yeah, Stinkface wants something more from me than to glare at me." She takes my hand as she rolls her eyes at me in disbelief and I walk her out into the hallway.

Enzo is walking out of his room next door at the same time in only a pair of basketball shorts and his eyes instantly go to Riona. "Wow."

"I know right? And you haven't even seen what's underneath the robe." I pat his shoulder as we pass. "Meet you down there. I just need to change."

Enzo reaches out and pulls Riona back against his body and out of my hold. "Then I'll make sure she finds the training room." His hand disappears under her robe and for the first time, I might actually be jealous of my brother.

Riona playfully swats his hand away. "No touching. I need to practice with your knives before I throw them at Matteo. I don't want to hurt him."

She pulls Enzo down the hall toward the stairs but looks back at me. "Hurry up."

The smile she gives me has me quickly heading to my room and removing my clothes because there was something dirty behind it. After I pull on my sweatpants, I rush down to the basement that is as big as the entire house.

This is our training room. Our weapons, shooting range, and targets are down here. This is also where Enzo's office and our cells are where we hold people that we need information from. Not my torture room though. That's in a different location.

Thudding sounds echo through the space as I walk to where our wood targets are. I find Riona throwing knives alone. "Where's Enzo?"

She points a knife toward Enzo's office door. "He said something about giving us alone time."

I look up at the camera above the door giving him a nod. Alone time, sure. He's going to be watching every second of this. "Are you done practicing?"

She gives me a wicked smile as she quickly turns and throws a knife hitting the bullseye right next to three other knives. "I think I'm good."

I walk past her and go to collect the knives. When I walk back to her, I catch her eyes running over my naked chest. "Like what you see?"

"Just thinking how dangerous it is for you to expose all those muscles. I could get distracted." She might be talking about my upper body, but her eyes are on my pants where they're definitely tenting.

"I'd happily die at your hands knowing it's because you couldn't get enough of me."

She takes the knives from me and sets them on the table. "Go stand in front of the target, hands flat against the wall next to your sides."

I follow her instructions, leaning back against the wall with my hands flat against the wood. Riona picks up a knife and flips it in her hand. "Don't move and this won't hurt too much."

"You better remove that robe before throwing that knife." She rolls her eyes at me but sets the knife down and unties her robe. "Do it slowly. Put on a show for us."

Confusion flashes across her face and I nod to the camera behind her and look up to the one above me in the corner. Her smile brightens, realizing Enzo is watching as she opens her robe with her eyes connected to the camera. She runs her finger up her stomach at the opening of her robe as her eyes connect back with mine, giving me her full attention. The robe slips from her shoulders and pools on the floor at her feet as I groan at the vision in front of me. She's perfect.

Slowly she picks up a knife and runs it across her thigh. "Ready?"

I give her a nod and she throws the first knife. The knife sticks into the wood right against my side. It's so close I felt the blade slide against my skin. I look down, shocked I don't see blood. "Matteo, don't move. I'm going to throw the rest really fast so I need you to stay very still."

"Sorry." I lean my head back against the wall and take a breath, calming myself. I don't know why this is turning me on, but having her eyeing me and taking my life in her hands has me wanting to bury myself in between her beautiful thighs.

Before I can even continue that thought, five knives fly at me within seconds. I don't even realize until it's done where all the knives landed. One is to the right of my hip. Another is on the inside of my left thigh. The third one is between my middle and ring finger on my right hand and the fourth is right next to my left wrist. But the one that has my attention is the one at my right shoulder because it cut me. A slight burn comes from the shallow cut as a few drops of blood run down my chest. "You cut me."

The sound of her heels against the floor has me looking up at her. Her hips sway a little more as she runs her hands down the curve of her hips. "Oops." She stands right in front of me and grips the knife. "I'll kiss it better." She pulls the knife from the wall and drops it to the floor.

Riona's lips touch my skin over the cut and her tongue runs over my skin, licking up my blood. She continues to kiss across my chest as her hands slide down my arms and she pulls out the knives at my wrist and hand. With those knives gone, I thread my fingers through her hair, tilting her face up so I can kiss her. She moans against my lips and deepens our kiss. Her hands move over my chest and to my side, removing that knife.

She pulls her lips from mine and smiles up at me. "Is this what you imagined?" She kisses down my chest as one of her hands goes to my hip, pulling out that knife, while the other rubs over my sweatpants along my hard length.

Before I can pull her back to my lips, she goes down on her knees and the last knife falls to the floor. Her hand goes into my pants and I groan at the feeling of her hand wrapped around my hard length. "Is this what you fantasize about when you pictured me throwing my knives at you?"

"One of them. Although it'd be a lot better if my pants were off."

She smiles up at me as she continues to pump me. "And you don't mind Enzo seeing you naked and me sucking your cock?"

I thrust into her hand at the thought of the scene she talks about. Enzo and I aren't strangers on sharing a woman and even Dante gets in on the fun sometimes. It's always a rush to see lust fill the eyes of the women, knowing my brothers want them to. But Riona has me frantic. I want whatever she's willing to give. Just me. Me and Enzo. Or all three of us. "Princess, Enzo can join us if it gets your lips wrapped around my cock."

Desire flames in her eyes as she rubs her thighs together. She's turned on by the thought of Enzo joining us. We'll definitely need to bring that to reality but right now I'm loving all her attention on me. She leans forward and places kisses along my abs until her lips reach the top of my sweatpants. With her free hand, she tugs my pants down, freeing my erection.

With my pants around my ankles, she continues kissing down to my cock and then she places a final kiss to my tip. I groan in pleasure. It's the best feeling in the world. That is until she licks up my length and then wraps her lips around the tip. "Oh fuck, Princess. You're amazing."

She takes me all the way to the back of her throat and sucks as she moves back to the tip. "So many compliments. You must really want this."

I grip the back of her head as she flicks her tongue over my tip. "I want everything from you."

She smirks at me. "You haven't given me enough compliments for everything yet." Her warm mouth surrounds me again as her hand wraps around my base, working my long length that her mouth can't cover.

I tighten my grip in her hair and she moans around me as I start to control her pace. Her eyes connect with mine as she takes me all the way into her mouth and I almost come just from the look of pure, hot desire and want in her eyes. She wants this. She wants me.

Her teeth graze against the underside of my cock and my hips involuntarily thrust forward, pushing myself deeper into her mouth, making her gag. I try to pull out of her mouth to apologize but her hand goes to my ass, pushing me further into her and she swallows around me. "Oh fuck." Riona picks up her pace, sucking me harder.

My balls draw up and I hold her head in place as I thrust into her mouth, chasing my orgasm. "I'm coming. Fuck. If you don't want me to come in your mouth, tell me now."

Instead of pulling away, she sucks me harder and swallows me down her throat again. I come hard down her throat and she moans around me, taking all of it.

She licks up every drop and I pull her off the ground by her hair and slam my mouth to hers. I don't care that I can taste myself on her lips, all I want to do is get her naked. I run my hands down her sides to the edge of her panties but as I go to push them down, she's pulled out of my hold.

Enzo gives me a cocky smile as he holds her against his chest and runs his nose up her neck where he nips her earlobe.

"Are you done watching?" I give him an excited smile, ready for this to continue.

"You had your time. It's my turn now." He picks her up and carries her away to his office.

"Don't worry, Princess. We can finish what we started later. You can find me naked in your bed."

She looks over Enzo's shoulder with a pleased smile and gives me a wink. "Can't wait."

Chapter Nine

Enzo

Riona is radiant! Absolutely breathtaking. I lean back in my chair, watching her on my center screens. Her eyes connect with one of my cameras and the smile she gives me has me hardening in my pants. Her robe slips off her shoulders as her eyes connect back to Matteo. When it hits the floor, revealing her gorgeous body in black lace lingerie, I lean forward wanting a closer look. God, she's perfect.

When I first saw Riona at the Gala, it was her beauty that I noticed but as I watched her throughout the night, she seemed so innocent and out of place. She didn't belong in a room full of criminals. She didn't belong in this dangerous life. But when I saw her at the club, I knew my judgment about her was wrong. She wasn't as innocent and sheltered as she looked at the gala. Seeing her now in only a lace bra and panties with stockings running up her legs as she throws knives at Matteo, I know she's made for this world. And she's going to rule over it one day.

Within a blink of an eye, all the knives are in the wall, holding Matteo in place, but it's not him that draws my attention. It's the sway of Riona's hips as she walks to him saying something. The cameras don't pick up sound but based on her smile as she reaches Matteo, things are about to get interesting.

I can't take my eyes off her as she kneels in front of Matteo and runs her tongue along his length. As she wraps her lips around him, I lean back in my chair and adjust myself in my shorts. She's intoxicating. I could watch her like this all day.

The only thing I would change is to have her kneeling in front of me. Her eyes look up at Matteo with so much fire that I can't resist sliding my hand into my shorts and wrapping my hand around my painfully hard erection. As she sucks my brother's cock, I slowly pump myself, giving myself some pleasure but not enough for a release. I don't want to come without her wrapped around me in some way. When Matteo comes, I'm out of my seat and heading out of the office. It's my turn.

Walking up behind Riona as she kisses Matteo, I softly wrap my arms around her middle, pulling her back. I run my nose along her neck, making her shiver and I can't help my cocky smile at her reaction to me. I nip at her earlobe as I grind my erection against her ass and she melts into me with a quiet moan.

"Are you done watching?" Matteo gives me an excited smile, thinking we're going to have her together, but I have other plans.

"You had your time. It's my turn now." I place a kiss behind her ear and whisper so she can only hear me, "Are you okay with that?"

She gives me a single nod and I pick her up honeymoon style and carry her into my office. Matteo says something to Riona, but I don't hear it because I only have one focus.

The door shuts behind us and I take a seat in my computer chair with her in my lap. Her back is against my chest and I hook her legs over mine, keeping them open for me. I kiss up her neck as I lightly run my hands all over her upper half. She sucks in a breath as I skim my fingers across her stomach and lets out a moan when I push her bra straps down her shoulders, freeing her breasts. When I just lightly brush my fingers over her nipples, she just lets out a frustrated groan. "Please, Enzo... stop teasing me."

I cup her breasts in my hands and roll her nipples between my fingers. She arches into my hands with a satisfied moan. "What do you want, Beauty?"

"Touch me. Make me come." Her head falls back on my shoulder.

I turn her face toward me and press my lips to hers. She opens for me and I deepen our kiss, showing her how desperate I am for her. Not wanting to ignore her pleas, I slide my hand down her stomach and underneath her panties where I rub a tentative circle over her clit. She bucks up against my hand as she hums in approval. I slide my fingers further into her panties and sink two fingers inside her. As I push them in and out of her, the heel of my hand rubs against her clit, making her squeeze around me. She breaks our kiss and lays her head on my shoulder, panting. "Yes... Oh god... I'm so close."

Her nails dig into my chair's armrest and she clenches around my fingers. "God, you feel amazing squeezing around my fingers. I can't wait for you to squeeze my cock like this."

"Yes." She reaches behind her to my shorts. "Please Enzo. Fuck me."

Who would ever say no to her when she begs like that? Within seconds, my shorts are pushed down just enough to free my erection and her panties are pushed to the side with my erection at her entrance. She holds me at her entrance, giving me a few pumps until she slides herself on me. God, it's the most beautiful feeling.

When she's seated fully on me, I wrap my arm around her waist, pulling her back against my chest and flexing my hips up. I don't have a whole lot of motion in this position, but I make sure my thrusts are powerful, hitting just where she needs to be brought back to the edge. I slide my free hand back underneath her panties and find her clit.

I rub rough circles over it, and she bucks against me, sending me further inside her as she squeezes around me. Oh shit. I'm not going to last long if she keeps doing that. She rides my cock as she gets closer to coming and her moans grow louder and louder. "Fuck, Enzo. I'm so close."

"I can feel it. You feel so amazing riding my cock. Come for me, Beauty. Scream for me." I pick up my pace, thrusting hard into her as I pinch her clit and she comes screaming my name and squeezing me so tight that I come with a loud groan.

Our bodies are covered in a mist of sweat as we both catch our breath, lounging in my chair. I slide out of her and adjust her in my lap so she's sitting on one thigh and her legs draped over my other. I run my fingers through her hair as she looks at me with a pleased smile. The space between us is eliminated as our lips move toward each other and collide in a slow, passionate kiss. When our kiss breaks, I run my eyes over her face, taking in everything because she looks breathtaking. Something inside me warms with her in my arms and her light smile directed at me. I don't want this to end.

No words are spoken between us as we look at each other, but they don't need to be. After a while, Riona leans forward and places a quick kiss on my lips. "Show me your security system so we can go to bed." She runs her fingers through my hair. "You've worn me out."

She gives me a cheeky grin and I chuckle. "Alright." I slide us toward the desk, and we quickly adjust ourselves so our clothes are back in place and her back is against my chest again.

After I log in, I just sit back and watch her get to work. She quickly pulls up my security program without even having to ask where it is, which confirms we need a stronger firewall. With the club and house using the same security, I can't have just anyone being able to get access. Especially with her here.

A black screen pulls up and she starts typing in code before looking over her shoulder at me. "You sure about this? With it being my code, it'll give me full access to your security anytime I want."

I run my hands down her stocking covered thighs and back up. "Are you going to use it against us?"

She shrugs her shoulders and gives me a mischievous smile. "Who knows? Maybe. It might be fun sneaking into your house and into your bed."

An image of her sneaking into my bed naked pops in my head and that seems like the best surprise. "I'd be okay with that as long as you're not there to kill me."

"No promises." She smirks.

I chuckle and lean forward, kissing her shoulder. After a second of her watching me making sure I'm not going to object, she turns back to the monitors and continues typing in her code. Several minutes later she hits a button on the keyboard and the code starts to scroll until it disappears. She leans back against my chest and lets out a long breath. I nuzzle my nose into her neck as I wrap my arms around her. "You ready for bed?"

She nods and I loosen my hold on her so we can both stand and I lock the computer. Riona has her hand outreached to me and I take it in mine. She leads me out of my office, up the stairs, through the main level, and up to the second floor. We both enter her room to find a sleeping Matteo. She heads to her closet to change as I take a seat at the end of the bed, waiting for her.

She walks out minutes later in a long nightshirt and heads straight for the bed. As she passes me, her hand runs across my chest and I follow after. I pull back the covers and she slips in and slides all the way to Matteo's back. She places a kiss on his cheek and I climb into bed next to her. She curls into my side and lets out a long breath. I place a kiss on her forehead as I wrap my arms around her and whisper, "Goodnight, Beauty."

"Goodnight, Beast." She places a kiss on my chest and almost immediately her breaths even out in sleep. Beast. I like the sound of that. She connected us and I hope she means it, even though she didn't say the words exactly. I don't think I'll be able to let her go.

Chapter Ten

Riona

No. Not again. Concrete and darkness surround me and right in front of me is Aisling, curled up on a dirty cot with a thin blanket partially laying over her. "Aisling," I whisper hoping to have some sort of connection to her. She doesn't stir so I walk to the side of her cot with her facing away from me toward the wall and reach out to touch her. I try to move the hair from her face, but nothing happens.

Wanting her to know I'm here somehow, I lay down in the small space at the edge of the bed and curl around her. I whisper to her how much I miss her and I'm going to save her as I run my fingers through her hair and rub my hand up and down her arm even though I can't actually touch her. I'm not sure how long I lay with *her but I get into a dream like trance until I'm jolted from it suddenly by two men standing over me and Aisling screaming, "No."*

The men move in on her, tightening the chain around her wrists that I didn't notice before, so her arms are held above her head and her blanket is pulled from her body exposing her in a dirty shirt and shorts. Her legs thrash around, trying to keep the other guy away from her but he grabs her legs holding them against the bed spread apart. He keeps her spread with his legs as he unbuttons his pants. She tries to fight against her chains and their holds as she screams.

My screams fill the air as well as I try to help but nothing I do touches them. The two of them chuckle as the man in between her legs bends over her with a wicked grin. "Your fight and your screams turn me on."

He pumps his erection looking over her and a shiver of disgust runs through me. I try to focus on his face but it's blurry. All I can see is his awful smile. I watch, laying there, unable to do anything as he rips her shorts and she screams.

Her screams quickly turn into mine and instead of us being in the concrete room, I'm now in the room of my tortured past. And instead of the blurry face over me, Tony DeAngelo's face is there as he chuckles. Pain shoots through me as the man I know is dead rapes me. "You're so perfect, my pretty Princess. Your pain is so arousing. Look at all this blood. You're going to be my new favorite toy. I'm never going to let you go."

I scream in terror as he continues to rip me open. Tony continues to draw pain from me as he uses me for pleasure. My name being yelled breaks through my screams, and I'm pulled from my torture.

I wake with a start to find someone holding my wrists in front of me and my body held back against someone. Panic takes over and I pull against the hold on me while screaming, "Let go of me."

Instantly all holds are gone and I quickly jump off the bed and back up into a corner. Now that I have space, I realize that it was Enzo and Matteo holding me and that I'm not in that awful room. I slouch against the wall and slide down it until I'm sitting on the floor with my knees to my chest and I wrap my arms around them.

Not taking my eyes off them, I watch them climb out of the bed and Enzo softly calls out my name as Matteo pulls on his boxers. Even though I watch them come over to me, I don't quite register it until Enzo reaches out and touches my shoulder. I jerk away from him with a small whimper and they both step back.

"Please don't touch me." My breath starts to pick up as the room starts to grow smaller.

Worry and concern takes over their faces. "We won't touch you, Princess."

The nickname has me tightening my hold on my knees as I think about the name Tony called me during the two awful weeks I was held by him. Memories assault me and I bury my face in my knees, trying to get a grip on reality. I can feel Matteo and Enzo's eyes on me, and it feels too weighted. "Can you leave? I need space."

"Of course." Enzo's calming voice washes over me and I have to fight back my sobs because I need them gone before I break down.

The second the door clicks shut I let out a gasp, trying to suck in air as I fall apart. It's been a while since my memories of those awful weeks have caused so much havoc. Normally they're just nightmares and don't feel so real. It was like I was back in that room. A room I haven't been in for eleven years. I feel like I relived every horrible minute of the torture by the time I'm able to surface from my panic.

When my tears stop and I'm able to breathe without the feeling of a hundred-pound weight sitting on my chest, I lean my head back against the wall. Rape is a torture that's both physical and mental and to go through it over and over again isn't something I'd wish on most people. And the fact that Aisling is going though it makes me sick. I need to find her.

I stand from my huddled position and my whole body aches. How long was I like that? I head into my bathroom and directly go to the shower and turn it on. As the water warms, I pull my night shirt over my head. Stepping under the hot water, my aches slowly start to dissipate, and I quickly move through my shower routine, making sure to spend extra time washing my body. I have to wash away those memories.

When I finish, I turn off the shower and dry off, heading into my connected closet. Needing to get out of the house and search for Aisling, I grab my favorite skinny jeans, a black tank top, and my black Converse. Once I'm dressed, I leave my room and head downstairs to find one of the guys. As much as I'm ready to get out of here, I'm not stupid enough to leave without one of them. They're hired to keep me safe and have my back. I can't help Aisling if I'm taken or killed.

I hear their voices coming from the living room so I head in that direction. When I enter the room, all three of them turn to me. "Hey, Princess," Matteo says hesitantly.

I give him a soft smile as I walk toward him, still getting a sickening feeling when he calls me that. "Hey. Sorry for my freak out." I sit down on the couch between him and Enzo.

Enzo moves closer to me but doesn't touch me. "You don't need to apologize. How are you doing?"

"I'm doing better now." Enzo sets his arm across the back of the couch, behind my head and I can tell it's killing him not to touch me. I lean my head back to rest it against his arm and he lets out a breath as his arm goes around my shoulders. Matteo must've been wanting to touch and comfort me too because his hand goes to my knee when I don't freak out about Enzo's touch.

"Did you have another dream about Aisling?" Dante brings my attention away from Enzo and Matteo's touch, back to the conversation.

"Yes and no. But I don't want to talk about it." He nods and leans back in his chair. "I actually came down to see if one of you would come out with me. I need to be out searching for Aisling. I'm not going to find her sitting behind my computer."

"I'll go out with you," Dante volunteers. "I need to follow up with some merchants that owe us some money and you can ask around."

I nod, feeling relieved that they aren't going to fight me on this. "What about Enzo and Matteo?"

Matteo squeezes my knee, drawing my attention. "We have other business to deal with. Unfortunately, Dante will need to go with you tonight as well."

I shrug my shoulders, trying to act like I'm not disappointed about them not spending the day with me. This is probably for the best. I can't get too attached. It'll help with me putting my walls back up around them. "Okay." I stand from the couch, removing myself from their touch. "I'll go grab my weapons. Are we leaving soon?"

Dante nods. "I'll meet you at the front door."

I leave the guys in the living room to head back to my room to grab my gun and knives. I need to find some information about who took Aisling today. It's been days and I'm still not any closer to finding her.

Chapter Eleven

Dante

Riona comes down the stairs with a gun holstered to her hip and a dagger strapped to each of her thighs. Man, she's a goddess. A perfect woman. She smiles at me as she loops her arms through the straps of a black backpack. "Are you ready to go?"

I step to the side and signal for her to go past. "After you."

She walks past me and we leave the house through the front door. "So, what's the bookbag for?"

"Oh, it has stuff I might need for tonight. I wasn't sure if we'd be coming back before then."

"We don't have to come back." I grab the car door for her. "Is what I'm wearing appropriate enough for what you have planned?"

She stands in front of me, looking me up and down. "You're wearing dark enough colors. We hopefully won't have to do too much if everything goes as planned."

She climbs into the car and I walk around the front to get into my black Audi Q7. When I get into the driver seat, Riona holds out her hand. I look at her hand and then her face, confused. "Do you need something?"

"The blindfold."

"Oh." I reach across the console and in between her legs to open the glove compartment. Riona squirms in her seat and I lean over further so my arm rubs against her thigh. Her breath catches and I smile up at her. "Do you not like me between your legs, Rose?"

Shocked, she smiles at me. "Are you flirting with me, Dante?"

"Maybe. You didn't answer my question." I pull the blindfold out and close the compartment, resting my hand on her thigh.

Her eyes darken with lust. "I'm not against it. I'm just surprised."

"Why? You're a beautiful and strong woman, why wouldn't I flirt with you?" I slide my hand higher up her thigh.

"I don't know. Enzo and Matteo were so open with their flirting from the beginning. You just seem irritated by my presence and being forced to protect me and find Aisling."

"Openly flirting isn't really my style but watching you with them earlier made me jealous. I wanted you to come sit with me." I close the distance between us and kiss her. It takes her a second to kiss me back but when she does, she deepens the kiss, trying to fight for control. Not giving it up, I bite down on her bottom lip, making her moan and she gives in. I pull back from our kiss to find her breathless.

She chuckles quietly as she leans back in her chair. "So, you're just going to take what you want now?"

I smile at her. "Yep. You don't have a problem with that, do you?"

She shakes her head. "And you don't have a problem with me sleeping with your brothers?"

Not at all. This won't be the first time we've shared a woman but it's the first time we want something more than just sex. Closing the distance between us again, I kiss her, showing her just how much I don't mind she's with my brothers.

Desire burns in her eyes as we separate. "I'm going to take that as a no. But I wonder, would you join us?"

I give her a knowing smile as I lean back in my seat not answering her question. "Put the blindfold on, Riona."

She gives me an excited smile as she takes the blindfold and pulls it over her eyes. "Just so you know, I like that you didn't answer my question. Now I get to imagine all the possible ways I can have all of you."

I bite back a groan as I adjust myself, thinking of her in between all of us naked. Whatever fantasies she has, I'll happily participate, but I also want her to myself as well. I put the car in drive and make my way off our property. "Just so you know, I wouldn't have made you wear the blindfold if you didn't mention it."

She looks at me without seeing me. "What?! Then why am I wearing it?"

I chuckle. "You're the one who asked for it."

"That's okay." She leans back and links her fingers on her lap. "I don't mind being blindfolded. I'm also open to being tied up."

I groan and grip the steering wheel tighter so I don't reach for her. "We need to change the subject or I'm going to pull over and see how far I can push your limits."

She chuckles. "You're no fun. If we can't talk about sex, then you need to entertain me somehow. Tell me about what the Russo family does. I pride myself in knowing all the families, but I don't know anything about you guys."

I merge onto the highway, taking us back into the city. "Well, we moved into the New York area about a year ago. We took over from another underboss that had been dormant for a while."

"I still never remember the Russo name ever."

"Well, thanks." I chuckle.

"Oh, I didn't mean it in a bad way."

"I'm just messing with you. We're a small organization here in New York. Our main organization is in Italy. We don't want waves here against your father." Our parents have history; while they aren't friends, my father doesn't want us to cause trouble. We don't need New York.

"It's best not to piss off my father or you would've met me a lot sooner."

I quickly look over to her. "Is that what you do for your father? Eliminate any threats?"

"Mostly. I also gather information at his meetings and parties since I'm invisible to all powerful men." Not to us. She shined the moment she walked in on her father's arm. Only idiots wouldn't notice her in a room.

"You aren't invisible. We saw you at the Gala with your fake smile and dancing with all the eligible men." I reach over and remove the blindfold.

She blinks rapidly until she focuses on me. "I don't remember dancing with any of you. I actually don't remember you there at all."

I know. We stayed out of sight all night. "We like to stay in the shadows. It helps with what we do."

"And that is?" Curiosity is all over her face.

"We mainly deal with money laundering through the club, information, and security. We help find people, follow people, and merchants pay us to protect their stores. That's what I need to do today. I have to follow up with some merchants that haven't paid and check on a few that were having problems to make sure it's all good now. We also have a small involvement in drugs and weapons but that is mainly just roll over from my father." I take the exit for Little Italy.

"How many people do you have underneath you guys?"

"About 75. Our people pretty much stay in Little Italy working as security. We have a few guys that work at the club as well."

"Wow you're a lot bigger than I thought."

"We like to stay under the radar. Worry about ourselves. At least that's how we want to run our leadership."

"Past leadership ran differently?" she asks.

"Yeah, they got too big for their britches, I think the saying is."

She chuckles. "So did you grow up in Italy?"

"Yes. We were there until high school, then we were shipped off to California for boarding school. We needed to be here to be ready to take over the American chapter. It's tradition. Only the oldest stays in Italy, so Armando is there ready to take over when my father is ready to step down, and we run the American groups."

"What other cities are you in?" Her eyes are on the side of my face.

"Chicago, Detroit, Los Angeles, Dallas, and a small organization in Miami and New Orleans."

"You're bigger than the Murphy organization, why don't you overthrow us?"

"Because we don't need to. We have a partnership with your father."

We pull into an alley just inside Little Italy's borders and I park the car. I look over to her to find her looking at me with such curiosity. "What?"

"I'm just shocked. You could easily take power over the city, but you don't. If my father had that kind of power, he'd take over the whole country." She looks confused because she'd only ever watched her father take.

"And your father's need to always get more power will eventually be his downfall." I can tell she wants to fight me on that but I can also see that she understands what I mean as well. I turn off the car and lean on the center console, looking at her. "I didn't mean that your father would be killed. It could be his people who force him out so Killian could take over."

"I know. Power is a deadly thing. Not just for the people seeking it." I know exactly what she means, but how she says it, I can tell she has experienced the bad part of power. I reach over for her hand, but she pulls back from me. "We should probably get out."

She grabs the door handle and opens the door. I climb out of the car as well and walk around to her side. She's messing with something in her bag as I walk up behind her. "I know you want to ask around today, but can you please try to lay low while doing it? We still don't know who took Aisling for sure, but Maxim is still trying to find you, along with the O'Brien threats. We can't let them know you're on the streets."

She stands, removing her gun holster and tucking the gun in the back of her pants. "I'll be smart about it. I'm just going to talk to the guys I know."

"Okay. These are the list of merchants I'm visiting. Will you please stay in contact with me as you move around?"

"You're not coming with me?" She looks at me confused because she knows what her father told us.

"Your guys aren't going to talk with me being your shadow. You're more than capable of protecting yourself."

She smiles at me with appreciation and nods. "I'll stay in contact, letting you know where I am."

Riona pulls a hat out of her bag and she pulls it on her head and then places sunglasses over her eyes. "Do you think this is low key enough?"

I chuckle. "Rose, you can never be low key. Your red hair is a beacon drawing everyone's attention."

She throws her hands up in the air. "Well, I can't change that."

"You definitely shouldn't." I reach forward and twist a strand of her hair around my finger. "I like your red hair."

She grabs my hand, stopping me from twirling her hair. "You're getting distracted. Let's go."

She steps closer to me to close her door and I drop my hand from her hair. We both walk out of the alley, but when we're about to go separate ways, I grab her hand stopping her. "Keep your eyes open. Your father still hasn't found out who released your location that night."

She gives me a nod, understanding that she needs to be careful and walks away from me down the street. I watch her until she turns a corner and then I turn and walk the opposite direction to handle my business.

Chapter Twelve

Riona

I feel like I've spoken to everyone in Little Italy today and haven't learned anything. No one has seen Aisling, Maxim, or Craig O'Brien. Or if they have, they aren't saying. Since it's getting later in the day and I need to start heading to Swartz's house, I send Dante a text letting him know I'm heading back to the car.

Blending into the dinner crowd, I walk down Mulberry Street trying to get to the car as quickly as possible. I turn down a small side street getting further from the crowd when the hairs on the back of my neck stand up.

Without drawing attention to myself, I scan the street in front of me trying to see if anyone looks suspicious. Nothing looks out of place and the few people that are on the street aren't paying any attention to me.

Ahead of me is a large storefront window so I keep my pace the same as I discreetly use the window as a mirror. I walk the length of the window, not finding anything that has put me on edge. I'm about to just chalk it up to everything going on when I see a man dressed in all black walking behind me and he's definitely watching me.

I pull out my phone and hit Dante's contact. Placing my phone to my ear, I wait for Dante to answer. "Riona?"

"Hi D! I know I'm late but I promise I'm just around the corner. Will you go ahead and order me a drink? I really need it."

"Riona, what's going on? Where are you?" Come on Dante, catch on.

"I'm a few blocks away on Bayard Street. Oh, I forgot to tell you my special friend is coming to."

Dante is quiet for a second and I pray he gets it. "Is someone following you?"

"Yes, that friend." I see the alley we parked in up ahead and I breathe a sigh of relief.

"I'm coming."

"No, that's okay. He can order when he gets there. I don't know what he wants. I'm actually turning into the alley now across from the bar. See you in a few."

I hang up the phone as I round the corner and Dante is there standing in a dark corner. I give him a smile as I pull out my gun from the back of my pants and move to hide behind the car for the guy.

Seconds later, my follower walks into the alley and I step out from behind the car as Dante steps out of his dark corner, slamming him into the wall. I raise my gun, aiming for the stranger as Dante holds the man against the wall. Seeing the two together, Dante is at least six inches taller and has a hundred pounds on him. When Dante pulls back the guy's hood, I see why. It's just a kid, probably no older than sixteen. "Please don't hurt me. I just wanted to give you information, Miss Murphy."

I almost chuckle at being called Miss Murphy by a kid, like I'm an old person or something. I step up in front of him and I see he is scared shitless. Lowering my gun, I touch Dante's shoulder, getting him to loosen his hold. Dante drops his arm that holds the kid to the wall and quickly pats the kid down before stepping back next to me. "What's your name kid?"

"Leo."

I cross my arms and step forward a little. "It was stupid of you to follow me like that. We could've killed you."

Leo's eyes widened. "I'm sorry... I just heard you were looking for information on Maxim."

Interesting. "I am."

The kid frantically looks between the two of us. "My family owns Bella Amor and last night I delivered dinner to Maxim. I can tell you where he is."

I look back at Dante to see if he thinks it's legit. He shrugs his shoulders silently saying 'what can it hurt?' Turning back to Leo, I ask. "What do you want for this information?"

The kid shakes his head. "Nothing." I nod for him to continue. "He's staying at 5001 Hicks Street in Brooklyn."

"Thanks, Leo." I pull out one of my cards that I always have on me. I only give these cards to people I feel might need my help one day. "This is my card. If you or your family ever need anything, give me a call."

The kid looks shocked, nodding while looking at the card. He knows this isn't just any ordinary business card. "Thank you, Miss Murphy."

"Riona. Now go on." Leo slowly walks toward the entrance of the alley, still looking at the tiny card. "Hey Leo." He turns. "Never follow anyone into a dark alley again. You never know what people's monsters look like." He stands up straighter, knowing we don't live in a pretty world and nods before leaving Dante and me in the alley.

When I know we're alone, I turn to Dante. "We need to go."

He smiles at me and holds his arm out for me to pass. "After you, Miss Murphy."

I flip him off as I pass. "Shut up."

He chuckles as we both climb into the car and head across town. "I already sent guys to the address the kid gave us. They'll watch for Maxim and once we get eyes on him, we'll move in."

"When did you do that?" Shocked, I look over at him.

"When you were giving the kid your card and a solid life lesson. By the way, why did you give him your card?"

"Because he is a kid and is bound to get into trouble, needing help."

He looks over at me. "Do you give out those cards a lot?"

"No, I don't." It's a feeling I get when I look at someone. It's like I can tell they're going to need help in the future.

"He could sell it. Your number for a favor is a high price." He doesn't understand.

"He won't. Plus, I know who I give these cards to."

"All of them?"

I nod. "I know which ones are outstanding. Most people I give them to call me pretty quickly." Typically, they're people I remove from one bad situation and willingly go back home to another.

Since we're running a little behind, I pull out my laptop and start going over the footage from the outside cameras, making sure nothing happened today. On fast forward, I watch the back door first, seeing nothing all day and then switch to the front of the house. Other than Swartz going to work and coming back, there is nothing, which is perfect.

Darkness surrounds us as Dante parks the car a couple streets over and he leans over the console to watch the video feed with me. I have all three cameras up and the microphone on from under the table as John Marshall steps out of his car. Two out of the six targets have arrived.

"Riona, that's the Chief of Police."

"I know."

"You can't kill the Chief of Police. He's in everyone's pocket. He allows us to do what we all do. I'm surprised your father is allowing this."

"First of all, my father has no say on what jobs I take. Second, I don't give a shit who it is. All I care about is what a disgusting piece of shit he is. Do I need to give you the full story of what they did to Tiffany so you can realize how much he deserves to die?"

"No." He looks away but I can see the conflict on his face.

"And she wasn't the only one. You saw the pictures of the basement in that house. That setup is from experience."

He turns back to me with a look that says he doesn't need further reasoning. "How do you plan to get away with this and every other illegal thing we all do from here on out?"

"I don't get caught. For this job, I have the Captain of the Fire Department and the new Chief of Police in my pocket."

"You already have the new Chief of Police in your pocket?" He's impressed.

"Yes. I'm not stupid enough to kill the men keeping me and my family off the radar without having his replacement willing to do the same."

He smirks. "I'm sorry for even questioning you. Who else will be here tonight?"

"The DA, Lieutenant Governor, a Wall Street guy, and a social worker for the foster care system." People of power shouldn't be as despicable as they are.

"This is going to rock a lot of boats with all these guys being murdered." He shakes his head in disbelief at how much this will change our city, as the people next in line are forced into their new positions.

"Which is why it's going to look like an accident. A gas leak."

Another car pulls up and Carter Winters and Zach Hanes, the DA and Lt. Governor step out. With the four of them inside, I turn on the gas and set a timer for an hour. "We have an hour."

Dante sets a timer too. "What if the rest don't show?"

"Then I'll go to their houses and kill them in their sleep." I have at least three plans for this execution. None of them will make it to morning.

"How will that look like an accident?"

I lean down and pull out a vial. "Poison."

He reaches for the vial and tilts it back and forth. "Non-detectable?"

I nod with an evil smile. "It simulates a brain aneurysm."

"Very handy." He looks impressed as he hands the vial back.

"Yes, it is. I normally always have some sort of poison on me. It's my preferred choice for killing."

"You aren't known for your poisons. You're known for your brutal, messy kills."

Yeah, I love sending a message in blood. "Those are only a small portion of my kills. The ones I want to hit the news. Other than poison, I'm very handy with a sniper rifle. But that is only about a handful of my skills."

"How many kills do you have?"

I shrug my shoulders. "Over a hundred. Not all are jobs. Some came from threats against my father."

"Wow. You would've had to start killing as a kid to have those kinds of numbers."

"14 actually."

"Why would your father start you so early? Even my father waited until I was 18."

"It wasn't his choice." I look at him with a blank expression because he doesn't need to know my trauma.

"What made you choose to be an assassin?"

"I learned you can't be weak in this life. So, I made myself strong." Another car pulls up at the house and Warren Lowe steps out. That means only one left. Looking at the clock, I see that it is just past seven. "Only the social worker is left."

"How much longer..."

Dante is cut off by Warren Lowe bursting into the house loudly. "I've been waiting for tonight all week. It's been a while since we've had our fun." The guys sitting around the table chuckle.

Raymond pushes an open chair back. "Grab a beer and have a seat. Thomas isn't here yet. He wanted it dark before he brought us our treat. He'll be here in a few."

I look to Dante as a sickening feeling fills my stomach. Their treat is going to be someone. And my guess is an unwilling someone. Dante has the same look that I do. "That isn't part of your plan, is it?"

I shake my head. "No, it's not."

"Are you going to stop the gas?" His panic is starting to match mine.

"No. They die tonight. Either before the fire or during."

As the guys discuss who they think Thomas Oz is bringing, I start digging in my bag for all my daggers and my poison accessories.

I wrap my hair into a bun and thread two hairpins filled with poison through it. "What's with the knitting needles and rings?"

I smile at him as I slip on two rings. "I think you know the answer to that."

He looks between all the accessories. "More poison?"

"I told you it was my favorite." He reaches his hand out to the needles and I move away from him. "I wouldn't do that. I don't have the antidote with me."

"You didn't poison yourself by putting it in your hair, how will a touch poison me?" His hand still hovers near my head.

"It's dried on the tip of the pin. If you break skin, you die. I didn't break my skin and I've been using these pins for years. I've learned not to poison myself."

His eyes widened in shock. "You've poisoned yourself before."

I strap my leg and waist holsters on. "Oh yeah. Multiple times. I had to learn. Plus, they were minor poisons. Making you tell the truth or sleep."

He chuckles. "I would've loved to see that."

"There might be videos…" Wait, I shouldn't have said that.

"Oh, I'm definitely getting my hands on them." He starts typing away on his phone.

"Who are you texting?" I lean over the console to see his phone, but I can't see the screen.

"Your brother."

"Oh no, you don't." I reach over, trying to grab his phone, but he moves out of the way. We chuckle as we wrestle each other for the phone. One second we're laughing and the next Dante turns to me and kisses me. I lean into him, deepening our kiss before I pull away from him at the sound of a scream.

Looking at the camera feed, I see a little girl probably around fourteen cowering on the floor as six men surround her. Fuck. When did they get here? Their voices filter through the speaker on my laptop as they openly talk about how pretty she is and what they want to do to her. I'm not going to let them touch her.

Handing the laptop to Dante, I throw open my door, ready to bust in there and kill them when Dante grabs my arm. "Wait. Look." He shows me the screen. "Only Thomas is taking her downstairs."

With us both quiet, I hear Raymond say, "Lock her up in the basement for now. No one touches until we're done playing. You know the rules. Winner gets first dibs."

Disgusting. At least they're going to be dead before the night is over. Thomas appears back on the camera. "She's locked in the cage, crying."

"Fuck, now my dick is hard. I can't wait to capture her tears and use them as I jerk off." John Marshall moves in his seat as he adjusts himself.

"What the fuck kind of kink is that?" Dante looks disgusted.

"One he'll never get off on again. I need to get her out." I look down at the stopwatch on my phone and see I have 25 minutes until the house blows. "Shit, I need to go."

I start switching out my poison weapons for my gun. "From the pictures Enzo took, there are windows in the basement that I can get in and out of without detection."

I grab my AirPods out of my bag. "I need you to stay here and watch them. Let me know if they head to the basement." Without waiting for him to agree, I step away from the car and close the door. As I walk down the street, I call Dante as I put one of the buds in my ear. "Fuck Riona, you don't have to do this alone."

"I'm not. You're on lookout duty. A very important job." I pass the camera looking at the outside of the house and smile at Dante, knowing he's not happy at being told to stay in the car.

"Don't mock me, Ri."

"I'm not."

"I don't believe you." I make it to the side of the house and I bend down next to the windows. I can't see anything inside which means there is some sort of covering on them that I didn't notice in the photos.

Pulling out my blade, I push the tip into the seal where the lock should be and slide the blade until the lock slides, unlocking the window. Soundlessly, I push the window up and the basement comes into full view. Right in the middle of the basement is the girl curled in a ball, crying.

Before climbing in, I tap on the window, getting the girl's attention and whisper, "Hey." The girl's head shoots up and she starts to whimper. "Shh. It's okay. Please don't scream."

"Help. Please help me." She cries quietly.

"I am. I promise. I'm going to climb in now." The girl nods.

Flipping onto my stomach, I slide in through the window feet first. When I'm hanging by my hands, I drop the final few feet, landing without a sound. Now that I'm standing in front of the girl, she looks me up and down hesitantly. I make sure not to make any sudden movements as I look over the cage, seeing a heavy-duty lock. "Shit."

Dante's worried voice rings in my ear. "What? What's wrong?"

"There's a lock on the cage and I don't have my kit with me."

"You don't have time for that anyways. There's only ten minutes until the house blows."

"Fuck." Time is moving too fast. I look around the room. "There has to be a key down here."

I scan the walls looking for a hook of some sort. It's so dark down here that I can't really see anything more than a few feet in front of me. Walking along the edge of the room, I head closer to the door because that is where I'd keep the key.

"You're going the wrong way. The key is by the table," the girl whispers.

I quickly walk over to the table with all the sex toys and tools laid out. Scanning the table, I find the key laying right in the middle. You know this actually is a shitty place to hold someone. They leave keys laying around. There weren't secure locks on the windows. And there isn't even a top to her cage. Anyone could climb the chain linked fence. Man, these guys are idiots.

Grabbing the key, I walk over to the cage and quickly unlock it. The girl stands to her feet as I quietly set down the lock and key on the ground. The noise upstairs grows larger as a man cheers and I use the noise to mask the sound of opening the gate. A loud squeak rings through the basement and the girl and I both freeze as everything goes quiet. "Dante?"

"You need to move. Three minutes." I wave my hand motioning for the girl to move.

"Did they hear?" I'm more worried about them coming down here right now.

"Yes. But they thought it was her screaming."

I grab the stool at the table and place it along the wall under the window. Looking over at the girl, I see how thin she is and how shaky. She's not going to be able to pull herself up. "I'm going to get myself through the window and pull you up, okay?"

She gives me a timid nod and I boost myself up on the stool and push and crawl my way through the window. As soon as I'm out, I quickly turn over, place my feet on the wall for leverage and reach as far as I can into the window. With one hand I barely reach her hand, but I grab onto what I can and pull. Once I've got her a little bit higher, I grab her wrist and pull. It's not a pretty or graceful rescue as the two us squirm and wiggle her out, but once she is, I'm on the move.

Pulling her to her feet, I take off running, dragging her with me. We just pass the back of the house next door when Swartz's house explodes, sending both the girl and me to the ground. Dante screams my name in my ear. "God damn it, Ri. You better have been out of that house."

I chuckle. "We're out. Come get us." I look at the girl lying next to me. "Let's get you safe." We both stand up and I help the girl to Dante's car. Leaving her in the backseat, I get into the passenger seat and we don't say a word as Dante drives us past the burning house. Rot in hell, fuckers.

I pull out my phone and text Dr. Gibbons one word: Done. Letting her know she and her daughter don't need to live in fear of Raymond Swartz and his sick friends anymore.

Chapter Thirteen

Riona

Firetrucks pass us and I turn in my seat, watching them fly down the road. All they're going to be able to do is stop the fire from spreading to the other houses. I can't help the smile on my face as we turn and the house goes out of sight. Looking at the girl curled up in the backseat, I grab my backpack and pull out a hoodie. "Would you like to wear this?"

She nods and grabs the hoodie from me. "Where are you taking me?"

"If it's okay with you, I was thinking we could go get something to eat. I could use a cheeseburger."

She nods timidly. "Yeah, that's okay."

I nod and look at Dante. "Do you know where Sally's is?"

He nods and turns on his blinker, heading to my favorite diner.

I look back at the girl. "What's your name, sweetheart?"

"Daisy."

"It's nice to meet you, Daisy. My name is Riona and this is Dante. We're going to keep you safe. Can you tell me how you ended up with Thomas Oz and in that house?"

"Mr. Oz is my social worker. He was supposed to take me to a new home."

"Are you in foster care?" She nods. "Do you have any family?"

She shakes her head no. "I've been in foster care my whole life. I don't have any family."

Dante pulls into the parking lot of Sally's and I'm happy to see it's not busy. "I have a change of clothes; do you want it?"

Daisy shakes her head. "I'm okay."

"Okay. Let's go inside. This is the best place to get a cheeseburger. I hope you're hungry." Daisy opens the door and I look at Dante. "How about you? You want a cheeseburger?"

"Yeah …" He looks at me with desire burning in his eyes. "And something else."

I chuckle at him. "Well, I'll make sure Sally puts a little extra special sauce on your burger." I open my door and step out joining Daisy.

She looks over at Dante, hesitantly. "Is that your boyfriend?"

Daisy walks beside me toward the diner and when we're far enough away, I whisper, "He wishes." She chuckles and I lean into her. "Do you want to know a secret?"

Her smile brightens. "Yes!"

"He's not the only one. His two brothers want me too."

Her eyes widen. "No way."

I open the door to the diner and signal for her to go in. "Yes way. And they're all hot."

"Lucky. I can't even get my crush to notice me."

"Maybe he's not worth it then." I smile at her as an older woman in a yellow waitress uniform walks toward us.

"Miss Riona, is that you?" I smile at Sally. "Oh, bless my heart, it is. It's been forever, Sweetie."

Sally pulls me into a hug and I welcome her comfort. "It's only been a couple of months. You know I can't go long without your cheeseburgers."

She holds me at arm's length. "By the looks of you, you need more cheeseburgers in your life." I roll my eyes at her and she looks over my shoulder. "Who do you have with you? Where's Aisling?"

My smile drops a little at the mention of Aisling and I feel Dante stepping closer behind me. "I'm Dante, this is Daisy." I'm thankful he steps in because I don't think I could lie to Sally.

"Well, it's nice to meet you both. Come on, let me show you to the best booth." Sally turns and walks to the back of the diner. I signal for Daisy to go ahead of us and I give Dante a quick smile. Dante's hand lightly sits on my back as we follow Sally and Daisy. I slide into the booth with my back against the wall and I'm facing the door and Dante slides in next me.

Daisy smiles across from us as she watches Dante slide over until he's touching me and his arm rests behind my shoulders. "He is pretty hot, now that I've seen him in the light."

I crack up laughing and look at Dante's shocked face. Sally chuckles quietly as she watches all of us. "I'm going to put your burger orders in. Waters okay for everyone?"

We all nod, and Dante turns to me. "You think I'm hot."

I smile at him. "Technically I said you and your brothers were hot."

He gives me a cocky grin and shrugs his shoulders. "I'm okay with that."

I roll my eyes at him and look at Daisy. "Daisy, I have an idea I want to run by you. Is that okay?" She looks up at me and nods as she sucks down her water Sally just dropped off. "First, I need to know, do you want to go back into foster care?"

She looks confused by my question. "Don't I have to? I can't live on the streets."

"Well, I have a different idea."

Daisy sits back in her chair and gives me her full attention. "Daisy, you aren't the only girl I have saved. Most of these girls are like you; they don't have any families and were in bad situations. I have a home with a trusted friend where these girls stay and we help them finish school, find jobs, and go to college. I want to know if you would be interested in staying at this house. You would still be in the foster system, but with my connections you'd never be moved from this house and all the money the foster care system pays goes into an account in your name for college."

Tears run down Daisy's face. "You'd really do that for me? Why?"

I nod. "I do it because I have experienced what dirty, disgusting men can do to girls and I know the support you need afterwards. I hope one day I won't have to save anyone from it but until then, I want there to be a place where you and they can feel safe." I feel Dante stiffen next to me and I adjust in the seat, feeling uncomfortable that he heard that.

She nods frantically. "Yes, I want to go there. Please."

I smile at her. "Before you agree, let me take you to the house so you can see it and you can meet Miss Claus."

There is a spark in her eyes as she thinks of the fictional character. "Like Santa Claus?"

I chuckle. "Yes, but no relation."

We both chuckle. "Okay. Can we still eat before we go?"

"Absolutely. I'm going to make a call really quick so Miss Claus knows we're coming." I look at Dante to move, but he is looking at me like he's still trying to figure out everything that I just said. Before he opens his mouth to ask questions, I shake my head no, telling him I'm not talking about it. He keeps his mouth shut but gives me a look saying he's going to ask later. We have a stare off for a second before he moves out of the booth for me to get out.

I slide out of the booth and Daisy is there in a hot second giving me a big hug. "Thank you so much."

I wrap my arms around her, hugging her back. She has obviously been through more than tonight to be this happy about getting out of the system.

Daisy eventually lets go of me and I give her a smile as I walk outside, pulling out my phone and hitting Sandra's number.

She answers in the first ring. "Hello Riona."

I smile when I hear her voice. We haven't spoken in a while. I try to keep my distance from them. "Hi Sandra. How are you tonight?"

"I'm doing good. The girls just finished dinner."

"Good." I don't know how she deals with so many girls.

"You have another one, don't you?"

"Yes, I do. Do you have room?"

"God, why does our world have to be so dark and shitty? Yes, of course I have room. This house of yours has like twenty rooms."

When we started this, I bought the biggest property on the market. It used to be a rehab facility before we made it into a home. "My question is more for you and if you can handle another girl."

"Yes, I can. You know I love these girls. How old is she?"

She's a saint. "I don't know specifically but she looks about fourteen. Her name is Daisy."

Her thoughts are spinning as she plans for the new arrival. "Okay. When can I expect you?"

"An hour okay? We're about to eat."

"That's perfect."

"Okay. See you then." I hang up and turn to look inside. Dante's eyes connect with mine instantly and a sense of safety washes over me, knowing he's watching out for me.

Sally is dropping off the burgers as I'm arriving back at the table and Dante stands, letting me back in. Daisy doesn't take a breath as she digs into her burger and fries. It looks like she's not even chewing before stuffing more food in her mouth.

When he sits back down, he leans into me and whispers, "I'm learning a lot about you today. You won't be able to get away from answering my questions later."

I ignore him because there isn't a chance in hell that I'm talking to him about my past. I dig into my burger after pushing my fries to Daisy. God, this is a good burger.

Chapter Fourteen

Dante

When we arrived at the mansion where Daisy will be staying, Riona asked me to wait outside since there are still some girls that aren't comfortable with men. So now I'm standing outside this saving grace Riona has set up for girls and all I can think about is what she told Daisy at the diner. She spoke like she's experienced what Daisy was about to go through. Has she been held captive? Has she been raped? Was she abused? Who the hell touched her?

I know she's not going to tell me and it's probably not my business, but I'm starting to care for her and there's something big in her past that's still affecting her. If this morning with Enzo and Matteo didn't show that, I don't know what does.

Knowing I'm going to need backup to get her to open up, I call my brother. "Hey man. How's Riona? I heard about the fire. I can't believe it really exploded." Matteo, of course, sounds excited about the destruction.

"Yeah, it did. We had a little hiccup though. They brought a little girl to the house."

"What!? Please tell me you didn't blow up a house with a girl in it."

"Of course not, Matteo. Riona saved her and is getting her set up at a house she owns for girls that she's saved. But we can get into that later. I need your help when we get back. Riona is going to try to get out of talking to me and I need your help in getting her to talk."

"About what?" I can hear his hesitation about making her tell us something she's not open to discuss.

"I think she's been hurt in her past. When she was talking to this girl earlier, it was from experience, without saying exactly what happened."

"Who the fuck touched her?" This is why I called him. I knew he'd want to know as much as me.

"I don't know. That's why I need your help."

"We'll be there. She's not getting out of it."

"Thanks, man. Will you tell Enzo?" Enzo won't be so gung-ho about this.

"Yeah. We're finishing here and will be waiting at home."

"Alright, see you soon." I hang up the phone and lean against my car, looking up at the house. This girl is so much more than she lets people see. Yes, she's beautiful and a true mafia princess, but she's so much more. The more we spend time with her, the more she shows us who she truly is, and I want to know every side of her. I want to know what makes her the amazing, strong, woman that she is.

Riona walks out of the house with a smile on her face. "Daisy all set?"

She nods and I open the passenger side door for her. "Yeah. She's really excited. I'm so glad those assholes haven't brought her down. She's going to be okay after tonight. Not all of them are."

I climb into the driver's seat. "Do you come here often?"

She shakes her head as she looks at the house. "No. I don't want to put these girls in danger because of their association with me. My name isn't even on the house."

I pull out of the driveway and start heading back to the house. "So where do the boys stay?"

"Fortunately, I haven't come across a lot of boys being abused. But the ones that I have, I've been able to place them with good families."

"And you can't do that with the girls?" That seems weird. I would think girls would be easier.

"The younger girls sure. High school girls are harder to place. That's why I found Miss Claus and started this house."

"So, who is Miss Claus to you?"

She looks at me. "She was an old teacher of mine in high school. Me and Aisling got close to her after her husband passed. She had always wanted kids and when we needed someone to take in these girls, we called her and she agreed instantly. Now she has tons of daughters that call her house their home."

She's a savior but doesn't even realize it. "So, you're helping out more than the girls."

"Something like that." Riona looks out the window and I know she's done talking. That's fine, at least until we get home.

Chapter Fifteen

Riona

I know where his questions are leading, so I end the conversation by looking out the window. I'm not going to tell him about my past. He doesn't need to know. With me distancing myself, we don't say another word on the way back to the house.

As we pull into the driveway, I realize that he didn't make me put the blindfold on, but I was too much in my head to even pay attention to what was going on outside.

What I do notice is Matteo pacing outside the front door and Enzo sitting on the stairs. I sit up straighter in my seat and look at Dante. "Is something wrong? Have you heard something about Aisling?"

He shakes his head. "It's not about Aisling."

"Then what's it about?" Before he even gets a chance to respond, my door is ripped open and Matteo is pulling me out of the car. "Matteo? What the hell? Put me down."

He throws me over his shoulder and heads for the house. "Nope."

I hit his back. "What the fuck is this all about?"

"Oh, you're going to find out." He walks in through the front door.

I hit his back again. "Put me down and we can talk about what's got you acting like a fucking caveman."

"Oh, we're talking." He sets me down in the living room, turns me to face Dante and Enzo, who are walking in behind us, wraps his arms around my middle, and sits down on the couch, taking me with him.

He traps my arms and legs with his as I squirm against him, trying to get free. "Why are you holding me?"

He growls. "Because you're going to fight us."

"I'm going to fight you anyways now." I try to pull my arms out of his hold as I buck upwards trying to break out of his arms.

"Ri, stop." I freeze in Matteo's arms at the sound of Dante's voice. When I look at him, my whole body turns to ice because I know what this is about.

"No." I shake my head. "No. I'm not talking about it. It's none of your business."

"Everything to do with you is our business," Matteo growls behind me.

I shake my head. "Not this."

"Everything."

"No." I buck against his hold again. "I'm not telling you about the darkest time in my life. You don't deserve to know that. You don't ever share anything about yourselves and every day I'm telling you something about me. I'm not telling you this. We're only together because my father is paying you to protect me. And when we have Aisling back and that threat is gone, my father is going to pull me back home."

I raise my hips up again and purposely slam them down hard on Matteo's dick, making him groan and lean forward. When I have his hold loose enough, I bring my arm forward to slam my elbow back into his ribs but Enzo finally speaking has me stopping. "I'm not really their brother."

I freeze in Matteo's hold as I look at Enzo who's leaning forward in his seat with his elbows on his knees. Enzo looks at me and all I can see is understanding and sadness. He's about to share something that hurts him. "I'm not really their brother. I'm their cousin." Knowing Enzo isn't finished, I relax into Matteo's hold, wanting to know this part of Enzo.

"My mother was their father's sister." He pauses and I have about a hundred questions, but I keep quiet. "When my mother was in college here in the States, she was raped by a football player after a party where she got wasted."

He takes a deep breath and rushes out the rest. "I'm a product of that rape. My mother couldn't stand the sight of me because her family wouldn't let her abort me, so she killed herself a week after I was born."

Dante finishes off the story. "My father adopted Enzo. We might not have the same biological parents, but he is our brother."

"What happened to the football player?" I ask, knowing Enzo was done.

"I think you can guess." Enzo looks me right in the eyes and I know the guy was killed for what he did. Probably tortured beforehand.

With my eyes locked on Enzo's, I give him a slight nod, silently telling him thank you for opening up to me. With him sharing such an awful story about himself, I feel my walls breaking. Just thinking about telling them my story and having to relive it has my hands shaking, so I close them in a fist and close my eyes to try to keep myself from breaking. I touch Matteo's arms and try to remove them, but he just squeezes me tighter.

"I can't tell you this story trapped in your arms." I look back at him, pleading with him to release me.

Matteo's face softens as he looks into my eyes, and he releases his hold. I stand up and I watch all of them tense like they think I'm going to run. "I just need space." I walk past Enzo and touch his shoulder. "When you woke me up this morning, I was in the middle of a nightmare of when I was kidnapped. And just like this morning, I need space while reliving it."

I walk to the chair in the corner of the room and sit down. All their eyes are on me. "Once I tell you this, you won't bring it up again. You won't ask for more details or ask questions. Okay?"

Enzo is the first to nod and then Matteo. Dante takes a second to agree and I know he doesn't like not being able to ask questions. When he does eventually nod, I lean in the chair and close my eyes. "When I was thirteen, I was grabbed while walking home from school, as a power play against my father. They wanted him to step down in exchange for me. I was held captive for three weeks and they were the worst weeks of my life. The first two weeks my captor, Tony, took my virginity and raped me continuously. He used to call me his pretty princess while holding me down and raping me. He loved my screams and cries. He would talk about never letting me go so he could have me all to himself.

"Eventually, after days of this, I broke. I stopped fighting, stopped screaming, and stopped crying. I just laid there, not taking my eyes off the hole in the wallpaper. Tony got bored of my zombie state and allowed his men to take me. From that day, I was rarely alone or without some disgusting man using me for their pleasure. But you see, the guys didn't like the zombie state either so they started shooting me up with different things. Speed, Ecstasy, cocaine, roofies. You name it, they tried it. Some made me responsive to them, others made me pass out, so I don't remember what they did to me. I just remember the pain and the marks on my body."

I take a breath and open my eyes to look at them now that the worst part of the story is over. They all look concerned and upset at what I've been through, but surprisingly, there is no pity there. "At one point, one of the guys gave me speed in order to get me to fight him but he was called away before he could finish. He left the room, leaving me alone, unchained, and very awake. I took the opportunity and escaped out of the bedroom window. I ran as far as I could and then I knocked on the front door of someone's house and begged them for help. I called my father and he came and got me. But by the time my father got to the house I was held in, it was empty."

Matteo stands up from the couch and starts heading for the door. "You're telling me those fuckers are still alive? Don't worry, I'll find them and bring them back so we can kill them."

I jump up from my seat and run to stop him from leaving. I step in front of him blocking his exit. "You'll be searching for a long time. So why don't you sit down so I can finish the story?"

He looks like a bull ready to charge. "They better be dead at the end of this story."

"Well, come sit down and see." I reach for his hand timidly, hoping to not freak out from his touch, after reliving the horrible weeks of unwanted touches. When his hand slides across mine and I don't go into a panic, I grab it and pull him back to the couch. We sit next to each other, and I notice Enzo and Dante staring at our joined hands.

I unwrap my fingers from Matteo's and lean forward with my hands out for them to touch. I could see the jealousy in their eyes that I was willing to touch Matteo. They each reach for my hands and interlock our fingers. After a few seconds, I pull my hands from them because it's uncomfortable to sit with my arms stretched out.

Sitting back on the couch I continue. "It took me a while after getting home to recover and eventually I pushed myself to leave my bed and I got into learning how to protect myself so I'd never be a victim again. After two years of training, I became the assassin I am today. And my first kills were Tony and his men. My father found them and captured them for me so I could torture them the way they tortured me. Well, not exactly the same."

I look to Matteo to make sure he's relaxed now and then I look to Dante because he's going to still want to know about the girls' home. "With what I've been through, I couldn't stand to think of others going through that. So, I killed men and women who took that choice away from someone. But with those kills, I found that a lot of the men, women, and children were being held captive and didn't have anywhere to go after they were rescued, so Aisling and I started a foundation to open homes for them. Dante saw the house the girls go to and the boys are adopted out. But we also have an apartment building the adults stay in. Some work for us in my burlesque club, at their choice. Some we've paid for them to go to college. But they're all there to get on their feet and to recover from their traumas."

"That's pretty impressive that you guys help these people build their lives again. Most people wouldn't care." Enzo moves over to me on the couch.

"Most people don't understand what I and these people have been through. I know the torture it is and I was lucky to have a family to help me through it. All I'm giving them is a safe place and a family that understands."

"It's still amazing what you do." Matteo rests his arm behind me on the back of the couch. "Thank you for telling us."

"Thanks for listening and not judging." I stand from the couch. "It's been a long day. I'm going to bed." I give them all a smile before walking out of the living room and heading to my room. I need a moment alone to push those memories away, because I can't have them rule my mind again. I jump into the shower to wash the day away.

When I'm done and I've changed into some pajamas, I find Dante sitting on the edge of my bed. Not saying a word, I feel his blue eyes tracking me as I walk to my side of the bed and climb in. Once I get comfortable, I look over to him and silently ask if he's getting in. Dante stands, removes his shirt and pants and climbs into bed so he's curled around me.

"My mother died in my arms. I wanted to go to a specific Blues soccer game when I was eight and I don't even know why now, but my mom took me. I can't remember why but for some reason we had to leave early and as we were walking through the parking lot, a man tried to rob us. We fought back and I got pushed, making me fall and hit my head. My mom turned her back to the guy to help me, but he pulled out a gun and shot her once, right in the back of her head. I held her in my arms as I screamed for help. It felt like hours before someone finally heard, but my mom was already gone."

I look back over my shoulder at him as I squeeze his arms around me tighter. "I'm so sorry. It's absolutely awful to lose your mom, but in that way, I can't imagine."

"We all have trauma, Rose. Just know that we'll always be there for you to fight it."

I nod and he leans forward to place a soft kiss to my lips. We sink into each other's arms, pulling what we need in silence, and I find myself slipping off to sleep, feeling at home in his arms. As my eyes grow heavy, his voice breaks the quiet holding me awake. "I have someone following the video footage from the parking lot. They're working on it 24/7, so we'll find where they took her soon." My body stiffens at mentioning Aisling and guilt fills me because I'm finding comfort in these men while she's alone and living a nightmare.

"Then what are we going to do?" That was our only lead.

"Follow her mom's past and we're going to show you our business."

I look back at him. "Why show me your life?"

"Because you've pushed yourself into our lives and we might not let you go when your father calls you back." He traces his finger along my jaw and across my chin.

"That statement could call for a war between you and my father." And I might be willing to start that war.

"Not if you stay willingly."

"We'll see." I smile at him because I think he knows I'm hooked on them.

"Yes, we will." He kisses my shoulder and I relax into his hold, falling asleep quickly.

Chapter Sixteen

Riona

"Riona."

"Aisling?"

"Riona." I swear it's her.

"Aisling?" Darkness is all I see.

"Ri. Save me."

"Aisling. Where are you?"

"Ri."

"I can't last much longer."

"Rose."

"Hide within yourself. You can survive this."

"Hurry."

"Ri. Wake up."

My eyes flutter open and I see Dante leaning over me, rubbing my arm. "Was I screaming again?" I feel really dazed, like I'm not fully awake but I don't feel like I've woken from a nightmare. I feel like I was actually sleeping deeply.

"No. I just got a call. There's movement in the house the kid delivered food to for Maxim. We're going in. Do you want to come?" He gives me a confident smile because he knows I'm coming.

"I wouldn't miss it."

"Thought so. Come on, get out of bed. We leave in ten." Both of us get out of bed and I go to my closet as Dante leaves my room, but before he does, he stops at the door and looks back at me. "You might want to put a dress in that backpack of goodies because we have club business tonight and who knows if we'll have time to come back."

My smile matches his suggestive one. Maxim and a night out with my three men, this is going to be a good day. Wait? My men? I shake my head, pushing away that thought for another time. I quickly throw on some leggings and a tank top and head to the bathroom to get ready. Before leaving my room, I listen to Dante's advice and grab one of my favorite dresses and heels and put them in my bag.

The guys are waiting for me at the bottom of the stairs and they're each watching me. Dante runs his eyes over me like he can't wait to rip my clothes off. Enzo has a concerned look on his face as he checks me over and when he sees my smile, his own pulls across his face. I guess he is used to me being a mess after being woken up.

Matteo has a wicked but excited smile, like he can't wait to get his hands on Maxim and have a little fun. He steps forward and holds out his hand. "Come on, Princess. We have a Russian to catch." I place my hand in his and he pulls me to him and wraps his arm around my shoulders. With his mouth right next to my ear, he whispers, "And maybe even torture."

The spark in his eye is wicked and I can't help but chuckle. "As long as I get to partake."

He leads me out of the house with Dante and Enzo behind us. "I'd never think to exclude you. I can't wait to see you make him scream. Be covered in his blood and end his miserable life. I'm getting hard thinking about it." He steps behind me to open my door and rub his erection against my ass.

I turn to face him and run my hands up his chest and skim my lips over his neck. "Maybe after he's dead, I'll let you fuck me next to his body."

He growls and I can feel it all the way to my core. "Deal."

I turn and climb into Dante's SUV and Matteo smacks my ass, making me gasp. Once seated, I glare at him but he chuckles, closing the door and climbing into the passenger seat. Enzo, who's sitting next to me, reaches for my hand and pulls me next to him. I happily slide over so my side is pressed against his and with our fingers laced, I lay my head on his shoulder. He kisses the top of my head. "How did you sleep?"

He cares that I'm rested, but what he's really asking is if I saw Aisling or had nightmares. "Pretty good. I was really tired. No nightmares but I heard Aisling."

He rubs his free hand up my arm. "What did she say?"

"To hurry up and save her. I think they're going to break her." I lift my head and look at him.

"We're going to find her. Our hacker is looking over the parking footage and should be done soon."

I nod my head on his shoulder. "I feel like I should be doing more."

He places his hand on my neck and runs his thumb across my cheek. "I don't think there is anything else we can do at this point. They need to reach out for us to work on any other leads."

I shake my head, making his hand drop because there has to be something. "What about her mom's family?"

"Well, we're pretty sure the O'Brien's have her, so I've been working on their family tree, trying to find something. But without names, I could've already found them but wouldn't know it because her mother was wiped from their family. I did find out that Craig is adopted."

"Wow, that's interesting. Maybe I should try my father again so we can get names." I can't believe he hasn't called me back yet.

Dante looks back at me through the rearview mirror. "Killian is meeting us at the house. You should get him to look into their names or at least ask your father."

My brother will be there? I've missed him so much. We haven't spoken since I left, so I have no idea where his head is at or how things have been at home.

Like Dante did yesterday, he parks his car in a dead-end alley in Little Italy, but what's different today is my brother's car is there as well. Not waiting for the guys to get out, I jump out of the car and run to Killian who is leaning against his hood. He stands as I get to him and throw my arms around his neck. His arms instantly go around my waist, hugging me to him. "Hi, Kill."

"Hi, Ri. It's good to see you."

We break apart and look at each other. "It's good to see you too. How's everything?"

He shakes his head with a solemn expression. "Not good. The house is different without you both there. Dad is almost never there and when he is, he's yelling at me or someone else. He's pissed about us arguing with him in front of his men about Aisling. He's keeping me in the dark on something and I don't think it's going to be good. I've tried asking some of my guys, but they're in the dark too."

I squeeze his arm. "He must be keeping it close. I wouldn't continue to ask around because anyone you ask now can't be trusted. Once we have Aisling back and I'm home, we can work on figuring it out."

"It's a problem for another time. Let's go get the Russian that should've never put a hand on you."

I smile up at him and Dante says, "Yes. Let's."

158

Turning, I see Dante, Enzo, and Matteo standing in a line in full gear. They look sexy as hell with bullet proof vests on, guns hanging off their hips and a rifle across their backs. They're not messing around. I feel really unprepared right now.

Kill moves next to me. "Wow. A little much, Russos. Don't you think?"

"We don't take chances anymore. Once you've taken a bullet to the stomach it's not something you want to experience again." Dante crosses his arms over his chest, looking even more bad-ass as he glares at my brother.

I look at all three of them, trying to figure out which of them has been shot. I've seen them all shirtless but I didn't see any scars. My guess is Dante because I didn't get a chance to really take in his muscular upper body when we were in the boxing ring. I wish I knew the story but it's not the time for that. I step toward them but I'm looking at Dante. "You got an extra one for me?"

Enzo raises his arm and I'm just realizing he's been holding one for me the whole time. I give him a smile and quickly slip it over my head. Dante comes up to my side and starts making sure it's tight enough and secured properly as Matteo walks back to the car and quickly returns with my backpack. He holds it open for me and I quickly pull out my harnesses for my guns and knives.

With them strapped to my hips and thighs, I holster my two guns and strap on my six knives. When I'm done, I look up to see all of them looking at me. Dante, Matteo, and Enzo look turned on, but my brother looks shocked, but it's not just at me. It's at me and the guys.

Not wanting him to ask what's going on with us, I look at him. "Are you going to load up?"

"Already am." He lifts his shirt and turns, showing two guns in the waistband of his jeans.

"Low key." I nod, accepting it because Killian is never going to be armed like me or apparently my guys. "How are we doing this? I think Killian should go to the front to cover it since he looks unarmed, while we go in through the back."

Killian nods along with Matteo and Enzo but Dante just stares at me, and I know he's having a hard time not being in control.

I lean my head to the side and smile at Dante. "You okay with that?"

One side of his lips turns up slightly and I know he's fighting a smile. "It's not how I'd do it. Someone will need to go with Killian."

I shrug. "Okay. I'll go with him. Are we busting in or going in quietly?"

"It's Bratva property, so I say let's bust in." Matteo and Killian chuckle as Dante gives me a wicked grin. I shrug my shoulders like why not.

"Okay." Enzo steps up with his tablet open to a map. "Here is the house. Killian and Riona, you'll turn right out of the alley, go two blocks, cross the street and walk up one block and the house will be right in front of you." I nod and I can see Killian nod as well.

"We're going straight out of the alley, up three blocks and then over so we can get to the back yard."

Dante and Matteo nod in understanding. "Beauty, here is an earpiece so you know when we're in the back." I take the earpiece from Enzo and put it in my ear.

Killian, Dante, and Matteo all step away from our circle. Matteo takes the tablet, putting it in the SUV as Killian and Dante lock their cars. I'm watching all of them when Enzo's voice rings in my ear. "Can you hear me, Beauty?" Looking at Enzo, I see him smiling at me, with a finger pressed into his earpiece.

I reach to mine trying to find how to talk back to him. Enzo steps forward and guides my finger to the button. I press down on it and smile at Enzo. "We should've used these the other night while you were watching Matteo and I."

Enzo runs his fingers down my arm as he whispers without using the earpiece. "Would you have liked for me to talk dirty to you as you sucked my brother's cock? Or told you how I'd like my cock sucked?"

I moan thinking about Enzo's sexy voice ringing in my ear as I pleasure Matteo. "I wouldn't have said no to either. Would Matteo have a problem with you controlling what I did?"

"He hasn't had a problem in the past."

Shocked, I look over to Matteo and I find him smirking at me and giving a quick nod. "Can he hear me?"

He and Dante nod as Enzo answers. "Yeah. The button turned on the mic. It's so you don't have to continuously touch your ear."

Oh god. I look to Killian just to make sure they didn't give him one too. Killian isn't paying attention to us as he is typing something on his phone. "He doesn't have one."

"Thank god for that." I give Enzo a small shove back from me. "You could've told me."

"Oh, come on, Princess. Don't be mad. I love hearing all your dirty thoughts."

I roll my eyes and step away from Enzo. "Are we ready?"

Dante chuckles. "Yeah, let's go."

The brothers walk down the alley in front of me and Killian. They give us a nod as Killian and I turn right onto the sidewalk.

We're quiet for a little bit, trying to not draw attention to ourselves but once we're a block down, Killian breaks the silence. "You seem to have had a change of heart about staying with the Russos."

I look at him, trying to act confused. "What are you talking about? I went willingly. They're hired to help with Aisling and to protect me. I wouldn't fight that."

He gives me a look, telling me he's not buying it. "I meant you don't seem to have a very professional relationship."

"What are you asking?" He'll need to ask it out right.

"Which one are you with?" He cringes with each word and I hold back my laugh. One thing Killian hates more than anything is talking about my sex life.

"That is none of your business."

Matteo's voice rings in my ear. "Oh, say me. Please say me. I'm the one who proposed."

The sound of a groan follow and then Dante says, "Shut up." I can only guess he hit Matteo.

"So, you're with one of them." Killian gives me a side smirk.

"I didn't say that." I can't force my smile down.

"I think it's Dante." Killian just calls it out so matter of fact.

"What?!" comes from Matteo.

A growl comes from Enzo as Dante happily chuckles.

"He was really worried about the vest and you were challenging him when the plan was set." Killian talks out his reasoning, but I can tell he's uncomfortable so I change the subject.

"Killian, can we focus? Who I'm with or not isn't your business and not what's important right now."

Killian nods and we cross the street as the house comes into view. "I'm going to show him who you belong to, Princess." I groan at Matteo's comment because if he does anything that clues Killian into what my relationship is with all of them, I'll kill him. We pass a car that has a guy sitting in it and I assume that's their guy. "We're across the street now. Just passed your lookout."

"We're climbing over the fence now," Enzo calls out.

I signal to Killian that we're good and cross the street. As we're walking up to the front door, I start looking around to make sure everything is clear and we haven't drawn attention to ourselves.

Seeing the street is empty, I turn to the door, waiting right off the front porch. "We're at the back door." Enzo's voice is in my ear again.

"We're at the front."

"Okay. On the count of three."

I nod to Killian to get ready and then Enzo and I count out together. "3... 2...1"

I watch as Killian brings his foot up and kicks the door in. The front door bursts open and I follow Killian in with my gun in hand. Immediately I hear the guys yelling and I raise my gun just in time to see a guy run around the corner.

At the sight of Killian and I, he comes to a skidding stop. "Oh shit."

"Damn right." Matteo comes around the corner behind the guy with his gun raised. Killian and I don't lower our guns until Matteo kicks the guy's knees in, making him fall to the ground. Matteo places his foot on the guy's back, holding him face down to the floor.

Dante and Enzo come up behind me. "He's the only one here."

"That sucks for you, man. Guess you're going to have to give us our answers." Matteo grabs both of the guy's hands and pulls them behind his back and then he picks the guy up by his wrists and shirt. Once the guy is on his feet again, Matteo pushes him the way he came. When I turn the corner, I see he was coming from the kitchen. And by the looks of it, he was cleaning.

I stand back as I watch Matteo and Enzo strap this guy onto one of the kitchen chairs and really look at him. The guy is dressed in high end jeans and a button-up with messy brown hair and when his brown eyes connect with mine, he has tears in them. "Please help me."

Matteo just chuckles. "She's the deadliest of us all. She's not helping you."

At that, the guy's face hardens and he glares at me. "Oh, I know who she is. She's Maxim's girl." He isn't some low-level soldier.

Matteo punches the guy in the face. "She's not his."

The guy chuckles. "Not now. But just you wait. One day, he's going to get his hands on you and you'll never escape."

Matteo reaches back to punch him again, but I step forward and grab his arm. "Let me. He's trying to get a rise out of me. So, let's see if he can."

Matteo matches my wicked smile and steps back. "I'd like to see him try."

Turning back to the guy, I pull out a knife from my thigh holster and twirl it on my finger. "I like to know the names of the men I torture and kill."

"You can call me Daddy. That way you can get used to it for when I'm balls deep inside..." Growls come from behind me, but I'm only focused on the guy in front of me as I slam my knife into his thigh.

His scream fills the room and I can't help my smile as I pull the knife back out. "So, Dickwad, how about you tell me where Maxim is so I don't have to cover this kitchen in your blood."

"Oh, I guess Russo dick isn't that good if you're already wanting in Maxim's bed."

I chuckle. "Does any girl ever willingly go into Pencil Dick's bed?"

He gives me a suggestive smile. "No, they don't. That's why they crawl into mine afterwards."

Gotcha. "Oh, so then you must be Victor. Maxim's best friend." His face drops and I chuckle. "You really need to learn to keep your mouth shut." I look back at Enzo. "Find his phone. It might have info in it." Enzo leaves the room in search of it and I look to Matteo. "You ready to have some fun?"

Matteo rolls his shoulders. "Oh, I'm ready."

"Hold on a second." Killian walks around the kitchen and grabs the hand towel. He walks over and shoves it into Victor's mouth. "His screams are a little loud and we're not in your torture room." I give him a nod in thanks, because he's right. We'll be doing a lot of damage before we'll ask any other questions.

"You have a torture room, Princess?" Matteo gives me a giddy smile.

My smile matches his. "Of course I do. I'll show you mine if you show me yours one day."

"I'll show you anything if I get to see any of you." His eyes scan over me and I can't help but want whatever he is thinking.

"Okay. I don't need to hear any of this. I'll go help Enzo." Killian leaves the kitchen.

"I bet he thinks I'm the one you're with now." I chuckle at his satisfied smile and turn to face Victor. It's time to get some answers.

After an hour of Matteo and I taking turns inflicting pain, Victor finally gave us the information we need about Maxim. Or at least what he knows. Maxim has been moving between the different Bratva properties in the city. Only staying for a day or two. Nobody in the Bratva knows where he is. He only texts Victor his last day at a place so he can come and clean the place so Maxim's father doesn't know he was there. Such a good best friend. Too bad he's going to die because of that. But first, I have one more question to ask.

Standing in front of Victor, I grab his hair and pull so his beaten and bloody face is tilted up toward mine. "I've got one more question before we end this. What was the Bratva's involvement in Aisling's kidnapping?"

Victor's eyes widen just a little. "Nothing. That was the O'Briens. We didn't even know they were at the club that night. Maxim just wanted you." Something crashes in the other room and I turn to see Killian is no longer in the kitchen. Another crash comes from the living room and I look to Matteo to end this as I let go of Victor's hair and walk out of the kitchen.

As I walk into the living room, I see Killian pick up a side table and raise it over his head to smash it. "Killian." I move so I stand in front of him. "What are you doing?"

Anger is radiating off him as he breathes heavily. "What was the point of all this? You just spent an hour torturing this guy and he doesn't know anything about Aisling?"

I hold my hands out at my sides, confused because he knew why we were here. "We're here looking for Maxim because he attacked me and to see if he was involved with Aisling."

"Who cares about him attacking you?" I step back as his words hurt. "Aisling is still missing. Going through god knows what. You were supposed to have found her by now. Instead, you're playing house with those boys and goofing off. Do you even care?" He takes a step toward me but I don't back up.

"Of course I care. I know what she's going through and we're doing everything we can. What are you doing to find her?"

"You're not doing enough," Killian yells in my face. I slap him across his cheek and when he turns his face back toward me there is hatred in his eyes. But before he can do or say anything he's pulled away from me and Dante is standing between us. "That's enough, Killian. You should go."

Killian doesn't look away from me until he turns and storms out of the house. I stare at the door, still hurt and shocked at what Killian said. How can he think that I don't care? How can he say I'm not doing anything? I guess maybe he's right. For the last day, I haven't been looking. Someone else has. I should be looking for new leads. Putting out more feelers to my contacts to see if they've heard anything. Have more of my people on the streets. Maybe some of my dancers could start asking questions.

My face is turned from the door, and I see Dante looking down at me with concern. "Ri, don't listen to him. You're doing everything you can." I just stare at him because I'm not sure I believe him. When I don't answer, he looks to his left and I see Enzo standing there. "Go with Enzo. He'll get you cleaned up enough that we can leave the house."

Enzo reaches out his hand and I willingly place mine in his. He leads me out of the room and to a small bathroom. "Let me get this off of you and then you can wash the blood off your face and arms." As Enzo takes off the vest, I stare at myself in the mirror. I have splatters of blood all over my arms and face. My shirt would be covered too if it wasn't for the vest.

I can see Enzo watching me through the mirror. He has a worried expression on his face. Needing to look away, I bend down and splash water on my face and wipe away the blood. When I stand, Enzo is next to me with a wet rag. He reaches for my arm and I let him clean the blood away. "He didn't mean what he said, Beauty. He's just upset."

"I know." I don't fully believe that though. Sure, he's upset. He misses Aisling. But he also meant what he said.

He reaches for my other arm and I turn toward him so he can clean it. "He's hurting and is just lashing out at the closest person to him. Deep down, he knows you're doing everything you can."

When he's done, I give him a weak smile. "Thanks."

I leave Enzo in the bathroom and head to the kitchen. But right as I pass the back door it opens and Dante walks in. "I went and got the car. Our clean-up crew will be here in a few minutes." I nod and instead of going to the kitchen, I walk past Dante and head outside.

"I'll be in the car." I can feel Dante's eyes on my back as I walk to the car. Once inside, I take a deep breath and pull out my phone to follow up with my contacts.

Chapter Seventeen

Dante

I don't like the look Killian put on her face. She's taking all the blame for everything. Which is why I made sure he knew I didn't like how he spoke to her. After a few choice words and a punch to the gut, I left him in the alley to drive back to his house.

Leaving her with Enzo, I was hoping he'd cheer her up but she still had the sad and deflated look about her as she walked out of the house. I watch her until she's in the car and then I walk into the house. "Alright let's go. Clean up will be here in a few. They'll make it look like no one was here." I walk into the kitchen where Matteo is washing his hands and Ri's knife. He looks back and nods to the now dead Victor. He didn't live much longer after Ri left the kitchen.

Matteo immediately took her knife and slit his throat. "Are we taking him with us?"

I shake my head. "They'll take him and dispose of him."

Matteo nods. "Okay let's go."

Enzo meets us at the back door with Ri's vest and we head to the car. I can see Ri's silhouette through the window and she seems to be looking out the window in a daze. I bump into Enzo and Matteo as they stop, looking worried for her. Matteo puts a giddy smile on his face and walks over to her window and knocks. When the window starts to roll down, he seems to perk up. "I brought you your knife." He holds it out to her with his head bowed like he's presenting a sword to royalty.

"Thank you, Matteo." There is a light spark in her voice but when Matteo looks at us with a sad expression, I know he didn't get her to smile.

I toss the keys to Enzo. "You drive." Without waiting for him to respond, I walk to the backseat and climb in. In one swift movement, I grab Ri's hips, lifting her and placing her on my lap so she's straddling my legs.

"What the hell, Dante?" She glares at me, but I'm mad too. She doesn't get to take all the guilt.

"You need to cut this moping shit off."

She tries to climb off me, but I grab her hips, holding her in place. "You don't tell me what to do. If I want to sit here and pout about what my brother said, then I can."

"No, you can't."

"Yes, I can." She hits my chest in frustration.

I grab her hand and link our fingers. "Why then? What did he say that was accurate?"

"I should be doing more. I haven't been looking for her in the last 24 hours." She's deflating, but that's not what I want.

"Bullshit."

"What?!" Fire sparks in her eyes, but she's not fully back yet.

I tilt her chin up so she's forced to look in my eyes. "Bullshit. You haven't done anything for her in the last day. Yesterday you were out all day talking to people, trying to get information on her and O'Brien. Last night, you had a job that gave you access to a doctor for when you do find her. And today, you eliminated someone who could have been a part of it. Now we know it's the O'Briens."

She holds my stare. "But none of that got me any closer to her and I'm not sure how much longer she can last."

"What else should you be doing?"

"I should be looking over the footage of..."

I cut her off. "Nope. I already have someone on it, working all day."

"I should've followed up with..."

I interrupt again. "Nope. Your contacts know to reach out to you once they hear something."

Oh, she's getting pissed. "I should've been out..."

"Absolutely not, you're..."

"Stop interrupting..." she practically yells at me.

"I will when..."

Ri lets out a frustrated groan and slams her mouth to mine, kissing me deeply. "Would you just shut up?" she mumbles against my mouth.

"Never. Not when you're doubting yourself." With one hand in her hair and the other around her waist, I pull her closer to me and deepen the kiss, making her moan against my lips. When we finally break our kiss, we're both breathless and the spark is back in her eyes. I tuck her hair that has fallen out from her ponytail behind her ear. "Killian will be calling to apologize later."

"What did you do?" She smirks.

I give her a cocky smile. "I might have punched him back in the alley and told him what a dick he was."

A grin forms on her face and a chuckle comes out of her, but Matteo is the one to say something. "Well shit. Now he probably thinks you're with Dante again."

She cracks up laughing and it's a beautiful sound. "He's not stupid. He knows I'm with all of you. He just doesn't want to accept it yet."

"All of us, huh?" I run my hands down her sides.

"Yes." She leans forward and presses her lips to mine. "Thank you," she whispers against my lips, but before I get to deepen our kiss, she pulls away from me and climbs off my lap, facing to the front with her ass in my face. Not being able to help myself I rub my hand up her thigh to her ass, but she quickly swats my hand away. "Stop it."

She readjusts herself so she's sitting on the seat. Matteo is turned in his seat looking at her and she reaches out and runs her finger through his hair. "Sorry my brother ruined our fun. Next time he won't be invited."

"If I can help it, these two won't be invited either." Matteo points to Enzo and I and our protests ring out. She just chuckles and leans forward kissing him. Their kiss is short as well and Matteo groans in disappointment. "Do you mind switching seats with me?"

"Absolutely not."

They both get out of the car and I'm a little disappointed she doesn't want to sit with me, but I also get that she pulls comfort from Enzo. Matteo holds the door open for her but it's just to slap her ass as she climbs in. This time though she's quick enough to backhand him across his chest. Without a second look at him and his dramatic gasp, she focuses her attention on Enzo.

Leaning over the center console, she whispers into Enzo's ear and I wish I knew what she was saying. Her lips are still moving when Enzo grabs her by the back of her neck and kisses her. When they break apart, they stare into each other's eyes for a few seconds until Ri backs off and settles in her seat. Enzo drives us to the club with their hands linked together.

Okay, I might be a little jealous right now. As if she can read my mind, she looks back at me and gives me the biggest smile. Okay, a little less jealous now.

"Are we going to the club?"

I nod. "Are you ready to dive deep into the Russo business?"

"Hell yes." She looks like she's ready to take on anything.

"This is your office?" I can't help my smile as Riona takes in our large office, with two large black desks, wood floors that match the club's, and the two couches set off to one corner.

"It's nice, isn't it?" I lean back against the front of my desk and watch her slowly turn in a circle. "When we bought this place, we spent a lot of money to add this level."

"It shows." She finishes circling and smiles at me. "What's through those doors?"

"The conference room. That's where we'll hold our meeting later." She nods and points to the door on the right. "Closet." And then the left. "Bathroom."

"A bathroom?" She moves over to the door and automatically the lights of the full bath turn on, illuminating the white walls.

"A full bath, really? How often do you use that shower?" She looks back at me questioning.

"More often than you think. This is our main office and sometimes things can get messy." Matteo and Enzo walk into the office carrying all of our bags.

"Very messy, Princess." Matteo lays our suit bags across the back of one of the couches and falls down on the other as Enzo walks to Riona and hands her book bag to her.

She smiles at him in thanks before looking back at Matteo. "I don't believe you. There is no way you kill people up here on a regular basis. It'd bring too much attention to the club." She slowly starts walking to him. "I think you bring girls that you meet in the club up here to fuck and that bathroom is just to clean up afterwards."

She is standing in front of him and he leans forward and runs a hand up the back of her thigh slowly. "Like I said, messy. Those girls are always dripping wet for us." Riona swats his hand away, but he's quicker and grabs her wrists. "You jealous, Princess?"

"Hardly." He gives her a cheeky smile like he doesn't believe her. Riona rotates her wrist he's holding and interlocks their fingers as she leans forward. "There's no need to be jealous of those girls, because they were before me. You're mine now."

"Hell yes I am." Matteo leans forward to kiss her but she stands up. "Come on, you can help me cleanup for this meeting."

She pulls Matteo from the couch. "Does that mean you're wet for me?"

"I guess you'll have to find out." As she walks to the bathroom with Matteo happily following, her eyes connect with mine and I see desire burning in them. With that look, I wish I was the one following her into the bathroom. Matteo is one lucky guy. And the smile that he gives Enzo and I as he closes the door tells me he knows it. With the door closed, I look at Enzo who's sitting at the other desk with his laptop open. "What are you doing?"

"Watching." He gives me a smile that is up to no good.

"You shouldn't do that if she doesn't know." I walk around the desk, not taking my own advice.

"Oh, she knows." Just as he says that, she blows a kiss to the camera in the top corner of the bathroom above the sink.

"Okay then. Have fun."

I walk away from him and grab my suit bag from the couch. "You don't want to watch?"

I shake my head. "The first time I see her naked won't be through a camera lens. She'll be laid out in front of me."

I leave the office for the downstairs bathroom just as the shower turns on. I need to be focused for this meeting tonight and listening to her moans through the bathroom door will be way too distracting.

Chapter Eighteen

Riona

Matteo's breath fans across the back of my neck as his hands slide up my sides. "Enzo was pulling up his laptop."

I lean back against him and hum as Matteo kneads my breasts in his hands. "Does it turn you on knowing he's watching?"

Realizing what he's implying, I look around for the camera until I see it in the corner above the mirror I'm standing in front of. With my eyes locked on the lens, I grind back against Matteo's erection and blow the camera a kiss.

"Yes, it really does." I grab one of his hands and run it down my body. Matteo knows exactly what I want and takes over, pushing his hand into my leggings and panties. His fingers find me wet and needy, and I moan as he rubs circles over my clit.

"You're so wet for us. Do you want to see, bro?"

Matteo pushes a finger inside me and my knees go weak. "Hold on, Princess. Let me show him how much you want us." He removes his finger from inside me and pulls his hand out of my leggings, showing the camera his glistening fingers. With our eyes locked in the mirror, he brings his fingers to his lips and sucks them clean. "You taste amazing, Princess."

I moan in response as I rub my thighs together. "Would you like another taste?" I hook my fingers into the sides of my leggings and panties and push them down my legs. Once they're off, my shirt and bra are gone next.

Matteo stands there for a second, mesmerized as he takes in my naked body. "You're gorgeous, Princess."

He reaches out to touch me, but I hold up my hand. "No, you don't get to touch me until you're naked." Matteo moves into gear, ripping off his clothes and I reach into the shower and turn it on.

Facing the camera so Enzo can see all of me, I pull my hair up in a high bun so I don't get it wet. "Touch yourself, Enzo. Will you come watching Matteo touching me, kissing me, and fucking me?" It's a question that I won't hear him answer and I really wish we still had those earpieces.

"Oh, his dick is already out and in his hand." Matteo steps in front of me, naked and my hands instantly reach out and run over his broad chest and tight abs.

"Maybe we should always be naked."

He chuckles. "I'm not going to say no to that. If you're always naked, it'll make tasting you so much easier." Matteo picks me up and places me on the counter.

"Just think about all the positions we could get into." He smiles up at me as he goes down on his knees and pushes my thighs open.

"Now let me get my second taste." Matteo dives in and takes one long lick before sucking my clit between his lips. His scruff rubs against my sensitive skin sending goosebumps up my body.

"Oh fuck." I buck up against him and he chuckles, sending vibrations right through me. I tangle my hands in his hair, holding him to me as I let my head fall back against the mirror. Matteo's tongue moves from my clit and pushes it inside me, sucking up my wetness. "Oh god... Matteo." I ride his face as he switches between fucking me with his tongue and sucking on my clit. I'm so close my body is vibrating.

"Open your eyes, Princess. Let Enzo see you fall apart on my tongue." My eyes instantly go to the camera and when Matteo nips my clit, I fall apart screaming Matteo's name.

Matteo sucks and licks me clean, until I'm jelly and I have to push him away. I pull him up my body and crash my lips to his, tasting myself on them. He deepens the kiss as I wrap my arms and legs around him. "You ready to shower?"

I nod and Matteo lifts me off the counter and his erection runs overs my sensitive clit, making me squirm in his arms. "Don't get my hair wet."

Matteo chuckles. "I got you. But we're not quite ready to wash up yet."

Matteo carries me into the shower, making sure to block all the water. His lips meet mine again as my back hits the back wall of the shower. I grind against him needing him inside me. "Matteo... please."

"What do you want, Princess? My dick buried deep inside you?" He kisses down my neck.

"Yes... please... yes!"

He raises his head with a heated smile. "Should we make a show of it for Enzo?"

"Oh god. Matteo, get your dick inside me now." I give him a challenging smile that he steps right up to.

He thrusts into me in one swift move, and I moan out from the amazing feeling of being so full. Matteo doesn't wait for me to adjust as he pulls back and thrusts back into me. I tighten my hold on him and capture his mouth in a desperate kiss. Matteo's thrusts are hard and deep, hitting me in the perfect spot.

Not being able to hold back my moans any longer, I break our kiss, leaning my head back against the wall. "Fuck, Matteo. You feel so good."

"Not as good as you feel squeezing around me." Matteo kisses down my neck as his hand slides up my stomach to my breasts. "I've been dying to have these in my hands and mouth."

His tongue comes out and licks my nipple and I arch off the wall, pushing my breasts further into his hand and mouth. "How sensitive are they, Riona?" He bites down on one and pinches the other and I moan, squeezing around him.

"Oh, you like a little pain. I can definitely work with that." A wicked, needy grin spreads across his face as his eyes lock to my breasts. He descends on them with his mouth and hand, drawing all the pleasure from my body until I come, screaming his name.

"Oh fuck, Princess. You're so tight I can't hold out." Matteo's thrusts become erratic until he comes, holding onto my thighs so tight I'm going to have finger bruises.

After a few moments of us just holding each other, Matteo starts placing kisses all over my face, neck, and shoulders. "You're so perfect. You were made for me. For us."

I bring his lips to mine and kiss him. "You're perfect for me too."

Matteo kisses me silly until I'm breathless and then he pulls back. "I think you're dirty enough now."

"I definitely need a good washing. Do you want to help?" I unwrap myself from him and he holds me until I'm steady on my feet.

"It's tempting but I can't be late for the meeting. Raincheck, Princess." He gives me a quick kiss before stepping back and under the water.

Knowing he's right, I keep my hands to myself as I clean myself. But it doesn't stop us from watching each other rub soap all over our bodies. I can feel his eyes travel down my body, following my hands. My breath quickens throughout the shower as the desire between us builds and it takes everything in me not to reach out for him. A deep growl comes from him as he turns off the shower and I know he's contemplating being late. Not a word is spoken between us as we dry ourselves.

My eyes lock with his as I wrap my towel around my body and take a step toward him. The tension grows with each step but instead of giving in, I just give him a quick kiss. "Can I have the bathroom to finish getting ready?"

"Absolutely." Matteo gives me another quick kiss before leaving me in the bathroom.

I look up at the camera and blow Enzo a kiss. "No more watching." I give Enzo a second and then I grab my bag, pulling out everything I need. It's time to look hot for my guys.

Chapter Nineteen

Riona

I give myself one last look in the mirror, fluffing my hair. I have to say I look pretty hot, even though I didn't have any of my makeup. Running my hand down my short, high-neck and long-sleeved black metallic dress, I turn from side to side. The guys are going to love this. Especially the full open back. I really hope this makes their mouths water and they won't be able to keep their hands off me.

Stepping into my favorite black stilettos, I grab my bag and open the door. All three of the guys are in their massive office, wearing suits. Matteo is lounging on the couch messing with his phone and he's really living up to his Mr. Sex Appeal name in a tailored black suit with a white button-down and black tie.

Dante is talking to someone on the phone as he stares out the floor-to-ceiling window overlooking the club. He looks all-business in his black suit, black button-up, and black tie. A dark god that I crave to ruin me.

I take a breath, taking my eyes off him to see Enzo smiling at me from behind his desk. I shouldn't be surprised he's the only one to notice I'm out of the bathroom. He stands from behind his desk and I take a second looking over my Mystery Man, my Beast. He looks hotter than sin in his dark gray suit with a blue button-up and he's not wearing a tie, leaving his top two buttons undone.

"Beauty..." He pauses just long enough, grabbing Matteo and Dante's attention. "You look amazing." Enzo walks around the desk and heads straight to me. He reaches his hand out to me and I lightly place mine in his. He brings my hand to his lips, where he places a kiss to the back of my fingers. "Let's see all of this dress." He spins me slowly and I know the moment each of them notices my back.

"Damn," comes from Matteo.

A whistle from Enzo.

And a growl from Dante.

"You're going to turn heads tonight, Beauty." Enzo pulls me up against him and kisses me.

Matteo jumps up from the couch and walks over to us and pulls me from Enzo. "You look gorgeous, Princess. But if any other guy looks at you, they're dead."

I wrap my arms around his neck and lean into him, loving being in his arms. It's like being hugged by a teddy bear. "Then you're going to be killing all night. When will you have time to dance with me?"

Matteo runs his hand down my back, and I shiver at his touch. "I'll make time."

I lean forward to whisper next to his ear. "How about you kill anyone who touches me tonight? I like people's attention. For them to wish they could have me but can't."

I can feel Matteo hardening against my stomach. "Fine, but don't test me tonight. I'll kill anyone who touches you."

Looking in his eyes, I nod. "No teasing. Got it." I lean up and he closes the distance between us, kissing me silly.

A growl comes from behind me, making us separate and I know it's Dante. Just to piss him off a little, I stay in Matteo's arms and run my fingers over his lips acting like I'm wiping off smeared lipstick that I'm not wearing.

Dante's not having any of it. Instead of waiting, his hand goes into my hair and he turns my head so I'm looking back at him. I give him an amused smile because I love testing his patience and making him jealous. Moving away from Matteo, I turn and face Dante, running my hands under his jacket, up his chest. "Do you need something, Boss Man?"

His lips turn up at my nickname for him. "I'm not Stinkface anymore?"

I shake my head. "Nope but I'm still trying to find the right one."

"I like Boss Man."

"I don't know." I wrap my arms around his lower back, feeling his gun, and lean into him. "Tonight, I think Dark God fits you better."

Dante slams his lips to mine, and I'd say he likes that one too. Dante doesn't break our kiss until I'm breathless. He runs his nose against mine, catching his breath. "You look breathtaking, Rose."

"You look pretty hot, yourself." I step back from Dante and look at all of them. "You all do." I look at Matteo. "I think I want to change my dress code choice."

Matteo smirks at me. "I'll wear anything you want as long as you're naked."

I chuckle. "I'll keep that in mind." Maybe I can get him to do a little role play for me. It's not normally my thing but it could be funny. Knowing that their meeting is coming up soon, I walk over to the couches and sit down. "So, who's staying with me during your meeting?"

Whoever it is, maybe we can have a little fun. Dante steps forward so he's in the middle of the other two as they look down at me. "You're going to be in the meeting with us. We need your specific skill set."

Intrigued, I sit up straighter. "Oh yeah? What skill set is that?"

"Poison and charm."

"Okay tell me more." I'm almost bouncing from excitement.

This meeting they have setup is with Jonathan Franks. Franks has his hands in several of the crime families here in New York because he runs the docks. Anything you want quietly brought into the city, you go to him. Personally, I've only heard about him a few times because my father uses him for drug transportation, but I'm not involved in that side of the business. So, when the guys tell me he also deals in trafficking, I almost lose it. They know I'm not okay with that. Enzo calms me down enough to not kill him tonight, but I make no promises for tomorrow.

Tonight, we have to focus on the Russo contract with him. He's trying to raise their cost on the drugs and weapons they have shipped through the docks and Dante is pissed about it. He thinks that Franks is trying to take advantage, thinking that the brothers are new and young. Dante is going to show him that they aren't to be messed with.

After Dante tells me his plan, they head to the conference room, leaving me to my poisons, because Franks and his son have just arrived. I quickly go through my bag and grab the poison I need and the jewelry to best conceal it. With the poison hidden in a ring, I slide the white gold and diamond hand jewelry onto my pointer finger and thumb. God, I love this piece of jewelry. It makes my hand look so dainty and cute.

    With everything ready, I join the guys in the conference room. As I walk through the door, all eyes turn toward me. Dante steps toward me with his hand out and I happily take it and slip him the antidote. I'm glad I brought it this time. "Franks... Junior, this is our girl, Ri."

    "It's nice to meet you both." I step toward the two Hispanic looking men as they both look me over. Junior takes my hand in his first with a charming smile and interest shining in his eyes. Gently I pull my hand from his, letting him know he doesn't have a chance in hell and turn to his father. Frank instantly makes my stomach roll as I force myself to shake his wrinkled sweaty hand as he undresses me with his eyes while biting down on his bottom lip.

    "You don't mind if she joins, do you?" Dante wraps his arm around my waist, pulling me a few steps back and away from Franks.

    Franks continues to look me up and down like I'm a piece of meat, with an intrigued, pervy smile on his face. "Not at all. As long as she sits on my lap."

    Three loud growls fill the room from my guys and I watch Frank's bodyguard reach for his gun because he can feel the anger radiating off them.

    Needing to defuse this, I chuckle. "You're funny, Mr. Franks. I'll be sitting with my guys." I step out of Dante's hold. "Now before we get started, how about some drinks?" I clasp my hands together in front of me and look at him sweetly.

"That would be lovely, sweetie. Scotch neat."

I give him a nod, holding back an eye roll and look at his son. "Same, please."

Oh, he's definitely not as creepy as his father. Too bad I'm going to have to poison him to get the leverage the guys need. I walk by them and around the massive wooden conference table, heading to the bar in the corner. As I pull out the scotch bottle, I look at the bodyguard. "Do you want anything? Water? Soda?"

He looks away from Franks for just a second to answer. "No thanks, ma'am."

I give him a smile and pour two scotches. With both poured, I switch the lever, opening the ring and releasing the poison as I carry the glasses by my fingertips on the rim. Everyone is sitting at the table as I set the drinks down and carefully maneuver my way around Franks' wandering hands.

A chair is left empty for me in between Dante and Enzo, and I head over to it, giving them a slight nod. As soon as I sit down, Dante's hand goes to my thigh, under the table, and I place mine over his. "Before we start…" Matteo raises his glass and myself, Dante, and Enzo follow. "To a hopefully long and profitable relationship."

Franks, being the sleazeball that he is, grins like he's just robbed a bank and got away with it and raises his glass. "Yes. To contracts, money, and a beautiful woman." He downs his glass in one gulp and I wish I would've poisoned his glass.

Nobody else drinks at Frank's toast and I notice Junior glaring at his father. "Miss Ri, I do apologize for my father."

Frank looks offended by his son. "Apologize for what?"

Junior just ignores him as I give him a nod, accepting the apology, and he raises his glass. "To business." We all raise our glass in the air and then take a drink. When I set my glass down, I move my hand back to Dante's on my thigh and draw the number ten on the top of his hand, letting him know he has ten minutes before Junior starts showing symptoms.

"Sweetie, why don't you get me another drink?" Franks holds his cup in the air. "I like to watch you walking around."

I dig my nails into Dante's hand, letting him know I'm reaching my boiling point. "Franks. You will not speak to our girl like that. She isn't your waitress. If you want another drink, get your ass up and pour it yourself." Dante glares at the man and Franks actually looks shocked. Well, he's not alone. I can't believe he just berated a business associate for me. When he doesn't say anything, Dante continues. "Now I've asked for this meeting because you're increasing our rates and I want to know why."

Fuck, why do I have to be turned on right now in front of this asshole? I shift in my seat slightly, trying to get a little relief, but Dante's hold on my thigh tightens, stopping me. "Mr. Russo, the rate increase is nothing personal. Based on supply and..." Whatever Frank's excuse is, it goes right over my head because Dante's hand starts stroking my inner thigh as his hand moves up my leg. Oh god. Is he really doing this? I must go still because Enzo leans forward and whispers in my ear right as Dante's finger runs over my wet thong and traces down my core. "Are you okay?"

I shift, crossing my legs and capturing his hand. He isn't going to make me come in front of these guys. I give Enzo a small nod, letting him know I'm good. Out of the corner of my eye, I see Dante's lips turn up in a smirk.

"You see Franks, I call bullshit on your answer." Dante slips his fingers into my thong and pushes it to the side. I try to squeeze my thighs tighter to stop him but all it does is spur him on. He teases me, just stroking my skin, but not going for anything that'll get me off. "You see, I have a lot of contacts that do business with you. And do you know what they said?"

He pauses as he glares at Franks, but he takes the pause to spread me open and rub circles over my clit. I bite down on the inside of my cheek so I don't moan out loud and draw attention to myself. I dig my nails into his arm in frustration, but he doesn't stop. "They told me that you weren't raising their rates. Actually, they say you never raise your rates."

"Mr. Russo..." Franks tries to give more excuses but Dante isn't having it.

"No." He pauses, pulling everyone's attention. "You tried to rip me off. Take from the Russo Family. I could take your life for that." Dante presses hard on my clit, building me quickly. "But I don't think that would be best for our business relationship. So instead, you're going to decrease your current rate by 50 percent. I think that will allow us to forgive you. Don't you think, boys?" He looks at Matteo and Enzo.

They both nod in agreement. Dante's eyes connect with mine with a mischievous smirk and I pull his hand away right as I'm about to come. As much as it pains me to do so, I'm not letting this asshole see that.

"Are you fucking kidding? I'm not lowering my rate. Who do you think you are, asking that?" Dante's eyes stay locked on mine as Franks boils across the table. The room falls quiet, waiting for him and he gives me a wink before turning to Franks.

"I think I'm the man who holds your only son's life in my hand." At that exact second, Junior starts coughing violently. He reaches for his glass, and I speak up for the first time since the meeting started. "I wouldn't do that if I were you. You'll only choke faster. Plus, there is probably more poison in there."

At that, Franks jumps up yelling and his bodyguard pulls out his gun. But this is what we expected, so at the same time, Matteo and Enzo stand, drawing their guns. Matteo has his aimed at the bodyguard and Enzo has his aimed at Franks. Dante and I sit back like we're enjoying the show and Junior is slouched over the table, giving me a pained expression, wheezing. I draw a five on Dante's hand letting him know he needs to move so we can give the antidote.

"Franks." Dante calmly pulls out the antidote from his pocket and sets it on the table in front of him. "Shut up and listen if you want your son to live." Franks shuts up. "Good. You're going to sign this drafted contract which now only gives you 5 percent of our shipments." Dante slides the papers that have been sitting on the table this whole time over to him. Franks stands, unmoving as he glares at Dante. When Franks doesn't move for the papers after a moment, Dante reminds him he has all the power. "Please take your time considering it. I'd say your son has three minutes to live. Is that right?" He looks at me.

I act like I'm thinking, tilting my head back and forth. "I'd say more like two."

"Okay fine, I'll sign. Please don't kill him."

"Sign first." Franks quickly grabs his pen and signs the contract. When he pushes the papers across the table, Dante hands me the antidote and I quickly stand and go over to Junior.

I pull him up from the table and lean him back against the chair. "Keep breathing, Junior." I open his mouth and pour the antidote down his throat. Once he's swallowed it, I head to the bar and grab a bottle of water. By the time I get back to the table, Junior is coughing again and I set the bottle in front of him. "You'll be okay in a minute. Just keep breathing normally."

Franks grabs my arm, leaning on the table, and pulls me to him. "You'll die for this girl. No one tries to kill my son."

I glare up at him without trying to pull away because I can feel my guys at my back. "Your threats mean nothing to me. But you should listen to mine. The first chance I get, I'm going to give you a visit and when I visit, I better find that you're no longer in the skin business. Because if you are, I will tear down everything you own and hold precious. Nobody sells skin in my city."

Franks laughs. "Who do you think you are? These boys don't give you that kind of power."

I give him a wicked smirk. "Oh, my bad. We weren't formally introduced. My name is Riona Murphy, but you may also know me by M."

Pure terror run through his eyes and he quickly let's go of my wrist and steps back. "Oh good, you know who I am. Now I'm going to say this one more time. No one sells skin in my city. If I find out after today you sell or traffic one person, I'll destroy everything, leaving nothing for your son after I kill you."

Franks nods and Junior steps up to his father looking almost back to normal. "It's time to go, Father."

They both turn to leave but I grab Junior's wrist, stopping him. "Sorry about this. I hope there are no hard feelings."

He gives me an understanding nod. "None at all. My father was an idiot to think he could play the Russos."

"If you ever decide to overthrow him, you have mine and the Murphys' backing, as long as skin isn't a part of it."

"How about if I need an assassin to do that?"

I'd happily do it. "Please call me. It'd be my honor."

Junior chuckles and coughs. "It was nice meeting you, Riona." He looks at the guys behind me and nods. "Russos." Junior meets Franks and their bodyguard in the hall.

I close my eyes and take a deep breath, letting the tension go. That was a crazier meeting than I thought it would be. Feeling a body up against my back, I open my eyes and look over my shoulder to see only Dante. "Where's Matteo and Enzo?"

Chapter Twenty

Dante

Watching her putting the fear of god in Franks from just her name was the hottest thing. Riona's confidence and power draws me to her. I want her attitude and sassiness directed toward me. She knows I like it too and she tries to get a rise out of me.

Matteo follows Franks and Junior out, making sure they actually leave, and Enzo goes into the office with the signed contract. Once we're alone, I step up to her back and I watch her body relax. She looks back at me with a small smile on her face. "Where's Matteo and Enzo?"

I wrap my arms around her waist. "Matteo followed our guests out. Enzo is in the office."

"So, we're alone?" She turns and wraps her arms around my middle, underneath my jacket.

"Yes, we are." I run my fingers down her back and she shivers at my touch. "Are you still wet for me?"

"If I am, will you finish what you started?" Desire flashes in her eyes, knowing my answer.

I quickly spin us and lift her up onto the table. "Are you still on edge, Ri? Do you need some relief?" I skim my lips down her neck as I pull her thighs apart and step in between them.

She moans softly and tries to grind up against me. "Yes... please."

I run my hands up her thighs, pushing her dress up and she lifts her hips so it gathers around her waist, exposing her lacey black thong. I rub my thumb down the seam and she bucks against my touch.

"Stop toying with me, Dante." She glares up at me in the way I love so much. "You've had me on edge the entire meeting in front of that perv. Finish what you started."

I growl, pulling her thong off and her hands go to my belt. She pushes my pants down just enough to release my erection and I thrust inside her. God, she can get me so worked up. She hooks her legs around me, digging her heels into my ass. The way she smiles up at me tells me she loves getting a reaction out of me. Her fingers go into my hair, and she pulls me to her until my lips graze over hers. "Fuck me, Dante."

I slam my lips to hers and do exactly what she asked. I fuck her hard and fast on our conference room table. The sounds she makes spur me on and I pick up my pace. I lift her leg higher to get a better angle and Riona digs her nails into my scalp and back. "Oh god... Please don't stop."

I kiss down her neck and grab her breast over her dress. "Not until you're coming all over my cock."

She arches into my hand and I rub my thumb over her pointed nipple. "Yes, Dante…yes."

Loving the sound of her moaning my name, I reach in between us and rub circles over her clit. Her walls tighten around me and I let out a curse as I feel myself rushing to the edge. "You feel so good squeezing around me. You're so close, Rose. Come for me. Let me hear you scream."

I pinch her clit and she screams out my name as she comes, vibrating beneath me. Her tight grip around me has me coming seconds later. "Oh fuck." I lay my head against her breasts as I catch my breath and she runs her fingers through my hair. "God, I could fuck you all day."

"If you can fuck like that all day, I'm down. But you might want Matteo and Enzo to join just in case you get tired."

I chuckle and look up at her. "What if you get tired from all the orgasms we give you?" I can feel myself hardening again inside her just thinking about a second round.

"That sounds like a pretty ideal situation to me." Ri leans up and pulls me into a kiss. I wrap my arms around her back and pull her up into a sitting position as I pull out of her. She groans at the loss of our connection and tightens her hold on me.

"Are you wanting a round two?" I slide my hands under her ass and squeeze.

"I wouldn't say no to it." She kisses along my jaw and I want to bury myself inside her, but I know I won't get a chance.

"Well, the guys aren't going to let that happen after hearing you screaming. They're probably rock hard for you." She looks around the room for cameras, almost giddy to think they watched. "They're off." I turn her face back to mine. "It's not something I'm into. The walls are thin, though, and they heard all of it." I pull back from her before I slide back in, tuck myself into my pants and get myself dressed.

Her cheeks turn pink as she rubs her thighs together and I know she's picturing them in the other room wanting her. God, I want to lay her out again and see how wet she is. But before I can even take a step towards her, there's a knock on the door, telling us our time is up.

"Come on, Rose. Let's have some fun." I hold out my hand for her and she takes it, sliding off the table. When she's back on her feet, she pulls her dress down and eyes my pocket.

"Well, if we're not going again, can I have my thong back?"

She holds out her hand for me to hand them over, but I shake my head. "They're mine now."

She gives my cocky smirk a stern look. "I won't have you leaking down my thighs all night so you either give me my thong and I promise not to clean myself up or I can go into the bathroom and wash you from between my legs." I growl, not liking the thought of her washing me away. When I don't make a move, she steps up to me, smiling because she knows she's won. She rises up on her toes and kisses me in victory as her hand goes into my pocket and she takes her prize. "I'll give them back to you back at the house."

I place my hand on the side of her neck, keeping her head tilted up. "Only if I'm the one taking them off."

"I think I can work with that." She turns out of my hold before I get a chance to kiss her and walks away from me to the office.

The door opens and Matteo is standing there waiting. "The club just opened. Ready to have some fun tonight?" He hooks his arm around her shoulders and leads her further from me.

She wraps her arm around his waist and answers while looking at me. "With you definitely."

She's not done with me yet.

Chapter Twenty-One

Enzo

Riona looks so happy tonight. I haven't seen her smile this big since the night she was here with Aisling, dancing the night away. Sure, she smiles and laughs with us but tonight she's carefree. I lean back in our private booth next to Dante as I watch her dance with Matteo. Well, dry humping is more like it. I watch as Riona grinds against Matteo's thigh as his hands slide down her back and grab her ass.

"They're magnetic." Dante leans forward on the table watching them.

"It's not just him and her. She has a pull to you as well. She riles you up just so you can let it out on her. She did it all afternoon to you until you snapped after the meeting. Or should I say during the meeting?" I look over at him with a knowing look.

It doesn't surprise me one bit that he knows I could pick up what he was doing to her under the table. "I know she does. She pulls me in with her challenging smirks and sassy attitude. But you two pull comfort from each other. You calm her when things get too much."

"She is perfect for us in every way." I look at him. "I'm not going to let her go after our end of the deal is done."

"I'm not asking you to," he replies, knowing exactly what I mean.

I nod and smile as I see Riona with her back to Matteo's chest and her eyes connect with mine. "Matteo will fight you on it."

"And you won't?" Her eyes shift to Dante.

"Nope, because the decision is hers. Us fighting won't matter." My eyes lock with hers again and she starts reeling me in, guiding Matteo's hands all over her body.

"They're baiting you." The growl in his voice tells me she's baiting him too.

"I know. They probably have a bet to see how long it'll take me to join."

"So, when are you?" He moves closer to the edge of the chair like he's about to get up.

"When she gives me a signal. Whatever they bet, I want her to win." I smile at her, letting her know she has all my attention.

Her lips part and her tongue peeks out, running along her lips. My dick hardens in my pants, and I lean forward adjusting myself. A satisfied smile pulls on her lips as she sees I'm hooked. I watch her every move as I sit on the edge of my seat, ready for her signal. I've watched her enough with him today. It's my turn next. Her face morphs into pure pleasure as a moan leaves her lips that I swear I can hear. I scan my eyes down her body and notice one of Matteo's hands isn't visible anymore. But I know exactly where it is.

"He's testing my patience," Dante growls next to me.

"She'd stop him if she didn't want it. You can see it all over her face that she wants this."

"People can see."

I let my eyes break from hers for just a second to scan the faces of the people around them. "There are dozens of people surrounding them focusing on their own desires. Not hers." I watch in slow motion as Riona's eyes fall closed, her teeth bite into her bottom lip and her hold on Matteo tightens. There she is, glowing in pleasure, surrounded by strangers, knowing our attention is solely on her.

When her eyes open, they're dazed but I don't miss her need for me reflecting in her eyes. I'm out of my seat in an instant and make my way to her, not caring who I push out of my way. I pull her from Matteo, and she instantly melts into me with her arms around my neck and her face turned up to me. I lean forward and place a quick kiss on her lips. "You've been naughty, Beauty. Dante is going to punish you later for that."

Her eyes are filled with so much desire. "I know but it's you I need right now."

I place a kiss on her forehead. "And what do you need?"

"You, dancing with me. Feeling your hands on me. Your body against mine." Her fingers run through my hair at the back of my head.

"I can definitely do that." My hands slide down her sides to her hips as I move us to the beat of the song. Our bodies never disconnect as we sway with each other. I get lost in her eyes as she stares up at me, drawing me in. Her fingers continue to run through my hair and everything around me disappears.

I lean forward and capture her lips into a soft kiss, but when she opens her lips and flicks her tongue against my lips, I break, deepening our kiss. Our tongues dance together just like our bodies, slow and sensual.

This isn't a kiss just to kiss. It's a kiss with feelings being expressed. And I show her just how I feel about her. Who cares I've only known her for days? I know how I feel. She is my orbit. All day she's on my mind when I can't see her. But when she's in the same room as me, she's the most important thing. My eyes never lose track of her.

She might think she's going home after all this and that's fine. I'll just be going with her. I hope she has a bed that fits four. Our lips break apart and my eyes open, connecting with hers. Her thumb runs across my cheek and I lean into her touch. "You have so much power over me, Beast. I don't think you realize how much."

She lays her head on my chest and I know she doesn't want me to say anything. I kiss the top of her head and take her hand that was on my cheek and hold it to my chest. I rock us back and forth to my own beat, not caring it's not the beat to the song playing.

"We're slow dancing." I can hear the delight in her voice.

"Yes, we are."

"But the music isn't right." She smiles up at me and my smile matches hers.

"Does it bother you?"

"No." She shakes her head.

"Good." I push Riona slightly away from me and pull our conjoined hands over her head and spin her. She giggles and I bring her back to me as I start moving us into a basic waltz. "I do own the place, so I can ask the DJ to slow it down if it bothers you that people are looking at us funny."

She chuckles moving with me as our steps start widening so we're taking up more space. "Well, if we're doing this, we need proper form." She shifts our arms so our elbows are up and out correctly. Riona lets me lead her around another square but then her focus breaks and darkness starts to consume the light in her eyes.

I stop us resting my hands on her hips. "What's wrong?"

She looks up at me, worried. "Do you feel that?"

I start looking around to see if I missed something that everyone else is reacting to, but everyone around us is just dancing. "Feel what?"

She's scanning the crowd. "Someone is watching us."

I look around again and only see Dante and Matteo watching us. "It's just Matteo and Dante."

"No, it's not. This is different. It's like I can feel their anger or hatred. It's chilling." Her head continues to swivel as she looks around.

I take another look around, still not seeing anyone looking directly at us. Not doubting what Riona is feeling, I grab her hand and start pulling her to our booth. "Let's take a break."

As we walk back, I watch everyone that we pass, ready to attack if someone goes for her. Dante and Matteo look confused as we reach them, and I step to the side allowing Riona to slide into the round booth first so she's sitting between me and Dante. "What's wrong?" Dante asks as his arm rests behind Riona.

"It's just a feeling." She leans into him.

"What feeling?" He looks between the two of us.

I place my hand on her thigh and she immediately links our fingers. "Not everyone is friendly here tonight."

Matteo and Dante look at me for clarity but when I don't give it, I hear Matteo growl. "Did someone say something to you or touch you?"

"No. That's why I said it was just a feeling." She glares at Matteo, and I squeeze her hand. She's wound up, ready for something, so I know she didn't mean to snap at him.

I watch as she takes a deep breath, trying to loosen the tension. She reaches over the table and places her hand on his forearm. "Maybe it was just someone being jealous that I get all you sexy men. It's probably best I stop flaunting it and sit in this dark corner with you instead."

I don't think she believes that, but she's definitely hoping that's it. "You're probably right. I'd be jealous if I saw you with me." Matteo smirks at her. "Our chemistry is something everyone..."

"Sorry to interrupt." One of our waitresses, Shannon, gives us an intimidated smile. "A gentleman bought you this drink." She slowly places the drink in front of Riona with a folded-up napkin. "He asked to give this to you as well."

Riona looks at her, confused, and then down at the napkin. Dante goes to grab it but she's quicker. A second after the napkin opens, Riona stills and goes cold. I quickly take the napkin from her and look at what's on it.

You've been missing for days.

You finally reappear and you're letting them touch you.

You're supposed to be looking for Aisling, not fucking your bodyguards.

She's screaming in pain and you're moaning in pleasure.

What would she say if she knew?

"What the fuck?" Who the hell wrote this? I look at Shannon to see her a few steps away. I yell her name and she turns back around. "Who the hell wrote this?"

I slam the note on the table as I squeeze Riona's hand, letting her know I'm here and not to take a word of this note to heart. Dante and Matteo read the note and they both curse loudly.

Shannon looks back to the bar. "I'm sorry sir. He's not at the bar anymore. I don't know who he is. Never seen him before."

"What did he look like?" I start scanning the crowd as she tells us.

"He was wearing a hat, dark shirt, and jeans. He was average looking. Cute but not attractive. He seemed tall but was sitting. Average build. I wouldn't have remembered him if he didn't ask me to come over here."

I give her a nod. "Thanks, Shannon. You can go."

Shannon quickly moves away, and I pull Riona out of the booth with me as Dante balls up the napkin and pushes it into the drink. "Let's go to the office. I want eyes on this guy."

The four of us move through the club as a group with Riona in the middle and us surrounding her. When we make it upstairs, I head straight for my desk. My laptop is open on my desk and I'm logged in before my ass hits my seat. Riona leans on the back of my chair with her hands on my shoulders as she looks at the screen.

Matteo leans on the front of my desk as I bring our security system up and project it on the large TV screen across from us. "Move back to thirty minutes ago. Focus on the bar."

"Yeah, I know." I'm entering in the time and bringing up the right camera feeds when Riona's hands slide off my shoulders. I look back at her to see what's wrong only to find Dante has brought his chair over and pulled her into his lap. She smiles at me as she kicks off her shoes and rests her feet on my thigh. I pull up all the cameras facing the bar and it plays. All our eyes are on the screen as we scan everyone looking for the guy Shannon described.

"Right there. Third camera," Riona calls out, pointing at the TV.

I pull that camera up and sure enough, there is a guy sitting at the end of the bar with a hat on. The guy is leaning against the wall, looking out past the bar to the center of the club.

"What's he looking at?" Dante asks and I'm pretty sure we all know the answer.

Bringing up a wider camera angle I see Riona, Matteo, and I on the dance floor just as I'm pulling her from Matteo. "Oh god. He watched me..." I run my hand over her ankle and shin trying to soothe her. "I feel gross."

A visible shiver runs through her and Dante wraps his arms tightly around her. Looking back at the screen, I watch Riona and I kiss and the guy becomes visibly angry as his grip tightens on his beer. Done watching this guy, I fast forward the feed until he gets up. I track him as he walks right by our table as Riona reads the note and leaves the club.

"I want his name, now." Matteo pulls out his phone and calls someone. "Get me whoever is working the door." He's called the bar manager.

I rewind the footage to find when the guy came in. The guy is talking to John, our bouncer, as he hands over his ID and thankfully John does what he's supposed to do. He places the ID under the UV light which also has a camera. I pause the image just as our bouncer walks in. "You called for me, boss?"

Matteo stands and turns to our employee. "What can you tell me about this guy?"

"Oh, he was a nice guy. We joked about having the same name. I made fun of how common his name was. Who names their son John Smith? If your last name is Smith, have a unique first name. He said at least it's not Jon Snow. What did he do?"

"Don't worry about it. Thanks for the information. You can go back to the door," Matteo instructs John and he nods and walks out.

We're all quiet as we stare at the screen, looking at the ID. "It's a fake." I look at Riona and she stands from Dante's lap and walks to the screen. She points to the hologram in the ID. "This is wrong." She points to the bottom left corner. "These are five-point stars. There are supposed to be more points."

"Well, damn." I fall back into my chair. "People just look for the hologram, not the specifics."

"I'm calling Zach." Dante stands and walks out of the room.

"Who's Zach?" She looks at us, confused.

Matteo walks to her and wraps his arms around her center. "He's our best friend, next in command, and forger. We met him in boarding school, and he hasn't left our side since."

"Is he this good?" She points to the screen.

Matteo chuckles. "No, he isn't. Not with IDs at least. Passports definitely." Riona slightly nods, acknowledging Matteo's comment. She sees something that she's trying to figure out. As much as I want to ask what, I keep quiet, studying the ID as well.

Dante walks into the room and he's not alone. "Riona?"

She turns and looks relieved to see Killian. "Kill, what are you doing here?"

"Looking for you." He walks over to her and pulls her away from Matteo and into a hug. They hug tightly and I barely hear Killian whisper, "I'm sorry, Riona. I shouldn't have said those things."

She rubs his upper back. "I know. It's okay." She pulls back from their hug and looks to the screen. "Do you recognize him?"

"Do you?" I sit forward in my seat, surprised that's her question.

"There is something familiar about him. Like he looks like someone I know but I can't place who." She looks back to Killian.

He shakes his head. "No, I don't. I do see what you mean though. There is something about him that makes you think you might."

She nods, still staring at the screen. "How about the address? I know that street name, but I can't think why or where it is."

Killian smiles. "One of your favorite restaurants is on that street. O'Malley's."

"That's it." I pull up the address on my map and it comes up right over a blue pin.

"Guys..." Everyone turns to me. "That address is an O'Brien property."

I move the map to the TV screen. "So, the note was definitely from O'Brien's people." Dante crosses his arms over his chest.

"So, Aisling could be there?" Riona looks at me, hopeful.

I shake my head. "Sorry, Riona. She's not there. Our guys cleared that place already. That's why it's blue. Red are properties we haven't." I zoom out showing twenty or so red dots.

She throws her hands up in defeat. "Of course it won't be that easy. I'm so tired of today. Can we go home?"

I can't help my smile as she says home. "Zach should be..."

"Talk about me and I appear." Zach bursts into the room with his arms out like he owns the place. He's your typical American jock, with shaggy dirty blonde hair and a body built like a tank. He steps up beside Dante and pats him on the shoulder. "So why have I been summoned?" He sees Killian and Riona. "Other than to meet the infamous Murphy siblings." He walks over to Riona and gives her his signature smirk that makes girls swoon. "It's a pleasure to meet you, Riona. I must say, you're more beautiful than people give you credit for." He kisses the back of her hand.

Instead of getting weak in the knees like most, Riona just rolls her eyes. "It's nice to meet you, Zach. The guys didn't mention you were a flirt."

"They never mention my best qualities." He shakes Killian's hand with a nod. "Okay, why am I here?" He looks at the screen. "Damn, that's a good fake."

"That's why you're here." Matteo steps up. "Do you know who did this?"

He shakes his head in awe. "Have no idea. Someone who charges more than me."

"How much do you charge?" Riona asks.

He shrugs. "$75 for ID."

She nods and smiles like she's chuckling to herself. "Then yes, they do charge more."

"Wait, you know who did this?" Dante is getting angrier by the second as he fumes next to me.

"Yes. My forger did. That's why I could point out the difference." She looks at him like it's not a big deal.

"Your forger?" They square off with each other.

"The Murphys' forger."

"Who is it?" he demands.

She shakes her head. "Sorry, but I'm not telling you. Their name doesn't matter anyways because they aren't local. No one really knows their location. You just order what you need."

"Very secretive," I comment. Never having to use your name is security.

Riona gives me an appreciative look. "Exactly. They don't even know our names. When you place an order, you send a picture telling them how to modify it, if needed, and the name and address." But they do know what you look like. If they're good enough, they could find you. This forger doesn't seem like the safest option. "Our forger isn't for underage students getting a fake ID. They service criminals only."

"Why didn't you mention this earlier?" Dante glares at Riona and she shifts her stance and crosses her arms, matching him.

"You didn't ask."

"Don't start, Ri." He points at her.

She hits his hand away. "Don't start? I told you it was a fake and you walked out of the room to call this guy. Why would it matter who made it? This isn't a common criminal that you can intimidate. They're the best forger in the world. What did you think, they'd give up their client list?"

"You don't know that they won't."

She throws her back with a laugh. "Don't be stupid."

"Okay. On that, I'm out." Zach starts moving to the door.

"Me too." Killian hugs Riona as she continues to glare at Dante. "Get some sleep. Your cranky side is coming out."

"Fuck you, Kill." Her glare turns to him and Zach chuckles by the door.

"Love you." Killian gives her a sweet smile.

She flips him off. "Yeah... yeah... same." Zach and Killian leave the room, leaving only us. Riona and Dante continue to glare at each other until Riona breaks it, moving around him to grab her bag. "Let's go."

"You're just done with this conversation?" He turns, watching her.

"Yes." She doesn't look back at him. "It's been too long of a day to hear you yelling at me over something stupid."

He huffs and runs his fingers through his hair. "It's not stupid. It could've led..."

She interrupts him, or, more likely is ignoring him, when she steps beside me and holds out her hand. "You ready?"

Quickly I shut everything down and grab her hand. She looks at Matteo as I stand. "How about you?"

"Hell yeah." He moves instantly, heading to the door.

"What? Are you ignoring me now?" She doesn't respond as the three of us head to the door. "I have the keys, so how are you getting home?"

Riona stops, let's go of my hand, and stomps over to him. When she's standing in front of him, she holds out her hand, silently asking for the keys. After a few seconds, he pulls the keys out of his pocket and places them in her hand. Her fingers wrap around them and she calls out Matteo's name before throwing the keys behind her, right at him. Matteo catches the keys effortlessly, but her eyes never leave Dante's. "You coming or not?"

He nods and she turns and comes back to me, linking our fingers and we all leave the club and head home. Riona is right, today has been long and all I want to do right now is curl up in bed with her.

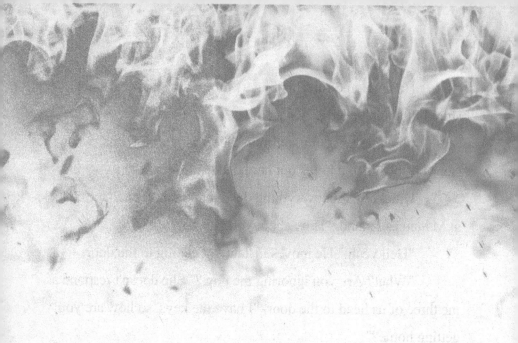

Chapter Twenty-Two

Riona

Sleep is definitely what I needed. Yesterday was long. Some amazing things happened, but the crappy seemed to outweigh the good. The idea that I'm not doing enough to find Aisling was thrown in my face several times. That's why I needed Enzo last night. I just needed him to hold me. Soothe me. The way only he can.

His arm is draped over my middle and his body is pressed to my back. I turn in his arms so I'm facing him and I run my fingers over his sleeping face. His hold on me tightens and I start placing kisses over his face. When my lips skim over his, his hand buries in my hair and he slams his lips to mine. I welcome the kiss, opening my lips when his tongue asks for access. Enzo rolls us so he's on top of me and I open my legs, letting him settle in between them. I feel his hard length grind against my core and I moan out, lifting my hips to feel more of him. He starts kissing down my neck as his hands go underneath my sleep shirt, pulling it up my body. "Good morning, Beauty."

"Good morning, Beast." I run my hands down his bare muscular back as I arch into him, rubbing my chest against his.

Enzo pulls my shirt over my head, leaving me in just my panties and his lips go to my nipples. A moan escapes me as my nipples peek and I tangle my fingers in his dirty blonde hair, holding him to me. I grind my hips up, wanting to feel him against me, but he's too far away. "Enzo..."

"Shh. I've got you." He starts kissing down my body as he pulls my panties down.

"I need you inside." I grab for his boxers, but he grabs my hand.

"Soon…" He brings my hand to his mouth and kisses the back of it. When his eyes connect back to mine, he smirks. "There's something I want to do first."

He places a kiss right over my core and I buck against his mouth as his tongue moves over my clit. "Oh god... yes."

I open my legs wider as his hands move down my inner thigh. "I've wanted my tongue inside you since yesterday when I watched you come apart for Matteo."

I hum, remembering how good Matteo made me feel in that bathroom and the feeling of Enzo's eyes on me. Our eyes connect as he looks up at me and I know he's remembering last night. "Did you like what you saw? Did you come watching me come on Matteo's tongue? Or did you come watching us fuck against the shower wall?"

His smirk grows as he lowers his face and places a kiss on my clit. I moan at his touch and he doesn't stop at that one kiss. He sucks my bundle of nerves between his lips and his tongue works beautiful magic until I'm a squirming mess. I'm breathless and on the edge of coming, needing more. I grip his hair and push his face against me.

Enzo pushes two fingers inside me and hooks them upward, grazing them over my spot and I squeeze around his finger. "Yes…I'm so close."

He scrapes his teeth across my clit and I come screaming his name, riding out my pleasure on his face. He kisses back up my body until his lips cover mine in a passionate kiss. "I came watching you come all over his cock, hearing your screams echo in the bathroom."

I moan at his answer and frantically push his boxers down, needing more of him. All of him. "Enzo... I need you inside me. Please." Enzo presses his lips to mine and kisses me like he's never going to let me go. I feel his erection at my entrance and I wrap my legs around his waist as he slowly sinks into me. I'm panting by the time he's fully inside me, stretching me in the best way. Our eyes connect and my breath catches at all the emotions I see in his eyes.

Emotions that I feel, but I'm too scared to say or even admit to myself.

I bring my hand up to his face and run my fingers along the edge of his jaw. He starts to move, thrusting into me slowly, building us up with soft touches and lingering kisses. But as I get closer and closer to the edge, his thrusts pick up and the power behind them has me moaning and squeezing around him. He moves my legs higher on him, changing the angle so he's hitting me exactly where I need him to.

My orgasm starts at my toes and it shoots up my body and stars form in my vision. My screams are muffled as Enzo slams his lips back on mine. His thrusts continue until I'm falling into a second orgasm and then he comes, groaning my name.

My body shakes from the aftershocks as Enzo lays on top of me. I run my hands up and down his back and he places soft kisses across my shoulder, up my neck, and to my lips.

I kiss him back, taking his comfort wordlessly. He slowly pulls out of me and my body follows him, not quite ready for our connection to break. "Let me make you breakfast." Enzo kisses my forehead before rising above me.

"I'll never say no to that." Reluctantly, I release Enzo from my hold and he sits up and pulls his boxers back on.

Enzo stands, grabbing his sweatpants he changed into last night and I stretch my body out with my arms above my head and my legs straight. Enzo's eyes move over my naked body and I smile up at him. He smirks at me while shaking his head. "You're addicting."

I slowly sit up and stand so I'm right in front of him. "Is that a bad thing?"

He grabs a shirt off the floor and pulls it over my head. Instantly Enzo's cologne hits my nose and I know it's his shirt. I slide my arms into it and look down, seeing that it hits right above my knees. "Not a bad thing. It just makes me want you always." Enzo takes my hand and pulls me out of my room.

I pull back at my open door. "Do I not get to put panties on?"

He looks over his shoulder at me with a smirk. "Nope."

I chuckle as I follow him down the hall and down the stairs where Matteo and Dante are already in the kitchen, working on getting breakfast. Dante is at the stove flipping pancakes and Matteo is making coffee and pulling out butter and syrup.

"Looks like you won't be making me breakfast."

"Raincheck?" Enzo looks down at me and I nod. He leans forward and gives me a kiss.

"Oh, look who has decided to join us." Matteo smiles at us as he tracks his eyes over my body and I feel like he can tell I have nothing on under this shirt. I rub my thighs together, hoping that he'll find out. Matteo moves toward me and Enzo steps away, giving him an opening. Matteo pulls me against him and buries his nose in the hook of my neck. "Hmm ... you smell like sex, Princess."

"I do?" I slide my hands over his chest and around his waist.

"It's one of my favorite smells on you." He runs his hands down my back and grabs my ass. He definitely knows I'm not wearing underwear now. He kisses my neck. "You're sitting next to me at breakfast."

I nod and give him a quick kiss. Dante calls out that the pancakes are ready, and I look to him, seeing him watching me. Matteo swats my ass. "Go make up with him." He walks away and takes a seat at the bar.

Dante and I stare at each other for a few seconds and I can tell he's trying to see how mad I am at him. To be honest, I'm not mad at him. I didn't like him yelling at me. I didn't like him implying I was holding back from them.

I take a deep breath and walk toward him until I'm right in front of him and my arms go around his middle. "Hi Stinkface."

He chuckles. "I thought you weren't going to call me that anymore."

I tilt my head to the side, looking up at him. "That was before you yelled at me."

He slides his hands up my neck and tilts my head back so our eyes are connected. "I yelled because a guy threatened you and you didn't tell us you knew who made his fake ID. Your safety is my top priority, and he was able to hurt you. Maybe not physically, but he still hurt you."

How can I be mad that he was upset because someone upset me? I rise up on my toes and kiss him. When I pull back, I smile up at him. "Sweet words won't always make things better."

"I would never think that." He smirks at me and he has very dirty things running through his mind. Things I'd happily allow him to do as an apology. He covers my mouth with his, kissing me passionately. "I'm sorry, Rose."

"I'm sorry too, Boss Man."

He gives me another quick kiss and we separate. I head to the empty seat next to Matteo and he pulls my chair to him until our sides are touching. Enzo hands me a coffee and I smile at him in thanks. As we eat breakfast, the guys talk about business but I'm not really paying attention to what they're saying because Matteo is teasing me with his hand.

He slowly moves his hand up and down my inner thigh, getting higher and higher every time. By the time he's skimming over my lower lips, I'm silently begging him to touch me where I'm wet for him. But instead of doing as I want, he removes his hand completely from me. I fight back a groan as I glare at him. His lips turn up slightly and I realize he's playing a game.

His hand goes back to my thigh and I stand from my seat, removing it. I'm not playing his game. I can feel their eyes on me as I leave the room and I hear Matteo chuckle as I hit the stairs. "She doesn't like to be teased."

God, he's lucky I like him or I'd have a knife in him right now for keeping me on edge. I walk into my room and head straight to the bathroom.

After a shower and completing my morning routine, I walk out of the bathroom with a towel wrapped around me. As I head to my closet, my phone starts to ring. Thinking it's one of the guys calling me down, I slowly make my way over to the side table but instead of one of their names showing up, Father is on the screen. I quickly grab the phone. "Father."

"Riona. I hear you've been trying to reach me about Aisling's mother."

"Yes. Does Aisling have a connection to the O'Briens?"

"Her mother's uncle was Carl O'Brien."

"What!? You had me kill Aisling's family?" I run my fingers through my hair in frustration. Aisling doesn't have any family other than us and I just made her family tree smaller even though it wasn't known.

"He wasn't her family. Carl was never involved in Aisling's life or her parents."

Frustrated, I yell, "They're blood."

"That doesn't mean anything. She is our family."

Rage builds inside me. "You can't call her family when you chose not to protect her. This is all your fault."

"I'm not having this argument with you again. I protected my own. You might not agree with my decisions, but you have to accept them. I'm the leader of this family, of this Clan, not you."

"How can you be our leader when we don't follow you?"

He growls in my ear. "Riona Murphy, don't make me enforce my power over you. It won't be pretty. Now if that's all your questions about Aisling's mother, I have to go." Before I can say anything else, he hangs up and I let out a frustrated groan as I punch my bed.

This whole thing is showing me a side to my father I've never seen before. He's never been a normal, loving father but he's also never been cold to me and Killian. I stand from my bed and stomp over to my closet to throw on some clothes. Once dressed, I head downstairs looking for the guys. When I don't find them in the kitchen, I call out their names. Seconds later I hear a faint "Down here."

I head to the door that leads down to their training area. As I walk down the stairs, I hear two sets of gunshots going off. At the bottom of the steps, I see Dante and Matteo shooting guns down an alley at targets. Matteo turns to me with a teasing smile on his face. "Did someone cool off in the shower?"

I flip him off and head to Enzo's office door. Opening his door, I stick my head in. "Hey, can you come out here?"

Enzo nods and heads toward me. When I turn back to Dante and Matteo, I find them standing closer. "What's wrong?"

I look at each of them. "I just got off the phone with my father. Carl O'Brien was Aisling's great uncle."

"Well fuck. That means Aisling is from two high-ranking families in your Clan." Enzo runs his finger through his hair.

"This is all my father's fault. If he hadn't asked me to kill Carl, Aisling wouldn't be in this situation." Needing to let out some of this anger, I move past Matteo and Dante and head to the shooting range. I pick up the first gun and aim for the target. I shoot until the clip is empty and then move to the next stall and aim for that target. Once that clip is empty, I move to the next stall which happens to be the stall where I threw knives at Matteo. I pick up the knives one at a time and throw them, imagining my father's face on the target.

A ringing fills my ears, and I don't realize it's me screaming until someone wraps their arms around me, pulling me back. "Princess, please calm down," Matteo whispers in my ear and I stop fighting against him. Dante and Enzo step in front of me and I see the concern written across their faces.

I take a deep breath and relax into Matteo's arms. "I'm fine. Just needed to let out my anger. My father put us at risk and didn't protect us. He knew they wanted revenge and only protected me. I'm who they really want. Why didn't they just take me? They got to her; they could've gotten to me. Maxim did."

Enzo answers me. "They couldn't get to you because we were watching you."

It just doesn't make sense. "Then how do you explain Maxim getting into the bathroom?"

A light growl leaves Dante. "We couldn't stop him because we were told not to interfere with the Bratva if he approached you."

"What? Why would he tell you that?"

Matteo holds me tighter. "Maybe because he knew you could handle that dick."

"I don't know." It doesn't make sense. Father told me Maxim dies the next time he touches me. Why wouldn't he have someone ready to take him after he attacked me? Why leave me open to being attacked?

"Well, I know one thing." Matteo loosens his hold around me. I look back at him, curious at what he's going to say. "You have crazy good aim, even when you're using your emotions."

I look at all three targets, seeing I hit the bullseye on all three and I chuckle. "I am pretty good."

Matteo kisses my neck. "Damn right you are."

Enzo steps forward and places his hand on my cheek. "You doing okay now?"

I nod, leaning into his touch. "I'm okay. Just had to release some anger so I didn't kill my father."

"Well let's look into Carl a little bit more. If Aisling is that closely related maybe then they had other reasons to take her." Enzo takes my hand and I step out of Matteo's arms and follow Enzo to his office. I can feel Dante and Matteo closely behind me so I know they're following.

I pull a second chair next to Enzo, but Matteo quickly takes it, pulling me into his lap. "We figured they took Aisling to torture you, but they could've taken her to remove her as a threat to Craig. With her link to you and Killian, they could be worried that she'll claim power and sell out to your father."

"Let's hope that's not the case because that means they're going to kill her." Enzo pulls up the family tree and adds Aisling's connection. Seeing it all connected and knowing her father's ties,

Aisling could be the head of two families. Could this be about power?

"So, you want this to be about you." Dante looks down at me as he stands between the two chairs.

I nod. "If that's the only other option. Yeah. If this is about me, eventually they'll reach out to trade. She has to be alive for that."

"But you won't be alive long after a trade." Enzo gives me a concerned look.

"That's something I'll worry about when it happens." I shrug my shoulders because I don't have a plan for after a trade, if it comes to that. I'd happily give up my life for Aisling, but they don't want to hear that.

Dante grabs my chin and turns my face so I'm looking up at him. "You won't die for her. You hear me. I'm not going to allow it."

"Sometimes you can't control everything, Dark God." I pull my chin from his grasp.

"This I can."

"Then we better find her before it comes to that." He nods and I look back to the O'Brien family tree. Something Matteo said earlier is bothering me. Aisling being connected to both families means that her engagement to Killian brings more power to my father.

I pull out my phone and dial Killian. "Who are you calling?" Enzo asks as I put the phone on speaker.

"My brother." I look at him.

"Hey Riona. You calling for a cleanup crew after tearing apart Dante?"

I chuckle as Dante growls, "Fuck off."

"Oh, he's not dead." He pauses for a second. "What can I do for you?"

"Did you know Aisling was an O'Brien? Actually, the rightful head of the O'Brien family now that I killed Carl."

"What?" I can hear the shock in his voice. "That doesn't make sense. Carl wasn't her father."

"No, but he was her mother's uncle."

"Fuck. This isn't good, Riona. Craig could kill her just from the threat of her. Shit... this is what Father has been gearing up for. He wants that power and he's using her for it." I can picture him pacing whatever room he is in.

"Well then he needs her alive for that."

He chuckles. "Looking at the bright side?"

"Something like that. You have to marry her for his plan to work."

"I'm marrying her no matter what."

"As soon as we have her, you can make that statement true. Talk to you soon, Kill."

"Soon."

I hang up the phone and I looked at Dante. "Who's this guy that was looking at the footage?"

"Are you not waiting anymore, Ri?"

"I was never waiting." Dante gives me a proud smirk at my comment. "He has to be close by now if he's really been working on it nonstop for two days."

"I'll give her a call." Dante brings his phone to his ear after dialing a phone. After a few seconds, I hear someone answer.

"Hey Carmen. I'm just following up on how the footage is going?" Carmen says something, but I can't make it out. "Okay, send Enzo the last car and we'll follow that one." Seconds later, Enzo's computer beeps. "Got it, Carmen. Thanks for everything. Let me know where yours leads."

Dante hangs up and Enzo pulls up his email. "She's down to the last two cars. We're taking the last one."

The footage pulls up of a black sedan pulling out of the parking garage not even a minute before Killian pulls in. "What are the chances they left right before Killian got there?" I look between them.

Enzo looks at me with hesitation. "I think it's easy to say you have a mole in the Murphy organization."

"Let Killian know. I'm going to grab my laptop so I can help in hacking street cameras." I'm out of Matteo's lap and up the stairs before they can say anything. I can feel it; we're close to finding her.

Chapter Twenty-Three

Riona

It took Enzo and I two hours to track the black SUV all over town. Not once did they stop somewhere but they definitely took the long way. Making unnecessary large circles. It's like they were making sure they weren't followed.

The SUV finally pulls into the driveway of an upscale townhouse on the edge of the city and I lean back in my chair, watching the SUV pull in and then disappear behind the garage door.

"Has Carmen found anything on her last car?" I look back to Dante and he shakes his head no.

"She texted a little bit ago saying she has nothing."

I look at Enzo. "Who owns this house?"

Enzo types away on his computer and pulls up his map of O'Brien properties. The black cursor of the townhouse we just watched the SUV pull into sits right on top of a red cursor. "That's where they took her."

Dante stands, bringing his phone to his ear. "I'm calling in Zach." I look back at him to ask him to let Killian know but he doesn't need me to. "I'll call Killian too."

I mouth "thank you" to him and he nods before walking out the door. Matteo stands next. "I'll go load the car. Do you need anything specific?"

"My backpack has my gun and knives. Will you grab that? I also need some clips."

"I got you." Matteo leaves Enzo and I alone.

"Let's run through the footage over the last couple of days. See if there's anything that we need to be aware of." Enzo plays the footage on fast forward since we have five days to get through.

I sit back watching the days go by with normal traffic and I wonder if maybe this was too easy. Enzo must sense my worry because he reaches out, grabbing my hand and linking our fingers. "What's going on in your head?"

I look to him and squeeze his hand. "It almost seems too easy. What if she's not there and it's a trap?"

He turns to me and pulls my chair close. "Would you rather we wait and get surveillance on the place first?"

That's a hard question to answer. "Ideally, yes, but if she's there, I don't want to waste a second sitting outside."

"Then if it's a trap, we'll kill everyone waiting for us." He smiles with confidence.

I love his confidence, but I'm worried about this. "And if it's a bomb?"

"We'll send Dante in first." He smiles at me, telling me he's joking.

I point at him playfully. "I'm telling him that."

"Go for it. Dante will die..."

"I'll do what?" Dante walks back into the room.

"I was just telling her that if there's a bomb, you'd go in first."

"Please..." Dante chuckles. "That's Matteo, not me."

Matteo walks in. "No way. Zach is the dispensable one. He'll go first." We all chuckle.

I look at Matteo. "Are we ready to go?"

"Yep. The car is all packed." Matteo nods.

"Zach and Killian are meeting us in thirty minutes," Dante adds.

"I'll move the footage to my laptop and we can finish going over it in the car." Enzo grabs his laptop and we all head upstairs and out of the house.

I climb into the backseat next to Enzo and find my backpack waiting for me. Dante pulls out of the driveway, and I blindly start strapping on my knives and guns as I watch Enzo's screen. We're halfway across town when the video feed shows live. "It looks like they're still there."

Enzo nods. "At least at quick glance. It also doesn't look like it's an ambush. Maybe six guys at most."

"We're meeting Zach and Killian a couple blocks away to go over how we're doing this." Dante looks back at me through the rearview mirror.

"It appears to be a three-story townhouse with a basement and a patio on top. If I can use your computer, I should be able to hack into city records for blueprints." I look at Enzo and he quickly hands over his laptop.

I get to work hacking into city records as I listen to them plan how this will go. By the time we're pulling into the parking lot to meet everyone, I have the blueprints of the house next door pulled up. The O'Brien's are smarter than I thought. They've gotten the property removed from city records so I can't pull their blueprints.

"Who's with your brother?" Dante asks as we're pulling to a stop.

I look up and can't help my smile as I see the twins standing next to their car in a t-shirt and jeans with their dirty blonde hair styled back. As soon as the car is stopped, I'm outside, jumping into the arms of Tanner. "Oh my god!" I let go of Tanner and hug Colton next. "When did you guys get back into the States?"

Tanner and Colton aren't only my brother's best friends, but mine as well. They've been there for me through everything, but our connection isn't always just friendly. For years, I have willingly allowed them in my bed to explore all desires and pleasures, but we've never committed to a relationship. Our love for each other never blossomed into more than friendship.

"This morning. Sorry it took so long getting back. We just heard last night about Aisling," Colton answers me as I step back from our hug.

"How are you doing, Firecracker?" Tanner runs a hand down my back and it's a touch I'm familiar with. But it's a touch someone doesn't like as I hear a growl come from behind me.

Colton chuckles as his hands rest on my hips. "Or should he ask who you've been doing?"

I smack his chest. "That's none of your business. All you need to know is it's not you two anymore."

They both gasp dramatically and act like I hurt them. I look at my guys and step toward them. "Tanner, Colton, these are the Russo brothers, Matteo, Enzo, and Dante." I point to each of them. "Guys, this is Tanner and Colton, Killian's best friends and his chiefs when he takes power. They do a lot of our weapon sales overseas, so they're off the grid most of the time." Enzo steps forward and shakes their hands as Matteo wraps his arms around my shoulders and presses his lips to my ear. "Who are they to you?"

I look up at him and smile. "We grew up together."

"And?"

"And we have a physical relationship when they're in the city."

"Not anymore." Matteo leans down and kisses me, staking claim.

I push him back, not liking his jealousy. It's not playful. "Stop acting like a dog. I'm not a toy you can piss on and mark as yours." I step out of Matteo's hold. "Colton... Tanner, I'm with them. We're..." I point between Tanner, Colton, and myself. "Not fucking anymore. You cool with that?"

They smile at me as my brother groans in the background. "Really, Ri? We had a deal."

I chuckle at my brother's discomfort. Tanner and Colton look at each other and then nod. "We're cool with that, Red. But can I get one last kiss? So I can store it to memory." Colton puckers his lips at me.

I shake my head at him. "No. You have plenty of memories for your spank bank."

"So true. I guess we'll be stopping by your club while we're here." My burlesque club also has a lower level for the sex club we open twice a month.

"I'm sure Bianca will be happy to see you."

A wide smile spreads across his face. "Ahh yes. Bianca is a close second to you."

"Okay I'm done with this. Can we talk about anything else? Where's Zach?" Killian steps forward, pushing his best friends back. Just then, Zach pulls into the parking lot. "Oh, thank god."

With everyone here, the energy changes and there's no more joking. Enzo starts out with all of us surrounding Dante's hood. He pulls up the map on his laptop. "We've tracked an SUV from the parking garage to this property. We believe this is where they're keeping Aisling."

I step up, pulling up the blueprints. "These are blueprints to the neighbor's house. So, you can see there's a garage with a basement, a main floor, top floor, and a rooftop patio."

"Do you not have their blueprints, so we know if there are any hidden rooms?" Colton steps forward, looking at the layout more closely.

"I didn't have time to find them. They're wiped from city records."

"You're losing your touch, Red. These boys making you soft?" He shakes his head with playful disappointment.

I flip him off.

Dante steps up, moving the plan along. "Riona believes they're holding Aisling in the basement so you..." He looks directly at me, "and Killian should cover the garage and basement. That way, if she's there, she'll see someone she knows." I give an appreciative smile. "Tanner and Colton, you can clear the first floor and we'll cover the top floor and patio." He points to his brothers and Zach.

Everyone nods and we all start gearing up. Once again, Dante straps a bulletproof vest on me and I see the worry in his eyes. "Which one of you was shot?"

His eyes look up at me. "I was. It was about five years ago. I'll give you the story at another time." When he's done, he moves off to get geared up and I go over to Matteo to get a few clips.

"You still mad?" Matteo looks down at me with sad eyes.

"No, Bear." I push up on my toes, giving him a kiss and he gives me the biggest smile.

"Bear?"

"Yeah, you're a big teddy bear but you can also be a grizzly bear." He growls but I can see he's not mad about the name; he likes it. I leave him at the back of the SUV and get into the backseat, finding Enzo sitting there checking his gun. Everyone else gets into their cars as Dante and Matteo get into the front.

As Dante leads us to the house, I reach over and take Enzo's hand, needing just a second of his calmness. He gives my hand a squeeze and then the second is over because Dante is pulling into the driveway with Killian and Zach's car behind him. We're all out of the car as soon as it comes to a stop and moving to the front door as a group.

I stand behind Matteo and Zach, with Killian next to me and Tanner and Colton behind as Enzo picks the front door lock with Dante ready to enter. We decide to go in quietly and not to alert whoever is inside; that way, if someone is with Aisling, they don't kill her before we reach her. Enzo stands once done and I grip my gun tighter. As soon as the door opens, we all filter into the house, and Killian and I head directly for the lower level. I know something isn't right as we step into the garage and the SUV isn't there. I look over to Killian. "An SUV should be here."

"It's too quiet here." Killian looks at me and we both have the same sinking feeling.

"They aren't here anymore."

"Let's make sure though."

I nod and we continue through the garage and into the connected basement. As soon as we enter the unlocked steel door, I'm instantly hit with the smell of blood and death. But what sends shivers down my back is the chains attached to the far wall.

This is where I saw Aisling get branded in my dream. "She was here."

Killian walks over to the corner of the room and picks up a dirty rag. He turns and holds it up and my breath catches. It's Aisling's romper from that night and there is blood on it. "This is hers, isn't it?" Pure fear washes over Killian and I've never seen him so broken.

I nod as tears pool in my eyes. We don't know if she's okay but we do know she went through a lot of suffering in this room. "Come on. She's not here. We need to figure out where they took her from here. Maybe the others have found something."

"What if they already killed her?" For the first time, my brother is looking to me for hope.

Without hesitation, I answer, "She's alive."

We head back upstairs to find Tanner and Colton in the living room. "No one is here."

"But they were." Killian holds up the dirty romper.

Colton, seeing Killian's despair, takes the romper and pulls out his lighter. He sets the fabric on fire and throws it into the fireplace. "This doesn't mean anything. Aisling is alive and you know it. Stay strong."

Matteo, Dante, Enzo, and Zach enter the room. "This place is wiped clean."

"They haven't been here for days." I look to Enzo. "We need to look back at the video footage. She was here that first night when she was..." The sound of static silences me and we all turn to the TV that's just turned on. I look at everyone, trying to see who has a remote in their hand. "Who...?"

An image comes on the screen and it takes me a second to recognize the older man smiling at me is Craig O'Brien. He's smiling like he's won. "Hello Murphy Princess. Or should I say M? You're not as great as I thought you'd be. I was expecting you two days ago. I guess Aisling isn't as important to you as she thought. Because of you, she had two extra days of torture." I feel Matteo, Dante, and Enzo move in closer to me. "Ahh, are they the reason why it took you so long?"

He looks off camera. "Aisling, do you want to see why Riona hasn't saved you yet?" Craig walks out of the camera shot and we hear a whimper before Craig comes back in the camera's view with Aisling, holding her by her hair. I reach out and grab Killian's hand, squeezing it, telling him not to react. Craig pulls her head back so she's looking at the camera and she lets out a scream in pain. Even though I'm not wanting Killian to react, my knees almost give out as I see the bruises on her face and her cut lip.

Craig steps into her space and runs his nose up her face. Killian growls and you can tell the moment Aisling hears it because her eyes focus in front of her and she lets out a sob.

Aisling drops to her knees as Craig sadistically laughs beside her. Killian tries to charge at the TV but Tanner and Colton grab him and hold him back. Aisling calling out pulls my attention back to her. "Kill, Ree Ree..." I look at her and see she's looking right at me. "Ree Ree. I want to go home. Please."

Killian continues to fight Tanner and Colton and they pull him out of the room. Craig laughs as he reaches down and grabs Aisling's hair again, pulling her up. "You hear that, Riona? She wants to go home. And I know just how you can make that happen." He pushes Aisling out of camera view and gives a command. "Take her back downstairs." I scan my eyes over the wall behind Craig, trying to see if I can see anything in the room.

His attention turns back to me. "I want you. Meet me at the Franklin Airstrip at 10pm and we'll do a trade. You for her. If you give yourself to me, I will let Aisling go at midnight in a different location." He gives me a cocky smile, knowing I'll die for her. "See you at ten." The camera feed shuts off and I immediately turn and walk out of the house.

Stepping out of the front door, I see Killian on the sidewalk, pacing and pulling on his hair. I walk over to him and stop in front of him. "Look at me." Killian takes his eyes from the sidewalk and connects them with mine. "Did you hear what she said?" I feel everyone surrounding us.

Pain pours from his eyes. "She said she wanted to go home."

I shake my head. "No, not that."

Zach speaks up beside me. "She said 'Ree Ree, I want to go home. Please.'"

I look at Killian, trying to get him to register. "Killian, she told us where she was."

He looks at me like I'm delusional. "No, she didn't. She's not at home."

"She called me Ree Ree." Come on, get it.

"So..."

"Killian, that's our code. Don't you remember?" I stare at him, trying to force him to remember.

He shakes his head desperate to know. "No, I never listened to you guys when you made up your codes."

I let out a frustrated growl. "Ree Ree is her code to get my attention. To listen for a code."

He still looks like he doesn't get the code. "She said she wanted to go home. She doesn't call the Murphy mansion home. You know that. And she didn't say please. She said peace."

I stare at him, hoping he'll understand. "Fucking Christ Riona, just spit it out."

"She's at our home. Our home away from all this. Our peace." I pause, waiting for him to catch on. "She's at the house she and I bought to make into our own home. She's on the estate."

"What!?" He doesn't believe it.

"After she said that, I looked at the room he was in and I'm pretty positive he was in the dining room, based on the edge of the photo frame I saw and the color of the paint on the wall."

"Then what are we waiting for? Let's go." He turns to leave but I grab his arm.

"I think we should wait." I look at the guys around me. "We should head back to the Russos..." I look at them for permission because I know they're secretive of their house. Dante gives me a nod to continue. "My laptop is there. I can access the security feed of the house. Then come up with a plan where half of us go to get Aisling at the same time I'll be meeting Craig for the trade."

"Trade?" Tanner questions.

"Yeah, he wants me for her. Tonight at 10pm at the Franklin Airstrip. Once he has me, he'll release Aisling at midnight at a different location."

"You don't think he'll move her until he has you?" Connor tries to figure out my plan.

"I think he'll release her from the house." I look around at everyone. "Let's go so we can get a plan together."

Everyone nods but I can see Killian is fighting himself not to run right to her. I squeeze his hand. "Trust me. If you don't like the plan once it's all laid, we'll head straight there."

Killian pulls me into a hug. "You aren't going to that trade."

Before I can even respond, he lets go of me and throws his keys at Colton as he climbs into the passenger seat. Everyone gets into the car they arrived in and I slide in beside Enzo, taking his comfort as I formulate a plan.

Chapter Twenty-Four

Matteo

Headlights are the only things that illuminate the Franklin Airstrip. One car pulls in from my right and one car pulls in from my left. I look down at my watch and see it's 10 o'clock on the dot. The doors on the SUV to my left all open and I watch as Craig O'Brien steps out of the passenger seat with three of his men. It takes everything in me not to just shoot him right now, from where I'm hiding, but one thing has me holding back. He's not leaving this airstrip with Riona.

Instead, he'll be leaving as one of our captives. I can't wait to get him back to my torture room and show him all my favorite toys. Maybe Riona will let me fuck her as we're both covered in his blood. I bet she will. Craig moves around the front of his SUV with his guys all standing behind him. He still has his cocky smile on his face, thinking he's going to get his hands on my princess.

My eyes catch movement behind Craig's car and I know it's Dante getting into place. The front doors on the car to my right open, drawing my attention. With the darkness of the airstrip, the only thing I can see is a woman getting out of the driver's side door in head to toe black with a hood up over her head and a guy climbing out of the passenger side. But I know exactly who they are.

She keeps her headlights on as they both close their doors but makes no attempt to step forward, using the darkness to conceal herself.

Craig's smile widens as his eyes land on her, not caring about Enzo and my hand starts to get twitchy as he starts moving toward her leisurely. He can't get too close to her or this is all going to blow up.

I lean down, taking in the scene before me through my scope. I adjust some of my dials, zeroing in on my targets. "I'm glad to see you do care for Aisling. She'll be happy to be let free out of her own personal hell. Too bad she'll never see her savior again. You'll be dead before she'll even get a chance to look for you. You're going to die screaming like my mother screamed over my father's dead body. Revenge is such a beautiful thing." Craig nods to his guys and they step forward, moving toward her.

That's my signal. Bang. Bang. Bang. Down each of Craig's men go, hitting the concrete dead. I look up from my scope to find

Dante with his gun pressed against Craig's temple and Enzo standing in front of him with his gun trained on Craig's chest. I stand from my hiding spot and loop my rifle over my shoulders.

I walk out of the hangar I was hiding in, and I can't help my smile as I approach Craig. "Guess you won't be getting your revenge." I take the butt of my rifle and smash it in his face, knocking him out. Dante steps back, allowing Craig to fall to the ground hard. Enzo puts his gun in the back of his pants and I swing my gun back over my shoulder.

"Wow this was a much more interesting night than I would've had at Mystique."

We all turn to Stella, who's grinning from ear to ear. Stella is the manager of Riona's Burlesque club, Mystique, and she looks exactly like Riona, except for the pink hair. At least from a distance. No one can be as gorgeous as my princess.

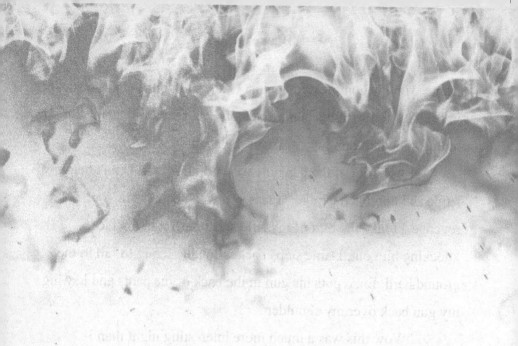

Chapter Twenty-Five

Riona

A couple of hours earlier

I walk into the dining room where the guys and I have been working to find Aisling. But for the first time, all the seats are filled. "Alright Red. Tell us this plan you have going on in your head."

I smile at Colton as I set my laptop on the table. "First, let's see if I'm correct at what Aisling was trying to tell me."

I bend forward between Enzo and Matteo and pull up the security footage of our estate. I don't have a lot of cameras set up yet because we're never there but I do have cameras on the gate, front door, living and kitchen areas.

"Why didn't you get an alert if someone is at the house?" Killian leans forward resting his elbow on the table.

"Full security isn't set up. I just put cameras up to keep an eye on the place. We're planning on doing a full remodel so I didn't see a reason until it was done."

The four camera images pull up and I can't help but smile. We found her. Thank you, Aisling, for sending me the signal.

I turn the laptop around and show everyone. "They're there."

"How do you know it's live?" Enzo asks because he found out on our drive back that they looped the video footage on the townhouse so we wouldn't know when they left.

"These are hidden cameras. They'd have to know they're there. Plus, they're wireless and they wouldn't be able to hardwire in."

"They could hack in," Tanner suggests.

I shake my head. "It's encrypted. They'd have to hack my computer to get access."

"Well then, they don't have access." Tanner leans back and crosses his arms over his chest, knowing my coding skills.

I give him an appreciative smile. "Now let me verify that Aisling is there." I rewind the footage to about an hour ago and I watch as they bring her out of the basement connected to the kitchen and to the dining room that I don't have cameras in. But that's okay because we know what happened in the dining room. Several minutes later, I watch them lead her through the kitchen and to the door leading into the basement. "Okay so she's there." I look at

Enzo. "Do you mind watching this to make sure they haven't moved her?" He nods and slides the laptop in front of him.

"So, I think we need to get Aisling at the same time as the meet up. Craig isn't going to bring her with him, since he plans to release her hours after he gets me." I look at everyone and they all are focused on me.

Well, everyone except Enzo. I'm about to continue when his head shoots up. "He left the estate right after talking to us." I look at him and he answers the question I'm about to ask. "Not with Aisling. Just him and three guys."

I nod, figuring out what this means. "That means he hasn't been staying there with her. There's no way to get them together before the meet up. We'll have to separate."

"Riona, you're not going to that meetup. Aisling is going to need you when we find her." Killian gives me a stern look.

"She needs to be at that meetup so Craig can let his guard down so we can take him," Tanner says.

"I have a plan for that. Stella, my manager at Mystique, is about my size and she has pink hair. She can pass as me if we keep her face hidden." I look to Dante, Matteo, and Enzo. "You guys have to keep her safe."

"Why us?" Matteo asks.

"Because he knows about us. He won't believe it's me if she shows up with someone else. You guys would be the ones that would follow me if I did go, right?"

They all nod but I can see Dante wants to argue. I silently plead for him to keep his arguments to himself because I know they're about him not being with me.

"I'm going to leave it to you to plan how you want to take Craig." I look at Zach. "Zach, you can go with them or come with us." He's really the only outlier. Killian, Tanner, and Colton are coming with me to get Aisling.

"I'll come with you. I don't think they're going to need me." He tilts his head toward my guys.

"Okay. I'm going to make a couple of calls to get Stella and my doctor ready, then we can go over how we're going to get into the house."

I step out of the room, sending a quick text to Dr. Gibbons letting her know I'm calling in my favor and she's on call tonight. Once that's sent, I pull up Stella's contact and hit call. She answers immediately, "Hey boss lady. What's up?"

A smile spreads across my face at her loud voice. "Hi Stella! I need to ask you a huge favor."

"Okay? You know I'll do anything for you."

This isn't a favor she should accept kindly. "This ask is dangerous, so hear me out before agreeing. You can say no, okay?"

"Okay. What's going on?"

"Tonight, Killian and I are going to get Aisling but I need to be in two places at once." Stella was one of the first people I called after Aisling was taken. She hears a lot as she strolls through the club each night.

"If this is about saving Aisling, I'm in."

"Thanks, but I'm not done." I take a deep breath. "At the time I'll be getting Aisling, I'm supposed to be at a meetup with the man that took her. He wants me to trade myself for her. That's where I need you to be. I need you to go as me. You won't be alone; my guys will be with you, but what makes this dangerous is if this man figures out you aren't me, he could try to kill you." I'm silent, letting her take in what I said.

"You said try. Are your guys going to keep me safe?" Dante walks into the living room, by himself.

"Yes. They won't let anything happen to you. You'll be their number one priority." I look at Dante as he gives me a nod from the wall he's leaning on.

"Then I'm in." There is no hesitation in her voice.

"Thank you. I'll send you a text with an address. Get here when you can. We'll go over everything then and get you dressed up so you'll look like me."

"Okay. I'll be there in a couple hours. I'll just get everything set at the club."

"Thanks again. See you soon."

I hang up the phone and Dante pushes off the wall and walks to me. Once he's within reaching distance I wrap my arms around his waist and lean into his body. "Tell me what you aren't happy with."

"I don't like us not being with you." His hands rub up my back.

"Do you have another plan in mind?" I'm open to other suggestions.

"Not one that makes more sense."

I smile up at him. "People that Aisling knows need to be there when we get her."

"I know. I just don't like us not being with you when something could go wrong."

"Everything is going to be fine. By tomorrow morning, Aisling will be safe and Craig will be dead or locked in Matteo's torture chamber." I know this will end tonight.

"Hopefully so. Will you just stay in contact with me?"

"If that'll make you feel better, absolutely."

"It will."

I nod, agreeing. "Stella will be here in a couple of hours, promise me you'll keep her safe. She was one of the first girls I saved, and her story is darker than mine. Nothing can happen to her." We found Stella in a high end brothel in New Orleans that was being run by her stepfather and stepbrother. The things they forced her and twelve other kidnapped women to do was unthinkable.

"I promise. Craig won't touch a hair on her head." I know he'd step in front of a bullet for her just because I asked.

"Thanks." I lean up and give him a quick kiss. "Let's get this all planned out." I take Dante's hand and lead him back to the dining room while I send off the address to Stella. It's time to get all the details in place because we only have five hours until the meetup.

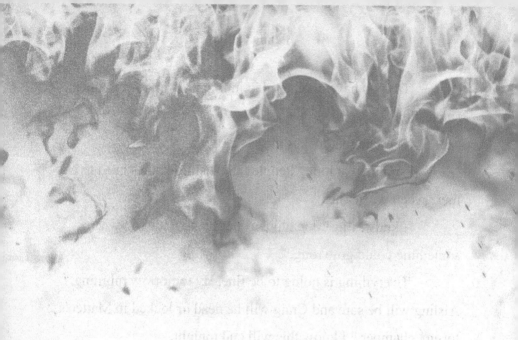

Chapter Twenty-Six

Riona

Our headlights flick off as we pull on to the street that runs along the side of the estate. The front gate is just out of sight down the adjacent street, but this is the closest road to the exit of my hidden tunnel. We're going in quietly, getting Aisling out and then we're going to make some noise. Every one of O'Brien's men are dying tonight.

I climb out of the passenger side of Killian's car and head to the back where Zach, Colton, and Tanner get out of an SUV. We're all dressed in head-to-toe black, with knives and guns holstered to us. We look lethal. "You guys ready to stomp through the woods?"

"Born ready, Red. Let's go get Aisling." Killian grabs Colton's shoulder as a silent thanks and we all head into the woods. Since I'm the only one that knows this entrance, I lead the way, making sure to keep my steps quiet. We're pretty far from the house but five people stomping through the woods can get noisy. The guys seem to have the same thought because other than hearing them breathe, I wouldn't know they were behind me.

Before I know it, my foot is connecting with the hidden steel door in the ground and a smile forms on my face. I look back at the guys. "We're here." Bending down, I start moving the leaves and pine needles off the door and open the latch, revealing the security pad. I type in my code and the door slides open to a dark tunnel where you can only see the top two steps of the ladder. "This tunnel isn't soundproof so we have to stay quiet in case someone is in the wine cellar."

They all nod and I grab my flashlight and turn it on, facing it down into the tunnel. I step onto the ladder and make my way down until my feet hit the floor. Each of the guys come down the ladder one by one and when we're all in the tunnel, I open the panel in the wall signaling the door to close. My eyes connect with Killian and he gives me a nod telling me he saw the code. If everything goes to plan, he's leaving with Aisling as soon as we get her and the rest of us are clearing the house.

Making sure to keep our flashlights low, we head down the tunnel. Since the house is closer to this side of the property, it doesn't take us any time at all to see the back of the wine shelves. A low light filters through the shelves and I click off my flashlight because the light should only be on when the wine cellar door is open. The guys turn theirs off as well and the tunnel falls into almost complete darkness.

I take slow, measured steps toward the back of the shelves making sure not to make a sound. With my breath held, I look through one of the openings, scanning the small room for someone. I let my breath go when the room comes up empty and the door is slightly ajar. All they have to do is close the door and the light would turn off. Instead, they're racking up my energy bill.

Reaching in through the hole, I grab the decoy bottle and twist. A faint clicking sound of the latch opening has me freezing for a second, making sure no one heard. When I don't hear anyone approaching, I pull my hand in and slowly push the hidden door open. These shelves are full of wine bottles so I make sure to move it smoothly. Not wanting to risk a bottle rattling, I only open the door wide enough for us to slip through.

The cellar isn't much bigger than a walk-in closet so once all of us are out of the tunnel, it's a little tight. I'm standing right by the door opening and I can see two guys standing outside the only other door down here. That's where Aisling has to be. Since the guys are standing at the end of the hall, I look at Colton and signal him to cover my back. Tanner steps up to the door as I pull out two knives from my thigh. I give Tanner a nod and he quickly pulls the door inward, and I step out, locking eyes on the guys as they turn toward the squeak of the door hinges.

A smile pulls at my lips as one knife leaves my hand and the other does the same seconds later. Before the guys even have time to react, my knives lodge into their necks. I step out of the safety of the room and Colton shifts behind me, covering the other end of the hallway. Both men fall to their knees, clutching their necks as blood spills from their mouths. Standing over the first guy, I bend down and pull out the knife. His muffled screams fill the hall as he looks up at me with fear in his eyes. "You should be scared. Hell is going to be torture."

I quickly and deeply slice across his throat and all the light leaves his eyes as his body slumps to the floor. Standing over my first kill of the night, I'm a little disappointed it wasn't messier. A groan comes from the guy next to me and I look over to find Zach plunging his knife in the guy's gut and slicing up.

He gives me a smile. "You don't mind, do you? I needed to get my hands dirty."

A dark smile forms on my face because I know exactly what he means. "Not at all. I like your style."

"You done playing?" I look behind me to find Killian there, not looking as excited as us.

I smirk at him and hold out my knife. "Not even close. You didn't want to get your hands dirty?"

He crosses his arms. "The most valuable lesson Lorcan has ever taught me is never get your hands dirty if you have people to do it for you." I roll my eyes at him. Killian isn't fooling anyone. He's just as lethal as I am. He never sits anything out.

"He says that because he's a coward."

Killian glares at me as I stand and wipe my knife clean on my pants. "Good thing you're not."

Muffled screams suddenly start and Killian pushes past me and barrels through the wooden door. I quickly rush after him, pulling out my gun, ready to find Aisling being brutally tortured by someone but instead I'm greeted with total darkness and deathly loud screams. What the hell? Those aren't Aisling screams. It sounds like five people screaming.

With my hand out in front of me I find the light switch and flick it on. The room illuminates, giving me a clearer picture. There is a dirty cot on the far side of the room and right next to it I see Aisling curled up in the corner with her head on her knees and hands over her ears, trying to block out the screams that haven't stopped.

God, how has she survived this. Slowly I move closer to her while calling out her name but it's no use. She can't hear me. I don't want to get too close to her without her knowing we're here, so I look to my brother and I find him frozen just staring. Suddenly the screams stop and I look back to see Tanner lower the handle of his rifle from a now destroyed speaker.

Her head shoots up at the silence and relief instantly washes over her face. "Ri?" Killian steps up beside me and tears stream down her face. "Kill?"

"Hi Angel." He steps in front of her and crouches down.

She hesitantly reaches out for his face. "Please tell me you're real."

He leans into her hand. "We're real. You're safe now."

He reaches out slowly and pushes her hair off her face. "Thank you for coming. I've been trying so hard not to break." A sob breaks from her and she throws herself at him.

"Oh Angel. You can break now. I've got you." Killian scoops her up in his arms and the sound of chains running across the ground has me noticing the metal cuff on her wrist. Killian looks at me and I step forward, pulling out a metal pin from my hair. Quickly I unlock the cuff and it falls to the ground, revealing the harsh red marks on her wrist.

Anger fills me at seeing more harm done to her. "Get her out of here. We'll meet you at the safe house. Dr. Gibbons will be there."

Killian nods and heads out of the room and I follow after. Aisling looks at me over Killian's shoulder. "Make them bleed, Ri."

I smile at the fight still inside her. "I'll paint the walls with their blood."

"Then we'll bulldoze..." A high-pitched beep rings out from somewhere in the room and Aisling's whole body shakes in fear. I slam the door shut the moment we're in the hall, muffling the sound. The crew upstairs must've heard me slamming the door because the dead guys' radios start going off.

I give Killian a nod and move ahead of him to join Tanner, Colton, and Zach at the bottom of the stairs. "Go... go now." When I look back, Killian and Aisling are gone.

Tanner looks at me and gives me a playful smile. "Ready for some fun, Firecracker?"

"Absolutely." I give them a deadly smile. Colton and Tanner immediately head up the stairs and Zach and I follow with guns in both hands.

Chapter Twenty-Seven

Riona

Blood splatters the walls as dead bodies lay on the floor. There were more men than I expected in here, but it still wasn't an issue for us. I walk across the open foyer to the two guys from the gate that made the stupid decision to run up here instead of away. Now they lay dead in the front doorway with bullet holes in their heads. Quiet surrounds me and it's a good feeling. No more gunshots. No more groans of dying men. No more yelling. All the O'Brien men are dead. I just know it.

I step over the two bodies and walk into the living room, finding Tanner and Colton. Tanner is standing close to Colton, doing something that I quickly realize is wrapping fabric around his bicep. "What happened? Are you okay?"

Colton smiles at me. "I'm fine, Red. It's just a graze. Nothing stitches can't fix."

I sigh in relief. "We'll get the doc to look at it. Where's Zach?" Tanner shrugs his shoulders. "He headed upstairs when we separated."

I nod and head that way. I'm ready to get out of here and to Aisling. She seemed okay but I need to hear it from her and the doc. I jog up the stairs and I'm about to call out to Zach when I hear a man's groan and the sound of wrestling.

Quietly I walk up the stairs until the hallway comes into view and I see Zach and a man wrestling. Fear courses through me as I see Zach on his back, fighting the guy for the gun. This isn't good.

A shot goes off and I quickly pull out my gun and fire two shots into the guy's back as I run up the final few steps. The guy rolls off Zach and I send another shot in his head just to make sure he's dead. Tanner and Colton come running up the stairs just as I'm kneeling next to Zach, who's groaning in pain as he grabs his shoulder. Blood starts to pool under him and I quickly press down on the bullet wound. "Shit. Tanner, give me something to apply pressure."

"I'm fine. It doesn't even hurt." Without thinking Tanner pulls off his shirt and hands it to me as Zach tries to push me away. His wince as I push the shirt to his shoulder betrays him and Colton calls him out on it.

"Yeah right." Colton kneels next to me by Zach's head. He takes over, adding pressure. "Let's roll him. I want to see if it was through and through."

Zach tries to help but it's really Colton and I that half roll him to see the exit wound. Another cloth is placed in my hand and I look up at Tanner to see him tearing up a bed sheet. I press the ball of sheet to his back wound and we pull Zach up to a sitting position. Tanner steps up and expertly wraps the strips of bed sheet around Zach's shoulder, holding the fabric to the wounds. "Alright, let's get out of here. I have more supplies in the truck."

Colton grabs Zach's uninjured arm and hooks it over his shoulder, supporting Zach as we make our way downstairs. I run down the stairs and to the front of the house where a bowl of keys sits. Grabbing the first set I find, I hit the alarm button and listen. We need a car to get to ours. Zach can't make it through the tunnel and the walk would take too long.

The alarm for the black SUV sitting out front goes off and I quickly run to it, getting in the front seat and turning it on. The guys are right behind me, climbing in. Once everyone is seated, I hit the accelerator and make my way down the long driveway. As I'm approaching the closed gate, I look back at Zach to see him very pale and barely keeping his eyes open. We don't have time to stop and wait for the gate to open. I'm ramming it. "Hold on." I push down on the accelerator harder and everyone grabs their oh shit handle when they realize I'm not slowing. We hit the gate with a loud bang, jerking us forward and the gate flies off the hinges.

"God, Red." Colton looks back at the destroyed gate. "You're going to have to completely replace that."

I shrug my shoulders. "I was going to have to replace it anyways. I can't have a gate that's easily bustable."

"True that." Zach groans in the back and I can't help my chuckle. Looking back at him in the rearview mirror, he tries to give a wink, but his eyes are too far shut.

I pull up to our SUV and jump out of the car without turning it off. Tanner throws the keys to me and I run to the driver's seat as they get Zach in the back.

Tanner gets in with Zach, grabbing his medical kit from the back. Colton jumps into the passenger seat and I take off down the road. I can hear Tanner working in the back replacing the shirt and sheets with actual bandages. I look at Colton. "I need to call Killian and the guys."

He nods. "I got you." He pulls out his phone and instantly Bluetooth pulls up with Killian's name. "Hey man."

I answer instead of Colton. "Killian, how is Aisling? Is she with the doc?"

"Doc said physically she's fine. She's still with her though."

"Okay great. We're coming, Zach was shot in the shoulder and Colton has a graze. We'll need her to also..."

"I'm fine. Tanner can stitch me up," Colton interrupts.

"Fine. We need her for Zach. It's not looking good." I chance a glimpse at him.

"Tell me what's going on so I can get her ready. How far out are you?"

"Fifteen minutes. He has a gunshot wound in the shoulder. Through and through. He's losing a lot of blood."

"Okay. I'll let her know."

He hangs up because he knows I don't have anything else to say. Immediately, Dante's name shows on the Bluetooth. "Colton, why the hell isn't Riona calling?"

Relieved to hear his voice, I quickly rush out, "Dante, it's Zach. He's shot."

"Ri? What happened? Is he okay?" Concern fills his voice.

I look at Zach in the back. His shirt is now gone and Tanner is pressing a shit ton of gauze on the wound but there's a lot of blood. "He's losing a lot of blood. He was shot in the shoulder. He should be fine if we can get the bleeding to stop. We're heading to the safe house now; Killian is giving the doc a heads up."

"Shit. We're on our way there. Does she need anything?"

"I don't know. We're about 10 minutes out right now." I weave in and out of traffic, wishing we were closer.

"Okay." I can almost see him nodding and coming up with a plan. "Ri?"

I look at the dashboard like I could see his face. "Yeah."

"How are you? How's Aisling?" I know it's killing him not being here right now to see that everything is okay.

"I'm fine. Aisling was badly beaten and they were torturing her mentally."

"Shit." Mind games can be the worst type of torture.

"Yeah." Mental scars are the hardest to overcome. They don't just heal. It's a daily fight to overcome them.

Enzo speaks up, saying exactly what I need to hear. "She'll be okay. She's strong." I wish he were here so I could hold his hand.

Zach decides in that moment to break the sad tension by finally making himself known. "Russos…" He sounds drunk, slurring his words with delirious excitement. "You should've seen me. I kicked some ass."

We all chuckle and Matteo's voice rings out. "It sounds like you got your ass kicked."

"Nah. He got a lucky shot. He died right after that."

"At least you killed him," Dante says.

"Oh, not me. Your girl saved my ass." A smile spreads across my face and if I wasn't driving, I'd give him a fist bump.

We pull into the neighborhood where the safe house is and I slow down so I don't draw attention to ourselves. I pull into the driveway and find Dr. Gibbons waiting for us. As I come to a stop, she rushes to the back, and they all help Zach out of the car but Zach's not leaving without the final word. "Bye guys! The pretty doctor is going to fix me up now." He looks up at her like he's dazed by her beauty. She just shakes her head at him and leads the twins to the house.

Silence fills the car and I let out a long breath. We made it. Zach is still alive. "You good, Rose?" Dante breaks the silence.

"Yeah." My adrenaline is slowly starting to drain and my body relaxes.

"Okay." I can tell that they don't believe me. "We're only a few miles out. Go inside, check on Aisling. We'll be there soon."

"Yeah okay. See you soon." I hang up at the mention of Aisling and sit up a little bit straighter. I need to see her.

I slide out of the car and look around, seeing how quiet this neighborhood is in the middle of the night. People here don't know the horrors my world has. They're lucky to not have to worry about the shadows that lurk in the night. I walk into the house to find Dr. Gibbons and Tanner in the kitchen working together getting a passed out Zach patched up on the dinner table.

The sound of Colton's voice has me looking to my right, into the living room. I find Killian cleaning Colton's arm as he tells Killian everything that happened after he took Aisling out. Killian sees me standing in the doorway and he gives a smile with a head tilt, signaling me to the back of the house. I give him a smile and head to the back bedroom. The door is closed and I give it a soft knock before opening. "Ash?"

I peek my head around the door to see a sleeping Aisling. She looks so peaceful and almost like normal except for the black eye and cut on her lip. I quietly slip into the room, close the door, and walk over to the bed. I reach out to push her hair out of her face when I see all the blood on my hands from Zach. I quickly withdraw my hand, step back from her and head toward the bathroom.

Looking in the mirror, I see I'm covered in blood. Earlier I wanted this, but knowing the majority of it is Zach's, I feel gross. I tear off my clothes quickly and jump into the shower, frantically scrubbing at my skin. Over and over, I lather myself in soap until the smell of lavender is almost too much. That's when I step out of the shower and dry off.

Since I don't have any clothes, I wrap the towel around me and head out of the bathroom. Feeling tired, I head to the bed and climb in next to Aisling. My eyes instantly go heavy as my head hits the pillow and I turn to face her.

"I'm sorry this happened to you. It's all my fault." A tear slides down my cheek and soaks into the pillow. I place my hand over hers in between us and a weight lifts from me. She's here and safe.

I didn't know I fell asleep until I'm woken up by someone lightly shaking my shoulder as they whisper my name. Opening my eyes, I see Aisling is still sleeping in the same position. She must be exhausted. I look over my shoulder and see Enzo sitting on the edge of the bed. He smiles at me. "Sorry to wake you, but Dr. Gibbons is leaving and I brought in your bag with a change of clothes."

I smile at him as I sit up. "Thank you. I'll be out in a moment." I give Enzo a quick kiss and I just want to relax into his arms. But now isn't the time. Enzo leaves the room and I slide out of bed and grab my bag. Throwing on my clothes, I head to the front of the house where I find everyone hanging out in the living room.

As I walk into the room, Dr. Gibbons stands up and walks over to me. She doesn't slow down until she has her arms wrapped around me in a hug. "Thank you so much for what you did. It's been months since my daughter and I have slept soundly and we now can because of you."

I hug her back. "You don't need to thank me. I need to thank you. Thank you for looking over Aisling and stitching up Zach." I look over at him lounging in the chair looking exhausted.

"Oh, this is nothing. If you need anything else, please let me know." I give her a grateful smile and she gives everyone a wave before leaving.

I walk over to Zach. "How are you doing?"

"Better. Just a little tired." He doesn't even lift his head, just looks at me over his nose.

"It's all the blood loss."

"Yeah. Luckily Matteo and I are the same blood type."

I look over at Matteo who's laying back on the couch next to Dante. I move over to him and sit on Dante's thigh because I don't want to sit on his lap if he's feeling weak. He definitely looks paler than normal. He doesn't seem to like that because he quickly reaches out to me and pulls me in his lap. "I'm the one who gave blood, not Dante."

I chuckle as I run my fingers over his prickly hair. "Such a hero, giving Zach your blood."

"I am a hero. And not because of the blood. I kept Stella safe tonight." He gives me a smile, believing himself to be the savior of the day.

Happy to boost his ego, I lean into him, wanting to hear it all. "You did?"

"Not by himself," Dante says, not liking me giving Matteo all the credit. "But yes, Stella is safe and at home. We checked your phone."

Matteo glares at his brother. "I'm the one who killed Craig's lackeys."

Dante happily glares back. "We were there too, making sure Stella was safe."

Enzo gets into the conversation before Dante and Matteo start arguing. "Everything went as planned. Craig didn't realize you weren't there and we have him waiting for you."

I smile at him and then Dante and Matteo. "Thanks for watching out for her."

"She's actually pretty cool. She said she'll be your body double whenever needed." Matteo pulls me closer and rests his head on my shoulder in the nook of my neck.

I chuckle. "She is pretty awesome."

Colton and Tanner stand up. "We're going to head out. We have a flight out tomorrow afternoon and need to get some sleep."

I go to get off Matteo's lap but his hold tightens, not letting me up. I shake my head at him and Colton and Tanner chuckle. "It's okay. We'll come to you."

Tanner comes over to me and gives me an awkward hug and a kiss on my head. Matteo growls at him and I hit his chest.

Colton steps up and kisses the top of my head as well, making Dante growl too. I give him a kick and Colton chuckles. "It was good seeing you, Red. Until next time. Maybe without these guys."

Dante and Matteo lose it, but I stretch out over their laps, preventing them from getting up. Colton quickly steps back, laughing. "Calm down. He's just messing with you."

Enzo chuckles at the end of the couch and I smile at him. I love them being possessive, but I also love that Enzo didn't get riled up at Colton's joke. Zach sits up in the chair. "Can I actually get a ride with you?"

"Sure, man. We'll drop you at your place." Tanner helps Zach up.

"Thanks." Zach says bye to everyone and the three of them leave the house.

We're all quiet for a moment and I look over at Killian. "Did she say anything before going to sleep?"

He shakes his head. "Just that she's fine and that she hasn't slept in days. Doc said she's not dehydrated or malnourished. The cuts and bruises are a couple days old. There is also a symbol carved into her hip but it's healing fine."

I look at Enzo when he mentions the symbol in her skin. If that was true, then so was everything else. "She didn't mention anything else? What other trauma she might have gone through?"

He shakes his head. "Anything else I wasn't in the room for and the doc wouldn't say."

I can see the worry in his eyes, and I get up from Matteo's and Dante's laps. I crouch down in front of him and take his hand. "She'll tell us what she went through when she's ready. She's sleeping soundlessly so she can't have too much trauma. Remember my nightmares?" When I came home after Tony, I didn't get a good night's sleep for months. My nightmares were every time I closed my eyes.

Killian looks a little less worried and I look around at everyone. They all look exhausted. "We should all get some sleep. It's been a long day."

Enzo stands and walks over to me. He wraps his arms around my middle as I stand. "Are you coming home with us?"

I shake my head. "I'm going to stay here with Aisling."

"Okay. We'll be back after we get some sleep. We have a prisoner you're going to want to see." He smiles with a promise of revenge.

"I can't wait until we have some fun with him." Matteo comes up to my side and nuzzles into the side of my neck.

Dante appears on my other. "But he can wait. A few days tied up won't kill him."

"You will." Enzo leans forward and gives me a kiss. Matteo leans in next and then Dante.

Killian coughs behind me and I chuckle. I step back from Enzo and look at Killian. "Can you make-out with your boyfriends somewhere else?"

"Yes, I can." I grab Dante and Matteo's hand and beckon Enzo to follow. The four of us go to the front door and Dante quickly pulls me into his arms and kisses me.

I run my hands over his abs and around his middle. When my knees start to feel weak, I pull back from him, but I'm instantly pulled into Matteo's arms. He slams his mouth to mine and I melt into him. I wrap my arms around his neck so I don't become a puddle on the ground. When we break apart to catch our breath, Enzo is there and I willingly go into his arms.

His kiss is slow and passionate, but I still get weak-kneed and breathless. He rests his forehead against mine and I smile at him. Reluctantly, I separate myself from them and watch them leave, wishing they could stay, but this is only a one-bedroom home. As the door shuts behind them, I hear Matteo say, "Killian called us her boyfriends and she didn't correct him. Do you think that means she's staying?"

I don't hear what they say, but I know the answer. Yes, I'm staying. A large grin forms on my face as I turn and lean against the door.

Killian walks out of the living room and smiles at me. "It's nice to see you happy."

What is he talking about? "I'm always happy."

He shakes his head, looking like he's not sure. "Not the same happy as when you're around them."

I smile at him, knowing he's right. They make me very happy and hopeful. He steps up to me and places his hand on my shoulder. "I hope you're prepared for when Father calls you home. He's not going to allow you to stay."

Why did he have to go and ruin the happiness by bringing up Father? I push his hand off me and move toward the hallway. "I'm a grown woman and I can live wherever I want."

He chuckles like I'm delusional. "Good luck with that." I flip him off and he only chuckles more. "Where are you going?"

"To bed. I'm sleeping with Aisling." His laughter fills the hallway.

"That's okay; I was planning on sleeping in the chair anyways."

I look at him confused. "Why?"

"I don't want her to wake up and freak out." I can see it pains him to keep his distance, but he's trying to do what is best.

"She's going to want you with her. So don't go far, okay?" I reach out and grab his hand.

He squeezes my hand back. "I won't."

We enter the room and I go straight to the bed as Killian goes to the chair on the other side of the bed. As I slide in, I face away from them, giving Killian his privacy to say goodnight.

A quiet peace fills the room as it sets in that the three of us are together again and safe. We're going to be okay.

Chapter Twenty-Eight

Riona

Someone bopping my nose pulls me from my deep sleep and as I crack my eyes open, there is a smiling Aisling looking back at me. Tears pull in my eyes as I pull her to me and we hug each other. "I'm so sorry I wasn't there to stop them. It should've been me."

"No, it shouldn't. He would've killed you. He would rant about how much he hated you."

I roll back from our hug and scan her face looking for any pain reflecting in her blue eyes. She might think that it would've been worse if it was me, but she definitely didn't have it easy. "Are you okay?"

Darkness fills her eyes and I know she's not. "I will be."

I grab her hand, giving her support. "I know you went through some dark things. I'm here for you."

She looks at me confused and I answer her silent question. "Whenever I slept, it was like I was there with you. It was so real."

Her eyes lock with mine as she tries to figure out what exactly I saw. Whatever she sees has her looking back at Killian who's sleeping. At least I think he is until his body relaxes when she looks away from him. "What did you see?"

"The night after you were taken, I was in the basement with you as you were chained to the wall. A man walked in talking about how you were family and you needed their mark on you. I was pulled from my sleep as he started cutting into your skin." I look past her shoulder as I continue not being able to look at her as I say the next part. "The next night you were in what I now know was our basement, sleeping on the cot. I curled up next to you and slept with you. At least until two guys came into the room. One guy held you down as the other..."

I can't finish that sentence. Not with Killian listening. And I know he is because his whole body tensed with anger. "I ended up getting pulled into my own memories and nightmares from that."

Aisling squeezes my hand and I know she's trying to give me support for my nightmares. "They didn't rape me." I look at her in shock because that isn't what I saw. "They were going to but Craig ended up coming in right before that guy was going to force himself inside me. Craig shot them both in the head for touching me." I can't tell you how relieved I am that she didn't go through the horrors I have, but it's weird that he was so protective of her. Killian gives up all pretending and opens his eyes. Aisling must've known he was awake because she reaches behind her and Killian instantly jumps out of the chair, taking her hand in his.

Aisling turns on her back to look at him. "The first two days were the worst, physically. After they took me and chained me to that wall, I was beaten. Not constantly. It was like a game. They'd come in individually, Craig and Davis. They'd either punch or slap me or they'd just fake it. They'd swing their arms back like they would and I'd flinch. Then they'd just leave. I never knew if they'd actually hit me or not. I'm not sure how long that happened but it eventually stopped. Then right before they moved me, Davis came in saying I needed their crest." She lifts her shirt showing us the scabbed marking. I know Killian has seen it, but this is my first time. It isn't pretty. I can tell she moved while doing it because the lines are jagged.

Killian runs his fingers over it softly. "Once it's healed, we can come up with a gorgeous tattoo to cover it. You won't even know that it's there."

She nods but I can see that she knows she'll always know what is carved into her skin. "As he did this, he told me all about how my mom was an O'Brien and that we were family."

She looks between the two of us, seeking the truth. "We found out a lot about your mom's past. I can tell you if you want."

She shakes her head no. "I don't really care. The O'Briens aren't my family."

I nod and she continues. "Once they moved to our house, they started the psychological torture. Other than the almost rape. That was the last time I slept. After that, either the lights were on with this annoying beeping sound or it was pitch black with the terrifying screams. I started hallucinating you guys rescuing me. I'd only get a break when they brought me food and water and then I'd have to listen to Craig rant about you and your father." She looks right at me. "I didn't realize where I was until he brought me out for the video call. That was the first time I was out of the basement. I'm so glad you remembered our code." Tears fill her eyes and I wish I could take the terror away.

"Well, you calling me Ree Ree brought it back quickly." I chuckle.

She tries to laugh but it comes out more as a sob from the pain. "Yeah, it is an obnoxious name."

She curls into Killian as her tears start flowing and I know they need time together. I climb out of bed and give them a smile. "I'm going to grab us something to eat." Neither of them says a thing as Killian pulls her to him and holds her tightly.

I find my phone and Killian's car keys in the kitchen and as I head out of the house, I see I have a few missed calls from my father and several texts from Stella and the guys from yesterday. Reading over the guys' text, I can't help my smile at how worried they were. I know it's only been seven days, but I've become really attached to them. I know my father won't be happy about me staying with them but he can't force me to not be with them.

I send out a group text to the guys to see if they want to eat with us before I back down the driveway. I don't know what's around here but seeing it's lunchtime, I just drive around trying to find something to eat.

I pull up Stella's contact and hit call. "Hey Boss Lady."

"Hi Stella. I just wanted to call and thank you again for last night."

"Oh, that was no problem. It was a lot of fun. Your guys kept me completely safe. By the way, they're super hot. Especially when they're holding guns and killing people."

I chuckle at her bluntness. "Yeah, they're fine as hell. I'm a lucky girl."

"Does that mean you're not with the twins anymore?"

I shake my head. "Oh god, no. That wasn't anything serious."

"Well, that's some interesting information."

Well...well...well. I never knew she was interested in them. If I did, I would've sent them her way instead of Bianca's long ago. "Do you want me to tell them to come visit you tonight? You can make your office into Room 7."

The bottom level of Mystique is a sex club that is only open twice a month, by invitation only. It gives the girls opportunities for release in their own controlled, safe environments.

"Don't you dare." I can hear her embarrassment through the phone.

"Alright, I won't but I'll send you their numbers if you change your mind."

"I won't." Maybe not tonight, but in the future, I know she'll call them. "Well, I should go. The girls are arriving and we have a new routine to learn."

I chuckle at her excuse to get off the phone with me. "Alright. Call if you need anything."

"I will. Call if you need a body double."

I chuckle. "Will do. See ya, Stella."

"Bye, Boss Lady."

I hang up just as I see a strip mall up ahead and I pull in when I see a Chinese restaurant. Cheap Chinese is always a good choice. My phone rings as I walk in, but when I see it's my father, I hit ignore. I order a ton of food because I don't know what the guys like and the cashier gives me a shocked look. I understand why when he hands over two full bags of Chinese food. I really hope the guys are coming or we're going to have leftovers for days.

When I get back to the house, I find Killian and Aisling cuddling on the couch, watching TV in the living room. "I got Chinese!"

Aisling jumps up from the couch. "Thank god! I'd kill for some fried rice and sweet and sour chicken right now."

"Good thing I got those, then." She follows me into the kitchen with Killian on her heels.

I start unpacking everything and Killian looks at me like I have lost my mind. "Did you get enough food?"

I flip him off. "I invited the guys over so I ordered one of all the combos."

"Do they each eat for three people?"

"Guys?" Aisling looks up from her container with a fork already filled with food.

I ignore Killian and smile at Aisling. "I got some gossip to tell you."

"Oh yay. I like gossip. Killian, leave us alone. I'm sure you don't want to hear the dirty stuff."

"You can talk about this later. I'm not leaving." He wraps his arms around her from behind and my phone starts to ring. "Is that Father? He's been trying to reach you."

"I know. I've ignored the calls." Looking at my phone, I see it's Enzo. I move out of the kitchen to answer. "Hey! Did you get my text?"

"Yeah, we did. Sorry we didn't text back but we've been dealing with your father's men as they came and packed you up."

Shock and anger courses through me. He had no right. "They did what!?!"

"All your stuff is gone." I can hear the irritation in his voice.

"How dare he?" He violated their space and forced his hand without discussing it with me. I know I've been ignoring his calls, but Aisling has only been safe for hours.

"Don't worry, Princess. I still have a pair of your panties." I bite my lip to stop myself from chuckling at Matteo and from the sound of him groaning as one of his brothers hit him.

"We're on our way to you." Dante sounds pissed.

"I didn't ask for this." They have to know that I didn't want to leave.

"We know," Enzo says, but I can hear the uncertainty.

"Okay. See you soon." I hang up my phone and walk back into the kitchen, fuming. "He had his men go to the guys' house and pack up my stuff. How did he know where they were? Who does he think he is?"

Killian shakes his head. "That means you're probably next."

"I'm not going back. He can't lock me away."

Aisling looks at me with concern because she knows I'm not going to be able to stop him. The sound of car doors closing has me running to the window to make sure it isn't my father's men. I won't go easily.

A smile spreads across my face as I see Dante's SUV sitting in the driveway and the three of them getting out. Looking back at Aisling, I smirk. "It looks like the gossip has come to you."

I move to the front door and open it just as they step on the porch. Enzo steps forward and gives me a kiss. Matteo is next as he whispers against my lips. "You're not getting those panties back." I chuckle and he smashes his lips to mine in a quick kiss before heading into the house. "Yay, Chinese."

I chuckle looking after him while shaking my head at his silliness. When I turn back to greet Dante, he has a stern look on his face as he leans against the porch railing with his arms crossed. "I'm sorry my father invaded your space." I step outside toward him and wrap my arms around his middle.

He lets his arms fall but he doesn't wrap them around me. "Did you know he was sending them?"

I shake my head no, squeezing him tighter. I need him to wrap his arms around me. "Of course not. He's been calling, but I haven't answered. I wasn't ready to tell him I was staying with you guys."

His hands slide up my arms until he wraps his arms around my shoulders, pulling me against him. "So, you were going to stay?"

I nod against his chest. "I've gotten a little attached to you guys."

He tilts my chin up and pushes my hair behind my ears. "We've gotten attached too." His lips move closer to mine, and I rise up on my toes, trying to close the distance between us faster. "Your father's men left a message."

Instant mood killer. I let out a huff and fall back down on my heels. "Let me guess. My father is calling me home."

He nods. "Yes. The threat is gone and you're to report home."

Report home. What am I? A soldier. "Well, he's going to have to find me and drag me home."

"Not going to happen if we're around." They'll stop anyone from taking me from them, I have no doubt.

I grab his hand and pull him inside, not wanting to talk about this anymore. Aisling is gushing over Matteo and Enzo and when she sees me walk in with Dante, she's shocked. "Oh my god. Three! I need to up my game."

"No, you don't." Killian pushes off the counter and pulls her to him.

She waves him off. "I can't believe you're dating contestants one and two."

I chuckle, remembering her dating game that night. The guys look at me confused. "That night, Aisling was trying to find me a guy to hook up with. Enzo and Matteo were the two guys that made the list." Dante huffs and wraps his arm around my shoulders holding me against his side. I pat his chest. "I'm sure you would've been contestant three if everything didn't blow up."

He leans down and whispers, "And I would've won."

A shiver runs through me as his breath tickles my ear. I step away from him before I ask him to show me what he would've done if he did win. "Alright, no more talking about contestants. Aisling, this is Matteo, Enzo, and Dante. Guys this is Aisling, my best friend."

They each step up and shake her hand. "It is nice to meet you," Enzo says.

"We're glad you're safe," Dante says.

"Craig will be dead by nightfall," Matteo says.

I pat Matteo's arm and chuckle. "Alright let's eat. And no talking about killing people."

He shrugs his shoulders. "Later then."

Yes. Later.

Chapter Twenty-Nine

Riona

After we finish eating, the guys sweep me into the car so we can have some fun with Craig. And I literally mean sweep. As soon as I take my last bite, Matteo has me in his arms, carrying me out of the house. I only have time to wave bye to Killian and an amused Aisling before the front door closes behind him. He doesn't let me go as he climbs into the back seat of Dante's SUV and places me in his lap so my back is leaning against his chest. The seat belt comes across the both of us and his arms wrap around my waist as well.

"This isn't very safe." I look back at him with an amused smile.

"We don't have to go far and I'm sure Dante will drive extra safe, right?" He looks at Dante who has just gotten in the SUV with Enzo.

"Nothing is going to happen to you." I give him a smile, knowing I'm safe in his hands.

Adjusting myself in Matteo's lap so I can see him, I run my fingers over Matteo's hair, feeling his short hair prickle my skin. "So, what are we going to do to Craig?"

His eyes shine as a wicked darkness fills them. "I've prepared all my toys. You can do whatever you want."

An excited smile pulls on my face thinking about all the possibilities. "We're going to have some fun, taking turns on him."

As Dante drives us to Matteo's playroom, Matteo whispers all the things he wants to do to Craig in my ear. I didn't know talking about torturing a guy could be such a turn on, but with Matteo, it is. He runs his hand up in between my thighs and I grind myself against his hand. "Are you wet for me, Princess? Is thinking about torturing Craig turning you on?"

Matteo presses his thumb against my clit through my leggings and I let out a moan. "*You're* turning me on."

"Matteo," Dante growls.

"Just ignore him." Matteo pulls me into a kiss as he rubs my clit in quick circles. "I bet I can get you off before we get there."

"I bet you can too," I pant.

Matteo pinches my clit, making me buck against his hand and sending me straight to the edge. He kisses up my neck and nips

286

at my earlobe. "You're soaking through your pants. God, I want to taste you so bad."

"Yes... please." Matteo slides his hand into my leggings and he pushes two fingers into me. My walls squeeze around him and he slams his mouth to mine as he pinches my clit again, sending me right over the edge. I moan out his name and he gives me a cocky smirk as he continues to rub my clit in rough circles, sending me into another orgasm.

I'm breathless when he pulls his hand from my pants, showing me his glistening fingers. He brings his fingers to his mouth and he sucks them clean. A moan escapes me, watching him, wishing he was between my thighs, licking straight from the source.

I pull him into a sloppy and desperate kiss, wanting more from him. Not caring about the seatbelt anymore, I unbuckle us and shift so I'm straddling his lap. My hands go to his jeans blindly, but before I can unzip them, someone else's hands are on me, pulling me out of the car. "No...we weren't done."

"Yes, you are." Dante sets me on the ground and his eyes burn with jealousy.

I press my body up against his and kiss along his neck. "Are you jealous, Dark God?"

He growls in response and crashes his lips to mine. God, I love his jealous side. Just to make him burn more, I break our kiss and step out of his hold to Enzo. Enzo takes my hand and leads me toward a warehouse. I look around, taking in the area because I don't even remember us stopping. Shoot, I don't even remember how we got here. Looking back over my shoulder, I find Dante fuming with Matteo chuckling next to him. I send him a wink and follow Enzo inside, feeling the other two close behind me.

I quicken my steps so I'm next to Enzo and lean over to kiss his shoulder. I don't want him feeling left out or like I'm using him. Enzo hooks his arm around my shoulders and pulls me into a quick kiss.

We walk through rows of shipping crates filled with god knows what until we come to another door that Matteo quickly runs to, opening it for us. He bows as we walk into the room. "Welcome to my torture room, Princess."

I chuckle and look around to find an empty office. Well, this wasn't what I expected. This can't actually be it. Enzo removes his arm from around me and bends down, pulling back the rug that covers the floor, revealing a trap door. That's more like it.

"This way to fun." Matteo climbs down the ladder and I go after him. I'm halfway down when his hands grip my hips, picking me up and lowering to the ground with my back to his front. He turns us with his arms around my waist and that's when I see the full torture room. Craig sits in the middle of the room, or should I say, hangs by his arms from the ceiling, with his toes barely touching the ground. On the right and left of Craig are tables filled with all kinds of knives, guns, and other tools.

Matteo skims his lips over my neck. "Do you like?"

I nod, amazed by the setup as I step out of his arms and head straight to the tables. There's literally every tool possible here. What should I use? Every item I see, I think of a great way to use it, but when I get to the knives, a calmness washes over me. Here is my tool. I wrap my hand around a knife that looks like one of mine and make my way to Craig.

"Wakey, wakey, Craig." I slap his face and he jerks awake. When he zeroes in on me and sneers, I grin happily at him. "How's it going, Craig? Comfortable?"

Craig spits at me and it lands at my feet. "I should've killed you the second I saw you at the airstrip."

I ignore him but on the inside I'm grinning, because he doesn't know I wasn't there. "You know what? You look like you're hot. Let me help you with your shirt." I place my hand down on his chest, holding his shirt down and I slice down his body, cutting through his shirt and skin. Screams fill the room and I cut deeper with a satisfied smile. His shirt falls open and blood runs down his chest as I take a step back. I'm impressed with myself at how straight the line is, going from neck to belly button, especially since he was jerking the whole time, trying to shake me off.

"You fucking bitch." Craig tries to lunge at me but all he does is cause his body to swing back and forth.

Matteo comes out of nowhere and punches Craig across the face, making him sway more. "You don't talk to her like that."

Heat spreads to my core and I rub my thighs together, turned on by Matteo. The look that Craig gives me as he stops swinging tells me he has so many other names he wishes to call me. Not affected by his hateful stare, I continue my plan. My knife slices into his chest and he doesn't quietly take his punishment. He screams and curses, calling me vile things as he tries to move away from me.

A few times he tries to kick out at me, but each time I just stab my knife into his thigh and then when I start carving again, my cuts become slightly deeper. When I'm finished, I step back admiring my work. Man, does my mark look pretty on his chest. Matteo wraps his arms around my middle from behind and he kisses my cheek. "Beautiful work."

"Thank you. Do you want a turn?" I look at him.

He nods happily as he walks over to his tables. "Alright Craig, my friend here is going to have some fun..."

"Friend?" Matteo interrupts.

"Oh sorry, Matteo. My guy. My lover. My boyfriend." I say each title as I stare off with Matteo.

"Future husband," he adds.

I shake my head and look back at Craig. "Once he's done, we're going to have a little chat."

"Go to hell." Craig kicks out again, but Matteo is there hitting his legs with a metal pipe.

I step back as Matteo proceeds to shatter Craig's legs with the pipe. "You don't get to touch her, you filthy piece of shit."

I lean on the wall next to Dante and Enzo as Matteo drops the pipe and grabs brass knuckles. Matteo proceeds to take his rage out on Craig, shattering rib after rib with each punch. When Matteo has broken every bone of Craig's from the chest down, he goes for the face and I push off the wall and walk up to him, running my hand up his back. He immediately relaxes and drops his arms to his sides.

I sidestep him and look Craig over. Bruises are forming on his skin that isn't covered in blood and a victorious smile comes across my face. He beat Aisling repeatedly, covering her body with cuts and bruises and now his whole body is the same.

"You know Craig, I can understand you being pissed at me for killing your father but the reason you're here now is because you took Aisling. You brought someone I deeply care about into this when your father's death was inevitable. He was a snitch. Someone else would've done it if I didn't."

Matteo goes back to his brothers as Craig lifts his head and I can see that his fight is gone. "He wasn't a snitch, you stupid bitch. Your father had mine killed because he didn't bow down to him when he asked to make a deal. Now your father will get what he wanted anyways, since you've killed everyone in his way. He orchestrated all this."

"You've lost everything because of you, not my father. You stupidly tried to go up against the Murphys. Their deaths are on your hands. But yours will definitely be on mine." My knife slides across his neck, splattering drops of blood across my face and he dies choking slowly on his blood.

Hands move across my hips, and I let go of the knife, letting it hit the ground as I lean back into Matteo's chest. His hands come forward pushing under my shirt as he kisses up my neck, sending a shiver through me. "Are you ready for our fun now?"

"Depends on what you have in mind." His hands slide up my stomach and he cups my breasts over my bra. I arch into his hands with a moan as I grind my ass back on his erection.

"I think you'd be down for anything, but first..." He pulls my shirt over my head and turns us so I'm looking at Dante and Enzo. "We need to get you out of these bloody clothes."

His hands lightly run down my body and I lay my head back on his shoulder so I'm looking up at him. "We?"

He smirks at me, knowing what I'm asking, but before he can answer, Dante is pushing off the wall and I can't look away from him. My body buzzes from Matteo's wandering hands and Dante's eyes and I pull him to me when he's close. Being sandwiched between them, I look up into Dante's blue eyes and silently beg him to kiss me. He crashes his lips to mine, and I grip his shirt pulling him closer. Matteo starts kissing down my neck and I moan out, loving both their lips on me.

Dante skims his lips down the other side of my neck but instead of staying there like Matteo, who's marking me, he kneels in front of me, taking my bra straps down with him. My breasts fall free and my bra falls to the floor seconds later with Matteo's help. His hand slides over my stomach and cups one of my breasts as Dante's mouth sucks on the other nipple. I fist Dante's hair, holding him to me as my eyes connect with Enzo's.

He watches from the wall and my whole body breaks out in goosebumps as everything clicks into place. I have all three of them here and I want all three of them touching me. I reach out for Enzo, but he just shakes his head.

"Let him watch, Princess. He'll join when he's ready." Matteo turns my face to him, and he crashes his lips to mine. My knees go weak and I wrap my arm behind his neck so I don't become a puddle on the floor. Dante's lips move down my body and Matteo takes both of my breasts in his hands. He grips them roughly before pinching my nipples and I grind back against his erection, needing more from them.

I don't know if Dante can read my thoughts or if he's as desperate as I am, because he slides his fingers into the edge of my leggings and pulls them down my legs, exposing me to them. I break my kiss with Matteo and look down my body to find Dante smirking up at me. He hooks my leg over his shoulder, spreading me open for him and pushes a finger inside of me. "You're so wet for us, Rose. So desperate for us."

Dante leans forward, licking up my wetness and humming against my clit. I buck against his face, gripping his hair tighter as I moan out, "Oh god, yes."

He pushes a second finger inside of me as he sucks on my clit. My back arches as I throw my head back on Matteo's shoulder and grind down on Dante's face. With hooded eyes, I look over to Enzo to find his pants undone and his hand wrapped around his erection, pumping himself slowly.

Matteo nips at my earlobe as he rolls my nipples in between his fingers. "You like him watching you. Seeing you being touched by his brothers."

Dante hooks his fingers inside me, running them along my upper wall and my answer comes out as a screamed moan, "Yes."

"Then put on a show for him, Princess. Make him come to you." My core squeezes around Dante's fingers at Matteo's words.

They want a show, I'll give them a show and take my pleasure from them while giving it too. I let go of my hold on Matteo's neck, sliding my hand down his abs to his jeans, and into his boxers. He's already hard as I wrap my hand around him and give him a soft pull. He growls next to my ear and nips at the sensitive spot he was sucking on earlier. I pump Matteo at the same pace that Dante's fingers thrust into me, bringing him to the edge with me. Dante hooks his fingers again and my knees go weak as my core clenches. "Yes... again."

Dante answers my pleas as he hums against my clit at the same time Matteo pinches my nipples and I fall into a pool of pleasure as I scream out their names. I'm not sure when my eyes closed as my body exploded with pleasure but I'm not ready to open them as my body buzzes from Dante's tongue still licking me clean and Matteo's hands roam my upper body.

Sensing my Beast is close, I open my eyes as he brushes his fingers over my cheek. Enzo's brown eyes connect with mine as he gives me a sexy smirk. "My turn."

He pulls me from between Matteo and Dante, picks me up, and places me down on the table. Whatever tools were there are now all over the floor from one sweep of his arm and I pull Enzo into a kiss. I wrap my arms around his neck and my legs around his waist, pulling him to me. His erection rubs against my center and I moan against his mouth as I pull at his shirt. He reaches behind his neck and pulls his shirt over his head, showing me his muscular chest and tight abs.

I take my time running my hands over his muscles as I memorize every inch of his body. A wave of pleasure washes through me, knowing that he's all mine. Looking into his eyes, I open myself up, showing how much I need him. "Enzo…" a quiet plea slips from my lips.

Enzo's eyes have the same wanting need I know mine have as he pushes his pants down more and he brings my knees higher up his sides. I lean back on my hands as I slide to the edge of the table, giving myself to him. His eyes run over me as his hand runs up my stomach and cups my breast. "You're so beautiful." He leans forward and brushes his lips against mine. "And you're all mine."

He pushes into me with a powerful thrust, and I groan out in pleasure, finally being filled. He pulls out and thrusts back in as our eyes stay locked and we breathe each other's air. His slow pace quickly picks up as our pleasure builds together and when I'm right on the edge, I lean back on my elbows to get better leverage so I can meet his thrusts. He grips my hips as his thrusts pick up, making my toes curl against his ass.

I squeeze around him as an early wave rolls through me and he removes one of his hands on my hips and presses on my aching clit. "Oh god... yes... harder." Enzo pinches my clit as he chases his release and I come screaming his name. He continues to fuck me as I ride out one orgasm and quickly fall into another and he comes with me, pressing his forehead against mine. Our lips meet in a slow kiss as Enzo lifts me off the table and I let my legs slide down his body until my feet touch the ground, breaking our kiss.

Someone presses up against me from behind and a shiver runs through me as their hands roam down my sides. "You're mine now, Princess." Matteo licks up the edge of my ear and I grind my ass back against his erection. Enzo steps out of my hold with a dirty smirk and I know he's not done watching me yet.

I look away from Enzo and up at Matteo. "What are you going to do to me?"

Pure desire fills his eyes and I clench my thighs together. "I'm going to fuck you so hard you won't be able to leave us."

I pull Matteo to me and he devours me in a kiss, pushing me back against the table where the cold metal presses up against my hot skin. "I'm not leaving you." I moan against his lips as his erection slides in between my legs from behind.

"Good. You won't want to after I'm done with you." Matteo kisses down my neck to my shoulder, where he nips at my skin and thrusts into me. I brace myself on the table as I widen my stance, welcoming him in. His hands run up my spine, bending me further over the table and as my breasts touch the cold metal, I let out a moan in pleasure. Matteo pulls out of me all the way to the tip as his hand wraps around the back of my neck and then he thrusts back into me with such beautiful power.

"Oh fuck." I reach out for the edge of the table in front of me, holding on as Matteo does exactly what he promised. He fucks me good and hard, to where if I wanted to leave, I'd be changing my mind. No sane woman would leave a man that can give you this much pleasure.

My body buzzes and I can't help the nonsense that comes out of my mouth as he shoots me right to the edge. I reach back for him, gripping his hip as his hand slides to my clit. I dig my nails into his skin as I fall into the most powerful orgasm ever. Matteo continues to fuck me, prolonging my pleasure until he comes with his face buried into my shoulder.

Matteo kisses down my back as he pulls out of me and I'm ready just to fall asleep in his arms. But I'm not done yet. My eyes connect to Dante who's watching us as he strokes his erection, which looks ready to explode. Matteo pulls me up from the table and circles me in his arms as I turn to face him. He's still wearing his clothes, with only his pants open. "You rocked my world and you didn't take off any clothes. I'm feeling a little undressed now."

His hands slide down my back side and take handfuls of my ass. "You're in the perfect amount of clothes." I chuckle as I lean up, placing a kiss on his lips and he smacks my ass. "You have someone else who wants your attention."

I step back from him and look to Enzo and then Dante, then back to Matteo. "I have three someone's." I hold up three fingers before turning my back to him and walk over to Dante.

He's still leaning against the wall but his eyes roam over every inch of my body. He doesn't reach out to me when I stand in front of him, holding my stare as he starts pumping himself faster. I push his hand away from his erection, taking the final step to him, and start pumping him. That seems to get a reaction out of him because his hand tangles in my hair and pulls me into a powerful kiss. My knees go weak from the pure passion between us and I break our kiss, letting my body bring me down to my knees. My eyes stay locked on his hungry gaze as I bring my face closer to his hard erection. I take my time licking up the underside of his erection and when I reach the tip, I suck on it like it's my favorite lollipop.

"Fuck, Rose." Dante grips my hair tighter, pushing himself further in my mouth until he hits the back of my throat.

We fight for control as I pull back to the tip, flipping my tongue over it before taking him all the way to my throat again. Dante holds me there, making me open my throat for him and I swallow around him with a moan, allowing him to take what he wants. A deep growl comes from him as he fucks my face and I run my nails down his ass as I push his jeans down while holding him to me. I want his release. I want the taste of him on my tongue. I tighten my throat around him as I graze my teeth along his underside and he pulls my head back, off his erection.

An amused grin pulls across his face as he shakes his head at me like I have been naughty and my core flutters with desire. I give him a wicked smirk as I dig my nails into his ass and he yanks me off my knees and into his arms. He slams me against the wall as he devours me with a kiss. "All mine." My arms and legs wrap around him as he lines himself at my entrance and thrusts into me.

I moan out his name, feeling full of him as I grip his hair and pull him back in for a kiss. He fucks me into the wall while gripping my ass so hard I know there'll be bruises. From the three of them, I'm going to be marked all over my body. And I can't wait to see.

Dante nips at my shoulder and kisses up my neck. "You've been teasing me all day. Making me watch you fuck my brothers. I want to be the last one to mark you as mine." He bites down on my shoulder again, leaving his mark opposite of Matteo's. "The last one to come inside you. My come will run down between your thighs, covering theirs."

I squeeze around him and I throw my head back, as I beg, "Please."

"You want me coating you with my come? You want to feel me leaking from you?"

I nod frantically, answering in time with his thrust. "Yes... yes... yes."

Dante rubs rough circles over my clit. "Come for me, Rose. I want you all over me as well."

I come screaming and Dante erupts with me, doing exactly what he said he would. I bring his face to mine and kiss him as we come down from our highs.

Dante pulls out of me and helps me lower my legs to the ground. My whole body feels like jelly after having the three of them, but it feels amazing. "The next time we do a sex marathon, can it be near a bed?" Dante chuckles as he tucks himself away and buckles his pants.

"Did we tire you out, Princess?" Matteo is bent down over Craig, who's now laid out on the ground in a pool of his blood.

"You try coming six times. You'd be passed out after number two."

"Not with you. I'd go nonstop." He gives me a wink before rolling Craig in a tarp. That's when I see my clothes are sitting in the middle of the blood. Well shit, now I don't have any clothes. Dante walks over to help Matteo and I head to Enzo and wrap my arms around him.

He hugs me to him and I place a kiss on his chest, right over his heart. "Can I have your shirt?"

I look up at him with a pout and he chuckles. He reaches behind him, pulling his shirt over his head, and I loosen my hold on him. With his shirt off, he holds it open for me and I slip my arms in. The shirt falls down my body and stops mid-thigh, covering all the important stuff. Enzo lets out a possessive growl as he looks me over and I do a little twirl. "You like what you see?"

He pulls me back to him. "Always. But this might be your new required sleepwear."

"I can work with that." I give him a quick kiss and go grab my shoes, which, by some miracle, aren't covered in blood. I stand from my crouched position after my shoes are on to find all of them staring at me with hunger in their eyes and I shake my head no. "Not going to happen."

Matteo adjusts Craig on his shoulder. "Then let's get out of here so we can find a bed for round two."

I'm exhausted but it doesn't stop my heart from racing, wanting another round. "Let's... and clothes."

"You don't need clothes for round two." Matteo looks at me like I'm silly.

We all head to the ladder and all the guys step aside for me to go first. "Nope. I'm not going up first, opening myself up to your wandering hands." I wave my arm out silently, saying after you. They each go up one at a time and I get to check out their perfect asses as they do. Truly, I'm a very lucky girl.

Chapter Thirty

Riona

Dante pulls up to the safe house and I lean in between the front seats and give him and Enzo a kiss. Matteo's hand runs up the back of my thigh and I quickly swat his hand away. "Stop feeling me up." I sit back and give him a kiss as well.

"It's hard not to when I'm around you." His hand goes to my thigh again.

"Well, I'm fixing that." I slide across the backseat, removing his hand and open the door. "I'll see you guys later."

I give them a wave and jump down out of the car. They have to go dispose of Craig's body, but I promised them I was theirs tonight, with explicit details on all the dirty things I want them to do to me. It almost started round two in the backseat.

In only Enzo's shirt and my tennis shoes, I run for the front door, while holding down the sides of the shirt. The neighbors don't need a peepshow. I'm sure they already have wild ideas about who keeps coming in and out of the house, but who cares. We'll be out of here in a few days.

I walk into the house and a whistle has me stopping outside the living room on my way to the room. Aisling is laying out on the couch and the TV is on. "What happened to you? You look like you've been railed by three gorgeous men."

"That's because I have." I lean against the doorframe.

"How are you walking right now?" she teases.

I chuckle. "To be honest, I have no idea. What are you doing?"

"Killian was called in by your father so he had to leave. I didn't like the quiet, so I came out here to watch TV."

I walk into the room and take a seat next to her. "Why did he go? Father knows you were rescued. He should let you guys be for at least a couple of days."

"He only went so he could pack yours and my bags. I need to get away from this life for a while and you're dodging your father, so I volunteered you to come with me."

"Don't you want to go with Killian?" I'm happy to go, but shouldn't he go?

"Of course I do, but he can't leave right now. Your father is up to something that has Kill concerned, but he'll come join us at some point."

"And how long are we going to be gone?" I just told my guys I'm staying.

"As long as we want." She must see my hesitation. "Are you going to miss your guys?"

I shake my head like I won't but I'm really trying to formulate a plan because I'm going to miss them. "If Killian is coming, then they can come at some point as well."

"That is true. Wasn't sure if you wanted space from them or not. You went from casual hookups or one-night-stands to living with your three boyfriends." She knows how serious that is and it's completely foreign to me.

"I don't know how it happened. It just did. We have this crazy connection. So far I haven't gotten tired of them yet."

She smiles at me. "You look happy."

"l am happy." I lean into her, giving her a big hug. "Especially with you here and safe."

Aisling pulls back from me. "I love you, but you reek of sex. You should shower."

I chuckle. "I don't have any clothes."

"Take some from the bag on the bed."

"Alright, I'll wash my men from me just for you." I stand from the couch.

"Your brother will appreciate it too." I chuckle and head back to the room. After grabbing some clothes, I head into the bathroom.

After my shower, I take my time to dry my hair and apply makeup. Even if I'm only wearing sweats, I want my guy's mouths to drop. Once I'm done, I give myself a final look over and I've got to say I'm looking good in leggings and a white t-shirt crop top.

Stepping out of the bathroom, I can tell something is off. The house is too quiet. I reach next to me and grab a hidden gun under the nightstand. All my houses have weapons hidden. Especially if I know I'm going to use them. With the gun in my hand, I make my way to the open bedroom door.

Once I step into the hallway, I know exactly why I have a chilling feeling. Three of my father's top men stand at the end of the hall. Cyrus, who's standing in the middle of Jake and Zeb, steps forward. "Riona, your father has been trying to reach you."

"I'm aware." I make my way toward him.

"You need to come with us." I slide past him without touching him and he knows not to reach for me, especially with a gun in my hand.

"If my father needs me, he should come collect me himself." Once I see Aisling is safe in the living room with Killian, I turn back to Cyrus. "I don't see him here. Please give him my message."

He crosses his arms over his chest, trying to make himself look bigger. "We're not allowed to come back without you. We've been given permission to use force if necessary."

I chuckle. "You couldn't take me without my permission, and he knows it. You'd be dead before you could even touch me."

Thing is, I don't want to kill these three. I actually like them compared to some of my father's older members. I look back to Killian who just left my father and he gives me a nod, telling me it's time to see my father.

"Alright let's go. I have plans tonight I'm not missing." I stick my gun in the back of my leggings and head for the front door. My father's men follow me out of the house and to their SUV. I open the passenger side door and climb in.

The drive across town is quiet. Not one word is said, which works well for me. It allows me to focus on why I've been avoiding my father. Over the last week my father has really shown his cards. The things he did and said came from a man I didn't recognize. He's always been a monster, but it was never directed towards us.

When we pull up outside the house, I jump out as soon as the car stops and head in through the front door, making sure it bangs against the wall. He wants me here, he's going to know I've arrived. I march all the way to his office and let myself in with a bang.

My father calmly looks up from his computer to me. "About time you came home."

"I'm not home."

He continues without noticing I spoke. "I have a job for you."

"What!?" I throw my arms up in disbelief. "We just saved Aisling and killed all of the O'Briens and you've been calling for a job?"

He stands from his desk and walks around it. "Yes. You're to kill the Russo boys."

"What!? No. I won't do it." I shake my head, not believing this.

"You will. I made a deal with them that I don't plan to keep. So, I need you to kill them so they don't retaliate." What kind of reason is that?

I look at him like he's lost his mind. Has he always been this murderous, sending me to kill for stupid reasons? "I won't do it. I won't kill the men who've been protecting me and helped me find and save Aisling."

"They only did that because they wanted power. A connection to us. Your hand in marriage." I flash back to that first day and Matteo asking to marry me. Then earlier today when he said he was my future husband.

"Maybe I'm okay with that."

Anger radiates off of him as he looks me over and I know he sees the evidence of their marks on my neck. "You let those boys into your heart. Don't you see they were just playing you? Their family has been trying to take control of this city and this isn't the first time they've used you to get it."

He'll say anything to get his way right now. "What the hell is that supposed to mean?"

"Tony DeAngelo." My heart stops at what he's implying. "Tony was a Russo. A cousin. Do you really think those boys care about you? They know what Tony did to you. They sat back and let it happen. Their father wants my power and those boys will do anything to get it." He sneers at me in disgust. "Just this time, they didn't have to rape you. You willingly opened your legs for them."

I pull my gun out and aim it right at his head. "You're lucky I still consider you family. People have died for less than what you just said. Watch how you talk to me. In a second I could make Killian the new boss."

My father at least has the brains to take a step back. At that, I walk out of his office and head straight to the garage. Needing to get out of here, I grab my car keys and head to my black Tesla. My mind is moving a million miles an hour and I feel like my fury is about to explode, but I don't know where to aim it. Sliding into the driver's seat, I grip the steering wheel and scream.

Did I let them fool me? Was this all just a manipulation to overthrow the Murphy Clan? If it was just the deal, I'd be okay with it. I want to be with them. But knowing Tony was their family, I question every touch, kiss, and loving word.

It takes me a while to get to the Russo house, since I first had to find a place I recognized from one of our trips. I park right behind Dante's SUV and open my glove box, grabbing another gun and a knife. Looking at Dante's SUV, an evil smile spreads across my face as I spin the knife in my hand, eyeing his tires. I'm vibrating as I storm into their house with my guns raised and they all turn, reaching for their guns. My eyes scan over each of them as I feel my heart break open. Please let it be my father lying.

Dante steps forward with confusion and distrust written across his face as he grips his gun tighter. "What the fuck, Ri?"

The only one that should feel distrust is me. I shift to face him and aim my gun just over his and Matteo's shoulders. "Did you guys know this whole time? Were you just playing me?"

Enzo steps forward but stops when I turn my aim in his direction. "Beauty, what are you talking about?"

"My kidnapping. Tony DeAngelo. Did you know before I told you?" Recognition registers on all their faces. "Am I a tool again, so your family can gain more power? I guess I should thank you for not raping me this time."

"Okay. Hold up. We weren't playing you." Dante moves closer and I keep my gun trained in his direction. "We knew nothing about your kidnapping until you told us. All you said was his name was Tony. We never knew our family was responsible for that."

"But you made a deal with my father for my hand in marriage to gain power."

Matteo smirks at me. "We made a deal for marriage because you're beautiful and captured our attention the night of the gala. We wanted time with you and yes, I wanted to marry you. I did ask that night, if you remember. We'd never force you into marriage."

My head starts to spin with what they're saying and what my father said. Who is telling the truth? I lower my guns and start walking backwards. "If I find you just lied, I'll kill you without my father's orders. And if your father did order for my kidnapping, tell him to up his security because I will come after him." I turn on my heels and walk out of the house with them following.

"Where are you going?" Enzo asks as I walk through the front door.

"Aisling and I are going away for a while. Get away from this life." I round the front of my car and look back at them. Worry and confusion is written all over their faces.

"Where are you going?" Enzo asks again as he clenches his hands into a fist and I know he wants to reach out for me.

"I don't know. But I don't want you following me."

I open my door and I'm about to get in when Matteo speaks. "Can I call you?"

Even though I'm not sure about them right now, I can't help my lips turning up slightly in a smile. "Maybe."

I slide into my car and drive away. In my rearview mirror I watch them run to Dante's SUV but stop when they see my knife sticking out of his now-flat tire. I swear I can hear Dante cursing my name as I pull out onto the road.

The further I run from them, the more the pain in my chest grows, but I can't stay. I don't know who to trust, including myself. I pull out my phone and call Aisling. "Hey."

"Hey. I need to leave now, tell me where we're going and you can meet me later."

"Go to the private airport; we're waiting for you there."

"We're?"

"Well, Killian is here until we leave, but we're crashing Tanner and Colton's flight. I knew you wouldn't want to stay in the city after talking to your father."

"You don't even know the half of it."

"Then I can't wait to hear what an asshole he is. See you soon."

I hang up and waste no time getting to the private airport. Distance is what I need.

I have to find a way to put some space between us...
Distance is what I need.

Chapter Thirty-One

Riona

It's been almost two weeks since Aisling and I arrived at Tanner and Colton's property on the Cliffs of Moher in Ireland. It's a fantastic place. The perfect place to reset and relax. It's only been Aisling and I here until two nights ago, when Killian showed up.

I walk out of my room, still in my pajamas, throwing my bedhead hair up in a messy bun as I head to the kitchen to get some coffee. Aisling is standing over the stove in her pajamas with her strawberry blonde hair tied in a ponytail as I walk in. "Morning!"

She looks over her shoulder at me as I pass her, heading to the coffee maker. "Morning, Ri. I'm making eggs if you want some."

"Yeah, that would be great. Thank you." I pour my coffee and add cream and then head around the island to take a seat on the bar stool. "Is Killian still sleeping?"

She turns off the stove. "No, he went to Galway this morning to pick up groceries and other things we need."

"It's just us for the morning, what should we do?" I smile at her, knowing the answer.

"What we do every morning. We eat here and then go sit outside as we drink coffee. You'll get your morning call from Matteo and, like every morning, you'll just let it ring." She puts a plate of eggs in front of me and takes a seat beside me. "Maybe you can change it up today and answer?"

"You know why I'm not answering." Everyday my reason gets weaker and weaker.

"I do, but I also think it's bullshit. You know those guys weren't playing you. Your father was making up things to get you to do his bidding." Ever since she found out my father left her to be taken, she's lost all trust in him.

"But what if he wasn't? What if I let them in and they're just using me?"

She grabs my hand and squeezes. "You need to go with your heart on this one. If it's true, then you'll kill them and I'll help."

I chuckle. "Wow. That's a big statement."

"Right. I don't kill just anyone." Aisling grew up in this life, so she has had to kill to survive, but she doesn't want that side of this life. She likes the business side and all the connections. That's why she and Killian are going to make a powerhouse couple once they take over.

"I feel so honored you'd kill for my broken heart." I squeeze her hand back.

"I'd kill for less for you."

"Same." I'd kill someone if they spoke ill of Aisling, but she doesn't need to know that.

I bump my shoulder against hers and we both smile at each other. It's been nice having time with her. Over the last couple years, with her in law school or with Killian, and me taking on jobs and running our businesses, we haven't had just us time for so long. It's almost like when we were kids. Hanging out all day, binging shows and movies at night, falling asleep on the couch.

After we finish eating, we both fill up our coffees and with our sweatshirts and blankets, we head out to the back porch. We each take a porch chair and bundle ourselves up so we can look out over the cliffs. Even though it's July and probably 100° at home, here it's in the 50's.

It's beautiful and peaceful out here, just listening to the water crash against the cliffs. "Do you think you'll start planning your wedding now?"

She smiles with so much excitement for the future. "Probably. I want something small. With everything going on back home, maybe we'll just elope here."

That would be perfect. At home it would be made into a big event. "That could be fun." My phone starts to ring.

"Oh look. It's 10 o'clock." Every morning Matteo calls me at this time, which means it's 5am back home.

"Shut-up." I stick my tongue out at her.

"You know what?"

I look up from my phone. "What?"

She holds my stare. "I think you miss them and really want to answer."

I give her a weak smile. "I do miss them."

"Then answer."

I shake my head no and the phone stops ringing. "Oh, too late."

"Phones go both ways." My phone starts going off again. "Well, it looks like he's not taking no for an answer."

I can't help but smile. She might be right. Matteo was the one who's called me the most. At first it was multiple times a day and then it started every morning. Dante calls me daily and his voicemails always leave me smiling because I'm driving him crazy. Enzo calls every night and leaves me a goodnight voicemail. He seems to be the only one who's allowing me time.

"I'll leave you to answer that." Aisling stands and walks inside.

I stare at my phone, fighting myself on answering it or not. The side of me saying to answer ends up winning as I reach for my phone right before I know it's going to stop. "Is there an emergency?"

"Princess!" A huge smile spreads across my face. "Yes, there is an emergency. I miss you and needed to hear your voice."

I shake my head but swoon over his answer. "That's not an emergency."

"Yes, it is."

I close my eyes and lean my head against the back of the chair. "Well, now that you've heard my voice, I'm going to hang up." But I don't actually move to hang up because I miss him too.

"You better not."

"Bye, Matteo."

"Riona!" I stay silent, holding back my laugh. "Princess?"

"I'm still here, Bear."

He growls. "That wasn't nice. Tell me where you are so I can come punish you."

"I'm not sure I want you to know where I am right now. My head is still a mess about all this." I'm afraid to see them because I know I'll fall into their arms, not caring if they were trying to trick me. That's how much I miss them.

"Ri, is it really a bad thing that one of us wants to marry you?"

"Before knowing me, absolutely. When you made that deal you knew nothing about me. At least that's how it seemed."

"We didn't know anything about you then, except that you drew all of our attention the night of the ball. And then at the club, you can't deny the chemistry that was between us and I'm guessing between you and Enzo and maybe even you and Dante. That deal was made after Aisling was taken and before you came home with us. You needed protection and to lie low and we wanted to get to know you. We didn't need money, so we made a deal for your hand in marriage, knowing we'd never force you into it. Even after everything between us, if you said you didn't want to ever get married, we'd accept that."

"You'd let me go if I wanted to walk away?"

"That's not what I said. I'd always follow if you tried to walk away. What I'm saying is, if you never want to get married, we'd be okay with that as long as we had you. Marriage is just a piece of paper in the end. A commitment can be made without it."

"The Murphy name is strong for just being associated with us. Marriage isn't needed to get our power and respect, just dating me will give you that." I stand up and walk out to the edge of the property and pace along the brick one foot wall marking the edge of the safety area for the cliff.

"Ri, at any point before your father put all this doubt in your head, did you question how we feel about you?"

"I know you like having sex with me; I don't know how you feel. But to answer your question: no, I didn't doubt anything you did."

"Princess, this isn't about sex for us. Would we be chasing after you, calling you every day, if it was just about sex or even power? You matter to us. We want to be with you. You have us all in a mess since you walked away and we'd fly to wherever you are right this second if you'd let us. Dante is all wound up ready to explode. Enzo is moping around and me, I can't focus on anything. I've spent the last two weeks just waiting for you to call or trying to figure out where you are."

I'm silent for a while, taking in everything he said. It's hard for me not to believe him and I really want to believe him. I've missed them too and it's been wrecking me to think they were faking it. "Princess, please tell me you believe me."

I think it over for another second and then I answer with my heart, hoping it won't blow up in my face. "I believe that you want to be with me, but what about Tony? That order had to come from somewhere. I can't just forget that your family had something to do with the darkest moments of my life."

"My father didn't give that order. I flew out to Italy and confronted him myself and he swears that it didn't come from him. I don't know where it came from and I can't deny Tony was family, but he's dead and I can promise no one from the Russo family will ever hurt you again. We'd kill them if they do. That includes my brothers and myself. We'd die before ever hurting you."

I'm silent trying to process everything and think of things to build my walls back up again, but I can't. As much as I'm scared to open my heart to them, I can't find a legitimate reason to keep them away anymore. "Okay."

He's quiet for a second and I wish I could see his face. "Like okay, okay?" His excited voice has me giggling as he asks for confirmation that we're good.

"Yeah, okay okay."

"Oh, thank god. Please tell me where you are. We'll get on a plane now. I've got to see you."

"I'm in Ireland, but don't come. I'll be coming home in a few days. I promise." That wasn't the plan, but it is now.

"You get 48 hours to show up at our door before we go hunting for you."

"Maybe I like being chased." I smirk.

He growls. "Get here and I'll chase your naked ass all over the house."

"Okay. Two days. Can you do me a favor?"

"Sure."

"Rub it in Dante's face that I answered your call and tell Enzo I'll talk to him tonight."

Matteo chuckles. "You're asking for a fight when you get here but I'll happily deliver the messages."

That's exactly what I want. "Alright I've got to go."

"See you in two days, Princess."

"You better welcome me with an earth-shattering kiss."

"Hell yeah, I will."

I chuckle. "Bye, Bear."

"Bye, Princess."

My cheeks hurt from smiling so hard as I end the call. I'm about to turn to the house and tell Aisling everything when I see a man in the reflection of my blacked-out phone. Instantly, I turn, throwing my phone at the guy, hitting him directly in the eye. I rush him as he clutches his face and I add my fist to it, breaking his nose and making him fall to the ground. I add another punch as I go down with him, knocking him out.

As I stand, I'm about to make a run for the house but I have a wall of men standing in front of me, blocking my way. As I look over the ten men, I recognize each of them as father's men. I step away from the down guy and stand in front of them with my arms crossed. God, I wish I had a weapon on me right now. This is going to be a hard fight.

I open my mouth to say something smart as my eyes connect with Cyrus, but Aisling calling out my name has my focus changing to the open door where Aisling appears. "Aisling..." She looks up from her phone and surprise and terror washes over her face. "Run!"

Aisling immediately turns on her heel and runs, and I charge at the man who's raising his gun at her but before I can get to him, he fires and I watch as Aisling's body jerks from getting hit but she keeps going inside. I jump on the man's back and snap his neck as I scream out. His body falls and I jump at the man next to him, tackling him to the ground and as I raise my fist to punch him, there's a pinch on the back of my neck. I turn to see Cyrus injecting me with something and my attention goes to him.

I throw my elbow back, hitting him in the shoulder, but the force isn't there. I shift, trying to put my body weight into the next hit but my limbs fall to my sides. Whatever he injected me with is quickly immobilizing me as I collapse on the ground. I'm able to turn enough to land face up, but as blackness fills my vision, I see a satisfied Cyrus standing over me. "Don't look so pleased. You'll die for hurting Aisling. You better hope she lives."

"It was only a tranquilizer. She'll wake up in a few hours. You'll be out longer. We don't need trouble on the flight."

My eyelids droop so I can only see a sliver of the sky above me. "That's okay. Once I wake up, you'll be the first one I kill and then Father." My vision goes black and I fight to stay awake, but it's useless.

"You have no idea how wrong you are." That's the last thing I hear as I'm swallowed by darkness.

Chapter Thirty-Two

Riona

Horns blaring and someone cursing pulls me from the darkness and a smile forms on my face. New York City. Home. I open my eyes to take in the entertainment the city always is, but I can't see anything. Something is over my head. Realization hits as I remember what happened and I freeze. I was taken by my father's men on his orders.

How long have I been out? How are we in the city right now?

A loud horn rings out from what sounds like the car I'm in and then I'm jerked to the right. I try to brace myself but can't as I feel the plastic ties on my wrist cut into my skin. Hands grip my shoulders and I fight myself not to jerk away as they set me up and back against the seat.

"Why couldn't we put her in the trunk? I'm tired of her falling over on me because this idiot doesn't know how to drive." A third hand pushes me back harder against the seat and I let my head fall back.

Two soft cushions brace my face and I know it's the headrests. It's uncomfortable having my hands squished behind my back, but it also gives me cover to try to get out of the ties. I zone out the guys bickering as I focus on my wrists, trying to stretch out the ties.

The man on my left shifts his body closer to me as a finger pokes my thigh and I freeze my movements. "Isn't she supposed to be awake by now?" The one on my right starts poking my face through the bag, hitting my cheek, nose, and eye. I let out a fake tired groan as I turn away, acting like I'm waking up.

"You idiots stop messing with her before she kills you." Cyrus.

I groan again, moving my head side to side like I'm waking up. "You scared of me, Cyrus?"

"I'd be a fool not to be." I almost wish that he was.

"Well, at least you're no fool. I'm still going to kill you."

"Well, you better do it now, it'll be your last chance." The car turns and then starts bumping down an unpaved road.

"Untie my hands so I can. You can even leave the bag on my head."

"Sorry, we have other plans." The car stops. "Aren't you excited?"

I shake my head. "Can't say that I am."

Four doors open and the guy to my right pulls me across the seat and sets me on the ground. He pulls me a short distance away and then hands grab each of my biceps as the bag is ripped off my head. The sun is bright, making me blink a few times, trying to take in my surroundings. I look at the two idiots who each have a hold on my biceps.

Past each of them, I see several men standing in a line facing forward. My attention is drawn forward at the sound of footsteps on gravel. I really should be shocked at the sight of my father in front of me, but I'm not. "Hello, my dearest daughter."

"Father. If you wanted to see me, all you had to do was call." I give him a sarcastic smile.

His hand comes out faster than I expected, slapping me across my face. "You will not speak to me like that."

The burn that takes over my right cheek is nothing compared to the hatred that burns inside me. How dare he hit me?

He stands in front of me with his arms crossed, looking at me with disgust. "It was time for you to come home. You're needed here."

"What for?" I glare at him.

"It's time for you to get married. Make the connection that your marriage was always supposed to make." My father looks back at the car behind him and both the back doors open.

"I thought you didn't want me..." I watch in horror as Ivan Volkov, the head of the Bratva steps out, followed by his mini-me, Maxim, in their identical black suits, white blonde hair combed back and green eyes staring at me. Ivan looks at me like he's pricing me out, while Maxim looks like he's gotten everything he's ever wanted. "No."

My father turns back to me and gives me a death glare. "You will keep your mouth shut."

My father shakes both their hands and I thought I couldn't hate my father more. "With your marriage into the Bratva, you're bringing a new business opportunity to the Murphys."

I can't help my snarky response. "What's that? Vodka?"

My father fists his hand, trying to rein in his anger. "No... Women. Men. Children. Skin."

"What!?!" I pull against the idiots' hold. "You're tarnishing the Murphy name by getting involved in that disgusting business? What's the matter with you?"

My father advances on me, grabbing me by my throat and squeezing. "What did I say about keeping your mouth shut?"

Even with my throat burning, I spit back a response, "You're delusional if you think Killian and I will allow you to buy and sell skin."

Evil pours from him as he looks at me like I'm nothing to him. "You won't be able to stop it, since you'll be locked up with your new husband."

My father releases me. "I'll never marry Maxim or any of the Bratva."

My father chuckles in an evil way that sends chills through me. "You won't have a choice." My father pulls his phone out. "But first, I need to tie up a loose end." His eyes connect with mine. "The loose end that you couldn't close."

Chills take over my body in pure terror as my father turns his phone toward me and I watch as Dante, Matteo, and Enzo get out of Dante's SUV and head into their house. "This was just a few minutes ago."

He walks to me so he's standing next to me. "You know, I had a feeling you wouldn't be able to do what needed to be done, so I had my men put into place a plan B when they went and collected your things." My father taps on an icon I recognize and a red dot appears.

I fight against the two men holding me as my father laughs with his thumb over the button. "I hope you said your goodbyes." Down his thumb goes and the house explodes in a fiery ball of flames.

Watch
IT BURN

E. MOLGAARD

Watch it Burn

The Set the World on Fire Duet

Book Two

By: E. Molgaard

Note to Readers

This is a reverse harem romance which means the female main character has more than one love interest and she doesn't choose between them. There are dark themes in this book that can be triggering such as kidnapping, abuse, threats of rape, rape, child abuse, torture, and murder. This book is darker than the previous book. Please feel free to message me directly if you have any concerns or questions

About the Book

My father betrayed me.

He took them from me.

And because of him, I'm now in the hands of the Volkovs.

They want me to be the good little princess and marry

Maxim. That's not going to happen.

I'll show them what a true Mafia princess I am.

Maxim Volkov and Lorcan Murphy are going to wish they

didn't cross me. Nothing is going to stop me from getting

my revenge.

Maxim is my enemy.

Lorcan is my nightmare.

But they will be nothing when I'm through with them.

Chapter One

Riona

With a wicked grin, my father laughs as he holds his thumb over the detonator. "I hope you said your goodbyes."

He presses his thumb on the red button and my heart shatters as I watch the home I was coming back to explode with Enzo, Matteo, and Dante in it. Fire sweeps over the top of the trees in the distance and I scream out knowing this isn't some messed up trick. "Nooo!" I hunch over in agony, pulling on the grips the two idiots have on my arms.

Their fingers dig into my skin and fury courses through me. With a vengeful scream, I break the ties on my wrists and rip my arms from their hold. I throw my elbow into the idiot on my right's throat, making him choke, and grab his gun, sending one shot each into his and the other idiot's chest. Before their bodies hit the ground behind me, my gun is aimed at my father's head. He killed them. He killed the men I love. I clench my teeth as I growl, letting my anger overcome me.

"Riona, no." Cyrus charges at me and I turn to him with a smile.

"I told you." I pull the trigger, shooting him in between his eyes.

Turning back to Lorcan, I aim the gun again at his smiling face. "You won't shoot me, Riona. I'm your father." I see Ivan and Maxim escape for their car behind Lorcan.

"No. Your betrayal makes you my enemy." I squeeze the trigger, firing as a body slams into me, tackling me to the ground. My shot misses by a few inches and I roar out in frustration as I swing my fist back into the man's face. Five men descend on me, wrestling me to the ground, getting the gun out of my hand and grabbing hold of my wrists and ankles, immobilizing me.

My father's black leather shoes appear in my line of vision and he crouches down by my face. "My sweet daughter, I know you didn't mean it." He reaches forward, petting my hair, and I pull away from his touch. "I can't wait until I walk you down the aisle."

"You'll never walk me down the aisle. Fathers walk their daughters down the aisle and you're no longer my father."

He grabs my face, turning it at a weird angle so our matching green eyes connect. "You're a mafia princess and you will act like it. You have no more freedom, Riona. You will make your husband happy. You will mother his children. And you'll do it all with a smile on your face."

I pull my face from Lorcan's hold and arch myself up so I'm looking up at him. "I am a mafia princess. Someone who can't be shackled. Someone who can't be tamed. Someone who'll kill anyone who tries."

Feet crunch on the ground behind Lorcan and Maxim looks down at me with a smile like he thinks he's won the lottery. Lorcan stands as Maxim crouches down in front of me. He reaches out for me, grabbing my hair and pulling me up so I'm on my knees with five men still holding me. "I'm going to have so much fun breaking you, Princess."

Maxim slams his lips to mine and I try to pull back from his disgusting mouth but his hold doesn't allow it, so I do what any girl would do. I bite down hard on his bottom lip, drawing blood and some skin as he pulls back. Maxim slaps me across the face and I spit his blood and skin from my mouth.

I chuckle uncontrollably as I look back at Maxim, Lorcan and now Ivan. "You're a little bitch. Someone who runs from a gun fight and gets his ass kicked by a girl will never break me." I continue to laugh as both Maxim and his father's faces turn red in rage.

Ivan grabs his son's shirt and yells at him in Russian. For the first time in my life, I wish I spoke Russian so I could listen to Ivan berate him. Maxim looks at me, breathing heavily and vibrating with anger. I pout at him mockingly, and I'm about to taunt him when I see Ivan swinging the butt of his gun at me. Before I even have a chance to react, it hits me on the side of my head and everything goes black.

Chapter Two

Riona

God, my head is pounding. I curl in on myself, holding my head in my arms and the mattress creaks underneath me, making my ears ring. I bite down on my lip, holding back my scream as I remember what happened, like it was a nightmare. The pain in my chest rips me open as I remember Matteo, Dante, and Enzo are gone. I was coming home to them, ready to see what being theirs would be like. Ready to fully open my heart to them and accept that I've fallen for three men that I've only known for a couple of weeks. Now it's breaking because I'm all by myself. Tears form in my eyes, wishing

I could kiss them one more time. Hug them one more time. Talk to them one more time. Tell them I love them.

"One hit to the head and you're already broken. I thought you'd be a little bit more fun." I bury all my emotions deep inside of me, locking them away so only rage is left. I lift my head, even though it's pounding, and take in the room I'm in, or should I say cell. It's just me locked in a 5x10 cement cell with a sink, toilet, bed, and side table. Sitting up, I glare at Maxim, who's standing outside the metal bars with a victorious smile, still in his suit.

"Why don't you come in here and see how broken I am?" I stand from the bed, facing Maxim, with my hands at my sides, trying not to sway on my feet. Silently, I dare him to open that door.

After a few minutes of us just staring at each other, Maxim proves he's smarter than I thought as he takes a small step back and nods at the floor. "Time to eat." I look down at the ground to see a metal tray with meat and potatoes along with a plastic cup filled with water. When I look back up, his lanky body is further back and his blue eyes gleam as he smiles at me. "Oh, and they did find three bodies in what was left of the Russo house."

Any hope that they could've gotten out vanishes and my body burns with deathly hate. I want them all dead. Maxim, Lorcan, Ivan, and all the men that were there are going to die at my hands. I scream as I charge at the cell door, ready to wrap my hands around his neck but he steps back, just out of my reach. He chuckles at me as I grab the bars and shake the door, screaming. Maxim turns his back to me and walks down the dark hallway to the stairs. I pick up the cup filled with water and throw it down the hall after him. "I'm going to kill you!"

I let out my rage on my concrete cell by picking up the tray filled with food and throwing it against the opposite wall. Picking up the only side table, I smash it against the ground until it's in pieces. My single bed is next as I flip the metal frame over and grab the middle of the thin mattress with both fists and tear it to shreds.

Screaming, I fall to my knees when there is nothing left to destroy. My throat is sore, adding to the pounding in my head that's now ten times worse, but my rage has my body vibrating. I need to calm down. Be smart about this. Maxim won't let me get close to him if I rage out every time I see him. I lean back against the cool wall as I try to take calming breaths. I might not rage out but I'm not going to lay back and do nothing. I'm going to fight.

My stomach growls and I'm pissed that I threw the food and water. Who knows how long it's been since breakfast with Aisling? I need my strength. Seeing a bread roll sitting next to the flipped over tray, I crawl to it. Not caring if it has dirt on it, I bite into it and savor it with small bites. As I eat, I take in the mess I made.

Stuffing from the mattress covers the floor, the bed frame is bent, but it's the shattered side table that has me smiling. Broken wooden legs and large shards of wood scatter the floor. A plan formulates in my mind. It's time to piss Maxim off and put fear in his men.

Gathering up the wood, I straighten up my cell and fortify it by pushing the bed frame up against the cell door. I won't have them entering my cell without me knowing it. I sit down on my makeshift bed with my back to the wall and stuff the pieces of wood under the mattress. Silence fills the cell as I lean my head back against the wall and close my eyes.

Images of Enzo, Matteo, and Dante walking into their house flash in my mind and I open my eyes, stopping the memory before I'm forced to watch them die. A tear rolls down my cheek and I quickly wipe it away. My whole body aches from the loss of them but I can't let it overtake me. Not here, at least. Pushing them to the back of my mind, I focus on my hate and how I'm going to get my revenge for them. The princess is no more, but the monster has come out to stay.

Chapter Three

Riona

Not being able to let myself fall asleep, I only rest my eyes while listening out for any signs that someone is coming. After a long while of only hearing silence, the sound of a door opening and footsteps echo loudly down the hall. My body stiffens, ready for anything, as the two sets of footsteps stomp toward me. Keeping my eyes closed, I tilt my head toward the cell door, listening as the footsteps stop in front of my cell. "Damn, she tore apart everything."

The sound of metal sliding across concrete and the smell of breakfast tells me they've brought me food. "Hurry up, man. I want to get away from her. Did you hear how she took out three guys at that meetup?"

"Yeah, but they took her down." I wrap my hand around the piece of wood I hide underneath my thigh. I'm about to kill two more.

I open my eyes, taking in the two lower level Sixes who are more concerned about their conversation than watching me. One is a meathead, all muscles and no brains. The other is a young guy with a slim build. He has every right to fear me. "It took five men..." The young one notices me looking at them and he chokes on his words.

A smile pulls across my face as I look at the meathead. "You should've listened to your friend." In one swift move, I throw the side table leg right at him, like it's a spear, and it impales him in the throat. He falls to his knees right in front of my cell as his hands wrap around the table leg like it'll stop his death. With a thin piece of the table top in my hand, I rush toward the cell door and grab the young one's shirt before he can react. With the sharp end, I repeatedly stab him in the stomach until he falls to his knees as well. I leave the piece of wood embedded in his stomach as he falls out on the floor with a shocked expression as he takes his last breath.

Looking back at the meathead, I move the turned over bed frame out of the way and crouch down in front of him. He's still on his knees, gurgling blood as the leg holds him up on the door. I smile as his panicked eyes connect with mine and he tries to say something, but it just comes out as a gurgle.

"Shh… don't speak." I wrap my hand around the table leg while the other goes to his shoulder. "I'll make this quick." I pull the leg out of his throat and immediately jab it into his stomach. I stab him over and over until I feel my exhaustion set in and then I give his shoulder a little shove. His dead body falls back on the ground next to his friend's and I step back, grabbing the tray of food. By some miracle, blood isn't covering the eggs and bacon but it's definitely covering my dirty pajamas and me. Setting the tray on my torn up bed, I go to the sink and wash their blood down the drain like it never happened.

Except it definitely did happen and I bask in that as I eat, facing their bodies, wondering how long it will take for Maxim to notice his guys haven't returned. Surprisingly, it only takes until I finish my breakfast before I hear more footsteps walking down the hall. "John, Nick, what's taking you so..." His question stops as soon as he sees the bodies and curses in disbelief.

Sticking my hand under the mattress, I grab another table leg, ready to attack again. With the leg in hand, I move so my back is to the wall he can't see. "Nick... John?" The third guy comes into view as he looks down at the bodies and I grip the leg tighter. When he looks up into the cell, our eyes lock and I see his terror as I move, plunging the leg into his neck. I pull the leg out and his blood sprays across my face as I chuckle with wicked glee. Not wanting to exhaust myself, I step back and watch him slowly collapse on the floor.

I walk backward all the way until my back hits the far wall, as multiple people run down the hall. Five men surround the dead bodies and the front of my cell with their guns trained on me, but I know they won't shoot. I crack up laughing, mimicking them as I raise the table leg covered in blood, pointing it at them as I slide down the wall. Fear takes over their faces and I know I look deranged, covered in blood with an evil smile on my face and a laugh of pure happiness.

With hesitant glances, the Sixes lower their guns and start collecting the dead bodies, but two of them keep their eyes on me as the other three drag the bodies away. As the last body is thrown over a guy's shoulder, I stand slowly, watching the last two men. Their bodies lock up as they fully face me with stern faces and I know they're trying to not show their fear. But I want to see their fear. Pushing off the wall, I run at them, screaming, and they both jump back and scurry down the hallway. The door slams at the top of the stairs and I can't help my satisfied smile as I step back to my bed and lay out on it. They'll be back down soon, for the next meal, so I need to rest up. Let's see how many I can kill before the day is over.

Chapter Four

Riona

I guess my punishment for killing three men is no food. I'm not sure how long I slept but it couldn't have been more than a few hours and I've definitely been up for a while. It's my stomach that is really telling me I've missed a meal. It's been growling for what has to be a couple of hours. Not only am I hungry, but I'm bored and as I sit here, I feel my rage decreasing and I can't have that. I need to find a way to entertain myself.

A wicked smile comes across my face as my eyes connect with the blood of the Sixes that had stopped spreading into my cell hours ago. That'll do. It's always fun expressing yourself through art.

I crawl over to the front of my cell and run two fingers through the thickened blood. Perfect consistency. I look at the empty walls, thinking they could use a little decorating. Bloody paintings of the different ways I could kill Maxim. Now, these aren't going to be pretty but I can draw some pretty good stick figures and weapons.

Let's see which killing I should draw first. Easiest to bloodiest, I think. I drag my blood covered fingertips across the bumpy concrete wall right by the cell door, drawing two heads, two bodies, four arms, and four legs. With my stick figures facing each other, I draw a line running from one figure's hands up to a point and down to the other where I draw a circle around the other figure's neck, completing the hangman image. Just so it's clear who's who, I draw long hair on the figure holding the rope and make a tiny little line, barely noticeable, in between the hanging figure's legs. I can't leave out his pencil dick.

I take a step back, admiring my work with a joyous smile. Oh yes, this was a good idea. It really brightens up the place. Gathering up some more blood, I look around at the empty walls. Where should I draw next?

Staring at the back wall, I know what's going there. The main masterpiece. My bloodiest vision. But that will be last. Turning to the wall opposite my other drawing, right next to the cell bars, I draw two stick figures. Me holding a gun to the head of a kneeling Maxim.

I draw every possible way for me to kill Maxim, scattering two walls with ten drawings. The back wall though only has one.

One stick figure. Maxim is written over top of the figure that has its arms and legs stretched out in a spread eagle, held by ropes.

But I'm not done yet. I scoop blood onto my fingers and drag them along the arms I drew, signifying blood pouring from his slit wrists. Next I draw my mark across the center of his body so even in death he will always know I killed him, I'm better than him, I'll never be his. Let's see what's next. Oh I know. Pencil dick will be no dick. I draw hedge clippers where the blades surround his little dick.

His fingers are next. Each one being cut off by the hedge clippers. Now if this was really Maxim, he'd already be close to death from blood loss and has probably passed out, so I would inject him with adrenaline so he'd be awake for the last part: removing his eyes. I mark an X over each eye since I can't draw empty eye sockets.

I step back to the middle of my cell and look at the massive drawing. Now I just need Maxim here so I can tell him how I'd cut up his dead body and scatter it all along the Hudson. But I won't call out for him. The blood needs to dry and I know he'll eventually come.

Washing the blood from my hands, I hum to myself no particular tune as I think about Maxim's reaction to the ways I'm going to kill him. I want him to cower in the corner and cry, but I know it'll just piss the entitled prick off. He'll have a hissy fit and hopefully come for me. That's when I'll kill him.

Chapter Five

Riona

It's official. I'm bored out of my mind. No one has been down to see me in what I think has been days, which also means I haven't eaten in days either. I need out of this cell so I can release some of this murderous energy. For the first time since I woke up here, I head over to the cell door and slide my arms through the bars. Blindly I run my fingers over the lock to see what I'm working with. My fingers run over a keyhole and I'm a little disappointed it's not an electric lock. That would've been easier to crack. I'd just have to bust open the lock face and rework the wires.

Pulling my arms back through the bars, I turn and eye the bent bed frame. Specifically, the metal netting that the mattress is supposed to sit on. I know how to pick a lock, but my problem is how I'm going to make the tools I need without any wire cutters. It's not going to be easy to break the wires with only my hands.

Turning the bent bed frame onto its legs, I climb on it trying to use my body weight to find a weak spot. The only problem is it feels like the wires are cutting into my bare feet. After only taking a few steps down one side, I can't take the feeling anymore and jump off. The impact of my feet hitting the concrete doesn't help the pain and I wince as I fall back onto my mattress. Lifting my foot up, I'm happy to see it's red with irritation and not a drop of blood is found. The last thing I need is to get an infection down here.

Leaning my head back against the wall, I let out a long sigh as I stare at the bed frame. Walking on the wires isn't going to work, so I'll have to break them by force. I need something strong and solid. A good size chunk of concrete would be nice right about now but of course there isn't one. These walls are solid as if they were just built. No cracks. No rubble. I'm going to have to just use what I have.

Reaching underneath my mattress, I grab a flat piece of wood from the table top. It's not a solid piece of wood since it was a cheap side table, but hopefully it'll be strong enough. Grabbing on to each end so the long flat side is at the bottom, I raise it over my head, while on my knees, and with all my power I bring it down on the edge of the bed frame where the netting isn't as tight. As the wood connects to the wires, it disintegrates in my hands, falling to pieces. The wires were like a saw cutting through the wood without any issue. "Fuck." I throw the tiny pieces of wood that are still in my hands against the wall and they join the scraps on the floor.

What else could I use? I look around my small cell, trying to think of something when my eyes connect with the two metal food trays that I stashed in the corner under the sink. I crawl across my bed and grab one of them. With the tray in hand, I weigh and test its sturdiness. This definitely won't break so easily. Once again, I get up onto my knees and raise my hands above my head but right as I'm about to bring it down the sound of footsteps stops me. Falling back on the bed, I prop my feet up on the frame, and start twirling the tray on the ground.

Making sure my face is neutral, I focus on the wall across from me, like I don't give two shits who's coming down here. I only look away from the wall when the person has been standing outside my cell for a few seconds. The Bratva Six stands tall outside my cell, holding a bowl of something, while looking all over the cell walls at my drawings, and a smile spreads across my face. "Do you like my drawings? I think I really captured Maxim and all his smallness. Don't you think?"

The Six doesn't look happy when he tears his blue eyes off the walls and looks at me. "He's not going to like this."

I shrug my shoulders because that doesn't scare me at all. What I care about is what's in his hands. I nod toward the bowl. "Is that for me?"

"Yes. It's oatmeal." Without looking away from me, he bends down and pushes the bowl into my cell. When he stands back up, he doesn't say another word as he heads back up the hallway.

Wanting the last word, I call out after him. "Next time you come, I'd like a washcloth and new clothes. These are kind of covered in blood." All I hear is an irritated grunt along with his faded footsteps. I don't move from my spot until I know I'm alone, but once I am, I quickly crawl over to the bowl of oatmeal and bring it back over to my bed. Not caring how it tastes, I start shoveling it into my mouth with the spoon.

To my disappointment, the food is gone before my stomach is full and I lick the bowl clean. I let my body relax and my hands drop to my lap with the bowl cradled in between them. The bowl wiggles in my hands and I look down at it, fighting back a laugh. They gave me a rubber bowl. I guess they don't want to give me any more weapons.

I throw it against the wall across from me and to my delight it bounces back to me. Oh, this could be entertaining. I throw it a couple more times before I set it to the side and grab the tray. With food in my system, my body aches a little bit less and my energy level is up. Moving from my bed, I move over to the end of the frame again and wait, listening for any sounds coming down the hall.

When all I hear is silence, I bring the tray up over my head and down on the edge of the frame as hard as I can. I want to scream out as the tray hits the wires, but I bite down on my lip instead. I don't want to draw attention to myself. Well, attention from my screams, because the frame sure makes a lot of noise as the side opposite of me lifts off the floor and slams back down. I wince at the sound and freeze, hoping it won't bring anyone down here.

Looking down at the frame, I see a decent size bend in the wires, and I feel hopeful for the first time. It might take a few times, but I think this could actually work. Actually seeing a way to escape, I bring the tray down on the same spot three more consecutive times. The third time, the tray breaks through three of the wires and I jump up in excitement, but the sound of heavy footsteps has my body going rigid.

Quickly, I set the tray on top of the hole I made as I casually start walking back and forth in my cell. I reach the back of my cell and turn, coming face to face with Maxim, in his tailored suit, looking all business, but not being able to pull off the ruthless dictator vibe his father holds. He looks furious as he takes in the mess I've made. His face is beet red and I swear he has smoke coming out of his ears.

"Hi Maxim! Would you like a tour of my cell? I decided to decorate the walls with all the ways I could kill you." I walk over to my first drawing and point to the tiny dick. "I even drew some parts to scale." I look down at his crotch and look back up, bringing my hand up measuring an inch with my fingers.

Maxim is vibrating with rage. "You ungrateful bitch."

"There is no need for name calling. I didn't call you pencil dick. Plus, I still need to show you my masterpiece." I move sideways and look back to the back wall. "This is how I'm going to slowly kill you." Maxim pulls a key out of his pocket and for the first time I see the cell door slide open. I take a step toward it ready to fight for my escape, but he sees me, pulls his gun out of the back of his pants, and aims it right for my head.

"I tried to make your stay down here comfortable, civilized, as I finished up some business that required me to be away. You thank me by killing my men, destroying your furniture, and drawing these grotesque pictures of me. Wishing death on your husband isn't very nice."

"Nice... Really?" I chuckle but it's cut off by Maxim slamming me against the wall and his hand going around my throat, while his other holds the gun at my temple.

"I was hoping you'd come to your senses on marrying me, but I guess I'm going to have to beat you into submission." Before I can even think about blocking a hit, Maxim hits me on the side of the head with the butt of the gun. I fall sideways, right into the sink, hitting my head again as I crumble to the ground.

Maxim yells out. "Someone, get down here and remove everything from this cell." I look up at Maxim and he smiles down at me. "You want to be a prisoner, then you will be." Footsteps fill the hallway, and I can feel other people entering the cell, but I can't see anything as my vision goes black. All I feel is pain.

Chapter Six

Riona

Fuck. My whole body hurts. What did Maxim do to me? I try
to roll over, but my head screams and the ringing in my ears
intensifies so I curl in on myself, cradling my head in my arms. I
groan out as pain pulses through my upper body and my chest aches
with every breath I take. I lay like this until my body turns numb and
then I let myself drift off, hoping sleep will help with the pain.

I'm not sure how long I've been asleep but it's long enough
that I can feel my muscles screaming from staying in one position
for too long. Fighting through the shooting pain in my head, chest
and my stomach, I stretch out my arms and legs as I roll onto my

back. I bite down on my bottom lip so hard I taste blood to keep myself from screaming, but it doesn't stop the tears.

Finding the strength, I bring my arms back down and rest them at my sides as I let out a struggled breath. Opening my eyes, one at a time, I'm happy to see that the lights aren't on but the hallway light casts a nice glow, allowing me to see my cell isn't the same as it was before I passed out. Everything is gone. I'm lying on the cement floor, looking up at the bare walls. Well, not completely bare. The walls are still tinted red from them scrubbing away my drawings.

Movement out the corner of my eye has me quickly looking at the cell door, and I wince at my pounding headache. My vision is a little blurry, but I recognize the guy as the one who brought me oatmeal. "About time you woke up. You've been out for at least a day."

I really take the time to look him over, actually noticing his nice suit that hugs him perfectly, showing off his muscular body and his brown hair swept back into a bun. He isn't just some low level Six. "And you've been standing there the whole time watching me like a creep." I slowly push myself up so I'm leaning back on my hands.

He's looking down at his phone as he types something. "No. Not just me. Since you can't be left alone without pissing off Maxim, you'll now have someone watching you constantly."

"Oh, did he not like my drawings?" I pout at him.

"You need to watch yourself. That mouth of yours is going to get you killed." He looks up at me, giving me a cautious look. Not him being cautious of me, but for me.

"He can't kill me."

"You're stupid if you believe that. Your marriage is preferable, but they'll kill you if you don't step in line." His phone goes back into his pocket, and he crosses his arms as he leans against the wall, facing me.

Sitting up, I slowly move so I can lean against the wall. "Then he might as well kill me now. I'll never accept this marriage. I'll fight it every step of the way."

"I hope you have a lot of fight, because he's going to try to break you. He's not going to give up so easily."

I look at him confused. It sounds like he wants me to fight and not give in to Maxim. Before I can ask, I hear footsteps down the hall, and a few seconds later another man appears with a paper plate and cup. He hands it to the man I've been talking to and then leaves.

When we're alone again, he steps up to the bars and brings his arms through, holding the plate and cup in each hand. I stare at him, shocked that he's actually handing me my food. I know I'm hurt but I could kill him if I wanted, without causing further injury to myself. Cautiously I stand from the floor and slowly walk to him, watching for any move he might make.

If he's going to put himself in a situation for me to get to him, I'm going to take it. Standing in front of him, I reach out slowly with my hands open, waiting for him to do something. He stands completely still, watching me, like he's waiting for me to try something. My fingers touch the back of his hand and I'm about to strike when he says something that makes me pause. "Kiera says hi."

A large smile forms on my face as I let out a chuckle. Kiera is Maxim's sister and one of my best friends, but no one knows it. Even though my father has sold my hand in marriage to the Bratva, we aren't allies, so my friendship with Kiera isn't allowed. But that has never stopped us. Once we met in high school, we bonded. At school, we were friends but when we went home on breaks, we were enemies, relaying false information to our fathers.

"Tell that bitch I said hi." I take the plate and cup from him and move back a few steps so I'm standing in the middle of my cell.

The guy chuckles. "I'm sure she'll like me repeating that."

I take a seat on the ground, and he steps back to lean against the wall again. "So you're just keeping her updated about me?"

He nods. "She knows Maxim's days are numbered and she's getting things in line. I'm here to make sure he doesn't take it too far."

"And yesterday wasn't too far?" I wave my hand down my body.

"He was stopped before he made permanent damage. You can take a hit, can't you?" He gives me a look that says he knows I can.

I shrug my shoulders as I take a bite of my sandwich. I can take a hit, but the head damage is what I'm worried about. I can't take much more of it, but I don't voice that. Instead, I focus my attention on the sandwich and not scarfing it down. I take slow bites and look back up at the guy. "What is your name?"

"Xavier."

"Why are you, Team Kiera?" Maxim and Kiera are twins and while Kiera is older, her father only sees Maxim as his heir. In our world, women don't lead, even though we can easily rally men to fight and work. Our world is so wrong. Kiera, Aisling, and I have always had a plan to rule though. Kiera was going to take over her family. Aisling and Killian are partners, so her power was never questioned. Me, I was up in the air, at least until I met them. With them, we all could have the city. Now, I'm going to tear the city apart to get my revenge. But one thing is definite. Aisling, Kiera, and I will make it out on top.

"He's an idiot and a coward. He'll lead us into the ground."

"And?" That's not enough to believe he's a part of Kiera's force. Everyone knows Maxim would never be able to lead this organization.

"She's been fighting for this. She knows what it takes. Even under her dad's nose and her barely being around, she has his men ready to overthrow them. All she has to do is say the word."

"I know all those things, but why do you choose her?"

"I've always followed her, ever since we were kids. Why stop now?" There's a softness in his eyes that I recognize. He loves her. Interesting. Does she know?

Not wanting to get into girl talk while I'm locked in a cell, I change the subject. "Does Maxim know?"

He shakes his head no. "He thinks the respect the men have for his father is just going to roll to him. That he doesn't have to work for it."

"Respect is earned."

"Yes, it is." He stares at me for a second and then nods. Do I have his respect? How did I earn it?

We're both silent as I finish my food and drink my water. When I'm done, Xavier's phone dings, and he pulls it out. I watch him closely, trying to read him to see who texted him. If he's connected to Kiera like he says, do Killian and Aisling know that I'm here?

There's no way they know where I am and are staying away. No way they know about the marriage without breaking down the door to stop it.

Why wouldn't Kiera tell Aisling if she knew where I was? Xavier pulls me from my doubt as he pushes off the wall. "My shift is done. Got other orders to follow. See you around, Killer." He heads down the hall as I sit there shocked. Killer was my nickname Kiera gave me in high school. She was the Chemist and Aisling was the Law.

Is it just a coincidence or could he read my doubt and gave me another thing so I believe him? I watch him walk down the hall as far as I can and listen to his footsteps until there's silence. The silence only lasts for a few seconds before another set sounds, heading in this direction. I guess Xavier was telling the truth about something. I'm not going to be left alone anymore.

Chapter Seven

Riona

It's been three or four days since I woke up from Maxim's beating. At least, that's how long I think it's been, based on the meals and shift rotations. And I'm losing my mind in boredom. I've walked every inch of my cell a thousand times now. When I'm not walking or sleeping, I'm also trying to stay somewhat in shape by doing exercises like crunches, sit-ups, planks, and push-ups. But it's weird being watched 24/7, doing everything. The only time I get some privacy is when they're changing shifts. It gives me five minutes of alone time to go to the bathroom.

Right now, the guard I hate the most stands outside my cell. He's the only one that doesn't keep his mouth shut, and all he spews is rude and nasty comments, which only builds my anger up. But what drives me crazy about him is that he chews gum. He chomps at it and when I don't hear his smacking, he's popping it. Every time it pops, I feel myself winding up tighter and tighter and I'm so ready to explode.

I walk across the front of the cell, next to the metal bars, and he pops his gum. I stretch out my arms above my head to hide the irritated tick that courses through me as I turn down the side wall and head to the back. With each turn I make, he pops his gum and I grind my teeth. I know he's doing it on purpose because as I look at him, he gives me a knowing smile as he pops the gum again. "Am I annoying you?"

"Actually, yes." I stop in front of him, only a foot from the bars. "Just your very existence annoys me."

He growls in irritation. "It annoys me that I have to stand here and watch you. I don't see what Maxim sees in you. You're just a used-up whore. You let Italian scum tarnish you. You will never be my queen."

I chuckle. "You're right. I'll never be your queen. Maxim isn't worthy to stand next to me. He is a tiny ant in this world, and I'll happily squish him before they even try to drag me down an aisle."

"You don't get to act like you're above Maxim." He charges at me, grabbing me by my shirt, pulling me up against the bars. Oh, he just made a mistake. "You'd be lucky to be married to Maxim and to be a part of this organization."

"So do you want me to be your queen or not?" I give him a cocky smile.

He grabs hold of my throat and squeezes. "Maybe I'll just kill you and save Maxim from a mistake."

With strain on my vocal cords, I spit out, "Or I'll kill you."

I grab hold of his wrist on the hand around my throat and twist it backward. He lets out a deep scream as he tries to bend backward to alleviate the pain. I wrap my other hand around the back of his neck and pull his head toward me, slamming it into a bar.

A loud ding rings out from his head connecting with the bar and he goes limp, but he's not out, just dazed. Letting go of his wrist, I grab the back of his neck with both hands and bang his head against the bar over and over again until he's knocked out.

God, I wish I had those broken table pieces right now. It'd be fun to gut him. I guess death by head injury will have to do.

With all my annoyed and frustrated energy, I let out a roar as I repeatedly slam his head into the crossbar. I don't stop until my throat is sore and my body is shaking from exhaustion. My arms are sore as I hold him up by his head and look at the damage I caused. Blood is everywhere, pouring from his caved in forehead, flattened nose, and busted up mouth. A smile comes across my face as I chuckle. I really fucked up his face, but I'm not done yet.

I lower his body down to the ground and kneel next to his head. Gripping the sides of his face, I lift his head and slam it back down a couple of times, cracking the back of his skull as well. Letting go of his head, it drops one last time and I fall back on my ass with a satisfied smile. He might not be dead yet but he's not waking up ever again and it feels good to release some of my anger. To physically beat someone to death has me feeling renewed and recharged.

Silence surrounds me and I hum at the peace of not having to listen to his annoying popping. Speaking of, where is his gum? Pulling his body closer to the bars, I pat down his body, checking every pocket. In his back right pocket, I find his wallet and the gum, and his left pocket has his phone. Bingo. As much as I want to get out of here by myself, I know I'm not going to without some help.

Sitting down next to the guy, I pull out a piece of gum and pop it into my mouth as I open his wallet. Hello Vlad. I look at him. "It wasn't a pleasure to meet you."

Throwing his wallet on his chest, I power on his phone and wait. It lights up on the home screen which is a picture of a naked woman. I look at the picture and shrug my shoulders. She's hot. Hopefully she's a model and not dating this asshole because he's not coming home tonight.

I press the home button, hoping I'm lucky enough for it to just open. Well apparently, I haven't endured enough, because the phone is locked and based on the phone model it's passcode only. Fucking hell. This phone is like ten years old. How's it even working, staying charged? Bratva are cheap asses if they can't give their men updated phones. I tilt the phone toward the little light above me, hoping to see his finger prints on the glass to know what numbers to push, but the screen is smeared, probably from him pushing it in his pocket.

I wish I had some of my tech with me because I could crack this passcode easily. Maybe I can guess it? Let's go with the most common.

1-2-3-4. Nope.

5-5-5-5. Nope

0-0-0-0. Nope.

2-5-8-0. Nope.

1-1-1-1. Nope.

Fuck, I'm locked out.

A countdown for a minute shows on the screen. Okay, I need to put a little bit more thought into his passcode. I reach through the bar for his wallet and pull it completely apart. Other than his driver's license, all he has in his wallet are three credit cards, a CVS card, and $20. When the countdown ends, I enter in his birth month and day.

0-4-1-7. Nope.

A five-minute countdown shows on the screen. I lean my head back against the wall and let out a long sigh. Next, I'm going to try his birth year. I flatten the gum in my mouth against my tongue and move it to the tip, blowing a bubble. I chuckle when it pops and a wicked smile comes across my face as I look at Vlad. I've got time to kill so I might as well have some fun. I roll my gum into a ball and spit it out into my hand. Reaching through the bar, I push the piece of gum into one of his nostrils. I chuckle to myself as I sit back and put another piece in my mouth. Once again, when the gum is soft, I roll it into a ball and stuff it up his other nostril.

The phone lights up as I sit back, indicating my five minutes are up.

1-9-8-2. Nope.

Thirty minutes start counting down. Just enough time for what I'm going to do next. I crawl over to my pile of trash from all my paper cups and plates my food has been served on. I grab two of the cups and a plate and slide back over to the cell door. Grabbing two pieces of gum, I pop them into my mouth and start chewing. As I chew the gum, I tear pieces of the plate off and roll them into balls. With half the gum I stick it to the bottom side of one of the cups and then press the cup to his smashed in forehead. Pulling my hand away slowly, I smile when it stays.

Oh, this is going to be fun!

I push his chin down, opening his mouth and placing the last cup into it. With the last of the gum in my mouth I use it as tape holding the cup in place with his upper lip.

Let the games begin!

Scooting back so I'm sitting in the middle of the cell, I cross my legs and grab a handful of the paper balls. "Alright Vlad. I'm going to play a little game. In your honor, I'll call this game Ball in Vlad." I chuckle to myself as I take my first shot, aiming for his mouth.

My shot falls short, not even leaving the cell and I pout. The paper balls are too light. I tear off a bigger piece, roll it up, and pop it into my mouth. Maybe if it's wet, it'll weigh enough.

My second shot reaches Vlad, but it hits his nose and bounces past him. Perfect. I throw a couple more pieces, alternating between his forehead and his mouth. I miss a few but I get one in each. Thinking the thirty minutes are probably about up, I reach for his phone. Five seconds is all that's left. Wow, great timing.

Trying his apartment number. 1-2-0-1. Nope.

One hour. Fuck. I'm running out of options and eventually someone is going to come down to change shifts.

I throw a few more balls at Vlad, sinking them into the cups I aim for. "Okay, let's make this interesting." I stand from my spot. "You stay there. I'm going to do some trick shots."

Yes, I know I'm talking to a dead body but I'm bored and he's much more likable like this. Acting like I'm dribbling a basketball, I shift from side to side. Doing a spin, I jump and shoot the tiny ball, aiming just for his face. My shot ends up hitting the bar, but it's actually a good thing because it rebounds and falls into the cup on his forehead. "Oh my God! Yes!" I jump up and down in victory. "I can't believe that actually worked."

Can I make any more crazy shots? I turn my back to the cell bars and throw a paper ball backwards. The ball goes way right and I chuckle. "That's not the magic shot."

With my back still to the cell door, I bend forward and throw between my legs. That shot misses too, going way past him but I don't care. This is the most fun I've had since my drawings.

Turning back toward the cell door, I take a step back and hold a paper ball in between my hands like it's a baseball. I wind my pitch back, bringing my knee up to my chest, and then throw my body into it. I act like I'm going to throw a 90 mph pitch but at the last second, I ease the throw, only lightly tossing it. The ball goes into the cup in his mouth. "Woohoo! Home run!"

I do a celebratory dance, laughing at myself. Maybe I'm going a little crazy. My dance turns into me just spinning around in circles, laughing. I don't stop spinning until I'm too dizzy to stand. Bracing myself against the wall, I try to right myself between taking deep breaths and chuckling.

When everything stops spinning and I've caught my breath, I look over to Vlad to tell him he's funnier than I thought but the words never leave my mouth as I find a man standing over Vlad's body. "Oh shit." I jump back slightly and stand straighter. "When did you get here?"

"During the twirling." He looks down at Vlad and shakes his head. "I hope you're prepared for what's to come." He bends down and places a cup and plate on the ground. He steps back as I step forward to grab the sandwich and water. I sit down in the middle of the cell and drink the water in one go. Killing Vlad and playing my game really made me thirsty. Footsteps sound down the hall as I place the cup down and pick up my sandwich. I pout as I bite into my sandwich as the guy grabs Vlad's shirt at his shoulders and starts pulling him away. Why is he taking away my fun?

"Is he dead?" The sound of Maxim's voice puts a bitter taste in my mouth, and I glare at the front of my cell where I know he'll appear any second.

"Not quite." Maxim appears, looking down at Vlad with disgust.

"Finish him off and burn his body." Maxim's eyes connect with mine and his lip curls in irritation. "You just can't behave."

I shrug my shoulders because I couldn't care less about behaving. "His gum popping really got on my nerves."

"How you feel doesn't matter."

I roll my eyes. "Why are you down here ruining my fun? Did you miss me?"

"Oh Riona. I'm here to play now. You've had your fun with my men. Now it's time for me to have my fun with you." A wicked smile pulls across his face.

"Oh please, come in here. We can see who's playing with who." I bring my feet under me to stand, but my legs give out and I fall back to the floor. What the fuck? I try to stand again but I can barely get them underneath me. "What the fuck did you do?" I look up at Maxim and he's blurry.

"It's just a small sedative." Maxim walks into my cell and squats next to me. I try to push him away, but I can't get anything to move as I lay on my side. "My fun is in a different room. Since you're not cooperative, this is the only way."

"I fucking hate youuu." My speech starts to slur.

"Go to sleep, fiancée." He pushes my hair from my face as my eyes get too heavy to stay open and I wish I could swat his hand away. His touch makes me sick. Everything goes black at the disgusting feeling of Maxim running his fingers through my dirty hair.

Chapter Eight

Riona

I wake with a start as I gasp for air, but I can't breathe.
Liquid fills my lungs and I choke on it as I flail around trying to
break to the surface. My hands hit something on either side of me
and I slide my hands along it until I find an edge. I try to pull myself
to the surface but something on my throat is holding me down. The
hold tightens around my throat and my eyes shoot open in panic as I
realize it's someone holding me down. I grip the arm of whoever is
holding me down and dig my nails in. I'm yanked out of the water,
and I instantly gasp for air, but I choke again.

Leaning over the side of what I now realize is a tub, I cough up the water I swallowed until I'm able to pull in a full breath. A chuckle has me whipping my head to the side where I find Maxim standing over me. I glare up at him as I grip the edge of the bathtub until my knuckles turn white. "Glad you're finally awake." Maxim walks away from me and for the first time, I notice the large white bathroom I'm in. The bathtub is along the back wall and on either side of me is a shower and a two-sink vanity. "Time for you to clean yourself up. You smell and I can't have you dirty for what I have planned." He opens the bathroom door and a small woman that looks my age with blonde hair walks in dressed in a maid's uniform. "This is Cassandra. She's your maid from now on. Cassandra, I want her showered and shaven within an hour." Maxim turns to me. "You won't give her any problems or I'll make your life a living hell."

"I'm already in hell. I have to look at your face."

Maxim walks over to me, grabs me by my hair and pulls me to my feet. As the cool air hits my body, I realize for the first time that I'm naked. Maxim's eyes scan over my exposed skin. "I can't wait to break you."

I ball my hand into a fist and throw a punch at his face but he catches it before he pushes me back and I slip, having to catch myself on the wall.

"Don't cause any problems, Riona, or it will be Cassandra who's punished." Before I can tell him I don't give a shit about his maid, he's out of the bathroom and I hear a lock engage. Great. Just another cell. Movement to my left has me looking at Cassandra as she turns on the shower with her back to me. I quickly climb out of the tub and grab for the ceramic soap bottle, ready to throw it at her if she comes near me.

Cassandra turns around, facing me, and when she sees me ready to attack, she holds her hands out, showing she means no harm. "Please Miss Riona. I'm not here to hurt you. I'm only following orders."

"I don't give a fuck about your orders. You aren't touching me."

"I promise I won't. Everything you need is in the shower. Please don't hurt me. I have a little girl."

My shoulders relax a little because she doesn't seem to be a threat. Cassandra backs away until her back is on the wall next to the door. I'm torn because the shower looks so nice and warm, but I need to try to escape. I look at the door next to her and she slowly reaches for the handle and shows it's locked. "They won't let us out until the hour is up."

I look at her, confused, because she almost sounds trapped as well. My want to shower ends up outweighing my need to find a way out but I make sure to not turn my back to her. The second the warm water hits my skin, I let out a moan and submerge myself under the spray. It's probably been about weeks since I've showered and I can't wait to get the dirt and grime off of me.

Not caring what bottle I grab, I squeeze the liquid into my hands and rub it all over my body, lathering myself. The scent of coconut fills the air as the dirty suds wash down the drain, but one wash isn't enough. I grab the bottle again and realize I washed my body with shampoo. Well, it's better than nothing.

Actually taking a second to look at everything in the shower, I find everything I could need. High end shampoo and conditioner, hair mask, body wash, body scrub, shaving cream, razor, and loofah. Oh, I'm going to use every bit of this. I hope their hot water doesn't run out.

I grab for the body scrub but movement at the corner of my eye catches my attention and I grab for the razor instead. Cassandra holds out her hands in mid-squat as she leans against the door. Fuck. I actually forgot about her.

"Sorry. I'm just sitting down." We watch each other as she slowly slides down the door and then sits cross-legged, while leaning against it. "Take your time. No one is getting in here without you knowing. I promise."

"Why do you care?"

"Because it looks like you need someone in your corner, someone to trust."

"I don't trust you."

"Not yet." She gives me a small smile before closing her eyes and leaning her head against the door. Just because she trusts me not to slit her throat while her eyes are closed doesn't mean I'm going to trust her. It's stupid to trust hired help. Their loyalty is bought, but right now, she's not a threat. Setting the razor down, I grab the body scrub and scoop a hefty amount into my hand.

I take my time scrubbing my body until I feel like a new woman. It's relaxing, feeling the tiny sugar crystals running down my body as the water washes them away.

I focus on my hair next, looking over at Cassandra every now and then, making sure she hasn't moved. She never does. She only opens her eyes when I finally step out of the shower. Grabbing a towel, we watch each other as I dry off. I slightly respect her for being just as wary of me as I am of her. "Lotion, brushes, and a hair dryer should be in the drawers." She points to the vanity.

I wrap the towel around my body and start searching the cabinets. Once again, anything I could possibly need is in these cabinets. Pulling out the lotion, I cover my body in it, loving the fresh clean smell with coconut.

I'm starting to feel like myself again and I can't wait to show Maxim who I really am. He'll regret removing the metal bars between us. I can't help my smirk as I brush my hair out and catch a glimpse of metal at the end of my towel at my chest. I adjust my towel, pushing the razor blade down a tiny bit because I don't want Cassandra to see it.

My eyes catch with hers in the mirror and she just smirks and shakes her head. I don't know if she saw it or not, but she doesn't say anything. I plug in the hair dryer and as I'm about to turn it on, I hear the door unlock. Cassandra hears it too and quickly jumps up from the floor and presses her back against the wall. The door opens and Maxim walks in, ignoring Cassandra and glares at me. "Time's up."

"Fuck off. You're ruining my time. I still need to dry my hair." I rotate the hair dryer in my hand.

"I don't give a fuck if your hair is wet or not. Lose the towel and come out." He looks me up and down with a disgusting smile. "You won't be needing it."

He grabs Cassandra by the arm and pulls her out of the room. Setting the hairdryer down, I tighten the towel around myself because there is no way in hell I'm walking out there naked. I slip the blade from my towel and place it between my pointer and middle fingers. Stepping out of the bathroom, I find a massive bedroom with a huge bed against the far wall and there are doors on each side of it. But the bed is what has my attention. The metal canopy over it has four loose chains hanging off each post with a cuff attached to each chain. Four cuffs to hold someone. Making them completely vulnerable. Maxim steps into view. "I told you to lose the towel."

I glare at him. "I told you to fuck off."

Maxim backhands me across the face and I shift the blade in my fingers, ready to attack but a whimper beside me has me stopping. Cassandra is standing there with two men behind her and one of them has his hand moving up her thigh and under her dress while the other one holds her. The look of pure terror tells me that his touch isn't wanted. Maybe I can kill him before Maxim can stop me. Maxim grabs my arm and I pull it away, glaring at him. "Don't touch me."

"No... No." Cassandra tries to get away from the man who has now lifted her skirt up and has his hands in her panties.

"Lose the towel and get on the bed or you're going to watch my men rape Cassandra here. They've been waiting to get their hands on her for a while." Maxim steps into my space and chuckles as he looks at what his men are doing to her.

Cassandra stills as tears form in her eyes and the asshole just smiles as he grinds himself against her, whispering God knows what. Based on how her body is shivering in terror, I bet it's not things she wants to hear.

I'm torn between fighting and complying. I want to tear that guy's arm off for touching her, but what if this is all an act? I don't know or trust this girl. Could this all be a ploy to tie me down? I'm not going to be chained down willingly.

"You're not going to save poor Cassandra. I thought rape was a no-no for you. You've killed several men because of it." I look at Maxim. How does he know that? "Your father told us about your extracurricular activities. It's too bad Cassandra doesn't fit your bill. It's a good thing I have someone who will make you comply."

The bedroom door opens and a naked three-year-old girl walks in with a creepy old man and Cassandra goes crazy. "Nooo... Cami... Nooo... Run." She lunges forward trying to get the little girl, but the creepy man picks her up and runs a hand down the little girl's front. Terror washes over me for this little girl, who's so innocent.

The two guys shove Cassandra up against the wall and the guy that had his hands in her panties earlier rips them and shoves his fingers inside her. The little girl screams for her mom as Cassandra screams, fighting the guys holding her.

Their screams have my heart breaking and I find myself taking a step toward the bed. I can't stand here and listen to them "Fine, okay." Everyone freezes at my voice as I look at Maxim. "I'll get on the bed."

I head to the bed slowly as I get myself prepared to be chained up without an escape. At the side of the bed, I look at Maxim. "Stop this. I'll do whatever. Let them go." Maxim has a wicked grin on his face.

"I said lose the towel."

That isn't something I'm willing to do with all these men here. "No. Not with all of them here."

"I don't give a fuck."

"Well, you should. How can you expect these men to respect you if you're willing to allow them to see your wife naked? If you get what you want, I'll be standing next to you when you take over and how can they respect us if they've seen me at my most vulnerable?" If I need to make him feel like we have a future, I will. I know I'm not going to be able to keep this towel on when I'm alone with Maxim, but I can keep it on with an audience. Maxim's face is red with anger at me defying him. "Get on the bed, Riona. Put the cuffs on."

I let out a breath in relief and turn to the bed. Rubbing my hand down my face, I push the blade into my mouth and hold it in between my teeth. I climb onto the bed and sit down in the middle. Grabbing one of the leather cuffs at the bottom of the bed, I look at a crying Cassandra and her cute little girl. I have to do this. I wrap the cuff around my ankle and buckle it. "Make it tight, Riona. I will take out your disobedience on them."

I really want to tell him to shut the fuck up, but I don't. I tighten the cuff with another loop and move to the next ankle. Once both my ankles are cuffed, I buckle each wrist and look at Maxim, silently tell him to let them go. "Ed, give Cami back to the nanny." I cough when he pauses because he knows he needs to say more. "And don't touch her again without my permission." The creep sets the girl down and escorts her out of the room. "Cassandra, go to your room and don't come out until I call for you."

The men let go of a disheveled Cassandra and she pulls down her skirt and quickly moves to the door to the right of the bed. As she passes, she mouths 'thank you' and my heart sinks because I was going to let them hurt her before they brought her daughter in. Once the door closes behind Cassandra, Maxim speaks one word: "Leave." The two men leave the room and when the door closes behind them, I hear a lock sliding into place. Maxim stands at the end of the bed and smiles. "It's just you and me now."

He pulls out a remote and presses a button and the chains attached to my wrist cuffs pull tighter. I'm forced from my sitting position, onto my back and my arms spread into a V above my head. A chill runs through me as I test the restraints and there is no pull. At least I can still move my legs. I slide my feet down the bed just to make sure but that was a mistake because Maxim presses another button and my ankles start pulling apart until I'm spread eagle on the bed.

Maxim climbs onto the bed and crawls in between my legs. "I really liked your idea of keeping the towel on." He's now over me where his face is just above mine. "Now I get to unwrap you myself." He runs his fingers along the edge of my towel over the swells of my breasts. I fight everything not to show fear or pull away from him. I can't show him weakness. He already knows one by threatening Cassandra and her daughter.

He pulls the towel open as he lowers his thin body closer to me. "If I fuck you, will you fall in love with me? That's why you fell for the Italian scum, right? You just need to be taken." I'll never love him.

He slams his lips to mine, but he quickly pulls back with blood running from his lips. I smile up at him, showing the razor blade. "You bitch." He backhands me across the face again, whipping my face to the right and I spit out the blade and blood before looking back at him.

"I'll never love you. You disgust me."

"Well, you don't have a choice." He slams his mouth to mine again and I rip my face away from him. "You can't stop this." His hands roam from my neck down to my breasts. As he gropes my breasts, I fight myself not to just check out. I won't give him that. He won't break me. I won't let another man haunt me. I glare up at him, making sure not to show him fear.

Maxim leans forward and sucks one of my nipples in his mouth as his hands move further south. "Are you wet for me?"

I chuckle. "I'm as dry as the desert."

He pushes two fingers in me and I'm barely able to keep my eyes from closing in pain. He rubs his thumb over my clit, trying to get me to give in, but I'd rather die than find pleasure in his touch. Maxim kisses up my chest to my neck as he unbuckles his pants. "I don't need you wet to fuck you. This way I get to tear you open and feel your pain. Watch you bleed, like it's your first time." Oh this is going to be just like my first time.

He sits up and pushes down his pants revealing his erect penis. I crack up laughing, seeing his penis for the first time. All the rumors are true. He does have a tiny dick.

Maxim lets out a roar as his hand goes around my throat and squeezes. "No one laughs at me." He thrusts into me and I'm thankful for his hold on my throat because it stops my scream from escaping.

While he is small in circumference, the unwanted entrance rips me open. It's like a knife covered in sandpaper tearing into my most sensitive skin. Maxim continues to thrust into me, and it feels like being stabbed over and over again. A tear escapes my eye and I wish my hands weren't bound so I could wipe it away before he noticed, but of course he sees and a proud smile comes across his face.

"Oh, poor Riona. You're not as strong as you think you are." He removes his hand from my throat and sets it next to my head as his thrusts pick up speed.

As soon as I have air in my lungs, I continue laughing. "You think that was from pain. I'm crying from laughing. I can't even tell you're inside me right now. God, I feel sorry for all your other conquests, but I guess they're luckier than me because they had Victor to come in after you to make them actually scream from pleasure. God, now I wish I didn't kill him."

I can feel Maxim soften inside me and he pulls out of me in rage. Seeing his soft dick that is even smaller, I chuckle. "Oh, does teeny weeny Maxim not like to be berated?" I pout at him.

"You shut your fucking mouth." Maxim climbs off the bed. "I'm so tired of hearing your voice."

Maxim goes to the dresser that is on the left wall and pulls out two things. He walks over to me and I see he's gotten some sort of whip and a silk tie. "Now I'm going to teach you to keep your mouth shut." He drops the whip next to me on the bed as he presses the silk tie against my lips and ties it around my head. As he tightens, it slides in between my lips and presses against my teeth, forcing me to open my mouth. He smiles down at me as he strokes my cheek. "This is a very good look on you."

He moves off the bed and grabs the whip-looking thing. As I get a better look at it, I see it's a flogger with leather straps that have three metal balls attached at the ends. The rage that is in Maxim's eyes tells me this isn't going to be pleasurable. He wants me to feel pain. He wants to punish me.

Maxim swings his arm back with the flogger and I try to ball up to block my body from the hit but I can't. The leather and metal balls hit my stomach with such force it knocks the air out of my lungs and my muffled scream rings through the room. Hits come right after the other as he lets out his anger all over the front of my body. By the time he stops, I feel like my skin's on fire. I'm in so much pain that my mind feels numb. I just stare up at the ceiling, trying to block out how much I want to break down and cry right now.

Moaning and grunting pulls my attention from the ceiling to Maxim who's kneeling next to me with his hand wrapped around his erect dick. Based on how fast his hand is moving, he's about to come. Not wanting to watch him come on me, I look back to the ceiling and think back to the night the guys took me to their club. Soaking in how good they made me feel, how much fun we had, and how being together made me feel whole.

The feeling of his come hitting my breast makes my stomach roll and I close my eyes to try to stop the bile. Maxim runs his finger through his come, spreading it across my skin. "Now you're marked as mine." The tie in my mouth loosens and is pulled away, but before I even get a chance to close my lips, Maxim pushes his come-covered finger into my mouth.

I try to pull my head away but he holds it in place. "Clean off my finger. Enjoy the taste of me in your mouth." I bite down on his finger and he quickly pulls his hand back and backhands me again. "You still haven't learned your lesson." He climbs off the bed and tucks himself back in his pants. "I guess I'll get to have some more fun with you tomorrow." Maxim walks around the bed and I track his every move as he stands by the door.

"Cassandra," Maxim yells.

A second later, Cassandra hurries out of her room, looking put back together. "I'm done for the evening. Do not wash Miss Riona. My seed stays on her until it seeps into her skin. You may loosen the chains but don't remove her cuffs."

Cassandra nods to Maxim without looking at me and he leaves the room. Once the lock clicks, I pull on the chains. "I need a bucket." Cassandra acts instantly, rushing to the bed, hitting a button that loosens the chains and grabs a trashcan by the bed. I lean over the edge of the bed and empty my stomach. When I have nothing left to throw up, I roll back on the bed and curl into a ball. At least I don't have his taste in my mouth anymore.

Tears pour down my cheeks as I let myself break for a second. A warm blanket covering me has me flinching and Cassandra steps back with her hands out in front of her. "Sorry. I just wanted to cover you. I'll leave you alone. Call out if you need me." I give her a nod and I pull the blanket over my head, and I get lost in the pain.

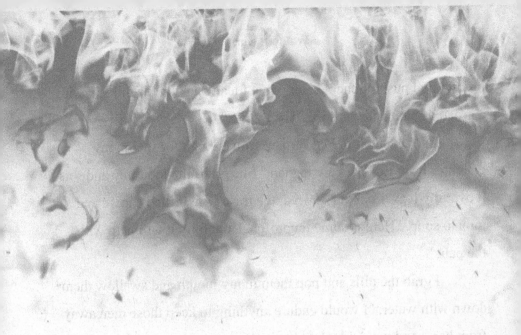

Chapter Nine

Riona

The soft sound of a door shutting has my eyes opening and my grogginess tells me I was asleep. I just don't remember falling asleep. Letting my guard down isn't an option here. With the blanket still over me, I straighten out from my ball and my body screams from the pain. "Oh fuck." Balling back up, I hope to relieve the pain, but my body only screams more at the quick movement.

"How are you feeling?" Fuck, I forgot about what woke me.

I pull the blanket from my face to find Cassandra standing beside me, pushing a tray of food on the nightstand. "I'm in a lot of pain." I slowly sit up and Cassandra rushes to my side, grabbing

389

pillows and pushing them behind me. I lean back on the pillows with a groan of pain and comfort. "Thank you."

"No, thank you. I can't thank you enough for saving my daughter from Ed. He's a vile man." She grabs the food tray and sets it over my legs. Looking down at the tray, I see grilled cheese and tomato soup. "Here is some ibuprofen. Hopefully it will help with the pain."

I grab the pills and pop them in my mouth and swallow them down with water. "I would endure anything to keep those men away from her...and you." I look at her in the eyes as I say the last word, telling her she has my trust and protection.

Cassandra breaks her stare and walks around the bed toward her door, and I can see her fighting herself. She's thankful but she feels guilty. Did she hear what Maxim did or is she just assuming? She disappears into her room for only a second before carrying out her own tray and dragging a chair behind her. "Do you mind if I join you?"

"Please do." I grab half my sandwich and dunk it into the soup. As soon as it hits my mouth, I moan out in happiness. God, it's so nice to have a real meal. "This is so good. So much better than the oatmeal and turkey sandwiches I've been eating."

"I'm glad you like it." She smiles shyly at me.

"You made this?"

"Yeah, I'm your cook for now. So you'll be eating a lot of eggs, pancakes, and grilled cheeses because that's all I can make." She chuckles.

"Anything warm is much appreciated. How did you get mixed in with the Bratva and Maxim?"

"I'm Kiera's maid, or should I say, was. I met her through some friends right after I found out I was pregnant, and she gave me a job. She didn't really need a maid, but she wanted to help out. Since she has been overseas for the last couple of months, I've been at home. A couple of days ago I was called in because Kiera was supposedly coming home soon so I needed to get her room ready. When I got here, Maxim grabbed me and threw me in that room," she points behind her to the room she disappeared to, "saying I was his future wife's maid now."

She was Kiera's maid. Does she know who I am? Does she know about Xavier? "How close are you to Kiera?"

Cassandra smiles. "I know who you are. And your friendship with Kiera."

I feel myself relaxing. I have a friend in this room. If Kiera trusts her, then I do too. "Do you have a way to contact her?"

Cassandra shakes her head no. "They took my phone."

"Well shit. When's the last time you spoke to her?"

"A couple of weeks ago."

I pout because she wasn't sent here by Kiera. "What day is it?"

"It's August 3rd."

Shit. It's been almost three weeks since I was in Ireland with Aisling. It's time to stop playing around. I need to get out of here.

"When you get a chance, can you get a message out for me? Can you reach out to my brother or Aisling and tell them where I am?"

She looks at me like it's an impossible ask. "I'm not sure when that'll be."

"It'll be before me. My guess is someone is going to be looking for you and your daughter when you don't go home in a couple of days."

"Yes. My husband will be expecting a call this weekend."

A call? "Where's your husband?"

"He's in the Army. Overseas."

"When does he come back?" Please let it be soon.

"Three months. He's been gone for nine."

Wow, I can't imagine. Just two weeks away from my guys was hard and I wasn't sure if I could trust them. I guess now that they're ... Nope I'm not going there. "I'm sorry."

"You don't need to be. He chose to enlist to provide for our family. We decided the four years are worth it for our little girl."

"Well, tell me about your little girl. I could use some happiness before Maxim decides to come back for a visit."

She smiles at me and then tells me all about Cami as we finish eating. I'm giggling at a story about Cami kissing a lizard when I hear the sound of my door unlocking. My face instantly falls flat as the door opens and Cassandra jumps off the bed. Maxim walks into the room with a wide smile on his face. "Hello, my beautiful wife, are you ready to have some fun?"

"Hello pencil dick. I'm ready to bathe in your blood after I slit your throat open, along with your wrists."

His smile drops as he glares at me. The door slams shut behind him, showing how pissed he is. "I guess you didn't learn your lesson. That's okay, it was quite fun putting some cracks in your wall. I'll break it today."

"You will never break me. You're too weak." He growls and pulls the remote out of his pockets. My arms and legs instantly pull apart and before I can react, I'm spread out without any possibility to move.

"Cassandra. Leave now." Cassandra quickly grabs our trays and hurries into her room. With one last look back at me, I see her wanting to step in, but I give my head a single shake, telling her that I'll be fine. She shuts her door and Maxim walks to the side of the bed and grabs my blanket. "Let me see my marks on you." He yanks the blanket off my body, and I look up at the ceiling because I have no desire to see what he has done.

"Oh, you look fantastic with all the small circular bruises across your body." He climbs onto the bed in between my legs and runs his hands over my stomach. I try to pull away from his touch and he grabs my waist, holding me still while pressing his thumbs into some of the bruises. Not wanting to scream out in pain, I grind my teeth together and inhale through my nose. "They'll be on your body for days." His hands move up my body to my breasts. "Everyone will know you're mine."

"I'll never be yours and everyone knows it. Everyone knows you're not man enough to be with me. I'd never bow down to a spoiled prince that thinks everything will be handed to him. I'd never marry into a weak organization that's going to fall apart under your rule."

He grabs me by my hair and yanks me up to the point where my shoulders ache from the stretch. "Can weak men do this? Look at what I did to you." He tilts my head forward and I see hundreds of round dark purple bruises scattered all over my front. You can play connect the dots on my skin with the harsh red lines from the leather straps, connecting them.

"Only weak men hurt women."

"No." He turns my face toward him. "Strong men make their women submit."

"You know you're weak. That's why you've tied me up, because you know I'm stronger than you. You're scared of me."

"I'll never be scared of you." He leans closer. "Do you want to know why?" I glare at him without saying anything, but he's not looking for me to answer. "I'm not scared of you because I know your weakness. I can control you."

I growl in irritation and spit in his face. I hate that he knows I'll do anything to protect others from enduring what I've been through. He backhands me across my face and I almost chuckle at how predictable he is.

"You stupid bitch. All you have to do is shut your mouth and take me happily." He throws me back on the bed and moves off the bed. He grabs something at the end of the bed. "Instead you make it hard." A long bar sits at the end of the bed and Maxim smiles wicked up at me. "But who am I to complain? I like marking you."

He clasps the bar to each of my ankle cuffs and then he unclips the chains. A smile pulls across my face. He made a bad decision, because even with my legs locked, he just gave me range of motion. I'm about to bend my knees and jam the bar into his face when he grabs the bar with both hands. "I'm going to need a blank canvas."

Before I can even comprehend what he means, he flips me over by my ankles and I scream out in pain. My arms feel like they're being pulled out of their sockets as they're forced to cross while my wrists don't move.

"Oops my bad." Maxim chuckles. The chains loosen but it doesn't release the pressure on my shoulders because Maxim is pulling me down the bed. I grab onto the sheets to try to relieve the pain, but the sheets just pull with me. My legs fall unexpectedly and the top of my feet slam into the hard floors, but my knees never hit the ground as the chains hold my upper body on the bed.

I quickly get to my feet and the pull on my arms loosens and I'm able to cross my wrists, giving me a little movement. Hands grope my ass and I freeze as Maxim runs his hands over my ass cheeks, kneading them. "Your ass is perfect." He removes his hand from me, but a second later it lands back on my ass with a loud smack. A heated tingle spreads across my cheek and Maxim instantly starts rubbing the tender area, not to soothe but to admire. "Your skin gets so red. It's beautiful."

He throws smack after smack on my ass, making the stinging intensify. His smacks are not teasing and fun. He hits me as hard as he can to inflict pain. I bite down on my lip to stop myself from letting him know he's hurting me. When he's done my ass feels like it's burning and even his soft strokes of his fingers cause me pain.

Maxim steps closer to me where I can feel his body heat covering my back. His breath brushes against my ear as he whispers, "Does the pain turn you on as well? Are you wet for me?" He runs a finger down my ass crack to my folds but all he finds is me dry.

Looking back as far as I can at him, I smile. "You could never make me wet."

"That's where you're wrong. You will come for me and then I'm going to fuck this perfect red ass." He brings his finger back up and pushes against my back hole. "Has anyone had your ass before?"

I chuckle. "My firsts are long gone."

"Good, then I don't have to prepare you for my cock. You'll either take me or I'll rip you in two."

His body weight moves off me and I hear him walking away. The sound of a drawer opening has me looking to my left and I watch his back as he messes with something.

After a few seconds he turns back to me, holding a large purple dildo with a clit stimulator. "I'll make you scream as you come."

He moves back behind me and I feel the dildo press at my entrance. I take a deep breath trying to relax to make this better for me, but nothing can stop the pain from him raping me yesterday and me being dry. Vibrations shoot through me as the vibrator turns on and I jerk forward trying to get away, but Maxim takes the moment to slam it the rest of the way in. I bury my face in the mattress and scream out in pain.

Tears run down my face and I grip the sheets, trying to focus on anything but the pain. When the clit stimulator moves to my clit, I rock back against the vibrations and for the first time I feel a hint of pleasure. The vibrations turn to a fast pulse and I fight myself to not moan out. While the pleasure is so much better than the pain, I won't give him the pleasure of coming for him.

Unfortunately, I can't help how my body likes the feeling as my walls tighten around the dildo. I pull against my cuffs, trying to add some pain because I can feel myself getting close as everything hits me just right. The vibrations speed up and I involuntarily buck forward, grinding my clit into the vibrations and let out a loud moan.

"You like it, don't you?" Maxim runs his hand up my thigh to my apex and I shake my head no. "It's okay. You don't have to admit it. Your body tells me you do. Can you feel your wetness running down your thighs?" He runs his fingers around the side of vibrator and I know I'm leaking out. Shame rolls through my body as it heats and I almost wish he was raping me with his dick, that way I knew I wouldn't give him my pleasure.

A cold sweat breaks across my skin as I try to hold back my orgasm but as the vibrations pick up again, I can't hold it back anymore as the overstimulation sends me into a painful orgasm. A scream rips through my throat but it isn't from the orgasm, it's from Maxim thrusting into my asshole in one powerful thrust, tearing me.

The pain is too much as he plows into my ass and I let myself slip into the place I haven't been since I was thirteen. Everything around me goes numb and blurry as I escape from the pain and weakness, staring off at nothing.

Chapter Ten

Riona

Something cold touching my face jerks me back to reality and I find Cassandra next to me. When my eyes move to her face, she lets out a sigh and presses a wet towel to my face. Seeing the heartbreak in her eyes has my walls breaking and I can't stop the tears rolling from my eyes. She just sits there next to me, giving me comfort by running her fingers through my hair and doesn't say a thing.

After a while my tears dry up and I'm numb to everything again. Cassandra runs her fingers through my hair one last time before she moves off the bed. "I'll be right back."

I don't respond or turn to watch her. Why do I need to? We're both trapped here. After a few seconds, I hear water running which has me looking over my shoulder. Cassandra walks out of the bathroom and the water is still running. "So I was able to convince Maxim to give me the key to the locks so you could take a bath." I sit up a little higher and the blanket I didn't realize was over me slides to the ground. Cassandra's eyes go to my bare skin and whatever marks Maxim has left on me. The pain on her face tells me it's not good, but the radiating anger tells me she's already seen it, probably when she placed the blanket over me. Maxim was definitely not the one to do that. "He only agreed because I assured him the cuffs would go back on after your bath."

I nod, knowing she needs my agreement before she can release me. I'd do anything to clean him off of me, even if it means being chained to this bed again.

She quickly unlocks my wrist cuffs and I try to stand but the pain on my backside has my knees buckling. I grab onto the sheets and Cassandra hooks her arm around my waist, holding me up. Looking down at the floor as I lean into Cassandra, I notice that the cuffs on my ankles are already gone. Cassandra helps me turn toward the bathroom and we slowly make our way toward it.

My whole body radiates in pain with each step and I can't wait to soak in this tub. But first I need to see what he did to me. Let it fuel my anger, because as much as I don't want to admit it and will never say it out loud, he broke me today. As we cross into the bathroom, I point toward the counter and Cassandra looks at me with concern. "Are you sure?" She knows I want the mirror.

I make myself stand taller. "Yes." I'm not weak. I can handle this.

As we approach the counter, the front of my body comes into view. Seeing all the bruises reflect back at me instead of looking down at them, they look so much worse and somehow they've multiplied. When the counter is close enough, I reach out for it for support and Cassandra steps away to turn off the water.

Looking at my face in the mirror, I barely recognize myself. The right side of my face is discolored from all the hits and I have dried blood on my lip and chin. I stand up straighter and take a breath, getting myself ready to see what he just did to me. "You don't need to see it. You can just wash it away."

"No, I need to see." I look back at Cassandra through the mirror and she gives me a nod.

"I'll wait outside. If you need me just yell. Salts are already in the water."

"Thank you, Cassandra." It's not just a thanks for the bath. It's a thanks for knowing I need to be alone. A thanks for being there for me. She gives me a smile as she backs out of the bathroom and closes the door.

Alone, I find the courage to turn around and my breath catches. My ass is a deep red but it's the distinct bite marks on each of my cheeks and the dried-up blood running between my cheeks that makes me sick. When the fuck did he bite me? The blood I kind of expected since he raped my ass, but the bite marks make it seem he owns a part of me. He doesn't own me. He can't.

I push myself from the counter and over to the tub. I grip the sides of it and carefully lower myself into the water. It's scalding hot but feels amazing on my sore muscles. Instantly, I submerge myself in the water completely and let out a scream silenced by the water. Reemerging, I let the water fall out of my mouth as I relax back with my head on the edge.

My ass stings as it rests on the bottom of the tub, but I push through it. If I have freedom as long as I'm in this tub, I'm not getting out until it turns cold. And when it turns cold, I'm going to drain it and refill it.

Cassandra sticks her head out of her room as I step out of the bathroom however long later. "I made us eggs and toast."

"Thank you." I point to the door on the other side of the bed. "Is this the closet?"

"Yeah." Walking toward the door, Cassandra quickly follows. "There's nothing in there that you need though."

"I'm not sitting here naked all day." I open the door and scan the room. This isn't a closet, it's a small apartment. It even has its own lounge. "Plus, I know what I'm looking for isn't in that dresser." I point behind me to the dresser Maxim has been pulling his toys from.

"You're going to make him mad and he's only going to take it out on you."

"Did he specifically say I need to be naked and tied to the bed?" I run my fingers over the row of hanging clothes until I reach the dresser.

"You should just comply with what he wants. I know you hate him, but it would be easier for you if you act how he wants."

I open the top drawer and find underwear. Pulling a pair on, I look back over my shoulder at Cassandra. "Acting like I want him would kill me inside." I open the next drawer down and find t-shirts. Grabbing the first one, I slip it over my head. "I can survive him beating and raping me. I have before. I won't survive kissing him. Faking my moans. Screaming through fake orgasms. Cooing at his touch. Acting like I love it. Love him." I shoulder past her and climb onto the bed. I sit cross legged in the middle of the bed against the headboard. I drape the blanket over my lap and reach for the first cuff.

Cassandra stands at the end of the bed watching with surprise. While I'll fight every touch and command from Maxim, I won't risk her safety. "I won't let him hurt you."

"I know." She walks into her room as I secure the second cuff.

She comes back out with a tray and sets it down in front of me. There are two plates full of eggs and toast and two glasses of orange juice. Before she grabs her plate and cup, I hold out my wrists and she locks the buckles. I look down at the eggs and then to the blackout curtains. "Is it morning?"

She nods. "Yeah, it's about 8am."

I look at Cassandra. "Do you mind opening the curtains?"

"Not at all." She sets her plate on the bed and goes over to the curtains. Blinding light shines through as they're pulled to the sides and I quickly have to look away. Only for a second though because I need to feel the sun on my face.

"Do you think I could convince Maxim to bring his torture time outside? It's been days since I've breathed in fresh air."

She chuckles. "I'd like to see you try. But his neighbors are too close. They could hear your screams."

I want to tell her I wouldn't scream just to spite him but we both know the trauma he's put me through and the screams that have come out of me. "How about I open the window for a little bit?"

"The windows open?"

"Look, there are bars on the windows. They're on all the windows throughout the house." She turns the latch and pushes up the window.

I breathe in the hot humid air and a smile forms on my face. We need to open the windows on a daily basis so I don't feel so claustrophobic all the time. With me being constantly chained, I'm not going to escape anytime soon. At this point, the only way I'm getting out of here on my own is if I annoy or piss off Maxim enough that he releases me. Maybe I should take the annoying approach now.

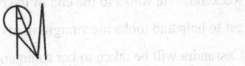

Cassandra and I get all day before Maxim pops our bubble of bliss and he's not the only one. One of the guys that was groping Cassandra the other day steps in behind him. "Cassandra. Key." Maxim holds out his hand for the key to my locks.

Cassandra walks over to Maxim, but I watch the other guy because I don't trust why he's here. Cassandra seems worried as well because she approaches Maxim as far away from the other guy as possible and stops at arms-reach away from Maxim.

She reaches out and drops the key into Maxim's hand but before she can pull away, he grabs her wrist and pulls her toward him and then pushes her at his guy. Cassandra lands in the guy's arms with her back to him and she instantly fights the hold around her. On instinct, I lunge forward to help her, but the chains stop me. "What the fuck, Maxim? You promised. I'm fucking chained to the bed."

"And I'll keep my promise if you continue to listen and keep your mouth shut." I bite my lip to keep my lips closed but I can't help my glare. I really wish looks could kill so I could watch Maxim fall to the ground dead.

A victorious smile pulls across his face and I grind my teeth together. "Good girl. Now you're going to follow what I say and if you do it without resistance, Cassandra will be released, untouched, and get to go home with her daughter and nanny for a long weekend." He walks to the end of the bed, which is as far as I could get to help and looks me straight in my eyes. "But if you resist, Cassandra will be taken to her room and my men will use her all weekend, raping her in every way." He pauses, holding my stare. "Do you understand?"

Making sure not to speak or show hesitation, I nod my head three times. "That's what I like to hear." He reaches out and strokes my bruised cheek and I freeze so I don't pull away. "Your fight gets me hard, but your compliance is a real turn on."

His hand slides from my cheek to the back of my head and he forcefully pulls me down so I'm lying flat on my stomach with my hands behind me and face right in front of his crotch. "Feel how much your obedience turns me on."

I look up at him, pulling on the cuffs and he smirks at me. Knowing how he means, I take a breath, looking over at Cassandra, needing to see the reason why I'm doing this. Her scared eyes look back at me and I scoot an inch forward pulling painfully against my cuffs and rub my face against his erection. "You're such a good girl today." He yanks my head up at an uncomfortable angle so I'm looking at his face. "Now don't move."

I give him a small nod because I don't have much movement with how he holds me. With my agreement, he drops my head and I face-plant on the edge of the bed, but I don't move or make a sound. Seconds later, my wrists are grabbed and pulled together making my back arch to relieve some of the pain. The pain from the pull only lasts a few seconds until my wrists are released and I fall back on the bed. I pull against my cuffs and I realized they're now attached, tying my hands behind me.

Maxim grabs onto my calf and pulls my legs to the side of the bed and then flips me over so he's standing between my open thighs and my upper body is laying on the bed. "Stand up, Riona."

Using my core muscles, I sit up on the bed and slide off, rubbing myself against Maxim because he didn't take a step back. Our fronts are pressed together as we glare at each other and I hope he can see all my unspoken words of hate and malice. "Go stand at the end of the bed and face the bathroom. I wait for him to take a step back but when he doesn't, I slide my body against his to move past him. God, I wish I could knee him in the balls right now.

Maxim follows closely behind me as I go to the end of the bed. When I turn to face the bathroom, Maxim is in front of me, unbuckling his pants. "Now kneel."

I hesitate for a second because I'll never willingly kneel before him but when he looks at Cassandra, I immediately fall to the ground on my knees. "Fuck, you look good on your knees. The only thing that would be better is if you were naked. But don't worry, you'll be punished for the clothes later." He looks at Cassandra and the guy and gives a nod. The guy instantly lets her go. "Cassandra, they're waiting outside for you. Have a good weekend but be back here Monday morning."

Cassandra looks at me and I mouth 'go'. She turns on her heels and escapes out of the room with the guy close behind her, closing the door with him.

It's just me and Maxim now. My obedience is over. Maxim grabs onto my hair, making me look from the door to him. "It's just you and me all weekend. We're going to have so much fun. But first I have one more hole to claim and then you'll be fully mine."

"How many times do I have to tell you? I'll never be yours. None of this is willing."

"I don't care if you're willing or not. You're mine. You'll be my wife in two weeks. You will provide me with children. I don't care if I have to lock you in this room for the rest of your life and only visit when I want to feel your warm walls swallowing my cock. It's time you accept your reality and open that mouth of yours."

I bite down hard, locking my jaw. He's going to have to pry my mouth open if he wants to put his dick in it. And if he does, I'll bite it off.

Chapter Eleven

Maxim

She is so beautiful there on her knees with her long red hair fanning out over her shoulders. She'd only look more gorgeous if she was naked but I'm also not complaining because my shirt looks hot as hell on her.

With one hand still holding her by her hair, I unbutton my jeans and slide down the zipper. "Open your mouth for me, Riona. I'll make it worth your while."

"The only thing I want from you is my freedom. Are you going to let me go?"

I shake my head no. "Never." I've had my eye on her for years and now that she's mine, I'll never let her go.

"Then my lips will never wrap around your itty-bitty weenie."

God, she pisses me off. I try to be nice and her fucking mouth always ruins it. I'll remind her how small my dick isn't as I ram it down her throat. I grip her hair tighter and she only shows her pain through her eyes as they slightly close. "Open your mouth, Riona." She glares up at me and I can feel her defiance. It only turns me on more. My dick grows painfully hard and I push my jeans and boxers down just enough to release it. Stepping forward, I rub the tip of my erection across her full lips. Just the feeling of her warm lips on me has my mind wondering how good this could be if she'd just give in.

"Open your mouth before I make you." Defiance shines in her eyes. I guess I'll have to make her.

With my grip on her head, I pull her closer to me, forcing my erection against her lips and with my other hand, I pinch her nose, cutting off her air. Riona fights against my hold and I can't help my smile as her face turns red. "I'll get what I want. Stop fighting it."

She tries to turn her face away, but my hold doesn't allow her to move at all. I don't know why she keeps fighting me. I always get what I want. Her fighting only hurts her.

Riona's red face starts to turn blue, and she finally gives in. Her lips part a sliver and I jam my cock into her mouth. I release her nose and I brace myself on the bed behind her as I continue to thrust into her mouth. Chasing my release, I get lost in the feeling of her lips wrapped around me, her warm mouth and saliva surrounding my erection, and the scrape of her teeth along the veins.

Feeling myself about to come, I shove myself into her mouth one more time and down her throat. She's going to swallow me. Holding her there, choking her on my cock, my balls draw up and I groan out in pleasure. But instead of feeling my blissful release, pain overwhelms me. I pull Riona's head back and off my cock and she looks up at me with a huge bloody grin. All I see is red as I look down at my bleeding cock from her bite. "You fucking bitch."

I grab her by her throat, pull her up to her feet, and push her against the bedpost. Using the bedpost as leverage, I continue to squeeze her throat, choking her as I raise her higher and higher off the floor until her toes can't touch.

"Your death will only make this deal easier. I only wanted you because I wanted a good fuck, but all you've been is trouble." Her body jerks against my hold but I'm not wavering. Fear flashes in her eyes as she tries to breathe and I can't help but chuckle. "The infamous Riona Murphy, the assassin M, is scared to die."

She tries to kick out at me, but I press my lower half to hers, preventing any of her kicks from having any real power. "With you out of my way, the girls in that boarding house will be the first group I present to your father. They'll go for a pretty penny and be a great start for your father to get into the business." Pure terror flash in her eyes as she tries to fight me off of her, but it's no use. She's not strong enough to fight me off. She only has seconds left and they'll be filled with fear.

Riona's eyes start to droop and I grip her throat harder, wanting the last thing she sees is me, the last thing she feels is my hand around her neck and the last thing she knows is that I killed her. She's mine alive and in death. Her body sags against me as she loses consciousness and I press my hand to her chest wanting to feel the last of her heartbeats.

As it slows, yelling comes from the hallway and I look to the door as a knock sounds. What the fuck is going on? I throw Riona down on the bed and head to the door as I push myself back in my jeans and buckle them. "What? I told you..."

Standing in front of me is my new right-hand man, Kristoff, but it's not him that stops me; it's the sound of gunshots.

"We need to go." Kristoff holds out a gun and I quickly take it. We head down the hallway, away from the gunshots, heading to the hidden escape. We hit the stairs on the east side of the house and Kristoff goes in front. When he hits the landing, shots are immediately directed toward him and I crouch down and move toward my father's office across from the stairs. Not waiting for him, I head to my father's bookcase and pull back the fake book, opening the hidden door. I grab onto the edge of the bookcase and pull it out and open.

Once I have it open enough to go through, I move around the door and stop. Standing there at the entrance of the passageway is my twin Kiera with her gun raised and aiming for my chest. "What are you doing? Move."

"Hi, Maxim." She tilts her head to the side and looks at me with such disgust. "Bye, Maxim." She pulls the trigger and I fall to my knees before everything goes dark.

Chapter Twelve

Riona

"Fuck. Beauty. What did he do to you?" I feel his touch as I fade into darkness.

"Breathe, Rose." His lips press against mine as he tries to breathe for me.

"I've got you, Princess." I feel like I'm floating as I'm being held in his arms. I try to open my eyes to see them but instead I'm drawn back into the darkness.

My car pulls up in front of their house and I'm beaming. I've missed them so much. Not waiting for the driver, I throw my door open just as their door opens. Not caring who's there, I run to the open door and throw myself at them. A grinning Matteo catches me and I smash my lips to his. His hold on me tightens and I melt into him. "I've missed you."

"I missed you too, Princess."

A comforting hand slides across my back and I know it's Enzo. I untangle myself from Matteo and go into Enzo's arms. He runs a hand up my spine and tucks a stray piece of hair behind my ear as we stare into each other's eyes. Not needing to say anything to each other, I know he can see how sorry I am for running and how much I missed him. He grabs me by the back of my neck and pulls me into an intense and passionate kiss. I stretch up on my toes and wrap my arms around his neck, bringing myself closer to him and pushing into his kiss.

A growl sounds behind me and I smile against Enzo's lips without pulling away. Dante's not having it though because his hands grip my hips and pull me from Enzo. I spin in his hands to face him, and they slide from my hips to my ass as I smile up at him and press my body up against his. "Hi."

"You ran."

"I know."

"You didn't answer my calls."

"I didn't."

"You know that drove me crazy, right?"

"I did."

"You're not allowed to run from us anymore."

I nod. "I won't."

Dante crashes his lips to mine, and I moan into it. He wants my submission, my promise, and I give it to him. I'm not leaving them. They're mine. When we break apart, there's so much relief and love in his eyes. I grab his hand and pull him to their front door. "Come on, let's go inside."

Just as I reach the door, Dante stops me. "You can't." He pulls me away from the door and the three of them step in front of me blocking it.

"What are you talking about? Why aren't..." Arms wrap around me from behind, locking my arms to my sides and pulling me away from them.

I fight against their hold but it just tightens around me. "Help me..." They just stand there watching.

"They can't help you." A cold chill runs up my spine as Maxim's breath brushes across my ear. "You're mine."

"No." I fight with everything I have, trying to get away from him. I can't be his. I'm theirs. Tears build in my eyes as I look to the men that stole my heart and plead with them. "Please don't let him take me."

All they do is stand there. Maxim stops several yards back and the guys turn toward the house and start walking in.

"You forced my hand." I whip my head to my left and my father stands there looking at me in disgust. "You were supposed to kill them." He pulls out his phone and realization hits me.

"No..." Panic fills me as I watch them disappear into the house. The hold around me is gone and I take off toward the house. "Get out. Don't go inside." The door closes behind them and I let out a scream, but it's drowned out by the explosion. I feel the heat of the fire as I'm thrown back away from the house.

I gasp awake and the only thing I can see is darkness. Where am I? I look around the dark room, trying to recognize where I am, but I'm coming up blank. Movement next to me draws my attention and I find someone sitting next to me. Instantly I try to move away from them, but my movement is sluggish and a sharp pain in my arm has me wincing.

"Ri?" The person next to me moves and seconds later a soft light fills the room from a lamp. Aisling sits forward in her chair and reaches for my hand. The feeling of her hand on mine has my whole body sagging into the bed. I'm safe.

Tears fill my eyes as I squeeze her hand. "Ash." My voice comes out as a wheeze and my throat feels like it's on fire. I bring my hand to it and flashes of Maxim's hands around my throat as he holds me against the bedpost flash in my mind.

"Shh... don't try to talk." With her free hand, she reaches over to the nightstand and grabs a glass with a straw. "Do you want some water?"

I nod and try to sit up more but she has to help me, stuffing several pillows behind me. Once I'm sitting up, she grabs the water again and brings the straw to my lips. I suck the water down until there's none left and the coldness soothes my throat a little. Aisling stands with the empty glass in her hand, and I reach out, grabbing her wrist. I don't want her to leave. With her here, I know this isn't a dream. "I'm just getting you some more water."

I shake my head no and she sits back down. Needing to know what happened, I force out one word, hoping she'll understand what I'm asking. "How?"

She sags into her chair. "How'd we get you out?" I nod and she looks toward the bedroom door. I look to the door and back to her because there is nothing there. What is she trying to figure out? I squeeze her hand, silently telling her to just tell me.

Aisling lets out a breath and looks back at me. "We had no idea where you were. We knew Lorcan took you, so Kill, Colton, Tanner, and I spent the first two weeks searching every property he has, trying to find you. We had no idea the deal your father made with the Bratva. We thought he had just locked you up as punishment.

"But a couple of days ago, your father called Kill and I to his office. When we arrived, he announced there would be a wedding. I thought he was talking about ours until he handed us an invitation that said you and Maxim were getting married in a couple of weeks. We went ballistic and that's when he told us about getting into the skin business.

"When we left, I called Kiera and she said she had eyes on you and she was on her way back to the city because it was time to take down Maxim. She promised us you were okay. Still fighting. At least until last night. Cassandra called her, worried about you, and Kiera called us saying it's time. We basically stormed the house with a few of Kiera's guys and got you. We brought you here and had the doc look you over." Aisling looks at me with pity and I know she knows what he did to me.

I harden my stare and shake my head, telling her not to pity me. A tear escapes her eye and she quickly wipes it away. "Cassandra told us what she thought you experienced. I'm so sorry you had to go through that again." I squeeze her hand, telling her I'll be okay. I'll be okay once I take Maxim's life.

"Maxim?" My throat burns saying his name. He tried to kill me. He's going to wish he was successful.

"Kiera got him. She's got him locked away, waiting for you."

I point to the door, and she looks at me confused. "You want Kiera?" I nod and she stands up and heads to the door. She opens it and sticks her head out the door. Silence is all I hear on the other side of the door, but I can't see anything since Aisling keeps the door pressed up against her. "She's awake. Kiera, can you come in?"

I hear footsteps approach the door and seconds later Kiera stands in the doorway. "Hey Killer!" I smile at her and wave. Aisling slips out of the room as the door shuts and Kiera takes a seat on the bed.

"Thanks." I wish my voice didn't sound like a gruff wheeze.

"You know I always got your back." I smile at her and nod. "You want to know where he is?" I nod again. "He's at your favorite place. My guys are keeping an eye on him."

I nod and look at the IV in my arm. I go to pull it out as Aisling walks back into the room with a glass. "What are you doing?" I pull out the IV and Aisling rushes to me to put pressure on where the needle was. She sets the glass down and opens the nightstand to grab a gauze and band aid. "You needed that for the pain." As she gets the bandage in place, I reach for the glass and down the water. Aisling stands next to the bed when she finishes and I throw the blankets off of me. Looking down at my legs, I'm glad I'm fully clothed in leggings and a t-shirt. "Where are you going?"

"Maxim."

"No, you need to rest."

I look at Aisling and Kiera who are standing next to each other beside the bed. I swing my legs over the side of the bed. "I won't rest until he's dead." I look at both of them, silently telling them I won't waver from this.

Kiera is the first to back down and I reach out for her. She steps forward and helps me stand. "Make him suffer."

I nod and look at Aisling and she lets out a breath. "Fine. You'll need shoes and you're not going alone. Your father is looking for you and her father is looking for you and Maxim."

I don't care about Lorcan and Ivan. It's time I get something I want. "He'll find Maxim. In pieces."

"Sit down." Aisling shakes her head as she bends down, picks up a bag at the end of the bed, and pulls out socks and tennis shoes.

Kiera helps me sit back down and then steps back toward the door. "I'll let the guys know." I watch Kiera's back as she leaves the room and Aisling moves in front of me.

"Who's here?" She kneels down and grabs my foot but I yank it away. "I can put on my own shoes."

"Stop talking." She yanks my foot back. "You aren't just going to shoot Maxim so save your energy for that." I let her take my foot and slide a sock on. "Tanner and Colton. Killian is out preparing for things." With my right shoe on, she switches to my left foot with shaking hands.

"Where are they?" Please tell me that Maxim lied to me.

Aisling looks up at me with sorrow in her eyes because she knows exactly who I'm asking about. "There was an explosion a couple of days after you were taken."

"I know that. I watched my father push the ignitor and saw the flames in the distance. Tell me they got out. Tell me they're okay. Tell me Maxim lied to me when he said three bodies were found."

Aisling has tears in her eyes. "I'm sorry. I can't."

I shake my head, not wanting to believe what she's saying. I know I saw the house blow up, but I could've sworn I heard them, felt them carrying me. Aisling slides my foot into the shoe and then envelopes me in a hug. "I'm so sorry, Ri."

"I want him dead, Aisling. I'll kill him for all this."

"Yes. Lorcan will die for his betrayal." My rage fills me as Aisling releases me from her hold and helps me to stand. On unsteady legs, I walk out of the bedroom and head in the only direction, down the hall, which opens into a large open space, holding the living room, dining room, and kitchen. I recognize this place as one of our safe houses on the edge of the city. As I walk into the open space, Tanner and Colton stand from the couch across from Kiera and make their way over to me.

Colton reaches me first and he pulls me into a hug. "It's good to see you, Red."

Tanner pulls me from his brother and gives me a tight hug. "You gave us a scare."

I step back from them, needing a little distance. It almost feels wrong knowing Dante and Matteo aren't here to growl at them for hugging me. I shake the thought from my head and smile at them. "It's good to be out of there."

"Shit, Firecracker. Your voice sounds awful." Tanner steps forward. "May I?" He points to my neck and I nod. Gently he touches my neck, but I still wince in pain. "Your vocal cords are swollen. You shouldn't try talking for a couple of days."

"I told her to stop talking." Aisling gives me a stern look.

"Let me get through today and I promise I won't talk for at least two days." Aisling rolls her eyes because she doesn't believe me. I shrug my shoulders because she might be right. I've never been good at not saying what I think. "Who's coming with me?"

Kiera stands. "I am."

"You going to say bye to your brother?"

"More like fuck you." We all chuckle and I follow her out.

We don't say a word to each other as we get into her car and she heads further out of the city. "So, I met Xavier." She looks over at me and I give her a wink. Kiera's cheeks turn pink and chuckle. "Oh my God."

She gives me a giddy grin. "Shut up."

"How long have you been together? Why haven't I heard about him?"

"We grew up together but didn't start anything until a couple of years ago. My father wouldn't approve, so we didn't tell anyone."

"Why?"

"Oh, come on, Ri. You know. The same reason your father wouldn't let you marry one of the twins. Our marriage needs to have a purpose. Marrying our own men brings nothing to our fathers."

She's right, but I hope she gets what she wants.

"So, do you love him? Not like the love I have for the twins, but real love?"

"Yeah. Real love." Her smile is so big that I can't help mine, but my heart hurts because I lost that love. "You loved them, didn't you?"

I look over to her and nod. "Yes, I did." I loved them. I just didn't realize it until it was too late to tell them.

"I'm sorry." I give her a weak smile before looking out the window. We're silent for the rest of the way as I wonder what my future will look like without them. Will I ever fall in love again? Will I just marry for connections? Maybe I'll just stay single.

I'm pulled from my thoughts when the car turns off. Looking out the windshield, I can't help my smile as I see Mystique sitting in front of me. Since it's in the middle of the night, it's in full swing and I wish I could go in to see how the girls are doing, but I have a man to kill right now.

Kiera and I both get out of the car, and I nod to Jon and Dave, my bouncers, as we walk around the side of the building to the entrance that leads to the basement. We walk up to the steel black door and I open the keypad panel. I type in 26-05-09, the days of the month Kiera, Aisling, and myself were born, and a handprint scanner pops open. I place my right hand on the scanner and the door unlocks. Kiera walks in behind me and closes the door. The lock instantly engages and the hallway lights up.

The hallway runs the length of the club and ends at an elevator with no other doors. As we approach the elevator, the doors open. Kiera steps in after me and I hit the B button. The basement of the club holds our sex rooms for our Thursday events but that's only half the basement. The other half is my sanctuary. The elevator door opens to my soundproofed torture chamber.

The large open space greets us and I can't help my smile seeing Maxim tied to a cross in the middle of the room. His head lifts from where it was hanging and he looks shocked to see me. Well at least what I can see of his face. His entire face is swollen.

"Yeah, you can't even kill me properly. It's a good thing I'm going to end your miserable life tonight. And I'll make sure you're dead."

"I'm sorry, what did you say? Speak louder." I grind my teeth together and school my face so I don't show my anger. Looking away from Maxim, I see Xavier lounging on the couch at the far wall. I put the couch in after Aisling complained about having to stand once while I tortured a guy for information on where a group of kids were being held.

"What happened to him?"

Xavier shrugs. "Maybe there were a few guys that wanted to inflict some pain for what he did to you."

I look over Maxim and I can see the anger inflicted on his body. "Killian, Tanner, and Colton came here while Aisling and I took you to the doc," Kiera explains, but this doesn't feel like them. They aren't this physical with the pain they inflict. If he wasn't dead, I'd say Matteo did this. I head over to the tables that hold all kinds of weapons and torture devices and run my fingers along the edge. When I reach the end, I turn back to Kiera and Xavier. "Where are the rest of your men? Surely Xavier hasn't been here watching this whole time by himself."

"You know I have no problem watching prisoners for hours." I raise an eyebrow at him silently saying 'really'. "Fine. I sent the other two up to the club. Kiera gave me a heads-up you were coming." I nod my thanks, because I don't want eyes on me when I kill Maxim. I look at Kiera and she understands my request without me saying a word. She grabs Xavier's hand and pulls him up from the couch.

"You guys can enjoy the show upstairs or you're more than welcome to use one of the rooms down here." I give them a suggestive smile and Kiera returns it, heading to the hidden door that leads to the other side of the basement. "Kiera, do you want to say anything to Maxim?"

She gives Maxim one look and then looks back at me. "Nope. I'm just here to collect his body and dump it on my father's front porch."

She waves her hand in front of the wall and the keypad lights up.

Seconds later, the wall opens after she inserts her code and they disappear into the other side of the basement. As soon as the wall shuts, I turn toward the center of the room and walk around until I'm standing in front of Maxim. "Do you remember the big picture I painted in blood on my cell wall?" I pause, looking into the one eye that isn't swollen shut. "That's what I'm going to do. Feel free to scream as loud as you want."

"Fuck you."

I chuckle and head to the table with the knives on them. "But first I need to return a favor."

I return back to him with a small dagger in my hand. "You tormented me for days, keeping me naked." I grab his shirt pulling it from his body and cut it open. "Your torment won't last for days though."

With swift cuts, I remove his clothes piece by piece until he's only in his boxers. The bruises that scatter his body really tell the story of what my brother and the twins did. I can see where fists connected with his abdomen and a pole struck his legs. But it's his blood-stained boxers that put a wicked smile on my face. "You know you did give me a first."

He tries to give me a cocky smile, especially as I grab the waistband of his boxers. "Oh yeah?"

I quickly slice my knife down his boxers at his left leg. "Yeah." I grab the right side of his boxers and slice down the side and his boxers fall to the floor. "You were the first dick I've bitten. I got to say, I left some pretty good damage." I chuckle at the clear teeth marks around his dick and the scrapes down it from him pulling away.

He tries to lunge at me, but he doesn't even get an inch because of the binds holding him to the cross. He has three on each arm and leg. I walk backward, away from him, to the sound system.

Linking the system to the club's, the dancers' music fills the closed space. "I do have one more treat for your dick. But it's not my first time. It is my second so you should feel special." Based on the song, I can tell Nina is on stage. "You really shouldn't have put your dick where it doesn't belong because you're going to lose it." Turning the volume all the way up, it drowns out the slurs Maxim's throws at me. Happy to finally get my revenge, I dance over to the table and grab the hedge clippers. These are exactly what I wanted. Just like my picture. I won't even have to touch his dick to cut it off.

I swing the clippers next to me as I move back to Maxim with a gleeful smile on my face. "I hope you're ready to scream." I know he can't hear me over the music because I can't hear me, but it doesn't matter. He gets the gist as I run the tip of the clippers up his thigh and under his soft cock. When it rests on the closed clippers, I bend down slightly, bringing the handle closer to the floor and open them. He violently starts to move, trying to dislodge his cock from the shears. I chuckle as it flops against the clippers like a wet noodle. It's time to cut the pasta.

Without even waiting a second, I forcefully close the clippers. His screams overtake the music and I chuckle as I open the clippers and his dick falls to the ground. Blood gushes out of the wound and spills onto the floor. Oh shit. I forgot how much blood there is when you cut off a dick. My last one was Tony's. I can't have him dying yet of blood loss.

Rushing over to the tables, I grab a large flat knife and a blowtorch. With the knife in front of the torch, I heat it until the blade turns orange and then I press the flat edge of the knife to the open wound, cauterizing it.

"Fucking hell..." Maxim screams and I only smile because I'm just getting started. Next go his balls, then I think I'll take his fingers before I drain him of his blood.

Holding his small ball sack in my hand, I look up to Maxim's face and see him crying. I press my body up against his and put my lips next to his ear without touching it. "Are you regretting touching me? Raping me?"

He nods through his sobs. "Good."

I bring the knife to the underside of his balls and slice up. Blood splatters all over my front as he cries. "I'm not going to regret anything I do to you."

Once again, I heat the blade, burning the blood off in the process, and then press it to the open wound. Instead of screaming, Maxim's head falls forward as he passes out. "Oh no you don't. I want you to be awake for all of this."

I head over to my locked cabinet that holds my guns and poisons and type in my code. The door unlocks and pops open and I quickly grab one of the many EpiPens I keep there for the only purpose to keep my victims awake when I need them to be. Tony taught me this. With quick precision, I jab the EpiPen into his thigh and Maxim gasps awake.

His eyes connect with mine and I shake my head. "You don't get to escape any of this. You'll die feeling all the pain." I grab the gardening shears and slide his right pointer finger in between the blades.

Chapter Thirteen

Riona

The ding of the elevator breaks through my trance as I carve my signature M across Maxim's torso. I had turned the music off a while ago after I was done cutting off his fingers. Looking over my shoulder toward the elevator, I see Killian walk out. "Hey."

Killian walks straight to me and pulls me into a hug. "Hey... really? You've been missing for weeks and that's the first thing you say to me?"

I hold my blood covered hands out making sure not to touch him. "I'm covered in blood."

He hugs me tighter. "Try again."

I wrap my arm around him, hugging my brother back. "I missed you too, Kill."

"Much better." He gives me one final squeeze before he releases me and steps back. "I'm glad you're okay."

I turn toward a now-dead Maxim and Killian stands next to me. "I am now." Maxim's body hangs from the cross with his blood covering every inch of his body.

"Is he dead?"

I chuckle. "If he's not now, he will be shortly. Want to help me cut him up?"

Killian looks at me with a gleeful smile. "Hell yeah." We each take a side of him, starting with unbuckling his legs. "So, who used the pole and who threw the punches?"

Killian looks at me confused. "Kiera told me that you guys let out your anger on Maxim."

He nods, like he's remembering. "Oh yeah. Colton, the pipe, and Tanner and I used brass knuckles."

I look at him skeptical, because I'm still not sure they did it. "That's not normally like you guys."

We move to unbuckle his arms starting at his wrists. "We didn't want to take anything away from you." I nod in appreciation, allowing my doubt to wash away. Aisling told me they were in that house when it exploded. So they couldn't have done this.

We work in silence as we finish unbuckling Maxim and we both step back, allowing his dead body fall to the floor. Seeing him land face-first puts a smile on my face and I only wish he was alive just to hear his wails. Leaving Killian to turn him over, I head to the tables and grab two freshly sharpened machetes. When I turn back around Killian has Maxim face up with his arms and legs spread out.

He takes a machete from me. "Since you got his fingers and manhood, can I go first?"

I look at him trying to hold back my laugh. "Manhood? You can't say dick and balls?"

"Hey. Just seeing it laying there has me in pain." Killian looks at the dick laying on the ground while covering himself.

I chuckle. "Yes, you can go first. But I get the head."

"Deal." I step back, giving him space. Killian brings the machete over his head and swings down right at Maxim's left knee. When Killian pulls the blade back up the lower part of the leg rolls to the side.

Killian steps back and I step forward. "You know I'm going to kill Lorcan for what he did to me and them." I look back at him. "Are you ready to take his place?"

He gives me a nod and I look back at Maxim as I bring my machete over my head and swiftly back down, right where his leg meets his hip. I pull the machete out and it's so satisfying seeing his leg detach from his body.

"We're not going to be able to walk into the house and kill him. It's going to be a war." Killian and I switch positions.

Not an all-out war but a strategic one. We'll back him into a corner, taking everything. "I know. We need to scare him first."

"Do you have a plan, Ri?" He gives me a smile, telling me he's ready for any plan I might have.

"Of course. Your guys are going to need to be ready to pull out once this goes down."

He nods, looking like the boss he is. "They've been ready since you were taken. They're just waiting for my word."

"How many do you have?"

Killian swings the machete down on Maxim's shoulder, detaching his arm. "About 60, but we'll have more when we take him."

"It's time to call in some favors." I look over at him and he nods.

"Call in some friends."

"Yes, and I have one I need to see in person." Killian is quiet as he looks at me and I know he knows I mean the Russos. It's not about asking for help. It's about apologizing.

He gives me a nod. "Tell me your plan."

As we finish dismembering Maxim's body, I tell Killian my plan to show our father he's not in control anymore.

Kiera and Xavier walk back into the room with their hair a mess, lips swollen, and clothes wrinkled as Killian and I are stuffing Maxim's body parts into duffle bags. "Did you guys have fun?"

"I had a lot of fun." Xavier pulls Kiera into his side and she swats at his chests.

"Shut up."

"They definitely used room three." Killian chuckles as he zips up the bag with the arms and legs.

"You say that like you know that room from experience." Kiera gives him a knowing look because we all know him and Aisling enjoy that room. It's a room setup to worship your partner. Massage oils, candles, whipped cream, chocolate syrup, blindfolds, feathers, restraints, and toys.

"Oh, I definitely know that room. I know all the rooms." Killian gives her a cocky smile. "Perks of being engaged to one of the owners."

Kiera walks over and looks down at Maxim's torso and head that's stuffed in the bag. "I can't wait for my father to see this."

I give her a cocky smile, knowing he's going to be furious. "Take a video for me."

"Oh, I'm already hacked into the security cameras." She bends downs and zips the bag shut. Xavier appears next to her as she stands and he grabs both bags and heads to the elevator. Kiera grabs my hand and squeezes. "I'd hug you, but you're covered in blood. I'm glad you're safe. We're going to go quiet for a little while because I can't get in a war with my father right now. But if you need anything, I'm a call away."

"Thank you." I squeeze her hand back before letting it go. My thank you has so much weight to it. I'd be dead if it wasn't for her and her people.

The elevator door opens and Kiera follows Xavier in. When the door closes, Killian steps up next to me and places a hand on my shoulder. "You go shower. I'll hose down the place." I give him a nod and head into the attached bathroom.

The light automatically comes on as the door opens and my breath catches. The mirror is right in front of me and I'm shocked at how bruised my neck looks. As I walk across the small bathroom to the mirror and vanity, I bring my hand to my neck. With my hips against the vanity, I tilt my head, taking in the damage Maxim caused. Seeing the outline of his fingers bruised on my neck makes me want to kill him again, but at least his death is permanent. These will fade.

Pushing from the counter, I turn away from the mirror and start stripping as I head toward the shower. Turning the water on, I let the cold water pelt my skin and wash Maxim away. As the water warms, I grab the soap and start scrubbing until my skin feels raw. When I step out of the shower, I'm no longer Maxim's prisoner. I'm back to myself. A fighter, not a victim who almost broke from her captor's hands.

Stepping out of the bathroom, dressed in the spare clothes I keep in the cabinet, I find all traces of Maxim gone. All that remains are our clothes we were wearing. "Your turn. Let's burn these clothes and head back to the house. I'm exhausted."

"I'll take those. We can burn these back at the house." Not really having the energy to argue with him, I hand over the clothes and lead the way to the elevator and out of the building.

Killian climbs into the driver seat of his charger and I get into the passenger seat. As my butt hits the seat, Killian holds out a phone to me. "To replace the other. Aisling had everything moved over."

"Thanks." I scroll through my messages and emails that I missed, making sure to skip over any from the guys.

"Aisling has been checking everything, making sure nothing was missed." Killian turns on his car and pulls out of the parking lot.

"So, for three weeks I wasn't needed."

"You were needed and missed." His tone has me looking at him, and I nod, knowing he'd always need me and come for me.

The sun is rising behind the house when Killian pulls into the driveway, but all the front lights are on. "Doesn't look like anyone slept last night."

"Do we ever sleep at night?"

"True." We both climb out of the car and I look around the neighborhood, seeing families waking up and having breakfast.

"What is it?" Killian is standing by the front porch while I'm still standing right outside the car with the door open.

"Do you ever wish our lives were like theirs? Normal."

He shakes his head. "We're not born to be normal. We'd get bored in that life."

"You don't think Aisling wants normal?"

"No, I don't. She wants less violence, but she loves this life. She loves us." I can feel him staring at me as I watch a couple say goodbye to each other as the man gets into the car. "Are you wanting out?"

I shake my head, wiping away any thoughts of wanting that kind of life. "No, I just wish we didn't lose so many people."

"Normal people die every day. Just in normal ways. If we die, it's for something we're fighting for. Come on, let's go inside." He waves me over and I close the door and head toward him.

Tanner, Colton, and Aisling look at us as we walk in. "We got donuts." Aisling smiles brightly at us.

"Thanks. I'll have one later. I'm going to bed."

I give them all a weak smile before heading into the room I was in earlier. I close the door behind me and climb right into bed. With my head on the pillow and the blanket covering my shoulders, I pull out my phone and bring up the group text with me and my guys. The only unread messages are from a couple hours after talking to Matteo.

Dante: We're coming, Rose.

My strong leader, rallying the forces.

Matteo: I still expect you at our front door in two days, Princess. You better fight.

Calling to the fighter in me. He'd be happy with how I fought through it all. A tear rolls down my cheek and it soaks into the pillow.

Enzo: You can get through anything. I love you.

My throat burns trying to hold in my tears as my heart breaks at his words. It's the first time any of them said I love you.

Matteo: He might have said I love you first but I asked you to marry me first.

I want to smile so bad at Matteo's jealousy, but I can't because we don't have the future he asked me for.

Dante: I'm going to be the first one to say it to you in person.

Not being able to hold back my sobs anymore, I bury my face into the pillow and let it all out. We'll never be able to say those words to each other. We'll never have our future together. I'll never feel their arms wrap around me, never melt into their kisses, and never hear their voices again.

Chapter Fourteen

Riona

An arm wraps around my waist and my skin prickles, pulling from my sleep. Panic starts to fill me, and I start to fight their hold on me. I try to roll away from them, but they don't let me. Their hold tightens. "Shh... It's just me." My body instantly relaxes at the sound of his voice. "Enzo?"

His body molds to my back and his warmth settles me. "I'm here, Beauty."

I curl into myself and cry. I need him. I need all of them.

My tears eventually dry and sleep starts to pull me under, but my body awakens when Enzo's hand starts drifting from my stomach, under my shirt and to my breasts. I moan from his touch and lean back into him. His lips skim over my shoulder and up my neck and I turn back to meet his lips. His lips skim over mine. "I knew I had to just wear you down."

My blood runs ice cold as my eyes shoot open finding Maxim and not Enzo. "No.... you're dead." I try to push him away, but I can't. I feel the cuffs around my wrists as I try to pull them apart. No. No. No. This isn't right.

Maxim moves on top of me as I try to kick away from him. "Does it feel like I'm dead?" His hand goes around my neck and he squeezes. "You can't kill me."

He presses his full weight on my neck and I try to scream but nothing comes out. This can't be happening. I thrash around, trying to get him off me. My vision starts to turn black as my body starts to shut down. Just as everything goes black, Aisling's voice is there. "Ri. Shh it's okay."

Suddenly Maxim is gone and I can breathe. My body flushes as the adrenaline rushes through my body and I take in large breaths. Aisling continues to soothe me by telling me I'm okay and running her fingers through my hair. The fear and nightmare slowly fades and I blink my eyes open to see Aisling sitting next to me but she's looking past me.

"I got her. Go." She looks back at me and her smile widens as our eyes connect. "Are you okay?"

No, I'm not, but I'm not going to tell her that. Instead, I change the subject. "Who was that?" I look behind me toward the door, finding no one.

"It was just Killian. You were screaming."

"Oh." I roll onto my back and stare up at the ceiling.

"You can talk to me about it, you know."

"I thought you wanted me to stop talking for my voice to heal."

"I want you to heal both physically and mentally."

"What do you want me to talk about? How I was held in a cell for weeks or how I voluntarily tied myself to a bed so Maxim could do whatever he pleased just to save Cassandra and her daughter from experiencing what I went through?"

Aisling lays down next to me and grabs my hand. "Tell me whatever you want. Whatever will help you heal."

"Talking isn't going to heal anything. Revenge and moving on will heal me." I pull my hand from hers. I don't need her softness now.

"Oh yeah. Who were you dreaming about then?"

I look at her and she gives me a knowing look. "I don't want to break, Aisling. Let me focus on this hate and rage inside me."

"You're going to have to break eventually. You can't bottle everything up."

"I lived through it once. I can live through this as well."

"Last time hardened you. I'm worried this time you'll shut it all off. All you'll be is hate."

"Maybe that's what I need to be. Look what happens when I open myself up to someone."

"You can't think like that." Aisling grabs my hand again and squeezes it. "Promise me you won't lose yourself in this."

Tears form in her eyes and I can't tell her I can't promise that. Losing them makes all of this so much harder. I think that's the worst part. If they were here, I know my heart wouldn't have this huge hole in it. "I'm tired, Aisling. We can talk about this later."

"Just promise me."

"I promise." I give her a weak smile and close my eyes. Aisling shifts closer to me as she cradles my hands in hers. I drift back to sleep with Aisling lying next to me.

"With you out of my way, the girls in that boarding house will be the first group I present to your father. They'll go for a pretty penny and be a great start for your father to get into the business."

I gasp awake, shooting straight up in bed, breathing heavily to pull air in my lungs as the panic from the dream leaves my body.

"Riona, what's wrong?" Aisling sits up.

"The girls." I scramble on the bed looking for my phone. "We need to get the girls out of that house."

"Hold on. What are you talking about?" She grabs my phone from the nightstand on her side of the bed.

I grab the phone and scroll to Miss Claus's contact. "Maxim must have been following me when I was trying to find you. He must've seen me go to the house when I dropped off Daisy. I just had a flashback of him choking me and he said he was going after them. They would be the first girls he'd sell for my father."

"It was just a dream." She looks at me concerned.

I hold her stare so she can see this isn't a delusion. "It wasn't a dream. I don't remember everything from when Maxim was choking me, but I just know that was real."

Aisling places her hand over my phone screen, stopping me from clicking on Miss Claus's contact. "Okay. It was real but Maxim is dead. The girls are safe."

"Do you really think Maxim kept that information to himself? Do you want to risk the chance? If he told his father or mine, they could still go after them. We need to make sure they're safe."

She lifts her hand. "You're right. We can't chance them."

I press call and the phone rings a few times until Miss Claus answers, "Riona, what's up? I'm just getting the girls ready for bed." Sounds of girls talking and running around come through the phone.

"Hi Sandra. Can you go into a room by yourself?"

"Riona, what the hell is up with your voice?" Concern fills her voice.

I lean my head back with my eyes closed, not wanting to get into it. "That's a long story."

"Hi Sandra!" Aisling says.

"Hi Aisling!" We hear Sandra tell the girls to brush their teeth and the sounds of the girls grow quieter.

Everything gets quiet over the phone at the sound of a door shutting. "Okay I'm in my room."

I look at Aisling and she nods for me to explain. "Okay. I don't want you to panic with what I'm going to say. You and the girls aren't in any immediate danger, and we'll have someone be there to watch the house tonight, but in the morning you and the girls are getting out of the country."

"What's going on?" I can hear Sandra's breaths pick up and I know she's scared, but I can't sugarcoat this.

"Your location has been compromised and I'm afraid some bad people have gotten their hands on it. We want you out of the house and town while we handle these people."

"Okay. Where are we going?"

That's a good question. "Don't know yet and I don't want anyone to get their hands on that information so you won't find out until you get on the plane."

"Okay. How long will we be gone? School starts back in two weeks."

Aisling leans forward. "We can't promise you'll be back by then. We'll get you a secure connection so you can reach out to the schools and get the assignments they need."

"Okay. When and where?"

I answer, "Be at the airport we've talked about at 9am. A plane will be waiting on the tarmac."

"Okay." There's worry in Sandra's voice but I want her to know we'll keep them safe.

"Hey, don't worry about tonight. You're safe. Someone will be there all night to make sure of that."

Aisling continues. "Just think about this as a vacation. The girls have been asking for one. Wherever you're at, it'll be fun and away from any danger."

Sandra takes a deep breath and I know she's settling. "You girls stay out of danger too."

Aisling says, "We will" as I say, "Not a chance." We all chuckle for a second until everything goes quiet.

I look up at Aisling with a somber look. "This is the last time we'll speak until this is all over."

"In that case stay safe. I expect to hear your voices after this. And that includes Killian, Tanner, and Colton."

"We'll call."

Sandra hangs up and I let out a breath in relief. The girls will be safe. Aisling leans back on the headboard. "Where are you thinking of sending them?"

Killian talked last night about calling friends to help so it's time I do that. "I'm going to call in a favor. We don't have properties that can hold twenty girls. But I'm thinking England."

Aisling smiles. "Tell Lady Tabitha I said hi."

"You know she'd punch you for calling her Lady."

"I know." She gives me a cheeky smile and climbs out of bed. When she gets to the door, she looks back. "We should probably get Killian's guys' families out of town too. I don't want Lorcan taking out his rage on them."

I nod. "They won't be able to leave until the night of though, or it could tip people off that something is about to go down."

"We'll make sure to stress that." She leaves the room and I pull up Tabitha's contact in my secure messaging app.

Riona: Hey Tabs, how are you? I need to ask a favor.

Riona: Btw Aisling says hello Lady Tabitha with a bow and all.

I chuckle to myself because I know that'll get her riled up. We met one summer a couple of years back when we were spending the summer traveling around Europe. One night we went to an underground fighting club and Tabitha was one of the fighters. After she beat the other girl, we bought her a drink and just hung out. We ended up spending a couple weeks at her castle. She might be the only woman who could beat me in a fight, but she taught me a lot of things as well.

Tabitha: Hey Ri!

Tabitha: Would you punch her for me?

Tabitha: What do you need? A fighting partner?

Riona: I need to fill your open rooms.

Riona: I need to get about twenty girls and their guardian out of the States for a while. Stuff is about to go down here.

Tabitha: These your girls?

She only knows about the girls and what I do because I had a job I had to do when I stayed with her.

Riona: Yeah. A shithead in my life found out about them. I need them safe while I end anyone else that might know.

Tabitha: Send them here. I'll be sure my driver picks them up from the airport.

Tabitha: They'll be safe with me.

Riona: Thanks. I owe you like a thousand times.

Tabitha: Maybe the next time you're in town, we can do a charity fight.

Riona: Only if you go easy on me.

Tabitha: No promises.

Tabitha: I have a meeting I'm walking into. Talk to you later. Send me the flight details.

Riona: Will do. Thanks again.

I close up her thread and pull up my pilots.

Riona: 9am tomorrow. 18 girls and 1 woman. No names listed. Bristol, England.

I climb out of bed and head to the bathroom. When I come back out freshly showered, I find one missed message.

Pilot: Thumbs up

Perfect.

When I walk out of the room Colton and Tanner are standing by the front door, looking like they're about to leave. "Hey, where are you going?"

"We're going to make sure Miss Claus and the girls are safe until they get on the plane." Tanner grabs his keys from the bowl and I see the two guns he's got in the back of his pants.

"Plus if she wants to give us some of her famous muffins, I wouldn't say no." Colton gives me a cheeky grin.

"I don't think she's going to have time to make muffins." I reach behind me and pull out a note I wrote for Sandra so she knows who to meet when the plane lands. "Can you give this to her in the morning? Tell her not to read it until after the plane takes off."

Colton takes the note from me. "Will do." I watch them leave and then I walk into the kitchen to make some coffee.

Aisling looks up from her laptop as I stand across from her. "You ready to book some hotels and getaways?"

I pour my coffee, adding a little bit of cream before walking around the island and sitting next to her in front of my laptop. "Yeah, but first..." I set my coffee down and swing out at Aisling, punching her with little force on the arm. "Tabitha says hi."

Aisling chuckles as she rubs her arm. "She's going to have a blast with those girls."

"Yeah, she is." I open up my laptop. "Okay, how many places do we need to book?"

"Fourteen. Several of the family are wanting to go together. Let's focus on houses." Aisling points to the paper setting between us. "Here's the families and the groups. I figured we'd book for two weeks, all over the country." She points to the paper above the others. "Here is a list of identities to book the places under and of course our corporate cards. For those that are flying, they'll have to use their fakes. Luckily, we have those records. Killian is out now, pulling cash to send with everyone."

"Looks like you have everything sorted." I give her a smile. "Let's go vacation hunting."

Chapter Fifteen

Riona

Killian walks in with a full duffle bag in one hand and pizza boxes in the other at around midnight. "I brought cash, food, and goodies."

"What goodies?" I look up from the house I'm booking.

He smiles at me. "Guns and ammo."

"Those aren't goodies. Chocolate and sweets are goodies." Aisling looks at Killian like he's crazy.

"Speak for yourself," I huff.

Killian walks over to the other side of the island and I reach out toward the duffle and signal for him to give it to me. He ignores me, setting the duffle on the ground and placing the pizza boxes on the counter. "Here are your goodies, Angel." He turns the top box around and inside is a chocolate chip cookie pizza.

Aisling is beaming as she blows him a kiss. "Thank you."

Killian walks around the island to her and gives her a kiss. "What can I do to help?"

"Serve me some pizza." I give him a cheeky grin and he flips me off.

"You can get your own pizza."

Aisling looks up at him. "Can you message the ones we finish with details and get the cash ready for everyone?"

"That I can do." Killian pulls a chair next to Aisling and she hands him our list. "How are we getting the cash to everyone?"

"That's up to you." I get up and walk around the island. I can't wait anymore to see the goodies. "We can do drop offs, pickup locations, or ship it to the houses."

I bend down and unzip the bag. Sitting right on top are bundles of twenties. There's at least $60k here. Grabbing them, I drop them onto the island so I can see the guns. Scattered at the bottom of the bag are all different types of handguns and pistols along with a ton of ammo boxes. A large smile pulls across my face as I skim my fingers over all the guns. "So pretty."

"You should see the rifles in my trunk." I look up at him fast when he mentions a rifle.

"You're hiding stuff from me." I pout at him, and he shrugs. "I need to test them out." He nods, knowing why I need to test them out. It's been a while since I shot a sniper rifle.

My stomach growling has me stepping away from the guns and grabbing plates from the cabinet. I set three plates down next to the two boxes of pizza. Setting Aisling's dessert pizza to the side, I open the bottom box finding a supreme pizza. Not my favorite but right now I could eat anything. Placing two slices on each plate, I slide a plate to Killian and Aisling each. "You did drop off food for Colton and Tanner, right?"

"Yeah. They got a meat lovers."

I take a seat back in front of my laptop with my pizza next to it. "Great. Were they bored out of their minds?"

"Not at all. They're planning how all of this is going to go down. Every little step and backup plans." Killian looks between the paper and his phone, sending out information.

"Have we figured out when all this is going down?" I take a bite and hum at how delicious it tastes.

"Not yet. Just waiting for a call from one of my inside men. It'll be in the next couple of days."

Days…that's not a lot of time. "There is so much that needs to be done." And I still need to find time to go see Zach.

"Well, we're about to get one thing done." Aisling waves the paper we've been working on at me.

"True." I type in the card information on the house I was booking when he arrived. "How many do we have left? I'm just finishing up the house on the beach for Adam, Jeff, and Harrison's fiancées and Alec's wife and little girls."

I reach out for the paper Killian is using and Aisling hands it to me. I quickly write down the booking information and scan the rest of the paper. "Only three left."

Chapter Sixteen

Riona

"Well, you've still got it." I look up from the scope on the sniper rifle and look to Colton who's lying next to me with his own rifle.

We've been in the woods on the backside of the estate for the last couple of hours. I've tested out not only the sniper rifle, but also the handguns and automatic weapons. Wherever Colton and Tanner got them, they're good quality.

I give him a wide smile. "Did you really doubt me? Were you hoping to get a chance to beat me?"

"Yeah, I was. You were rusty at first."

"Never." I chuckle and it actually feels good. It feels normal. "Do you want to go another round?"

"Definitely." He grabs the walkie-talkie next to his rifle. "Can you set five cans on each log?"

Tanner's voice sounds out. "Again? Really? You can't beat her."

I bite my lip to hold back my laugh as Colton growls. "Just set up the cans."

"Fine but we're done after this." Colton chuckles and looks over at me. "Seems someone is getting bored with target duty."

"Can you blame him?"

He shrugs his shoulders. "I guess not. We're having all the fun."

I look through my scope and watch Tanner set up my cans. As if he can sense me looking at him, he looks up and smiles. I smile to myself. They have both been great this evening, making it feel like old times. "I want to go see Zach tonight. Are you still in touch with him?"

"Yeah. He's at the club most nights." The club. Their club. I figured that's where he was with them gone, but it never really hit me I'd have to go back to the place I met them. The place that holds such a special spot in my heart. I look away from him and out toward the woods. "I can ask him to meet you somewhere else."

I shake my head. "No, that's okay."

"If you're not ready to go..."

Luckily Tanner interrupts him. "Okay, you're both all set."

Colton holds my stare for a second as I silently tell him to drop what he was about to say. He drops his eyes from mine and I know he won't bring it up again.

"Okay, thanks. Make sure to note I'm about to kick Red's ass."

Tanner chuckles. "I'll make sure to note it when it happens."

I look through my scope, making sure Tanner is out of the way. "You ready?" I ask Colton without looking at him. I adjust my aim slightly, noticing the wind change as the sun is setting in the background. "Yeah, let's do this. Five cans. One second between each shot."

I move my gun a centimeter so the cross is aligned with the yellow dot on the metal can. "3..."

"2..." he continues.

"1..." We both fire our first shots as one. As we trained so many times, we both make a quick but tiny adjustment before we fire again. We do this three more times and then I pull away from the scope and smile at Colton. "So in sync."

"Just like always." Colton grabs the walkie talkie. "Tell me, bro. Tell me that I beat Red." Colton's voice echoes through the woods as we both turn toward where it's coming from as footsteps sound out. Tanner appears from the darkening woods. "Sorry to disappoint but Firecracker won."

"How the hell would you know that if you're here?"

Tanner gives me a smile. "Because she always wins. Now come on, let's get out of these woods."

456

Tanner holds out his hand to help me up and then we quickly dismantle the rifles and fold up the blankets. "Who wants Sally's? I'm starving." Tanner throws the duffle full of weapons over his shoulder and we head out of the woods.

"Yes. Sally's. I haven't had her cheeseburger in forever." Colton makes a show of rubbing his belly. "But after we eat, we're going to Silas."

Tanner looks over his shoulder at me confused but before I can say anything Colton answers the silent question. "She wants to see Zach."

Understanding flashes across Tanner's face and he gives me a nod. "I could go for a drink."

"Or five," I add. I would love a night to just forget.

When we reach Colton and Tanner's SUV, they get into the front as I climb into the back. As we drive out of the estate, I get a glimpse of the house in the distance. "Has the house been cleaned out yet?"

Tanner, who's in the passenger seat, turns to look back at me. "Yeah, the bodies were removed and the blood cleaned up that night. The next day the whole house was cleaned. Killian and Aisling have had some guys out fixing up the place too. They wanted it ready for when you wanted to move in."

"Move in? Why does it sound like they aren't coming? This is our property."

"Well, they figured they'd move into your father's house after all this."

457

"Oh." When we bought this property, it was supposed to be for all of us. Aisling and Killian were planning on building a house on the back of the property. I guess with my father's betrayal, him stepping down is more accelerated than we originally planned. I love this property so I don't want to give it up, but living out here all by myself isn't something I want either.

"We can be your roommates when we're in town. Just think of all the fun we could get into." Tanner turns in his seat and squeezes my knee.

The three of us together is trouble. "We wouldn't get into any good fun."

"Don't we know it." We all chuckle as Sally's comes into view. It looks busy.

As soon as the car is parked, we're all climbing out, but my reflection has me stopping. "Oh shit. I can't walk in there with all these bruises. Sally will lose her shit." I can't believe I forgot about them.

Tanner walks to the back of the car and reappears a second later. "Here." He hands me a hoodie. "This will cover most of it."

I quickly pull it on and pull the hood over my head. It'll at least cover me until we get to the booth.

The door chimes as we walk in and I hear the regular welcome from the waitresses. "Welcome to Sally's. Please sit anywhere that is open."

We head to the back of the diner to our normal spot, which is luckily open. As I slide into the booth, making sure the bruised side of my face is toward the wall, I hear Sally's voice calling out Tanner and Colton's names. They sit in the booth across from me and I slide my hood off just as Sally reaches us. "It's so good to see you boys. Oh, and you brought Riona with you. How are you..." Her words are caught in her throat as I feel her eyes on me. I keep my face down, not looking at her but she isn't having that. "You look at me, little girl."

I respect Sally so much that I would never disobey anything she said. Slowly, I look up at her and when she sees the healing bruises she gasps. "Who do I need to kill for putting their hands on you?"

I smile at her threat to kill someone for me. "Someone who no longer exists in this world."

She gives me a proud nod, knowing I killed the person that hit me. "I'll get you all your usuals."

Sally turns and walks away muttering to herself. "She scared me there for a second." Tanner looks at us with wide eyes.

"She was a whole different person. Makes me wonder what her past was like." Colton's eyes follow her to the back.

"Not pretty is my guess." I look back to the men across from me and take a big breath. "But I'll never ask her." They shake their heads, agreeing. We all know to never bring up people's past traumas.

As we walk up to the bouncer at Silas, he gives us each one look and ushers us in. I guess Tanner's call to Zach when we left the diner is the reason for that. The club is packed as we make our way through the hundreds of people to the back. As we pass the bar, flashes of Enzo and I standing there flirting come to mind. My skin breaks out in goosebumps just thinking about how he made me feel. We walk by the exact spot and I can practically see us standing there waiting for the bartender to notice us.

I bump into Tanner's back when he stops abruptly which pulls me from the memory. Hands instantly go to my waist and I know it's Colton steadying me from behind. Tanner looks back at us with wide eyes as a group of drunk girls sway past him. "Sorry."

He starts moving again and I grab onto his shirt, following after him. My eyes track the group of girls to the dance floor and I can almost feel Matteo's hands roam my body as he danced with me. My body sparks just thinking about it.

Before I know it, we're walking down the back hallway, past the bathrooms, to the door that leads upstairs. With the darkness surrounding us and the music going quieter, a pit starts to sit in my stomach. Zach is waiting for us at the end of the hallway, looking like the boss he is, now that they're gone, in a suit with his blonde hair styled back. I push past Tanner and hug him. Zach and I aren't super close but right now I need some connection to them and he's the closest thing I got.

I don't know if he feels the same about me, but he hugs me back just as hard. After several long seconds we finally release each other. "It's good to see you, Riona. But I have to say you've looked better."

I chuckle as I look down at my tank top, leggings, and sneakers. I took off the hoodie when we left the diner because it was too hot and I didn't care about everyone seeing the bruises here. "I'm sorry I didn't get all glammed up for you."

"Well, next time you better." We both chuckle and then he waves us into the open doorway. "Come on up." I move past him and head up the stairs. I can hear the guys saying their hellos but I don't look back because my eyes are locked on their office door. When I reach the door, my hand hovers over the handle because I'm not sure I can go in there.

"I'm in the conference room." Zach saves me and I let out a breath. The next door is open but as I step into the conference room my heart stops as I'm hit with memories of me and Dante.

"This is where I've been working." I jump at the sound of Zach's voice, realizing I've made my way to the end of the table, where Dante and I first had sex.

"Do you want anything to drink?" I pull myself from my memories and turn to find all the guys standing by the small bar.

"Yeah, I could use one."

Seeing Zach and hanging out with him and the twins was nice. It felt normal, like it was a couple of weeks ago and everything was good. But every time I smiled, I thought about Matteo's big bright smile when he was excited, Enzo's calming touch, or Dante's eyes when I would tease him.

Eventually Zach had a club situation that he needed to fix, so we left him, promising to hang out again. Now as we walk through the club with the music blaring, I'm not quite ready to lose the happiness I feel. Maybe I need to go back to the old me before I met Matteo, Enzo, and Dante. What better way to do that than to connect with Tanner and Colton like we used to?

As we pass the dance floor, I grab both their hands and pull them toward it. "Dance with me."

My smile is filled with fake excitement as I walk backward with a sway in my hips, pulling them to the middle of the floor. I see the hesitation in their eyes probably reading my fake desire, but I don't care. I need to feel something. Letting go of their hands, I close my eyes and lose myself to the music. If they want to join, that's up to them.

I can feel their eyes on me as I sway my hips to the music before one of their hands finds my hips. Their body presses up behind me and I grind back against them as their lips brush against my ear. "Is this what you wanted, Red?"

A second pair of hands touch my waist as Tanner presses to my front so I'm sandwiched between them. Opening my eyes, I find Tanner's face close to mine and my breath catches with anticipation. At least until a cold shiver runs down my spine to the pit in my stomach. Panic rips through me at their touch and in disgust with myself. I quickly push them off and walk away with them calling out after me, but I don't stop. I need to get out of here. As soon as I step outside, I take in a deep breath of air, but I don't stop walking.

"Ri, wait a minute," Tanner calls after me. When I reach their SUV, I finally stop and rest my head against the cool window.

"Red, did we do something to upset you?" There is so much worry in Colton's voice.

"No, I swear you didn't do anything I didn't ask for. It's just me."

"Talk to us." I feel them standing behind me and I'm relieved they don't try to touch me.

"I panicked and I don't know why."

Colton places his hand on my shoulder. "Red, look at us."

I shake my head. "I don't want to talk about it."

Tanner steps next to me and leans against the SUV. "Firecracker, you've been through a lot without any time to process it. It's okay to freak out; we just want to be there for you."

I take a deep breath, building up my wall and turn around to face them. "I don't need help with processing anything. I'm over all of it. All I care about now is taking down my father."

Once I get my revenge, everything will be fine. I'll bury it with my father's dead body. Colton opens his mouth to say something but luckily all our phones chime, stopping him. We pull out our phones and I can't help but smile at Killian's text. Just what I needed.

Killian: It's happening tonight.

Chapter Seventeen

Riona

Headlights appear in the distance on the road I know my father would take to get to the warehouses for the drop off he's expecting. "He's here," Colton's voice rings through the earpiece we're all wearing.

He looks over to me with an excited smile. "You ready for this, Red?"

"Most definitely." Colton and I have been laying up on the roof of one of the warehouses for an hour, waiting for this moment, while everyone else is either waiting in the warehouses or down the other road, waiting for my father to arrive.

Looking through my scope, I watch my father's sedan drive down the road with two SUVs in the front and back of it. He's bringing a lot of guys with him. I guess he's excited about his first shipment of skin from the Bratva. He's going to be furious when he finds out the FBI seized the semi-truck about two hours ago on I-78 from an anonymous tip. A wicked smile pulls across my face as I imagine my father's head exploding in anger.

The line of cars stop in a row, facing the other side of the lot where the semi-truck is expected to show. Right at 2 am, I hear the sound of the semi-truck we borrowed and I watch as my father and his men step out. As the semi-truck comes to a stop 50 yards away from my father, there's only silence as he waits for the driver to step out. He's about to have a rude awakening. Shifting my sniper rifle toward the semi-truck, I watch as Killian and Tanner climb down. Quickly switching back to my father, I chuckle at the shock on his face.

"What the fuck are you doing here?" my father's voice comes through the open microphone Killian is wearing.

"To see your face when you realize your shipment of skin has been seized by the FBI." Killian stands in front of him with a confident smile on his face and his arms crossed over his chest. My father's face turns red as he sneers at my brother. I can almost see him vibrating with anger.

"You worthless piece of shit." Our father pulls out his gun, aiming it at Killian's head and everything gets chaotic for a few seconds as Killian's guys barrel out of the warehouses and surround my father and his guys. The only person who doesn't have his gun out is Killian because Tanner is right next to him with his gun aimed at our father's head. For the first time ever, I see the power pouring out of Killian. He's the boss he's been trained for his whole life.

"Do you really think this would stop me? I don't need those girls to start up my sex trade. I'll just grab some girls off the street. Maybe even start with pretty little Aisling." Our father's wicked smile grows sinister as he tries to get a reaction out of Killian. But Killian doesn't need to react because I will.

My finger squeezes the trigger and the bullet flies through the air and hits the ground right in between his feet, making him jump back. Fear flashes in his eyes but only for a second. "What the fuck was that? You going to kill me and take over? My men will never follow you. You will never..."

"Enough," Killian's voice booms, cutting off our father. "We're not here to kill you tonight. That would be too easy."

At that Colton and I take out the four council members standing on each side of our father. They were my father's highest-ranking guys and the first to support anything my father wanted. As the four dead bodies fall to the ground, the undercover soldiers of Killian's that arrived with our father change their aims and hold their guns to the heads of the other soldiers.

My father spews insults at Killian as Colton and I stand from our positions and sling our guns over our shoulders. But when we emerge from the warehouse, my father grows silent. A smile grows across my face as I close the distance between us and stop next to

Killian, making sure I'm standing slightly behind him. Killian has barely said a word but he's ruling this meeting, showing everyone he's running the show.

My father's stern expression starts to crack as he actually takes a look around and realizes how weak he is. His face is bright red as he glares at me. "You shot at me." His gun moves to my head and I don't flinch.

"You kidnapped me, killed my boyfriends, and sold me to the Bratva. You're lucky I didn't kill you. But don't worry, I will. I just want you at your lowest and begging for your life."

"I'm your father. I raised you."

"And I'm only doing what you taught me. Taking my revenge for the actions you took against me."

"My actions. You're the one who disobeyed an order," my father screams at me as he stomps his foot on the ground. He's crumbling in anger that his kids would stand against him. I look at Killian and we both share a secret smile. Our work here is done.

"Let's go," Killian commands and we both turn our backs on our father with Colton and Tanner and head into the warehouse that has our cars on the other side.

"Don't turn your backs on me, you disrespectful children. I'll kill you for this." One gun cocks back and then several others do the same, telling us our father took action to shoot us and Killian's men weren't allowing it.

When we get to the SUV, Killian and I jump in the backseat as Tanner and Colton get into the front. As Tanner pulls us away from the warehouses, I smile over at Killian. "Well done, Boss."

Tanner and Colton both nod and say, "Boss."

A strong smile forces on Killian's face as he leans back in his seat and pulls out his phone. Let his reign begin.

Chapter Eighteen

Riona

"Are you sure you don't want me to go with you?" I look over to Aisling as she drives me to the airstrip the following evening. Word has spread around about last night and slowly people have started turning their allegiances to Killian. Hopefully by the time I come back, all of them have or they're going to get an unpleasant visit from us, either making them kneel or eliminating them.

"I'm sure. I need to do this on my own." She looks at me skeptically and I know she's worried about me going to Italy to see Lorenzo Russo, the head of the Italian Mafia and Dante, Matteo, and

Enzo's father. "I'm not going to break in front of their family. I don't let anyone see me fall apart."

She gives me a weak smile as she grabs my hand and squeezes it. "Just promise to call if you need to."

"I promise." She pulls into the private airstrip and the only plane waiting is ours with the flight attendant waiting at the bottom of the stairs. Aisling puts the car in park next to the plane and the flight attendant goes to the trunk to grab my bag.

Turning to her, I give her a smile. "I know you're worried about me, but I need to do this alone. It's only for a few days and then I'll be back ready for our next part of the plan."

She pulls me into a hug. "Call if you need me."

I hug her tighter. "I will." We release each other and I climb out of the car and head to the airplane.

At the top of the stairs, the flight attendant greets me, "Hello Miss Murphy! Can I get you anything to drink before we take off?" He follows me to my seat.

"Hi Martin! Can I please get some water?"

"Of course. Bottle or glass?"

"Bottle."

He heads to the bar area and grabs a bottle of water and then hands it to me. "We'll be taking off in a few minutes."

"Thank you, Martin. I'm going to the bedroom in the back once we take off, so just relax."

He gives me a nod and leaves me alone. Buckling my seatbelt, I lean back in the chair, looking out the window to the dark runaway with the city lights in the distance. The pilot's voice comes on over the intercom. "Miss Murphy, the doors are closed and we're taxiing now. Our flight will take 8 hours and 15 minutes, meaning it will be approximately 10:15 when we land."

The plane starts to back up, before turning and heading to the runaway. I never look from the window as the city flies by as we rush down the runaway and tilt up, gliding into the sky. As soon as the plane levels off and New York is a small blip on the ground, I unbuckle my seatbelt and head to the back bedroom. These last couple of days I haven't been able to get a full night's sleep with everything that needed to be done and because of the nightmares, but tonight I'm going to sleep. From my bag, I pull out the sleeping pills Doc gave me and pop one in my mouth. Swallowing it down with water, I climb into bed and curl into the middle. Within minutes, I feel myself falling into a deep sleep.

As my driver pulls up to the Russo property, a sense of deja vu washes over me. The light brick grand villa with greenery running up the front wall seems so familiar. The car stops at the iron gate and I roll my window down for the guard approaching the car. "Hello, I'm here to see Mr. Russo."

"And you are?" He looks over like I'm a threat, and I smile, appreciating his caution.

"Riona Murphy."

He's quiet for a second as he looks at one of the few cameras and waits for approval. After several seconds the gate starts to open and the guard steps back. "Mr. Russo is waiting for you. Have a good day, Miss Murphy." I give him a respectful nod and roll up my window.

My driver pulls up to the front door where two men are waiting. One looks like the butler, with his black tux and white shirt, while the other looks like he's ready to kill me with the gun hanging off his hip at any misstep. My eyes connect with my driver. "This shouldn't take too long."

He nods as the butler rushes to the car and opens my door. "Hello Miss Murphy, welcome to the Russo estate. My name is Richard if you need anything."

I climb out of the car and give Richard an appreciative smile. "Thank you, Richard. Is it okay for my driver to wait here while I meet Mr. Russo?"

"Oh Mr. Russo insists that you stay here for your time in Italy."

Shaking my head, I wave him off. "Oh, that's not necessary. I already have a room booked in the city."

"He insists. Your room is already being prepared."

"Umm, okay." I turn and look at my driver. "Tim, you can go. I'll call you when I'm ready to be picked up."

He nods and opens his door. "I'll just grab your bag."

Both Tim and Richard head to the trunk and I close my door. "Thank you."

They both say, "You're welcome, Miss Murphy." Richard carries my bag to the front door. "I'll take this up to your room, Miss Murphy. Paul, here, will escort you to Mr. Russo's office."

"Thanks again, Richard." Paul holds the door open for me. "Paul."

"Miss Murphy," he answers as I pass him and step into the foyer. So, he's not as chatty as Richard. I follow Paul through the house, taking in every room we pass, awed by the classic design and antique furniture.

When we reach a closed door in the back corner of the house, I know we're standing outside Mr. Russo's office. Paul knocks once before opening the door and gestures for me to go in. I slide past Paul and walk into the office to find an older gentleman sitting behind a desk. When he looks up, my breath catches at how much he looks like Dante, or should I say, Dante looked like him. Their facial features are exactly the same, but he doesn't have Dante's blue eyes. They're brown instead and my heart weeps looking at eyes that are identical to Matteo's.

Standing in the middle of the room, I feel Paul behind me but my eyes are on the man in front of me. "Miss Murphy."

"Mr. Russo."

"Are you here to kill me?"

A giggle slips out, but I quickly shut it down as I sense Paul drawing his weapon and my hand instantly goes to my knife, stuck in the waistband of my jeans but I don't pull it out. "That depends. Is what Matteo told me true? You had nothing to do with Tony kidnapping and raping me?"

"That is true. That was not done under my orders."

I release my knife, showing them I mean no harm, but I think Mr. Russo already knew that. "I'm here to apologize for my father killing your sons. They died because of their involvement with me."

"You're here to apologize on your father's behalf?"

"No. I'm here apologizing for being the reason they were killed."

"Sweet girl. What your father did isn't your fault and you shouldn't hold the burden of it. Your father did what he did for power over you. I learned a long time ago that your father would do anything for power." Lorenzo stands from his desk and walks around it toward me. "Would you mind walking the grounds with me?" There is a softness in his eyes that makes me want to trust him, but it also reminds me of my father's softness, which I now know wasn't real. "I believe there are a few stories I need to tell you."

I tilt my head to the side, curious. Every time I envisioned how this conversation would go, not once did I think he'd offer to tell me stories about my father. "What stories?"

Mr. Russo looks to Paul. "This is a talk between Miss Murphy and I." Paul nods and leaves the room. Mr. Russo walks to the French doors and opens them. "Are you coming, Riona?" Mr. Russo looks back at me before stepping outside and I quickly follow behind him.

We walk side by side across the patio and down the stairs silently and I would be amazed by the gardens if I wasn't so preoccupied with what he wants to tell me. It feels like minutes pass while I wait for him to speak and I actually open my mouth to ask him when he starts. "Your father and I used to be very good friends and allies when we were younger. So close that it was supposed to be arranged that you would marry my eldest, Armando. You even came to visit with your family one summer. But even on that trip, Dante, Matteo, and Enzo were the only ones you would play with. So, it shouldn't have been a surprise when my boys told me about you and how you captured their attention."

"I thought your place looked familiar when we drove up. How long ago was that? I don't remember you or them." I look up at him wondering if what he says is true. And if it is, how come I don't remember it?

"You were probably three or four at the time."

"That would've made Armando a young teenager. No wonder I didn't want to play with him."

Mr. Russo chuckles. "That's true and he wanted nothing to do with you as well. You know, being too cool to play with a toddler."

I smile up at him. "And his future wife." He nods. "Is that why the arrangement didn't work out?"

Mr. Russo frowns. "No, your father was the reason. As we got older, he wanted more power and would do anything to get it and then with how he handled your mother's situation, I cut ties with him completely." What does he mean about my mother's situation?

"That's when I appointed Tony to New York. Since the day of your mother's funeral, I haven't spoken a word to your father. But as you're very much aware, our organizations got tied up together five years later." He stops walking and turns to me. "This next part is going to be hard to hear, so if you don't want to know, tell me now."

I look up at him and I know whatever he has to say next is about my kidnapping and it has the power to possibly break me but I can't not hear it. If I walk away now, I'll always wonder what he was going to say. "Tell me."

"Your father's organization was growing and threats against him and his family were growing as well. Killian had already been a part of the business, but you, his little girl, was happy, innocent, and weak." My whole body starts to shake as my breath quickens.

"So, he did the unthinkable thing, putting you in danger, hoping to toughen you up."

"Stop skirting around it and say it." Anger filters through my words but I'm not angry with him.

"Your father paid Tony to kidnap you."

"To rape me?" I need this clarification.

"I don't think there were limits. He wanted you to come out a warrior." My heart breaks knowing all my trauma and nightmares are because of my father. A man I thought loved me and would die for me.

"When I heard about this deal, I was disgusted by my old friend and my own family. Taking away your light is a sin that could've destroyed you. I ordered Tony to let you go right away and to return here. I know now that he didn't let you go. I'm sorry for that and for my family's betrayal. I was the one to ship Tony to you when I heard you became... lethal and were looking for your revenge."

I stare off across the expansive ground trying to process that my father is the reason Tony got his hands on me. He's the reason I couldn't sleep without nightmares for months. Why I couldn't leave my room for weeks. As I think back to how broken I was, I remember now how my father never comforted me as I cried, how he would come in every morning to see if I was going to leave my room that day, how he'd call me a crybaby. I remember the first time I left my room, he pushed fighting classes on me and when I would cower in the corner, he would get angry and leave, calling me a disappointment. How did I forget this? How did I overlook them? Instead, I drew from the memories of his approving smile when I would take my instructor down or hit my targets.

As I stand there trying to process everything, I slightly hear Mr. Russo telling me he'll give me some space and for me to come find him when I'm ready. I think I made some sort of sound acknowledging that I heard him, but who knows. When I feel his presence leave, my knees buckle and I fall to the ground. My father never loved me. All he wanted was a weapon. I knew his deal with the Bratva outweighed our bond as father and daughter but before a month ago, I would have sworn he loved and cared for me and wanted me to be happy. Now I can see it was all fake to keep me in his pocket and to be used whenever needed.

I'm so caught up in my despair that I don't even notice someone approaching, so when they touch my shoulder, I startle and my reflexes take over, throwing a punch. My knuckles connect with their chin and they groan out in pain. "Shit."

I jump to my feet and almost crash back down to the ground when I see the man in front with dark features and light blue eyes. "Dante?"

A cocky smile forms on his face as he moves his jaw left and right. "God, you can throw a punch."

Really taking in the man in front of me, I notice how his hair is graying and he has thick worry lines in the center of his brow and deep crow's feet. This isn't Dante. It must be Armando. Realizing it's really not Dante, my heart sinks because I could really use them right now.

"I'm sorry to have spooked you. My father sent me out here to let you know lunch is ready. I'm Armando, by the way."

"Riona. Sorry for punching you."

"It's okay. I shouldn't have touched you when you didn't respond to me calling out your name." He gestures for me to come with him, and we walk back toward the house. He rubs his jaw as we walk. "I'm actually proud my once-arranged wife can throw such an impressive punch."

I chuckle. "You shouldn't have dismissed me so easily when I was three."

He chuckles too. "Please don't hold a grudge. At that age, the only girls I cared about were in my Playboys. Maybe you'll give me a chance now."

Knowing he's kidding, I smile at him. "I've already hit my quota of Russos."

"Well, damn." We both laugh as we enter into the large dining room where Mr. Russo is already seated and food is placed in front of three place settings.

"Come on, let's eat before the food gets cold."

Chapter Nineteen

Riona

As our lunch plates are removed from the table, Armando's phone rings and he stands from the table. "Please excuse me."

He answers the phone as he walks out of the room, leaving Mr. Russo and myself. "Mr. Russo..."

"Please call me Lorenzo."

"Lorenzo, I believe you had more you wanted to tell me."

"I do, but I wanted you to be able to process what I told you earlier."

"I don't think I'll ever really be able to process the fact that my father was the reason for both of the darkest moments in my life.

That is why I'm going to kill him. But first I'll take everything from him. That will be my therapy, my peace." He gives me a nod in understanding. I open my mouth to ask the question that's been on my mind since he briefly mentioned her, but I quickly slam my mouth closed when Richard and some staff walk in to start cleaning up.

"Why don't you come to my office with me? We'll have privacy there."

We both stand and I follow him out of the dining room and down the hall to his office. Neither one of us says a word until we're both sitting down with his desk between us. "You mentioned my mother earlier."

"Yes, I did."

"The situation you mentioned, was it about her death?" He nods. "I was told my mother and Aisling's father were killed by a rival in a car accident. They were trying to lead the rivals away from us."

My mind quickly flashes back to that night and how frantic she was as she woke me and Aisling up. She had pure fear in her eyes as she brought us into Killian's room. Her last words to us as she kissed our foreheads were, "I'm so sorry, my loves. Please know I love you with all my heart. We'll be back for you when we can."

"I feel you're about to tell me that wasn't the truth."

Lorenzo shakes his head. "There was no rival. Your father killed your mother and his right-hand man." Feeling my heart ripping open just a little more at the truth, I sit quietly waiting for him to continue. "Drew and Callie were having an affair and your father found out."

"So what, they were running and left us behind?"

"Oh God no. They were running to get help. To come here. Your father was becoming more and more ruthless and they were worried for your safety. He was making so many enemies. When they went to run, their only focus was you kids, but they couldn't have taken you when they knew he was coming after them. They trusted the wrong person with their affair and escape plan and your father intercepted them on their way to the airport. I'm not sure how they died but they never made it here and news of their death quickly reached me."

"So you don't actually know he killed them."

Lorenzo looks at me like I'm talking nonsense. "Do you really think your father didn't have a hand in their death?"

If he would have told me this a couple of months ago, I wouldn't believe it, but now that I know my father and what he really is, I have no doubt that they're dead because of him. He might not have killed them himself, but he gave the order for them to be run off the road.

I saw the pictures of the crash so I know that's how they went. He must see the realization come to my eyes because a softness comes across his face. Knowing this and everything else makes me wonder what else he has done. Craig did say my father orchestrated everything. Did he really orchestrate Aisling's kidnapping? At this point I wouldn't put it past him.

"I can see there's a lot going through your mind right now."

My view focuses back on Lorenzo. "You can say that. My father is more of a monster than I thought. I always knew he was one. Shoot, I'm one. You have to be, to be on top, but this is another level." I pause, taking in my own words and look at the head of the Italian Mafia. "How much of a monster are you?"

Lorenzo looks at me with a stone face but he isn't mad at my question. "As you said, we all are just a little bit, especially to be in my position and I'll never be voted father of the year, but I love my boys. I would never put them in direct harm. I brought them into this life at a young age to harden them but to also make them stronger. To make sure they survive it. To outlive me." But three of them didn't because of me. I don't voice that, but I do suck in a breath as my chest tightens.

Looking away from Lorenzo, I shut my eyes, trying to not cry. He stays quiet, allowing me my moment and when I'm able to pull myself back together, he has a soft smile on his face. "That's enough of the serious talk. We need to have some fun. When you showed up, I was going to cancel but I think it's just what we need."

"What's that?"

"Will you allow Armando and myself to escort you to a charity gala tonight?"

Shocked by the unexpected invitation, I try to decline. "Oh I don't have anything for that."

"No worries. Richard will get you something."

As if he knows we're talking about him, he walks into the office. "Sir."

"Please have a dress ready for Riona for tonight." I look between the two of them as they plan, realizing I didn't actually say yes, but obviously Lorenzo wasn't going to take no for an answer.

"Yes, Sir. Should I request Tanya and Wanda?"

"Absolutely." Lorenzo's smile widens. "Riona, you're going to be pampered this afternoon. Please relax and make yourself at home."

Knowing I'm being dismissed, I stand and walk over to Richard. We both leave the room and Richard closes the door behind us. "Please follow me to your room, Miss Murphy. Tanya and Wanda should be here shortly."

We head up the stairs on the right. "Do I have time to shower before they get here?"

"They're here for you. Shower and they'll set up in your room." Richard shows me to the first door on the right but I notice three other doors along the hall. I wonder who stays in those. Not wanting to be nosy, I step into the room Richard opens the door for and I see a massive suite with a king size bed, vanity, couches, a closet and a bathroom. "Well, this is better than the hotel I booked."

He chuckles. "That's good to hear. I'll leave you to your time. Your dress will be delivered at 6."

"Thank you, Richard."

"You're very welcome, Miss Murphy." He leaves my room, closing the door behind him and I move to my bag, sitting on the bed, and pull out my bathroom stuff.

A knock on my bedroom door has Tanya, Wanda, and myself turning from the vanity mirror. That must be my dress. Wanda leaves us as Tanya finishes pinning up my hair. These last few hours have been amazing. Tanya gave me a massage, Wanda gave me a mani and pedi, and then they both fixed my makeup and hair. "I'm going to put these in the closet." Through the mirror I see her carrying two bags and a garment bag.

More bags than I expected. "What is all that?"

"I think a dress, shoes, and underwear."

My eyes widen. "Richard picked out underwear for me? That's kind of creepy."

They both chuckle. "Oh no. He just called their personal stylist and she picked out everything."

"Oh good." I let out a breath in relief.

Tanya places her hands on my shoulders. "Alright, you're all set. Go get dressed and we can do any final touches."

I stand from my chair and head to the large walk-in closet. Closing the door, I drop my robe. Bending down, I open up one of the two bags, finding an adhesive bra and a matching nude lace thong. I step into the thong and pull it up my legs. After attaching the adhesive bra next, I look at myself in the mirror. I'm glad Richard didn't hand pick these because I don't ever think I'd ever be able to look at his face again. A sliver of royal blue catches my attention and I notice the garment bag is unzipped. I step over to it and pull it open, revealing a gorgeous all-royal blue satin gown.

I slip the thin straps off the hanger and slide the zipper on the side of the dress down. With the dress open, I carefully step into it and slide it up my body until the straps sit on top of my shoulders. Stepping back in front of the mirror, I zip up the dress and my breath catches. This is definitely not one of my princess gowns. It's simple but sexy as it hugs my body all the way past my hips, showing off my curves. The high slit shows off my left leg, the deep v shows just enough cleavage, and the open back just takes the dress to a new level. This is the kind of dress that I would have killed to wear at one of my father's events but never could to keep my princess image intact.

I grab the nude heels from the second bag and step into them. Standing straight, I run my hands down my sides, really taking in everything. I really look like a vision with my natural makeup covering up the fading bruises and my red hair curled and pinned up. I really wish my guys were escorting me tonight. Thinking of them in their suits from the night at the club after we killed Victor, we would've looked killer all together. Tanya calling out pulls me from my wishful thinking. "Riona, it's getting close to the time you need to leave."

I open the door and both Tanya and Wanda smile at me in awe. "You look beautiful," Tanya says.

"Amazing. You'll have everyone's attention tonight," Wanda adds.

My smile widens at their compliments. "Thank you."

Wanda steps up with a pair of diamond earrings in her hand. "Here, put these on."

Bending forward to look into the vanity mirror, I put the earrings on. When I stand back up, Tanya hands me a small clutch. "Lipstick and your phone are already in it."

"Thank you so much. This afternoon has been much needed and you ladies have made it perfect."

"We were happy to pamper you. Now get out of here. Mr. Russo is waiting for you." Wanda moves me toward the bedroom door. I give them each a hug before rushing out of the room and down the steps.

Chapter Twenty

Riona

Lorenzo and Armando come into view as I walk into the foyer and my smile widens with how handsome they look in their classic black tuxes with white button-ups.

Armando is the first to see me and he lets out a whistle. "Wow, you clean up nice."

Lorenzo turns to me with a proud smile. "You look beautiful." He steps forward and sticks out his elbow for me to take.

"Thank you both. You look very handsome." I lightly place my hand on the top of his forearm and Lorenzo escorts me out of the house with Armando behind us. The driver opens the back door of a limo that's sitting in the driveway and Lorenzo doesn't leave my side until I'm sliding in. I go to slide across the seat, but the door closes next to me and I watch the driver and both Russos walk behind the back of the limo. Armando is the first to enter through the other door and he sits on the bench that runs the length of the limo, leaving the seat next to me open for Lorenzo. Once we're all seated, the driver closes the door and gets into the front cabin. The wall is already up, giving us privacy, so when the limo starts to move, I look over to Lorenzo. "Is this event for your dark business or the all-eyes-on-you business?"

Armando chuckles. "What?"

"Criminal business or legit business?" I clarify.

"A little bit of both, but mainly legit. Everyone we will speak to will know who I truly am, but that business won't be discussed tonight."

I nod in understanding. "What is this gala for?"

"Support for those who have been abused, either physically, mentally, or sexually."

I smile because this is exactly a cause I've spent a lot of time and money on. "That's a good cause and one I hold dear to my heart."

"That's what I figured. I'll have to introduce you to the lady that spearheads this organization and event."

"Please do. I'd love to help her in any way I can." I haven't done a lot in Italy, but I'll happily provide my services anywhere.

"You can speak openly with her as well. She is a widow of one of my underbosses."

"Interesting." I nod, intrigued.

"Yes, she really is." A blushing smile comes across Lorenzo's face, and I wonder how interesting he really thinks she is.

Before I know it, we're pulling up in front of a hotel and my door is opened from outside. Camera flashes start going off as I stand from the limo. This isn't anything new for me so I step forward and give them a casual pose with my right hand on my hip and my left leg forward, showing the slit. A hand touches my mid back and I look to find Lorenzo and Armando standing next to me.

The three of us make our way past the photographers and into the hotel. Black and white marble floors and crisp white walls greet us as we walk into the St. Regis Venice. I'm in awe of how grand this place looks. My heels click across the marble as Lorenzo guides me toward the left where hundreds of people are gathering in a ballroom. As we step into the ballroom my amazement continues as I take in the white clothed round tables, the beautiful carpet and the greenery running up the walls.

My awe must be written all over my face because Armando chuckles next to me. "This is nothing, wait until you see the gardens." He points to the right at the several open patio doors and all I can see past the stone patio is green. "They have a maze."

"Wow. This place is spectacular."

"Your parties aren't this elaborate?"

"Oh, our parties are elaborate, but nothing this breathtaking."

"Well, thank you," a woman's voice comes from behind us.

The three of us quickly turn around and I'm met with a beautiful older woman dressed in a gorgeous silver beaded gown with her gray hair pulled back similar to mine. Lorenzo's smile widens. "Hello Camilla. You have outdone yourself again." He steps forward and places a kiss on her cheeks. When he pulls back, I swear I see hearts in their eyes. Looking to Armando to see if he sees it too, he looks like he's holding back a chuckle and now I'm fighting mine as well.

Lorenzo speaking again pulls my attention back to him as he stands at my side again. "This is my guest for the night, Riona Murphy. She is visiting us from New York."

Recognition flashes across Camilla's face. "Riona, this is Camilla Moretti. She's who's heading this event and the organization I was telling you about."

I step forward with my hand out. "It's nice to meet you. This place looks spectacular." Camilla slides her hand in mine, and we lightly shake each other's hands.

"It's nice to meet you as well, Riona."

"I know you're greeting everyone now but later on in the night I would love to talk to you more about your cause. I have a similar organization back in the States and I would love to offer my services if you ever need it."

"I would love that. So, what brings you to Italy? Is the arrangement between you and Armando back on?" She looks between the two of us.

Knowing she's talking about the arranged marriage Lorenzo and my father apparently setup when we were kids, I quickly say no but I'm surprised that Lorenzo and Armando answer so quickly as well, echoing my no.

As I look back at the two of them, we all chuckle but Camilla looks worried that she offended us. Lorenzo is quick to relieve her stress though. "Riona is just a family friend visiting."

"Oh, I'm sorry for assuming." She steps forward and talks low like it's only the two of us that can hear. "Are you looking to meet someone tonight? I can definitely point out all the available men."

I chuckle. "I'm not looking to meet anyone. I'm not going to be in town for long."

"Okay. But if someone catches your eye and you need an introduction, you let me know." She looks past me and she quickly stands taller and places her greeting smile across her face. "Oh please excuse me, I have some more guests to greet."

She steps up to Lorenzo and places a kiss on his cheek and he whispers, "Save me a dance."

She beams back at him before leaving us and I can't help but chuckle as I look at how smitten he is as he watches her leave. He looks back to me once Camilla is talking to a couple with a questioning look. "What?"

"You have a crush on Camilla."

Armando hooks his arm around my shoulders. "It's not a crush. They're fucking on the regular."

492

My hand slapping his stomach and Lorenzo's hand hitting the back of his head has Armando groaning in pain. "You don't speak about Camilla like that." His anger slips from his face as he smiles at me. "Camilla and I have been involved for a while."

"Oh. Why do you keep it quiet?"

"We don't. We just don't broadcast it. Especially at her events. Not everyone agrees with my lifestyle."

"I under…" An older gentleman cuts me off as he greets Lorenzo, shaking his hand and immediately starting into a conversation about investing. I look at the man like he has three heads because it's very rude to interrupt our conversation and to just assume Lorenzo wants to be talking to him.

Armando chuckles beside me. "Come on, Ri. Let's check out the maze."

Armando's arm slips from my shoulders and he places his hand on my mid back as he escorts me through the crowd to the open doors. Right before we step out onto the patio, I notice a group of women that are eyeing Armando with dreamy eyes but when they look at me their glares are deadly. "You're definitely turning the ladies' heads tonight. Do you need a wing woman?"

"Wing woman?" We step off the patio and onto the gravel and I link my arm through Armando's for support. The last thing I need is a twisted ankle.

"Yeah, I can play it so many different ways. I can talk to all the ladies, finding the best one, if there is a certain girl you want, I can go talk you up, or if you want to make someone jealous, I can act like your girlfriend."

He chuckles as we step through the entrance of the maze. "There are a few ladies I don't want attention from so I might have to use the girlfriend idea to keep them away."

I chuckle. "I'm okay with that. What is the situation with the girls that we just passed?"

He looks at me with wide eyes. "Stay far away. I slept with one of them several years back and she faked a pregnancy to try to lock me down."

"Lock you down?" I look at him like he's ridiculous and shake my head.

"What? I'm a hot piece of ass here. Plus, with my connections, I have several women after me."

"Okay. We'll keep the gold-diggers away from you."

"What's going to be our signal?"

"Signal?"

"Yeah, so you know if I want you to get all handsy or to step back."

"Handsy? I'm not getting handsy with you. How about if you don't want to talk to her, you grab my hand or put your arm around me, and if you do, we stay separated?"

He nods, weighing it in his head. "That should work."

"But don't call me your girlfriend to anyone."

"Are you that grossed out by me?"

I chuckle. "No. Once you call me your girlfriend, it will spread throughout the entire party."

He nods in agreement. "I like all this fake stuff. Should we come up with a big fight and you storm off when we're ready to leave because my dad will stay all night?"

"I'm not fake fighting. You let me know when you're ready to go and I'll fake jet lag, asking to leave."

"That's not fun. Do you want a signal for if you want to talk to someone or not?"

"I'm not going to want to talk to anyone in that way."

"Well, men are going to try. Do you want a 'help me' signal?"

"I'll be okay. I can take any man down to his knees if they cross a line."

He looks me up and down. "I believe that. I also believe my brothers willingly got down on their knees for you."

"It went both ways." I give him a wink and walk away from him with his mouth open in shock as I see the maze opening ahead.

He chuckles as he jogs to catch up with me. "Are you sure you don't want another Russo?"

His arm comes over my shoulders, pulling me against him and I quickly push him away. "Not a chance."

As we approach the patio, Lorenzo walks out with three drinks in his hands. "Figured you were out here." He hands me a glass of champagne and Armando takes one of the glasses of bourbon in Lorenzo's other hand. "This guy has the whole maze mapped out in his head."

I look over at Armando, realizing we did make it through pretty quickly. "How many times have you been through it?"

"A few. I found an aerial view of it and memorized the path."

"Why?"

"I can't get caught getting lost in a maze. Plus, it impresses the ladies." He gives me a cocky grin.

"That you cheat."

Lorenzo chuckles. "No. They just think he's smart and figured it out."

"You know Lorenzo, you should take Camilla in there. I bet she wouldn't mind getting lost with you."

He just shakes his head at me. "You're trouble. Come on. Let's go in. Dinner is about to be served."

With Armando at my side, we follow Lorenzo back in and to the table. As we approach the table, Camilla is already sitting down with two young couples. The seat next to Camilla is empty so I go for the one that will have me in between the Russos. Lorenzo pulls out my chair for me and as I sit, he introduces me to the other couples. "This is Marco, Angela, Sara, and Luca. Sara and Marco are Camilla's children." He takes his seat to my left as Armando takes the one on my right. "And this is Riona Murphy, a family friend from New York."

"Oh, we know who Riona is." Sara leans forward with a smile on her face. Oh man, what is she about to say that has gotten me noticed all the way over here. "Colton and Tanner are good friends and business clients. They've given us so many stories of all the trouble they get into with the Murphys."

Phew, nothing too bad then. They must be in the business of selling weapons. "Any trouble we have gotten into was because of them. They were the ones that came up with the ideas."

Marco chuckles as he rests his arm on the back of Angela's chair. "That isn't surprising. How are they doing? We haven't seen them in a while."

"They're doing good. We have some trouble back home that's taking everyone's attention."

"Then what brings you to Venice?" Luca asks with a narrowed gaze at me.

"I needed to speak with Lorenzo."

"About?"

"Boy, that is none of your business." Lorenzo's voice rings across our table but quiet enough not to draw attention.

Luca nods at Lorenzo and relaxes back into his seat. "My apologies."

Sara reaches under the table for him and they smile for each other. "Please excuse him. It's not every day we see a Murphy sitting with a Russo. Plus, your special skills are a little concerning."

My back goes straight as she discreetly mentions me being an assassin and my hand instinctively goes to my thigh where my blades are normally but not tonight. It seems now the open knowledge of my activities has spread internationally. Armando discreetly grabs my hand under the table briefly, having me look at him. "No need to worry about this Murphy. She was about to be a Russo too, if Matteo had his way." I give him a grateful smile for his support. "Plus, if she wanted Dad dead, she wouldn't have announced herself at the front gate this morning. She would have just let herself in."

Everyone seems to relax from that statement and just in time, since the servers surround our table, placing our salads down. Needing a distraction, I grab my fork and take the first bite of my salad. As I'm chewing, Armando leans over to me so I'm the only one to hear him. "Are you sure you don't need a 'help me' signal?"

Not expecting him to say that, I choke on a laugh and cover my mouth so no food comes out but of course the sound draws the tables attention. Lorenzo looks at me with concern. "Are you okay?"

Grabbing my napkin, I cover my mouth and nod. "It just went down the wrong pipe, right Ri?" Armando gives me a playful smile as he starts hitting my back lightly like I have something lodged in my throat.

I glare at him until I swallow and am ready to speak. "I'm sorry. Something Armando said shocked me and caused the choking."

"What did he say?" Sara asks.

"Oh, just something about being his beard for tonight."

Lorenzo and Camilla look confused but the other four snicker with me as Armando gives me a death glare. "Not in that way. She's just going to help keep the clingers away tonight."

"The male clingers?" Luca has a humorous grin on his face as he reaches across Armando with his fist out and I bump mine to his which has everyone laughing.

Armando continues to glare at me. "Now see if I help you when the prince gets his hands on you."

"Ohhh Arie, don't be upset. It was funny and we all know you aren't gay," Sara says as she tries to hide her smile behind Luca's shoulder. "No woman should have to deal with the prince without a little help."

I look between them, knowing I'm missing something. "Who's the prince?"

Angela leans forward. "He's not here yet. He'll arrive after dinner. He's too good to eat with the commoners. He just comes to schmooze with all the available ladies."

Sara has a look of disgust on her face. "He acts like he runs this country, but he has no power and barely has a title. He's just a descendant from the last king."

Camilla scolds. "Ladies, that's enough."

Sara looks at her mom like she knows actually what they're talking about. "Oh, come on Mom. You know we're right."

Camilla stares off with Sara but instead of saying anything she decides to ignore us and continue talking to Lorenzo. Sara looks back at me, scanning my upper body. "You're definitely going to catch his attention tonight and you won't be able to tell him no. My best advice is to get the dance over with and then walk away."

"Why won't he dance with you?"

Angela and Sara both hold up their left hands showing off their wedding rings. Looking down at my empty fingers, I bump Armando's arm with my elbow and give him a sweet smile. "Please give me a ring so I don't have to dance with the creeper."

"You told me you didn't want me to call you my girlfriend but now you want to be engaged? No." He holds my stare, and I can tell he's silently saying payback is a bitch.

"Fine." I look at Sara and Angela. If I have to deal with this prince, then Armando is going to have a miserable time too. "So, tell me ladies, which of the desperate women here tonight wants Armando's attention the most? The one he's most cringey over." A wicked smile pulls across my face.

"Oh, easy," Angela says as she searches the room.

"Don't you dare." Armando tries to sound forceful.

"Oh, there she is," Sara announces.

"Sara, I swear to God. You better not." I bite my lip, holding back a laugh and I see Luca and Marco doing the same as I follow Sara's look.

"Okay you see the girl with black hair three tables back? The top of her dress is sheer showing her bra." My eyes scan the table and I know exactly who they're talking about. Wow, this girl is trying way too hard.

"She has had a lot of work done." I can only see the top half of her body, but there is no way her boobs are real, she definitely has lip fillers, I wouldn't be surprised if her nose was redone, and her hair is definitely not naturally black, since I can see a sliver of blonde at her roots.

"Is that not your thing?" I look at Armando and he's still glaring at me.

"Amelia used to look so much better before she had all the work and she's a really nice girl that doesn't deserve you messing with her." I look at him, confused. There's definitely a backstory with them. Filing it away to ask him later, I look for the girls I saw earlier. I find them sitting next to Amelia's table. "How about the girls at the table next to hers?"

"Oh, they're all awful." Angela scrunches up her nose. "Total mean girls but the worst is the one in red." I spot the girl she is talking about immediately. She's beautiful with her long wavy blonde hair, flawless makeup and revealing, but not distasteful dress. The way she's demanding everyone's attention at her table, even cutting them off, tells me she's a bitch.

"Oh perfect. She looks like she'll drive you crazy in two minutes."

Armando looks panicked. "I don't have time now to get a ring. How about I cut in halfway through the song?"

"Deal and maybe we can try to hook up the two awful people." I give him a smile.

"A challenge. I like it." Sara looks eager to play matchmaker.

Before I know it, the servers are collecting my only-touched-once salad and setting a dinner plate in front of me with chicken, risotto, and green beans. We all dig into the delicious smelling food and all that's discussed after that is business, family, and final summer vacations.

By the time our dessert plates are removed from the table, I'm stuffed happily. The band started up several minutes ago and people started slowly making their way to the dance floor.

"Riona, would you mind having the first dance with this old man?" Lorenzo holds his hand out for me and I take it.

"You're not an old man." I stand from my seat.

He gives me a warm smile. "That's nice of you, but at my age, I'm old."

"How about nicely aged?"

He chuckles. "That does sound better."

With my hand in his and my other on his shoulder and his on my waist, he leads us around the dance floor and I get flashbacks of Enzo dancing with me at the club. "Did you teach your sons to dance like this?"

"No, my wife did." A loving look washes over his face.

"Enzo and I waltzed once… to a rap song." I chuckle at Lorenzo's shocked face.

"How did that work?"

"We were very off beat."

We both chuckle. "Did you ever dance with Dante or Matteo?"

"Dante, no. Matteo, yes but it wasn't as classy as this."

He shakes his head. "No need to say more."

We dance for a while without speaking and all I can think about is how much I miss them. I'm so in my head thinking about them that I don't realize I said that out loud.

"I know you do."

I look into Lorenzo's eyes and I see sorrow in his eyes. "It's still not real for me yet. I don't know if it's because of what I've been through, or I just don't want it to be. Sometimes I sense or feel they were there." Tears build in my eyes, and I take a deep breath to try to push the emotions down. "I know it sounds silly."

Lorenzo rubs my arm. "It's not silly. It's just how you're processing everything. You're looking for them because you want them there."

I nod. I want them here more than anything.

"How about a drink?" He changes the subject and I'm thankful. I don't want to cry here.

"Yes, please. Something strong."

"Bourbon coming right up." We walk off the dance floor and head to the closest bar. The bartender pours us two glasses of bourbon and I quickly grab mine and swallow it down with a wince.

I slam the glass back down on the bar and point to the glass. "Another, please." Lorenzo chuckles and takes a sip of his. I point to him with narrowed eyes. "No judging."

"I wouldn't dare." With my glass refilled, we step away from the bar and look over the crowd. Camilla is working the room, Armando is talking with Sara, Luca is with a group of girls hovering close by, and Marco and Angela are on the dance floor.

"I hate to say this but you have gotten the prince's attention."
I look at Lorenzo and he tilts his head to the right. A small group of
people gather to our right but one of the gentlemen is looking over at
us. He's a tall and lanky man but when he smiles at me, any hope
that he isn't as bad as they said goes out the window. And it only
gets worse when he runs his eyes down my body and adjusts himself
in his pants. Oh my God, what a pig.

"Can I have your jacket? I feel like I need to cover up."

Lorenzo moves to take off his jacket but the prince starts
heading our way. "Oh no, he's coming over. Do you have any
weapons in your jacket?"

He has an amused smile on his face. "No."

I wave it off and try to hide behind him. "Then keep it. Make
sure your son knows he has one minute or our deal is off."

Lorenzo chuckles just as the prince reaches us. "Hello, Mr.
Russo."

"Hello, Prince Silvio. May I introduce my family friend,
Riona."

"She's a breathtaking friend. Miss Riona, it's my pleasure."
He reaches for my hand and kisses the back of it.

I quickly pull my hand away from his and discreetly wipe his
spit off on my dress. "Hello, Prince Silvio."

"I would love to have a dance with the most beautiful woman
in the room." He thinks his grin is charming, but it sends a cold chill
down my spine.

"Oh, well you should definitely ask her." I scan the crowd behind him looking for the blonde in the red dress. When I see her, I point behind him. "She's over there."

He chuckles and doesn't even turn around. "I'm talking about you."

"Oh, well Lorenzo and I were in the middle of a conversation."

"I'm sure you can continue it later." He's too insistent.

"My boyfriend really wouldn't like me dancing with another man."

"You were dancing with Mr. Russo."

"He's a family friend." Lorenzo looks amused as he watches us go back and forth as I try to find a way out of this.

"I can be a very good friend of yours."

My stomach rolls at his hidden meaning. "Not that kind of friend. He's like a father figure."

"You can call me Daddy if you like." Bile actually comes up my throat and I swallow it back down.

"Prince Silvio, she's a respected member of my family; you will not speak to her like that. Riona, please go dance with the prince so he can leave us alone." Lorenzo looks like he's about to kill the prince so I down my glass of bourbon and Lorenzo takes my empty glass.

Prince Silvio holds out his hand for me to take but I ignore it and walk to the edge of the dance floor. He doesn't waste a second, pulling me against him and placing his hand on my lower back.

Grabbing his hand before it goes lower, I bring it back to my side and put as much distance between us as my arms will allow. "We don't need to be so modest." He steps closer to me and I try to step back but run into another person. Without an escape, I'm forced into close proximity with the prince. "I know you want me."

He moves his hand down my bare back again and I quickly grab his wrist and twist. "I don't care who you are. If you touch me again, I'll kill you faster than you have time to scream and walk away like a ghost before anyone realizes something is wrong."

A familiar growl from behind me has the hairs on the back of my neck stand up. Pushing the prince away, I quickly turn around looking for him. Through the couples dancing, I get a glimpse of his short dark hair and start pushing my way through the crowd. Just as his back comes into view in a clearing, I'm pulled to the right. I go to throw a punch but stop myself at the last second, realizing it's Armando. "What's wrong? Where are you going? I was coming to relieve you."

I look back to where I last saw Matteo at the edge of the dance floor but find no one there. Maybe I was seeing things. All the alcohol and talking about them must be messing with my head. "I couldn't stand another second with Prince Sleazeball and I needed some air."

"Then let's go to the patio."

I nod in agreement, and we head outside. We find an open table and sit down. "He told me I could call him Daddy in front of your father."

Armando spits out the drink I didn't realize he was taking a sip of. "No, he didn't."

"Oh yes, he did. Your father was pissed." I give him an entertained smile.

"Man, I wish I had that on camera."

"You also missed me threatening his life."

"Oh please, tell me what you said." He leans closer.

"Just that I could kill him before he could scream and walk away without anyone noticing."

He chuckles. "I bet he pissed himself."

"I didn't stick around to see." With a big sigh, I lean back on the chair. "I think I'm ready to leave." I roll my head to the side, looking at him.

"Then let's go back to the house." Armando stands from his seat and holds out a hand to help me up. "Let's go tell Dad we're leaving." We head back inside and find Lorenzo where I left him with Camilla at his side. After saying our goodbyes to him and promising to call Camilla, we head out of the hotel to our waiting limo with a valet standing by the back door.

Chapter Twenty-One

Riona

Armando walks with me to my room and I feel myself quickly draining. Today has been so long, it's hard to believe I've only been in Italy for 12 hours. "Thanks for tonight. Going to the gala with you and your father has been the brightest moment in the past week."

"I'm glad you had a good night. Even if the prince ruined the end of it."

"Are you kidding me? Threatening him and seeing the fear in his eyes was fun. I just wish I stuck around to see him run scared of me."

He chuckles as we reach my door. "Or you could've turned him on even more. He probably likes to be demeaned since he holds himself to such high standards."

"Oh God. Now you made me nauseous."

He shakes his head and chuckles. "Goodnight, Ri. See you in the morning." He turns to head back down the stairs.

"Isn't your room one of these?" I look behind me to the three other rooms.

"Why, were you planning to sneak into my bed later?"

"You wish."

He shrugs. "My room is on the other side of the house. These are Matteo, Enzo, and Dante's rooms."

I look to the three other doors on the hall and I'm immediately drawn to them. Letting go of my doorknob, I move to the door across from mine. As I twist the knob, I know Armando has left me alone and I appreciate it.

The door slowly opens and even before turning on the light, I know this was Matteo's room as his woodsy scent hits me. Reaching into the room, I find the light switch and flip it up. The two lamps turn on next to his bed, illuminating the room, and my breath catches. I was expecting a clean room with the bed made and everything in its place but instead the bed is unmade, knives and other weapons are scattered over every available surface, and clothes are thrown everywhere. It's like he was just here.

Pain shoots through my chest as the hope he's here dies knowing he isn't. The mess must've been from when he was here confronting his father about Tony. Tears burn in my eyes as I step into the room and grab the first shirt I find on the floor. I bring the shirt up to my nose and inhale his smell. His cologne fills my nose like he wore this shirt today.

With shaking hands and tears running down my cheeks, I unzip my dress and let it fall to the floor. I pull his shirt over my head and as his shirt falls over my body I can almost imagine his arms wrapped around me. Needing to have something from all of them, I leave Matteo's room and go to the next.

My knees almost give out as I open the next door and Enzo's clean laundry scent hits me. My tears start falling faster down my face as I take in his room that I can only see from the brightness on his computer screen. His room is just like I expected. It's tidy and the main focus being his computer screens that are rotating through city skylines. Being in his room, a sense of calmness fills me and a sob breaks from me. Even with Matteo's shirt and the feel of Enzo from his room, I still have a piece missing. I need all three of them.

Grabbing one of Enzo's pillows, I bury my face in it, soaking in his smell as I leave his room and go across the hall to Dante's room. Pulling my face from Enzo's pillow, I let the smell of Dante's aftershave surround me as well. Using the light from the hall, I move to his bed and climb right in surrounding myself in his sheets. With the feeling of them surrounding me, I let myself break from how much I miss them and wish they were actually here to hold me.

"We'll see you soon, Rose." Soft lips press a kiss to my temple and I sink further in the bed with a moan. As he pulls away, my body follows and I roll over, facing the door. My eyes crack open as light falls on my face and I see him standing in the doorway. "Dante." My eyes close again as exhaustion takes over. A smile pulls on my face, feeling his lips on me still. It's so nice knowing he was here.

I'm about to slip back into darkness when I shoot up in bed. "Dante?" I stumble out of bed with sheets tangled around my legs and somehow make it to the hallway without falling. The hallway is empty when I get there so I run down the hall to the stairs. There's no way he had time to get all the way downstairs. The stairs are empty and I stand at the top of the steps in silence. Hope quickly drains from me and tears roll down my cheeks. I feel like I'm going crazy. I'm seeing them and it's only making everything worse.

The hope and then the disappointment is breaking me. I can't stay here anymore. Turning back to the rooms, I quickly grab my dress from Matteo's room, my shoes and clutch from the floor outside my room, and close myself in my room.

I stare at the made up bed and throw my dress and heels on it. I'm not going to be able to get any more sleep. Pulling Matteo's shirt from my body, I head to the bathroom. As soon as his shirt hits the floor, a cold chill runs through me and all I want to do is pull it back on and never take it off. I can't do that. I need to start moving on without them. No matter how much I want them to walk through the door, they never will.

Pushing that sad thought out of my head, I unpin my hair and remove my bra and thong before stepping into the shower. Turning on the shower, I let the cold water hit my body until it warms up. Only then do I start my shower routine. I take my time washing and conditioning my hair and then I grab my body wash and lather it over my body. Once I rinse it all away, I turn off the shower and dry off.

With the towel wrapped around me, I step up to the mirror again. As I stare at myself in the mirror, I silently tell myself that it's time to let them go and grieve. Everyone has told me they were in that house when it exploded and me imagining them is only going to drive me crazy.

With one big sigh, I look away from myself and finish getting ready. I leave the bathroom a while later with the towel still around me, my hair dried and pulled up into a messy bun, makeup done, and Matteo's shirt and my dirty underwear bundled up in my arms. My bag is still sitting on the bed, opened so I throw the dirty clothes in it and grab some clean ones.

Once I'm dressed in my oversized t-shirt and jean shorts, I grab my phone for the first time since before the gala. I have a few messages from Aisling and Killian asking for updates and giving me updates but it's the time that catches my attention. It's just past 6 o'clock and I look toward the window, seeing just a slight glimpse of light. Sunrise will be soon. Quickly, I pack up my bag and leave it on the bed before quietly slipping out of my room, down the hall and stairs, and out the back patio.

As I walk through the garden, I spot a guard every now and then but I ignore them. At the edge of the garden is a big grassy area and I take a seat in the middle of it and lay back. Looking up at the sky, it slowly turns from dark blue to light and when orange starts to filter in, I sit up ready for the sun to peek out onto the horizon. As the top of the sun rises into the skyline, the whole sky lights up in this beautiful mixture of blue, orange, and yellow. A smile spreads across my face as the sun rises higher into the sky signaling a new day.

After a while, the large sun is fully exposed and the orange disappears and only yellow surrounds the sun. That's when I pull myself up from the grass and make my way back to the house. Once I enter through the back, I head toward the kitchen. I'm in desperate need of coffee.

Surprisingly there's no one in the kitchen when I enter, but I do find a full pot. Opening the cabinet above the coffee maker, I find the mugs and pour myself a hefty cup. I find creamer in the fridge and pour one drop in my coffee. Grabbing a stirrer from next to the coffee maker, I walk around the island and take a seat on the barstool as I grab a banana from the fruit bowl in front of me.

As I finish off my banana, I take a huge gulp of my cooling coffee and let the caffeine soak into my bloodstream. Richard walks into the kitchen a couple seconds later and he doesn't even flinch when he sees me, making me wonder if he knew I was already here. "Morning, Miss Murphy."

"Morning, Richard."

"Would you like me to make you breakfast or refill your coffee?"

"I'm okay Richard but thank you. Is Mr. Russo up yet? I'm rescheduling my flight to today and I wanted to say bye before my driver arrives." Which reminds me, I still need to let him and the pilot know about the change of plans. I pull out my phone and send a text to the pilot first since he has more to prepare with the change.

"Our driver can take you whenever you're ready." I look up at Richard and set my phone on the table. The driver I hired has already been paid for three days. He won't care if I call him again or not.

"Thank you."

Richard nods. "To answer your question, yes, both Mr. Russo and Armando are awake and in the office."

I quickly finish off my coffee and stand from the barstool. I grab the banana peel and the dirty cup to throw away and wash but Richard's hand is placed over mine. "I'll get those. You go talk to Mr. Russo."

"Thank you for everything, Richard."

"It's what I'm here for, Miss Murphy." He pats my hands before grabbing the peel and cup from my hands. As he turns his back to me, I leave the kitchen and head to Mr. Russo's office.

Mumbled voices sound behind the door so I knock. A second later the door opens and Paul is standing in front of me. "Miss Murphy."

"Paul. Can I speak with Mr. Russo?"

"Riona, come in," Lorenzo calls out to me and I step forward but Paul doesn't move.

"Do you have something to say?" I stare up at him, with a glare.

"No." He glares back at me.

"Then move." I give him a 'don't test me' look.

"Paul, move before she puts you on your ass." Armando appears behind him and places his hand on his shoulder. Paul finally steps back and I eye him as I pass. Once inside, I turn to Lorenzo as I hear Armando and Paul leave. I don't speak until I hear the door shut behind me. "I just wanted to thank you for everything."

"You're leaving?" He looks at me confused.

"Yes, it's time for me to go home."

"Okay. Please know you're welcome here at any time." He walks around his desk and pulls me into a hug. I wrap my arms around his middle, loving the fatherly hug. It's something I never knew I missed.

When I pull back, I smile up at him. "Hopefully next time all your men will know I mea no harm to you."

"Oh they'll definitely know. You're family now. Which is why I'm sending these guys back with you." He nods behind me.

The hairs on the back of my neck stand as I hear a door at the back of the office open. My heart beats rapidly as I turn toward the back of the room and see Dante, Matteo, and Enzo walk into their father's office.

Chapter Twenty-Two

Riona

My whole body runs ice cold as I see them and it feels like time freezes as I take in the sight of each of them. Are they real? I want to reach out and touch them to make sure I'm not imagining them, but I stop myself as it clicks that they're alive and they weren't there when I needed them the most.

Hiding all the emotions I'm feeling from seeing them here, I turn back to their father and give him a nod, silently showing him my thanks and appreciation. As much as my heart is happy and hurt right now, I'm glad they're here. He gives me a small smile which tells me I'm not hiding my emotions as well as I was thinking.

Not wanting to break in front of him, I turn heading for the door without looking at them. As I exit out of his office, I can feel them following. I don't make it very far before Dante pulls me into a sitting room. I know it's him before looking at him because he's the only one who would handle me this way.

I swing around and push him, but he only moves a step back and doesn't let go of my wrist. "Don't touch me." I try to pull my wrist from his hold but he just grips it tighter. Frustration builds in me as he won't let me pull away, so I push into him instead. With my hands flat, I push him as hard as I can on his chest. He takes a step back, bracing himself as I continue to hit him. "Was this a game to you?" I hit him again. "You just wanted to see me break?"

I hit him again, but it isn't as hard as I actually start to break. "Not only did I have to go through all the things Maxim did to me but I also had to lose you as well." I grip his shirt in both hands as I sag into him, crying. "I needed you and you weren't there."

Dante lets go of my wrist and wraps his arms around me, holding me against him as I break down, feeling everything. My legs give out, but Dante doesn't let me fall as he scoops me up into his arms and I don't even realize he moved until he's sitting down and situates me so I'm straddling his lap. "Rose, we're so sorry. We never meant to hurt you." His hands rub up and down my back, trying to sooth me. "We wanted to be there for you so bad. To hold you. To help you. To let you break." A third hand touches my back and I stiffen, not expecting another touch until I realize it's one of my guys. They quickly withdraw from me and I let go of Dante's shirt to reach for them. My hand finds Matteo's large, callused hand and I place it back on my back with my hand resting on top of his with our fingers locked. On my other side, I reach out for Enzo's hand, and he intertwines our fingers together.

Feeling all three of them, my sobs turn to relief that they're actually alive and here. "I missed you so much."

Dante kisses the side of my head. "We missed you too."

Matteo places a kiss on my shoulder and rests his head there. "Everyday."

Enzo kisses my other shoulder and rests his head there. "Counting down the seconds until we could see you again."

They all stay like that, finding any type of connection to me until I'm able to pull myself together enough to lift my head from Dante's shoulder. Sitting back on his thighs, I look to my right because I'm not ready to face Dante yet. Matteo's strong jaw is now covered by a short beard and his deep brown hair has grown longer, but his brown eyes are still open and happy. I unlink my fingers from his and lift my hand to his cheek. "This is new." I run my nails through the short dark hair, feeling the softness compared to normal prickly beard and he leans into my touch. "Do you like it?"

"Yeah, I do." He grabs my hand and kisses my palm.

Looking over to Enzo, I see he hasn't changed at all. His blonde hair looks perfect as usual with the longer hair combed back and to the side but it's his brown eyes that I seek out. They're the window to his emotions and I couldn't take it if they had changed. His eyes connect with mine and all I see is love and calm. Relief flows through me and I lean forward, resting my forehead against his. We both stay quiet as I breathe in his air, connecting with him again.

After a while, Dante gets impatient waiting for my attention, and he starts rubbing up and down my thighs. I pull back from Enzo and look at Dante. I saw him when I was pushing him, but now I really take him in. He looks just like he normally does, put together with a stern face and determined bright blue eyes, but I can see how tired he is. I pull my hands from Enzo's and Matteo's grip and place them on either side of Dante's face. His eyes close as I rub my thumbs across his cheeks. "Have you been sleeping, Boss Man?"

He opens his eyes and they're so filled with emotion. "Not very much."

"How about you tell me what happened, how you are alive, and then we can sleep on the flight home?"

He nods and I slide my hands from his face and down his neck. "There is something I have to do first." He grips the back of my neck and pulls me to him. Our lips crash together in an intense kiss that has tears running down my cheeks again. I have them back. I'm whole again. A growl sounds to my right before I'm pulled from Dante as Matteo's lips smash to mine.

Matteo demands so much from our kiss, but I happily submit to him. A soft touch running down the back of my neck has me pulling away from Matteo and rotating until I'm looking at Enzo. We stare at each other for a few seconds before he leans forward, pressing his lips to mine. Our kiss is slow and deep as we both pull what we need from the other until it becomes frantic; that's when I pull away from him.

Their hands start to roam my body and I have to swat them all away. "Stop distracting me and talk."

Matteo gives me a wicked grin as he skims his hand across my back and under my shirt. Before I can swat his wandering hand away, he grips my hip and pulls me from Dante's lap and into his so my back is to his chest and his arms are wrapped around my middle. Not wanting to be disconnected from any of them, I stretch my legs out across Dante and Enzo's laps and get comfortable.

Dante places his hand on my lower thigh. "I got a call from Killian almost as soon as Matteo got off the phone with you." All the chaos that has happened seemed to have started that morning while I was in Ireland and they were back home. It's hard to think I was so happy and was ready to come back to them. "One of Killian's guys asked him to meet up in Galway that morning. When Killian met him, he informed Killian that he was one of the guys that came to collect your things and while he was there, he was ordered to plant a bomb."

He pauses as I take in the fact that my father had been planning to kill them even before I said no. He knew I wouldn't do it. "Your bedroom was at the center of the house. Perfect location to take us and the house down."

"That was a day before my father blew it up."

"Yes, well this guy also informed Killian that your father was making a move against us, soon, but first he was coming for you." I think back, remembering Aisling calling out my name as she came outside. He must've texted her to warn us. "When Killian wasn't able to get into contact with you or Aisling, we knew he had already gotten you. So instead of staying away from the house, we came up with a plan with our father and Killian. We would let your father win or at least think he did. It would be easier to look for you as a ghost than to have to constantly look over our shoulders."

I try to sit quietly, waiting for them to tell me how they knew when he was going to do it, but I can't. "Have you lost your fucking minds? You're telling me you walked into your house not knowing if my father would blow it up or not?"

"Not exactly." Enzo adjusts on the couch so he's facing more toward me but keeping my feet in his lap. "We knew he wouldn't just do it. He wanted it to be a show, to send a message, and the message could've only been for you." I shake my head; they couldn't have known that definitively. He could've blown it up at any point and just showed me the wreckage.

"We were hoping we could get you while he was making this show." Dante rubs soft circles on my thigh as he stares down at them.

"That's not how it worked out though. I watched you walk into that house and it exploded minutes later."

Matteo's hold tightens around me. "We always knew we were the bait so we had to walk into that house but something you and nobody else knew was we had a fortress underground that had a secret entrance."

Dante looks up at me. "As soon as we entered that house, we booked it to that room. It's just outside the house's walls, so while we felt the bomb, the walls didn't crumble around us."

"As you stated, it didn't go as planned and we weren't able to get you. Killian's guy got word that they were moving you and the meetup was at the back of the property. Killian, Tanner, and Colton were there to get you, but it was just a decoy." Enzo grips my ankle and runs his thumb over my skin.

I state the unspoken words. "He knew Killian was trying to get me back."

Dante nods. "After that, we spent the next couple of weeks following your father around, hoping he'd lead us to you."

"Your father isn't very observant," Matteo says next to my ear.

I nod, agreeing. "He's blind because he thinks he's indestructible." One thing doesn't add up if they weren't in the house.

"Maxim told me there were three bodies found in your house."

"Three guys you killed when getting Aisling. We burned their bodies and paid off the Fire Chief and coroner." Dante smirks at me. "You're not the only one with connections."

"Did Lorcan go anywhere interesting?"

Enzo shakes his head no. "He mainly stayed at home or visited his businesses. He did have a few lunches with the Bratva and Maxim, which should've let us know they were working on something."

"So you were there when everyone came and got me?"

"Yeah, Princess. I carried you out myself."

I knew I heard them. I look back at Matteo. "You also beat up Maxim before I killed him. I knew it wasn't Killian's style."

He nods. "We all happily partook in that. We thought you were dead when we got to that room and saw you sprawled out on the bed." There is so much pain in his eyes that I want to look away but I don't. I'm sure I looked dead and knowing the feeling of thinking they were dead, I know it would've broken them, knowing they were too late.

"You were barely breathing." I look to Dante. "And all the bruises, I almost killed him."

"He needed to die," Enzo continues, drawing my gaze. "The only reason we left him breathing was because we knew you'd bleed him out making him live through every tortured moment."

I nod. That's exactly what I did. "I planned his death multiple times while he held me. Even drew them in blood on the walls of my cell." I smirk remembering his reaction.

"What happened while you were with Maxim?" Matteo presses his lips to my shoulder.

I haven't been able to tell anyone what happened because I didn't want to break. I didn't want to be lost in the trauma without an escape. But with them here surrounding me with their love and support, I know they're my escape. They'll hold me together so I don't break.

"I'll tell you everything but won't go into detail about the last three days. I don't want to think about them and I'm pretty sure you got an idea of what happened from Cassandra and how you found me." They all nod and I take a deep breath. "When I got off the phone with you." I look back at Matteo briefly before continuing my story, telling them every detail of my fight and capture, how I woke up in the SUV, how I watched my father kill them, how I fought again, and finally how my days went in my cell until I was moved to the room. They all stay quiet as I tell my story and as the words come out, I start to feel lighter. Yes, the worst of torture happened within those last three days, but I don't think I need to talk about every detail to heal. I need these three men by my side and their love and comfort.

Chapter Twenty-Three

Riona

We didn't stay long after I finished telling my story, and, as Richard promised, a car with our bags and a driver was waiting outside the Russo villa for us. Matteo takes the passenger seat as Dante, Enzo, and I slide into the back. They each have one of my hands in theirs as we ride quietly to the airport. I lean my head against Enzo's shoulder and he kisses my forehead. "How are you doing?"

"Okay. Still surprised you're here. I keep thinking I'll wake up and you'll be gone again." I squeeze their hands, just proving to myself that they're here.

"We're never leaving you again." Matteo turns around with a wicked smile. "And you don't need to worry about something happening to us because I'm taking you with me. We'll rule Hell together."

I smile at him, loving his devotion to me. In life and death. The unspoken commitment between us reminds me of their last texts confessing their love. I lean forward and press my lips to his and whisper against them so only he can hear me. "I'm yours in life and death and one day I'll make that vow to you as you slip a ring on my finger."

The only indication that he heard me is his hand burying in my hair and him deepening the kiss. When we pull apart with huge smiles on our faces, I slide back in my seat and rest my head on Enzo's shoulder again. I can feel Dante and Enzo's eyes on me, but I ignore them. They don't need to know what that was about.

The driver pulls onto the airstrip not long after that, and when he stops outside my plane, I let go of Dante's hand and slide out with Enzo. The driver stays in the SUV so I pull on Enzo's hand, stopping him. Knowing we don't have long before our privacy is interrupted, I pull him to me and kiss him. "I saw your text from the day I was taken." I freeze as our eyes connect and I see he knows what I'm talking about. "I love you too."

Enzo's smile is so wide as he crashes his lips to mine in a knee-weakening kiss. He pulls back from our kiss with so much love and excitement in his eyes, but I place my hand over his mouth, stopping him from saying the three words I want to hear him say. "You cannot say it yet."

His eyebrows draw together in confusion for a second before realization hits him. He nods and I remove my hand. "He has until we land in the States."

"He better not take that long." Enzo chuckles before placing a quick kiss to my lips. Dante and Matteo are waiting at the bottom of the steps for us when we walk around the SUV. Matteo has a knowing smile on his face like he knows what we were doing while Dante looks irritated and hurt that he's missing something. Not letting go of Enzo's hand, I head up the steps with Enzo behind me and his brothers behind him. My pilot, Peter, is waiting at the top of the steps for us. "Hi Peter. Thanks for moving up the flight." Enzo continues into the plane along with Matteo and Dante so I can speak to Peter.

"No problem, Miss Murphy."

"I do have one more change up. We need to change our destination and those three men were never here."

He nods. "Understood. Where are we going?"

"Not far from New York. Bridgeport, Connecticut."

"Sounds good. I'll make the change." He turns to go back into the cockpit as I head further into the plane to take my seat. I'm happy to see the seat open next to Enzo and I fall down into it while pulling out my phone. I send Aisling a quick text on our new destination before shutting it off and placing it in the table cup holder.

Martin walks over to us after he closes the door. "Hello, Miss Murphy. Can I get you or your guests anything to drink while we wait for departure?"

"I'll take some water." The guys order their drinks and Martin walks away.

"With us going home, I'm guessing you're wanting to stay dead." I look at each of them.

They all nod, but Dante is the one who answers. "For now."

"Who knows you're alive?"

They look at each other and I can already tell I'm not going to like their answer.

Matteo leans forward so his elbows rest on his knees. "Killian, Aisling, Tanner, Colton, Zach, and Kiera."

"So everyone knew but me. Why couldn't I know?"

Martin comes over and drops off our drinks. I look at Dante because I know he has the answer and he waits until Martin leaves us. "There's no great reason, Rose."

"Well try." Irritation fills me because I was left out.

"Only people who needed to know knew. Your group needed to know in order for all of us to find you. Zach needed to know because he was being our face. Kiera only knew because we went to get you." Dante states the facts but not the reason.

"And I didn't need to know?"

"Not at that time. After finding you, we were only in New York for 24 hours before we had to leave for Italy. Our father wanted us out of the city after the attack, but he allowed us to stay until you were safe. He wanted us home and if you knew we were okay, you wouldn't have let us go. You only know now because you wowed our father by showing up here."

Hurt fills me, thinking I could still believe they were dead. "So if I hadn't come, you wouldn't have come back to New York or told me you were alive."

"No one was going to keep us from you for long, Princess." Matteo gives me a serious look, telling me he would have fought his dad to be with me again. I hold Matteo's stare as the plane starts to move and Peter's voice rings out. "We're set to take off next. Our arrival time is 3:40pm in Bridgeport, Connecticut."

"Bridgeport?" Enzo asks as we buckle our seat belts.

"We can't just fly into New York City with three dead guys. My father still has eyes everywhere in the city. Eyes that are looking for me."

He nods as he takes my hand and I take a deep breath right before we take off down the runway. We're going back home to take down my father and kill him for all the sins he's committed. And after this trip, he has a few more added.

Once we're in the air, I unclip my seatbelt. "Alright Boss Man. It's time to get some sleep."

"I don't need to." Dante gives me a look like he's going to fight me but I'm ready.

"What else are we going to do on a nine hour flight?"

"I can think of a few things." Matteo's eyes scan up and down my body.

"Not right now." Dante opens his mouth, but I place my finger to his lips as I bend over his legs. "Are you really going to turn down alone time with me? If so, I'm sure one of your brothers wouldn't mind taking your place."

Dante growls with jealousy. I got him now. I give him a smile, silently patting myself on the back, and he grinds his teeth, knowing I can work him up so easily. He stands and I stand up straight with him so we're only inches from each other. "Let's go." He waves for me to go first.

"Yes, let's." Matteo goes to stand as well, but Dante stops him.

"No. My time."

My core heats up at him claiming his own time with me. If he wasn't so tired right now, I might've taken him right here, but he is and I really just want to sleep in his arms. I walk around Dante and over to Matteo. "Later." I lean over and give him a quick kiss. I look at Enzo and he has a knowing smile on his face. As I walk past him, he pulls me into his lap and kisses me. I feel all the words he's not allowed to say yet, at least until I'm pulled away from him and into Dante's chest.

"They don't know how to share."

I grab his hand and pull him back to the room. "Oh, and you do?"

"Not at all; that's why I get my own time with you." He crowds me as soon as the door closes behind him and kisses me. There's so much desire in our kiss, I almost lose myself in it.

At least I do until he tries to remove my shirt. That's when I break the kiss and step back. "We're sleeping."

"We can do that naked." He tries again and I step out of his reach.

I give him a 'come on' look. "No, we can't." If we're naked, there is no way we won't keep our hands off each other.

I walk over to the side of the bed and take off my shoes, shorts, and bra. Pulling back the covers, I climb on the bed so I'm on my knees and give him a 'you coming?' look. He quickly pulls his shirt over his head and removes his jeans as I lay out in the middle of the bed. In just his boxers, Dante climbs into bed with me. He immediately pulls me to him so he's on his back and I'm curled into his side with my head on his shoulder. I place a kiss on his chest before relaxing with my hand over his heart.

For several minutes we don't say a word as he runs his fingers up and down my hip. "I missed you so much, Rose. Having you gone, then kidnapped, and then staying away from you felt like I'd never get a moment like this ever again." I move so I'm looking up at him with my chin on top of my hand, on his chest, and he runs his fingers through my hair. "You're my everything. The reason for me to live, love, and fight." I lean up and press my lips to his.

"I think you have something to tell me before one of your brothers beat you to it."

He chuckles. "I guess I do." He sits up slightly and rotates so I'm lying on my back and he's over me. "I love you, Ri."

I smile brightly up at him. "I love you too, Dante." His lips are on me in an instant and I happily moan into our kiss as I wrap myself around him.

He lowers his body over mine so I can feel him everywhere. His growing erection rubs against my wanting center and my whole body runs ice cold. Images of Maxim over me flash in my head and I go still. I pull my lips away from his and run my hands down his back, hoping he doesn't notice the change in my body. I'm not so lucky though as Dante pulls his whole body away from mine and he looks down at me. Concern is written all over his face as he takes in mine. Whatever he sees there stops him from saying anything. Instead, he moves us so I'm on my side again and curled into his side, with my leg over his and his arms wrapped around me.

"Sleep, Rose." He presses a kiss to my head. "I've got you. Nothing and no one will touch you again."

Feeling safe in his arms, I let myself drift into darkness.

Chapter Twenty-Four

Enzo

It's such a relief having her here with us again. The weeks we were apart while she was in Ireland were hard, but the weeks no one could find her were unbearable. I barely slept and it constantly felt like someone had their hand in my chest, squeezing my heart. When we did find her and had to watch her fight through her trauma and mourn us, I had a pit in my stomach knowing I couldn't go to her and comfort her.

That's why I only lasted 30 minutes before I stood from my seat and walked to the bedroom with Matteo right behind me. I needed to be near her. That's how I find myself lying next to Riona with Dante on her other side and Matteo laying in between her legs with his head on her stomach. Needy, but a lucky asshole.

I woke up a little while ago with a sleeping Riona in front of me and I haven't been able to look away from her. She's breathtaking even with the yellowing bruise on her cheek and outlines of fingers across her neck. She looks like a queen after a battle and we would happily bow to her any day. As I watch her dream, her face starts to scrunch up in pain as a whimper slips from her lips. She told us most of what happened to her while she was with Maxim, but I know the worst parts are what she's keeping locked up.

Not wanting her to be dreaming about that, I reach forward and run my fingers along her face. "Shh. You're safe, Ri." I lean forward and place a kiss on her forehead.

"No," Riona yells out and swings out hitting my chin.

"Beauty, you're okay." I grab her wrists, trying to stop her fighting but it only sets panic in her features.

"No. Stop." She tries to pull her wrists from my hold as her body jerks and legs kick out.

Matteo and Dante both wake. "What the fuck?" Dante looks shocked, seeing us in bed.

"Let me go," Riona screams, still living her nightmare.

Matteo wraps his arms around her thighs trying to stop her legs from kicking out. "Princess, it's just a dream. We're here."

"Don't touch me!" she screams.

535

Dante grabs Riona's face so she's facing him and he yells back, "Wake up."

Riona's green eyes open with pure terror in them as she breathes hard. It takes a few seconds for the fog of her nightmare to lift and she finally recognizes us. Tears well up in her eyes. "I'm sorry." We all release our holds on her, giving her some space and she reaches up to touch my chin but stops herself. "I hit you."

A tear rolls down her cheek and I quickly wipe it away. "It's okay. It wasn't that hard."

She reaches out, touching my chin. "I don't believe you. It's already leaving a mark."

I grab her hand and kiss the back of it. "I'm fine. I'm more worried about you."

"Who were you fighting, Princess?" Matteo runs his hands up her thighs and she jerks away from the touch as a haze flashes in her eyes. Matteo sees it too because he jumps up and sits at the end of the bed so he's not touching her.

"I'm sorry. Don't go." She panics at him retreating and reaches for him, but he doesn't move, only taking her hand in his.

"What did he do to you?"

She shakes her head with her eyes closed as tears stream down her cheeks. "All I feel is his touch. The nightmares bring it all back as if I'm in that room again."

Dante takes her other hand. "Tell us what we need to do to erase him from your body and mind."

"I don't know." Worry seeps through her voice like she doesn't think it will go away any time soon. I can't have her thinking that.

"How about we try something?" She looks at me hoping I'll have all the answers that will soothe everything. I don't but I'll try anything.

She nods. "Whatever you want."

I shake my head. "No, whatever you want." I hold my hand out to her with my palm up. "You control our touch."

She looks at my hand for a second and looks back up so our eyes connect. "You think this will work?"

I shrug my shoulders. "If you get uncomfortable or have flashbacks, we'll stop. If you want our touch, let yourself control it."

"I want your touch more than anything." She shifts on the bed so sheets fall off her and she's kneeling in the middle of the bed.

"Then take what you want." Matteo holds his hand out in front of him as well. Riona takes each of our hands in hers and she brings them to the tops of her bare thighs.

The feeling of her warm soft skin against my palm has me moving closer to her but making sure not to touch her. With our palms resting on her thighs, she takes a deep breath and closes her eyes, soaking in our touch. She slowly starts to move our hands up her legs and her grip tightens as her breath shortens.

"Open your eyes, Rose." She follows Dante's command and he turns her chin so she's looking at him. "Stay with us. Keep your eyes open." She nods. "You have all the power."

She holds his stare as she raises our hands up her outer thighs, and over her curvy hips. As she moves our hands under her shirt, she slams her lips to Dante's. The air around us turns from a tame curiosity to full blown desire. I have to fight myself not to reach out for her with my other hand as she moves my hand up her stomach and my fingers skim across the bottom swell of her breasts. Matteo shifts closer to her and I wish I could see where he was touching her as well. She must be able to read my mind because she releases our hands to grab the hem of her shirt, and when she pulls back from Dante's lips, she pulls her shirt over her head.

Her eyes connect with mine as her shirt is thrown somewhere in the room. "Don't stop." I hold her stare for a few seconds before I look down at her gorgeous body, finding my hand cupping her breasts, Matteo's hand sliding down her side, and her guiding Dante's up her inner thigh.

Raising my gaze back up her body, I zero in on her breasts. I run the tips of my fingers over the top swell of her left breast and down the center between them before circling back up the other side, moving closer to her nipple. With each circle, her nipples grow harder until they're hardened points. As my fingers flick across her nipple, she lets out a moan that has me hardening in my boxers.

Wanting both hands on her, I hold out my other hand for her and she happily takes it and sets it on her other breast. Riona arches into my touch and lets out a happy sigh as I roll her nipples between my fingers. The grip she has on my wrist tightens as she starts to rock her hips and I look down to see her thighs spread for us and her panties pushed to the side.

Dante has her open for us so we can watch as he thrusts his fingers inside her and rubs her clit with his thumb. Matteo's hand continues to roam her body, feeling every inch he can and she arches into his touch as he moves. Her moans start to get louder as she draws her pleasure from us and I can't look away from the beautiful goddess we get to call ours. Her cheeks turn flushed and her hips rock faster and I know she's close. Putting all my attention back on her breasts, I flick her nipples with my thumbs before pinching them and she comes with a loud moan that I'm sure the entire flight staff can hear. Dante prolongs her orgasm with his fingers deep inside her as I softly caress her breast and Matteo slides his hands down her sides.

When she comes down from her high, she looks at the three of us with a pleased smile on her face. She leans forward and captures my lips with hers but before I deepen our kiss and get lost in her, she pulls back. "I need to be..." She turns to Dante and kisses him just as deeply and quickly. "Marked as yours..." She turns forward and stares at Matteo for a second before climbing into his lap and kissing him too. "Inside and out."

Instead of pulling away again, she continues to kiss him as she runs her hands across his chest and down his arms. She grabs each of his wrists and sets his hands over her hips and sides of her panties. "Take these off." Matteo, not needing to be told twice, rips her panties from her body.

A happy smile forms on her face and Matteo beams back at her. "Now you all need to get your cocks out." Pure desire shines in her eyes as she looks up at me.

Not wasting a second, I stand from the bed, seeing Dante doing the same, but it's Matteo's movement that I watch as he quickly picks Riona up, making her squeal and positions himself on the bed laying back with Riona straddling his hips. "Take what you want, Princess."

Riona slides her hands down Matteo's abs and hooks her fingers into the edge of his boxers and pulls them down just far enough that he's exposed to her. She wraps her hand around his erection, and he lets out a pleasurable growl as she pumps him. Not wanting to miss out, I drop my boxers and kneel on the bed next to her. She smiles up at me and wraps her hand around the base of my cock. My eyes close as I groan, loving the feeling of her hand wrapped around me. Her hands slide up my length to the tip and she rubs her thumb over the head, making me thrust into her hand.

Her moans have my eyes opening and I take in Riona with her head thrown back as she rocks her hips against Matteo's erection. Matteo has a firm grip on her hips as he looks up at her like the goddess she is. "You feel so good, Princess. Keep doing that. Get yourself worked up." She moans at his words and grips me slightly tighter as she pumps me faster.

Dante runs his finger along her jaw and she smiles up at him. "Can I kiss you, Rose?"

She takes her hand off Matteo's chest and wraps it around the back of his neck, pulling him closer to her. "Always."

Dante crashes his lips to hers and I can feel her getting lost in us as her hand loosens on me. I wrap my hand around hers helping her and I look down to see Matteo's controlling her hips. With my free hand, I run it up her arm, over her shoulder, and down her back as she leans into my touch. Dante and her break apart but they don't look away from each other as she runs her hand down his chest and abs.

I skim my hand down her back toward her ass and her skin breaks out in goosebumps. My hand skims over the swell of her ass and as my fingers track her seam, her hand grips my wrist, stopping me. Fear shines in her eyes as she looks at me. I lift my hand from her ass and she lets go of my wrist. "I won't."

I lift my hand and place it to her cheek as I rest my forehead against hers. "I'm sorry."

"Kiss me, Enzo, and make it better." I lean forward and press my lips to hers. It isn't a deep kiss, but I give her everything, letting her take whatever she needs. She pulls back from me with the spark in her eyes as she reaches out blindly to her other side, wrapping her hand around Dante's cock. We both groan as she strokes us at the same time and I'm shocked I didn't even notice she stopped. A smile tilts her lips up as she faces Matteo. "Come here."

Matteo follows her invisible pull as he sits up and kisses her. She moans against his lips as she rocks against him with the same pace she's taking us.

"Matteo, I need you inside me."

"Fuck. I'll give you anything, Princess." I look down at her body and watch as she slowly slides down Matteo's erection. The moan she lets out has me almost ready to explode. She must feel it because she gives me a sexy smirk as she squeezes me a little bit more. Matteo supports her at her hips as she starts to ride him, finding her pleasure.

"Oh God. I need more. Please touch me." Matteo doesn't waste a second as he buries his face in her breasts and licks her between them before capturing a nipple between his lips. I take her other breast in my hand, kneading it before rolling her hard nipple between my fingers and Dante tangles his hand in her hair, bringing her mouth to his. She hums in pleasure at all of our touches as we work together to make her come. Her movements start to speed up and become a little jerky and I know she's right on the edge. I look at my brothers and their eyes are focused on her, knowing she's there too.

Matteo slides his hand over her stomach to where she needs him and starts rubbing her clit. "Come for us, Riona. Scream for us."

Dante pulls away from her lips and she does exactly what Matteo asks. She comes screaming and we all follow after her. I come all over her hand and breasts. Matteo falls next with a loud groan as he thrusts up into her. Dante holds on last as he turns her face toward his cock. "Open your mouth, Rose. Taste me."

She leans forward and opens her mouth with her tongue out. Dante strokes himself with his tip against her tongue. He comes with a curse a few seconds later and she swallows his release and licks him clean. We all collapse on the bed as we catch our breaths but don't stop touching her. Matteo runs his fingers through her hair, getting it out of her face. "You're amazing, Princess. So strong. So beautiful."

I rub her back, making sure not to go lower than mid-back. "Ours."

Dante rubs up and down her arm. "Yours."

She smiles at each of us. "Always. I love you."

I lean forward and give her a quick kiss. "I love you, Beauty."

Dante turns her chin toward him and kisses her too. "I love you, Rose."

Matteo smiles at her. "I love you too, Princess." He captures her in a deep kiss, but it doesn't last long. Riona's eyes start to droop as she cuddles on Matteo's chest, and I can feel exhaustion hitting me as well.

Silence falls over us as I close my eyes. Riona's hand slides to my chest and I take it in my hand. Everything is just perfect. "A yes to my proposal and I love you all in one day. Best day ever!" Matteo breaks the silence.

"What!?!" Dante whisper yells and I don't open my eyes. "You told him you'd marry him?"

Riona's voice is soft and sleepy as she answers. "Yes and no. Can we talk about it later?"

Dante sighs. "Fine, but I'm marrying you too."

"Okay." She smiles lovingly and falls back into silence as she squeezes my hand letting me know that I'm included. I fall asleep knowing I have the woman I love back in my arms and one day I'll call her my wife.

Chapter Twenty-Five

Riona

Aisling's leaning against a black SUV as the door to the plane opens and the stairs lower. She's beaming as she walks toward me, meeting me at the bottom of the steps. "Someone looks freshly fucked." She pulls me into a hug and I wrap my arms around her, chuckling. I'm not going to deny it. For the first time in a while, I feel like myself again and it's got everything to do with them. How they showed me how much they love me and gave me control to push past what Maxim did. Well, not all of it. I still have some healing to do but I know my guys will help me through it.

We pull apart and she smiles up at the plane. "Looks like you have a few stowaways."

I smile up at them as Matteo walks down first. "Well, someone had to entertain me. I forgot to bring a book."

She chuckles and gives each of the guys a hug. "Glad to see Papa Russo decided to let go of the leash."

"We're not dogs." Dante smirks, but it doesn't reach his eyes.

"When he says come, you come. He says stay, you stay." She looks at him like she proved her point and then a joking smile breaks across her face. Dante matches her smile and she waves toward the SUV. "Come on you wild wolves, we have a city to get back to." We grab our bags and carry them to the SUV.

"Did you get a new car?" Matteo takes my bag from me and I head to the passenger door.

"It's borrowed. We're being followed and I didn't want to take any chances taking my car." Aisling gives me a look, telling me things are ramping up.

"Has Lorcan retaliated since the drop?" I climb into the passenger seat as the guys get in the back so they can't be seen with the tinted windows.

Aisling climbs into the driver's seat. "Other than trying to follow us, no. He's been locked up in his house."

"What's he doing? He has to be planning something." It's weird that he's just sitting and waiting.

Aisling looks hopeful. "Maybe he's given up. We've been taking everything from him."

"What have you been doing?" Dante asks from the back.

"We haven't had to do much. After word got out about the other night, basically all the dealers and suppliers turned on Lorcan and reached out to Killian. It's not a surprise since Killian has been dealing with that side of the business for years. The ones that aren't willing to turn against Lorcan are being dealt with by Tanner and Colton. The boys have been busy blowing up shipments, leaving tips for the new sheriff, or killing the more violent ones."

I notice Aisling hasn't said what she's been doing. I know she's not sitting at home watching TV. "What have you been up to?"

She gives me a wicked smile. "I have been using my law degree. Killian now owns all the properties under your father's name, all the accounts, and all other assets. The only thing your father has left is his house."

Wow, he literally has nothing. "Does he know this?"

Aisling shrugs. "I don't know. I filed the name change on the deeds yesterday and his POA, giving us authority over all assets which I have moved to new locations or accounts."

"So sneaky." I'm so proud and she gives me a cocky smile.

Enzo leans in between the seats. "How did you get his signature?"

She shrugs like that wasn't a problem. "I believe you know an excellent forger."

"Zach," Matteo confirms.

Aisling nods. "That's him."

"You're an evil genius." Matteo gives her a wicked smile.

547

"Why, thank you." She gives him a proud grin.

"What about the families?" I ask.

"It's happening tonight. Killian's called..." Both our phones chime, cutting her off and I quickly pull it out to see what it is. A text from my father appears on my screen with a formal invitation to a party. I look up at Aisling and then back at the guys and they look confused. "What is it?"

Aisling hands her phone back to Dante as my phone starts to ring and an unsaved number flashes across my screen. No one unsaved calls this number. While it's my personal line, it's also my M line and no one calls me that I don't know. I hit answer and hold the phone to my ear. "Who's this?"

"Miss Murphy? I mean Riona. They took her."

My back goes stiff as I recognize the freaked out voice of the kid from the alley a couple of weeks ago. "Leo?" I look back at Dante and recognition flashes across his face. "Leo, what's wrong?"

"They took her." Leo's breathing heavy. "I don't know where she is."

"Took who?"

"They took Phoebe."

"Leo, I need you to calm down and explain."

I can hear the traffic outside and his heavy breath. He lets out a long groan. "You have to find her."

"I'll find her. Tell me what happened." I put the phone on speaker so everyone can hear.

"Phoebe and I were hanging out at her house after school when these two guys burst into the house and started beating up her father, yelling at him about owing them money. One of the guys grabbed Phoebe saying they're taking her as payment. I tried to fight them off. Phoebe was screaming so loud. They knocked me out and when I woke up, they were gone. They took her. You have to find her."

I can hear his sobs. "Okay Leo. I'll find her. Do you know who took her?"

"They said he owes the Murphys." My heart sinks.

"Fuck." This isn't good. "I'll find her and bring her home. Text me your address."

"Okay. Don't let anything happen to her."

"I won't." I hang up the phone and look at everyone. "My fucking father. He's planning to sell these kids at his party. We need to get them out tonight." I look at Aisling. "We've cleared out all his properties?"

"Yes," Aisling confirms.

"Warehouses?"

"Yes."

"Buildings... Businesses?"

"Yes, and yes."

Where are they? "He wouldn't bring them to the house."

"No way." She shakes her head.

I look back at the guys. "Franks." Franks and his son, Junior, run the docks and we met during his meeting with my guys. I told

Franks I'd take everything from him including his life if I found out he continued to transport skin into New York.

Dante nods. "Him or the Russians."

Enzo shakes his head. "The Russians wouldn't put themselves in the middle of this. Risking you guys tearing apart their business." With Maxim dead, there's no way Ivan would still be partnered with Lorcan. They'll try to survive this fight by separating themselves.

I give them a deadly smile. "Call Kiera to confirm. I have a son to threaten."

After the meeting, I took the initiative to get Junior's number because I had a feeling I'd need to make this call one day. Junior answers on the third ring. "Hello." There isn't a hint of question in his greeting.

"Junior."

"Riona! I've been expecting your call. Took longer than I thought. Your people are slacking on relaying information to you, but I guess you have been busy." I can picture the cocky smile on his face.

"Is your throat still bothering you? That's the only reason I would think of why you didn't call me with this knowledge yourself." In order to get what my guys wanted during that meeting, I poisoned Junior so he couldn't breathe.

"I don't work for you, Riona."

"True, but you knew the deal. Now you'll get to watch me destroy your whole life. Do you think your sister will cry as I kill you and your father in front of her?" He isn't in control. I'll make him beg for his life if he doesn't give me what I want.

"Now, now, there's no need for that. I have a deal for you."

Why would I want a deal when he couldn't hold up our previous deal? I'm curious, though. "It better be a fantastic deal."

"What's better than getting what you want?"

"And what do I want?"

"My father's head on a platter. The girls he has stored for your father. No more trafficking in the city."

He has my interest. "That does sound promising. What do you want?"

"I want my father's empire and having you help me get it is even better. I want to watch him piss his pants as you corner him. You understand wanting what your father has, don't you?"

"No. I know something about revenge. My father crossed me and made the mistake of thinking I'd forgive and forget. You better keep that in mind."

"I have no plans to cross you. I think our partnership could be very beneficial. Even outside of business. I'm sorry to hear about the Russo brothers. If you're ever lonely, my bed is always open for you." Really. That's not going to happen.

"Let's just get through this deal and we can discuss future business at another time." I sidestep the comment because I don't need the three men behind me to get all possessive right now.

"That wasn't a no."

Well, he's not letting it go. I look back at my guys and Dante's eyes lock with mine. I do like their jealousy. "Junior. I don't know where you heard I mix business with pleasure, but I can assure you that I'll never find myself in your bed."

Growls come from the backseat as I face forward with a pleased smile. "Understood. You can't blame me for trying."

"I expect a text with the location of the girls within the hour and a location and time for you to meet me with your father. If you double cross me, Junior, it won't just be your father's empire in flames. I'll tie you and your whole family in one of those warehouses and watch you burn inside."

"No need for threats, Riona. I just sent you the location plus some. Talk to you soon."

I hang up the phone and a text comes through with a pin drop, a code, and a link to their security cameras. "We have the location. It's time to get loaded up."

Chapter Twenty-Six

Riona

Killian's newly acquired weapons warehouse from our father is quiet on the outside as we pull up, but the door immediately rolls up revealing two of his men. Aisling slowly drives into the warehouse, waving at the two men. I chuckle to myself.

"What?"

"I see you have your queen wave down."

She reaches over and hits my arm with a chuckle. "Shut up. I was just waving hi. They're risking their lives for this fight."

"Yes, my queen." I bow my head to her and she rolls her eyes.

"I hate you." She sticks her tongue out at me and I do the same to her.

"No, you don't." She pulls up next to my brother's SUV and we both get out, leaving the guys hidden in the car since there are a few men walking around.

Killian, Colton, and Tanner's heads snap up from what they're looking at on the table when we walk into the office. "Did you get that invitation? Does he really think we're going to play nice?" Killian stands up straight and watches us walk over to them.

"Of course not. He has bigger plans than that. Like selling local girls." I drop the bomb we found out.

"What the fuck?" Tanner growls.

"I just got a call from one of my contacts and his friend was taken from her home a couple of hours ago by Lorcan's men as payment for her father's debt. She's a kid."

"Fuck." Colton runs his fingers through his hair.

"I should've seen this coming." Killian slams his hand on the table and Aisling moves closer to him, running a hand up his back.

"No one knew he was this evil, taking girls from his own backyard and selling them at a party." Who's he even inviting that would buy them?

It doesn't matter who because this party is Lorcan's introduction to selling skin. He wants everyone's support, so he's going to give them to his guests. "We need to save these girls, tonight." I stand in between Tanner and Colton and look down at what's on the table; a blueprint of one of our restaurants in the center

554

of town. Aisling told us after Junior's call how Killian called a meeting with the Murphy Clan families tonight. "But you don't need to worry about this. You have a meeting to hold."

"I can move the meeting. The girls are more important." Killian tries to roll up the blueprints, but I place my hand on it.

"They are, but you getting all the families on your side is important too. Especially with the party in two days. Aisling and I can handle the docks."

The door behind me opens and Matteo, Dante, and Enzo walk in with hats sitting low on their faces. Matteo smiles at me. "Got bored waiting in the car."

I chuckle and look back at Killian and the twins. "Plus, we have these guys, and Junior has given us the location and access to the security cameras."

Colton and Tanner walk up to the guys and they exchange man hugs. "I see Red didn't kill you for faking your death."

"She wasn't happy about it," I answer for them and glare at Tanner and Colton. "Since when are you all buddy-buddy?"

"We spent a lot of time together looking for you." Enzo moves closer to me, taking over the spot Tanner was standing at.

"Oh, so you're okay with them having their hands on my body as we danced the other night."

Growls come from Matteo and Dante who are still standing by the door, and I can't help my smile. "You're already starting trouble, Red." Colton chuckles as he walks by, messing with my hair as he goes to stand on the other side of the table next to Killian.

"And it's trouble we don't need tonight." Killian glares at me as he leans on the table looking stressed.

I raise my hands up in surrender. "I'm sorry Kill. Don't worry about the girls, we have it. Look..." I pull out my phone and open the security feed Junior sent me. "There are only four guys."

Killian takes my phone and looks down at the feed from the outside of the warehouse. Hands touch my hips as I feel someone step into me so my back is pressed to their chest. A shiver runs through me as their lips skim across my ear. "Do you not want us to be friends with them?"

Matteo steps to my right as Tanner rounds the table to stand next to his brother and I lean into Dante as he wraps his arms around me, holding me to him. "I do want you to be friends. I just liked how growly and possessive you'd get when I was around them."

"I'll always be growly and possessive about any man touching you. Even my brothers sometimes, but I think you know that. Which is why you torture me." He nips at my earlobe.

I love how he loses himself in jealousy when I purposely give more attention to Enzo or Matteo. A fire lights in him that's so fucking sexy. "I do know that." I look up at him with an innocent smile and he chuckles, lowering his face to mine.

"Ri, really..." I look away from Dante before our lips touch to find a stressed-out Killian and everyone else looking at us.

"Sorry Boss, were you saying something?" I give him a mocking look.

"You keep acting like there's nothing to worry about. These cameras only show the outside. Lorcan's whole army plus Franks' men could be in there."

"Oh, I have no doubt there are men inside, but a whole army won't be in there. We'll go in quiet and take everyone out and then save the girls." I walk up to Killian and touch his arm. "Don't worry about the girls. We got this. We just came here for weapons, to get the bus, and hang out until dark."

"And to change," Aisling adds with a cute smile, making everyone chuckle. "Ri's right, Kill. You need to focus on your meeting. Saving these girls is something we're good at." She gives him a quick kiss and walks to the back room where we keep back-up supplies for when we couldn't get to the house, ending the discussion. He watches after her until she's out of sight and then he looks at me.

I cut him off before he can say anything. "You heard her." I walk past him to follow Aisling. "Get the guys some clothes... and something to cover their faces."

I leave them and join Aisling in the back room where she's changing into black leggings and a black shirt with a bulletproof vest underneath. Shedding my clothes, I start pulling on the same outfit. "Are you going to bring your bow tonight?"

"That was the plan. I have some taser arrows ready. Figured it would be fun to watch Lorcan's men get a little twitchy." I chuckle because it will be funny.

Fully dressed, I stand behind her and let my smile fall. "I think we should go in quiet. No gunshots. I don't want to alert the guards inside or scare the girls."

Aisling looks back at me through the mirror and nods. "What about when we're inside?"

"Only if there are no other options."

She stares at me for a while and then shrugs her shoulders. "If you're trying to not scare the girls, then you'll need to hold back on the knife work. Walking in looking like Carrie will give them nightmares."

I chuckle. "Then I better stock up on my poisons and sedatives." Aisling walks over to the opposite wall where our weapons are. She pulls out her arrows and starts screwing on her custom taser heads. Opening the drawer in front of me, I start pulling out and strapping on my holsters. My dagger holster wraps around my upper thighs. My gun holster wraps around my hips. My syringe holster straps around my left forearm.

With my holsters empty, I walk across the room toward Aisling as I pull my hair into a high ponytail. Aisling hands me a gun as I stand next to her and open the drawer with my daggers in them. There's no way I'm leaving these behind. We hand off guns and daggers to each other until our hip and thigh holsters are full.

She grabs her bow and quiver and hooks them over her shoulder and I open another drawer and pull out eight syringes filled with lethal doses of poison or anesthetic and slide them into the holder. I face Aisling, looking her over as she looks me over as well.

When our eyes connect, a smile spreads across our faces. "It feels good to be geared up again."

"It's been a while since we've had something this big. Stay vigilant, Ash."

"You too. We're all coming home tonight."

"Maybe in the morning. I do have one person to kill tonight." Franks.

She chuckles and pulls me into a hug. "I love you, Ri."

"I love you too, Ash." We pull apart from each other and head out of the room. The guys all turn to us and I zero in on my guys who look sexy geared up in all black with guns hanging off them.

Killian pulls Aisling into him as I go over to my guys. Matteo smiles at me as he looks me over like he wants to consume me. "You look deadly, Princess. I can't wait to see blood spattered all over you."

I step into him and his arms instantly wrap around waist as mine go around his neck. "Minimal bloodshed tonight but I'll let you get dirty with me when I kill Franks later." I feel Dante and Enzo moving closer, but they don't touch me as I focus on Matteo.

Matteo brings his head forward and skims his lips across my ear. "Deal. I can't wait to see you rip him apart."

"Does the thought of me killing Franks turn you on?" Matteo grinds against me, showing me just how turned on he is.

"Everything about you turns me on." His hands move to my ass and squeezes.

"Hey, stop touching my sister's ass." I turn around in Matteo's hold and subtly grind back against his erection.

"Don't look if you don't want to see it." I stare off with Killian until he cracks.

"Just keep it PG in front of me, would you?"

"You're so boring since you've taken power."

He rolls his eyes at me. "Would you just tell me what your plan is tonight?"

"Fine." I walk up to the table and set my phone down with the map of the docks up. "This is the warehouse we're hitting. There are four guards on the outside, two covering each end. Aisling and I are going to cover each end of the warehouse. We'll do it quietly with tasers and anesthetics. Enzo is going to partner with Aisling and Dante and Matteo will be with me but when we get inside, they'll stay along the edge until we get everything under control. We don't want the girls freaking out. Which is also why we're not going in guns blazing. Only shoot if necessary. We don't need to scare these girls any more than they already are."

"What are you going to do with the girls after?" Killian asks.

"I don't know how many there are, but we'll do what we always do. The girls that want to go home, go home. The girls who don't or don't have a home, we'll find a place."

"I know you don't want to scare the girls, but your lives are more important than Franks and Lorcan's men. Shoot them if you have to."

"Don't you worry Kill. Ri and I already made a deal that everyone will be home tonight." Aisling smiles up at him and hugs his arm.

"By morning," I point out and everyone chuckles.

"Hopefully the meeting won't be too long, so if you need us, call. I have all the heirs on my side, so if the fathers don't want to follow, their heirs will take over." With Aisling being a part of two families and the twins from another, Killian just has to convince three families.

"Well, it sounds like we have tonight under control." Let's hope it all goes to plan.

Chapter Twenty-Seven

Riona

Two men dressed in all black with rifles across their chests are standing by the closed metal roll-up door. I don't recognize them as one of Lorcan's men so they must be Franks. I tuck back behind the warehouse wall that's sitting a couple buildings away and look at Matteo and Dante, who look very much like the guys guarding the warehouse. An excited smile comes across my face as a plan formulates in my head.

"What wicked thoughts are going on in that beautiful head of yours?" Matteo's smile meets mine and I know he's in for whatever I have in mind.

"You guys are going to be a distraction to draw them away from the warehouse so I can get behind them."

"What kind of distraction?" Dante grips his rifle tighter.

I tell them my simple plan of them acting like they're replacing the guards and they nod in agreement. In the dark shadows, I creep my way around the building that is shielding us as Matteo and Dante wait for me to get into position. Crouching down low, I peek around the corner of the building to make sure nobody's walking between the buildings. Luckily for me, none of the warehouses line up in a perfect grid so as I run between the buildings, the guards can't see me. When I get to the back of the second, I'm now about a hundred yards behind the guards. Turning on my mic, I whisper to the open line with everyone. "Aisling, are you ready?"

"Yeah, I'm ready."

"Matteo and Dante go. Aisling, give us 60 seconds."

"Got it," Aisling agrees and I shut off my mic before crossing the space between me and the warehouse holding the kidnapped girls. I plaster myself up against the side of the warehouse and slide along it toward where the guards will be just around the corner.

Dante and Matteo walk out of the darkness quietly chatting with each other looking like they're supposed to be here. I hear the moment the guards notice them by the shift of their guns. My guys don't even look toward the guards that have stepped away from the door with their guns raised.

"Whoa..." Matteo acts like he's just now noticing them as he stops abruptly and holds up his hands. "We come in peace, dudes." He folds his fingers down until he's holding up two peace signs. I bite my bottom lip to hold back my laugh at his ridiculous acting and based on his smile, he's pretty proud of himself.

Dante steps up next to his brother with an unimpressed look on his face as his rifle is held lightly in his hands, ready to shoot if he needs to. "Relax guys. We're here to replace you. Your shift is over."

I pull out two syringes from my holder, making sure they're sedatives, and take off the caps as the guards look at each other and then back at Dante and Matteo. "Our shift isn't over until dawn."

"We're just following orders." Dante shrugs his shoulders as I slip around the corner and behind the guards that are a few steps ahead of me. "Take it up with Franks if you have an issue." Dante and Matteo step aside like they're going to let the guards through but I'm right behind them plunging the syringes in their necks before they can take a step.

My sedatives are fast but not instant and the guards turn toward me, staggering as they try to put distance between us with their guns raised. I don't even flinch or try to go for my guns because they bump right into Dante and Matteo who quickly disarm them and lower them to the ground as they fall unconscious. I walk up to them, pulling out some zip ties with a victorious smile on my face. Dante and Matteo's smiles match mine as they grab the ties. Seconds later, loud curses and groans come from the distance. "That's Aisling. Her taser arrows are no joke. We need to get inside now."

Dante, understanding my urgency, agrees. "Yeah, if there are any guards inside, they know we're here now."

Dante and Matteo hover close behind me as we head to the side door on the left of the rolling door. With my hand on the doorknob, I press my mic on and tell Aisling and Enzo, "We're heading inside."

"So are we," Enzo says.

"We need to spread out, covering as much space as possible. Aisling, go to high ground." She'll be our overhead view, helping us locate all the guards.

"Got it," Aisling answers. "We go in on three."

I grip the door handle tighter and look at Dante and Matteo, who are standing on either side of the door with their masks up and guns ready. "1…" I grab my gun as well just in case their guards are on the other side of the door.

Aisling finishes the count and I fling the door open with my gun raised and my heart racing. As I scan the area around me, I relax, not finding guards waiting to greet us. Gunshots ring out on the other side of the warehouse making me pause. "Aisling... Enzo?"

Worry washes through me when their mics only give feedback and the gunshots stop. I point to Dante and Matteo, signaling them to take opposite sides of the warehouse and I'll take the middle. We need to get to them. We move with our guns high to our spots and as I look to them to signal them to go, Enzo calls out through the mic, "Our shots."

A couple seconds later, Aisling speaks, "In position. I see five. Enzo, one is to your right behind the boat." I let out a breath in relief, hearing their voices.

Knowing Aisling will let us know when we're close to a guard, I move further into the warehouse checking around every boat, piles of wood, and pallets of boxed parts. They're using this warehouse as a boat workshop but if you look close enough you can see the storage boxes for drugs and weapons. Are these Lorcan's? I want to inspect them more but that's not what we're here for.

I look around another pile of wood with crates surrounding it, seeing Dante moving along the wall. I smile at him when he sees me and he winks. He actually winks. I can't believe Mr. Stinkface winked at me. Heat runs through me and I can't wait to get him alone so I can show him how much that wink affected me.

"Matteo, he's coming up behind you." Aisling's worried voice cools my thoughts and I turn, trying to see Matteo or someone else. A loud grunt and wood falling has me moving to help Matteo. I don't get more than a few steps before Aisling's voice rings out again with an impressed chuckle. "Oh, never mind, you got him." I sigh in relief and keep moving further down the center of the warehouse.

"Dante, you have one walking through the pallets." I look ahead, seeing pallets on either side of me and pick up my pace.

"Ri, you have one in the pallets as well."

The guard steps out of his hiding place before she even finishes, and I stop next to a boat that sits right next to the pallets he stepped out of. I recognize the man as one of Lorcan's guys but I don't know his name. "Hello Princess. Your father's going to reward me greatly for bringing you to him." He raises his gun, aiming at me. "Now be a good princess and don't put up a fight."

I chuckle as I lower my gun because he's not going to shoot if he wants my father's approval. Reaching for one of my knives, I twirl the knife in my hand. "You'll be lucky to keep your life when my father realizes that his women have been taken."

The guard's eyes go to my knife and I use that distraction to throw it. My knife hits its target and the guard screams as he drops his gun and clenches his hand over the one with my knife in it. An object flies right over my shoulder and I whip around just in time to see another guard, about a yard from me, go down with a taser arrow right to his chest.

His screams match the other guard's as his body convulses on the ground. Silence fills the warehouse as he passes out and I look back at the other guard to see why he's quiet. Dante's standing over the lifeless body and I notice the guy's neck twisted at an unnatural angle. "His screaming was annoying."

I chuckle at his comment because I can practically hear him saying 'he was being a little bitch.' I turn back to the guard that's no longer twitching from the electric current running through his body and rip the arrow from his shirt and zip tie his wrist together. When I stand back up, Matteo, Enzo, and Aisling are walking toward us with guards being dragged behind them.

I smile at Aisling and nod to the guy behind me. "Thanks for that."

"I'll always have your back." Aisling looks at all the guys as Enzo, Dante, and Matteo start pulling the guards from outside in. "Half of these guys are Lorcan's. The other half has to be Franks'."

I look over the pile of dead and unconscious bodies, knowing Lorcan's anger will be taken out on them. "They'll all be dead by morning."

"Then why don't we kill them now?" Matteo drops the last guy to the ground.

"Lorcan will take his rage out on them instead of us." I walk over to him. "As much as this is war, we can't have any emotional attacks on us that could take one of us out. I prefer all attacks be from us and planned."

"Okay, Princess." He hooks his arm around my shoulders. "Let's get these girls out." We head to the far-right corner where a door supposedly leads to an office. But really it leads to a hidden hallway that runs the length of the warehouse with cages along the wall.

Before we open the door, I turn to my guys. "It's probably best Aisling and I go in alone." I look at Enzo. "We'll need to get out of here fast. Will you go get the bus and pull it up to that door?" Enzo nods and Aisling hands over the keys. "The gate code is 1852." Enzo leaves and I look at Matteo and Dante. "Will you open the roll door and keep a watch out?" They both nod and Dante turns with his rifle across his chest and he starts walking through the warehouse. Matteo heads to the roll door and starts looking around for how to open it.

Aisling opens the office door with her gun raised and I quickly follow behind her, holding mine up as well. Lights flick on as the door opens and I freeze as flashbacks of my own cell come to mind.

These are definitely more like cages than cells. Steel bars run along the hall that seem to make a dozen small cells. Aisling and I lower our guns and holster them as we slowly walk along the hallway. The first few cells are empty but we can see girls huddled together further down. We approach the first occupied cell to find a little girl around 10 years old with pale skin, messy blonde hair, and a scared expression on her face. She's curled into the side bars holding onto another young girl around the same age but with dark brown hair and tan skin. I can't see this girl's face because it's buried in her knees.

Aisling crouches down to the girls' level and calmly tells them, "You're safe now. We're taking you home."

I move past Aisling and continue down the hall. Some cages have two girls in them and others there's just one. Each cage I stop at I let the girls know that they're safe. There's a total of eight girls here as I reach the last occupied cell, halfway down the hallway. There could be so many more and a cold chill runs down my spine.

Two teens look up at me, scared, and they remind me of myself at that age, right after Tony. I'm about to ask what their names are when someone calls out my name from the end of the hall. Recognizing the voice, I run to the last cage, finding Stella standing there at the bars. "Stella?"

Someone stands behind her. "Bianca? How are you here?" I look down at the cell door and pull on the steel lock, knowing it won't budge.

"Why wasn't I told you were missing?" Surely someone from the club would've called me when she didn't show up.

"We're supposed to be in St. Thomas right now," Stella huffs, pissed about the missed trip. "We were taken the day we were supposed to leave."

"My boyfriend sold us. They grabbed us as we were picking him up." Bianca looks up at me with a hurt expression.

Fury courses through me as I pull out my phone. "You better mean ex-boyfriend. Never mind, it doesn't matter; he's dead anyways." I press Matteo's contact.

"I need keys or bolt cutters now." I hang up before he can respond and run my hand over my hair, taking in the condition of the girls. Their clothes are dirty and torn and I can see faded bruises on their faces. "Are you okay? Did any of them touch you?"

They both shake their heads no but Bianca folds in on herself as she hugs herself tighter. I need to get them out of here. They were supposed to be safe with me and instead my family caused them further trauma.

Stella is the opposite of Bianca as she stands with fiery confidence. "The first night it was just us and they tried but we fought back." A happy smile comes across her face as she thinks of it. "Someone pretty high up came in during that and chewed out the guys, saying we were supposed to be unmarked. After that, all they did was bring in new girls and sometimes food and water."

"How long have you been here?"

Stella shrugs. "What day is it?"

"It's Tuesday."

"Then three days."

Fuck. "I'm so sorry I didn't realize you weren't okay."

"Don't apologize. This isn't your fault. It's Keith's fault. I want him to suffer for selling us and just standing by, watching them grab and drug us." Fire burns in her eyes and I know she wants her own time with him and I'll give her that.

Bianca has somehow made herself smaller as she huddles in the corner silently and I'm worried about her. Keith's betrayal is hurting her. She was in love with him from almost the moment they met a couple of weeks ago.

Before I can say something to her, voices come from the start of the hallway just before Colton and Tanner walk in. "Reinforcements are here." They each have bolt cutters in their hands. Tanner stays with Aisling and starts cutting the locks on that side as Colton comes to me.

He stops in his tracks when he sees who's in the cell in front of me. "Shortcake? Bianca? What the fuck? Who do I have to kill?"

"Hi Chip, you're looking good." Shortcake? Chip? Since when did these two get this cozy with each other?

"Blossom?" Tanner walks over and Stella smiles at him.

"Dale." Blossom? Dale? What the hell? I take the bolt cutters from Colton and quickly cut the lock.

Before the lock hits the ground, the twins have the door open and they both go to Stella. Okay… something is up there. I leave them to take care of Stella and Bianca and help Aisling cut open the rest of the locks and coax the girls out of the cages and out into the warehouse. I bypass Killian as I lead the girls toward the van and I give him a smile. His meeting must've gone well with how quick it was. I can't wait to hear how they bowed to him.

With my back to the van, I call the girls' attention to distract them as the guys carry the still alive guards into the hallway to lock them away. "Hi ladies. My name is Riona and this is Aisling and the men moving around are our friends. I know you're probably scared and have lots of questions but right now we need to get you away from here and to someplace safe. You all look hungry and I bet you'd like a nice burger. Would you be okay going with Aisling and Killian to Sally's Diner?"

The young girls all perk up at the mention of food but the older girls still look hesitant. "We just want to get food and water into you and figure out if you're safe to go home. I promise all of you who want to go home will be sleeping in your beds tonight. The ones who don't feel safe to go home will have a safe place to stay."

Some of the older girls relax a little but not all of them. Stella steps through the girls to stand next to me. "These are good people and they mean every word they're saying. I've known them for years and it isn't the first time they've saved me. Those of you who want to go home, will. Those who don't have a great home life, they'll take care of you, give you anything you need."

The last of the girls seem to realize we won't hurt them and I let out a slow breath in relief. Aisling steps forward. "Okay let's get on the bus." The older girls take the younger girls' hands and lead them to the bus.

One of the teens though doesn't move in that direction, instead she shyly comes to me and Stella. "What if I have somewhere I want to go instead of home?"

"Phoebe?" She looks shocked and I take that as a yes. "You have a very good friend that was very worried about you. Leo calling me after you were taken is the only reason why we're here. We wouldn't have known you girls were here otherwise."

Tears stream down her face and I pull her to me and wrap my arms around her. She breaks in my arms and I rub my hand along her hair to soothe her. "It's okay. You'll be okay. We're taking you to Leo."

Phoebe pulls her head back and her face is all red. "Really?"

"Really. Would you like to talk to him while we finish everything here?" She nods and I pull out my phone and click the unsaved number and hand it over. "Don't wander off."

Phoebe nods as she takes the phone and I hear Leo answer. "Did you find her?"

"Leo." Phoebe walks toward the rolling door but doesn't walk out of the building. She takes a seat at the chair that's sitting there and tries to reassure her best friend that she's safe.

With the girls in the bus, and Phoebe occupied, we all gather together. "What's the plan, Ri?" Killian asks.

"You two take the girls to Sally's. Give her a call on the way over so she can close for everyone else. I want the place empty. Aisling, you know what to do." She's going to find out who's safe to go home and reach out to our contact with the police to get them home. She'll also tell them the story on how they were saved where we weren't involved. The ones that don't want to go home will go to the apartments with some of our girls until Miss Claus gets back.

Aisling nods and touches my arm. "I got them." She grabs Killian's hand and they climb into the bus and drive off.

I watch them go and give Phoebe a quick glance to make sure she's okay before turning back to the group. "Tanner and Colton, you will take Stella and Bianca home and then I need you to pick up a sorry excuse of a man. They'll be able to give you an address. Please deliver him to my special room under the club."

They nod but don't move so I continue talking to my guys. "You guys are coming with me." I smile at my guys and they smile back at me. "We have a girl to drop off and a Franks to kill." Their smiles turn from flirtatious to furious about Franks.

Someone grabs my hand and I look to find Bianca next to me. "Can I talk to you for a second?"

"Absolutely." I wave off everyone. "You guys go and get into the cars. We'll be out in a second. Phoebe?" She looks up. "Will you go with these three to the car? I'll be there in a second." She nods while still talking to Leo and stands from the chair, waiting for my guys to reach her before following them.

When we're alone, I turn to her and give her my full attention. "What's wrong?"

"I think I'm done. I'm ready to move on, maybe go home." She looks up at me like I'm disappointed in her.

I step closer and touch her arm in comfort. "The whole point of me being here to help you is for you to move on one day. You aren't indebted to me and whenever you or anyone is ready to move, I'll be there to hug you goodbye and give you anything you need to get settled into your new life."

She looks shocked. "You aren't mad?"

I shake my head. "Absolutely not. I'll miss you but I want you to be happy."

"I think I'll be happy back home, living the small-town life."

"I believe you'll be happy there." I pull her into a hug. "I'm sorry I didn't protect you like I promised."

She squeezes me tight. "You couldn't have known my boyfriend was a dick. You can't keep everyone safe all the time."

We pull back from the hug. "I can try." I give her a playful smile and she chuckles. "Just promise me you won't leave without saying goodbye."

"I promise." I squeeze her hand before letting go and we head out of the warehouse, and I make sure Bianca is safely in the twins' car before going back to close the rolling door. Enzo's waiting outside the open back driver side door for me and as I climb, I run my body against his and place a quick kiss to his lips.

I slide into the middle seat next to Phoebe and she smiles coyly at me with a deep blush. "Here you go." She hands me my phone as Enzo climbs in on the other side of me.

I lean over to her and whisper, "You should try that with Leo." Pure embarrassment washes over her face and I chuckle silently as I turn to Dante in the driver seat. "Take us to Little Italy."

Chapter Twenty-Eight

Riona

Dante parks out front of the last house I'd ever expect to see again. Phoebe opens the door and runs toward the house as flashes of the night I escaped from Tony's guys blurs my vision. Looking down the street, I can see myself in a long, dirty, torn shirt, knocking on every door trying to get help. This house was the only one with a porch light on. It was a beacon to safety.

The front door opens as Phoebe gets to the porch and I can see the same woman that opened the door for me several years ago. She embraces Phoebe in a hug and I unconsciously slide out of the SUV and start walking toward the front door. Enzo calls out my name, wondering what I'm doing since we were only supposed to drop her off.

"I just need a minute," I say without looking back.

Leo appears in the doorway and pulls Phoebe from his mother. The way he holds her and places a kiss to the top of her head shows how much he loves her and the way she melts into him with a content smile on her face says she feels the same. I'm glad we were able to find her before anything could happen that would dim their view on the world.

Mrs. Sorreno steps out onto her porch with a welcoming smile. "What a beautiful, strong woman you have grown into." She opens her arms out wide. "Come here."

I take the last couple of steps and wrap my arms around her center. She wraps her arms around me and warmth surrounds me. "It's good to see you, little one." She squeezes me tighter. "Thank you. Thank you for everything."

I pull back from our hug to tell her that no thanks are needed but she cuts me off from speaking. "And I mean *everything*." The way she says everything tells me she knows what I've done.

Once again, she doesn't let me say anything, which is fine because I have no idea what to say. "Please promise you'll stop by the restaurant soon." She nods toward the SUV. "You can bring your guys with you."

I look over my shoulder to see my guys all watching us. Well, that's not good; the tint is supposed to be darker. We need to get out of here.

I start walking backward to the car slowly. "I promise. We'll be by soon." I wave bye to her and turn to close the distance between me and the SUV.

"Oh, and tell those boys when they're ready to be raised from their graves, Little Italy will welcome them back with open arms." I freeze halfway to the car and look over my shoulder to this sweet woman. She gives me a knowing smile, telling me she has at least a hand in the dark and discreet world I live in.

I climb back into the SUV and shut the door, finding my guys all looking at me. "What?"

"What was that?" Enzo looks concerned, sitting between me and the window.

"Do you remember me telling you when I escaped Tony that a couple helped me?" They nod. "This is the house I came to; she and her husband helped me."

"Wow." Dante sits back in the driver's seat, looking forward. "Small world."

"No kidding." Matteo turns and faces forward as well.

"And I think she knows I'm their anonymous investor. As soon as I was able to function enough to sit up in bed, I looked into them and found out they had a family restaurant that was struggling so I created an anonymous business, moved all my money into the business account, and sent them a check to help them with their restaurant."

Dante shifts the car into drive and Enzo pulls me into his side. "That was very nice of you. When was the last time you saw them?"

"That night. I wasn't in good shape mentally when I got home, and by the time I was able to function, I was in training so I kept my distance. After a while they were just in the back of my mind."

"Your life moved on." Enzo takes my hand and I lean on his shoulder.

"Or it shifted into a darker, bloodier world."

"A world that you reign over." Enzo kisses the top of my head.

Matteo looks over his shoulder at me, with a loving smile. "A princess."

"A queen," Dante corrects.

Matteo mouths 'princess' with a playful smile and I smile brightly at him, showing him how much I love being his princess.

Enzo's lips move against my hair as he whispers, "Beauty."

We're quiet as Dante drives us back toward the docks and my eyes start to droop closed. My meeting with Franks is going to be short. I don't have enough energy to torture two men tonight. Dante's voice has my eyes shooting open. "We're going to need to make an appearance soon."

I sit up from Enzo's shoulder and stretch out my neck and back. Looking out the window, I see we're almost to the docks. "We weren't careful tonight."

Dante looks at me in the rearview mirror. "I didn't mean to wake you."

I wave him off because I shouldn't be sleeping. "Mrs. Sorreno told me that Little Italy is ready for you guys to rise from your graves whenever you're ready."

"I'm thinking we should show up to your father's party." Dante's eyes hold mine.

"You didn't get an invitation." I give him a teasing smile, knowing they're going with me.

"You did." He narrows his eyes at me, knowing I'm instigating.

"If you want to come with me, then you're going to have to ask me." He smirks at me, and I smile back at him, excited about a date with all of us. It'll be our first official date.

"Rose, will you please be our date for Lorcan's party?"

"Yes, I would love to be your date."

"It's going to make a big splash with you walking in on our arms."

"I'm used to everyone watching when I walk into Lorcan's parties."

"We're very aware." Matteo turns around and runs his eyes over me. "You had all our attention at the Annual Gala. But I have to say, the ballgown look isn't quite you. Now the dress you were wearing at the charity gala you accompanied my father to was very much you."

He's not wrong. "I didn't pick out that dress."

"We know." Enzo smiles at me.

"You picked it out." I look at the three of them, trying to figure out who did.

"We might have given the shopper a few tips." Enzo slides his fingers up my thigh, and I know it was his idea for the slit.

I chuckle and grab his hand before it goes any higher. "You get no input on tomorrow's dress."

"Why not?" Matteo looks sad and confused.

"So you can be surprised." I give him a sexy smile because I want to pick a dress that'll make their jaws drop. Dante turns down the street that meets the road the docks' entrance is off of. "You can stop right up here."

Dante slows but I can see his confusion at my request. "We're coming with you."

"No, you're not. Junior will be with me, so you can't be seen."

His eyes darken at the thought of me alone with Junior. "Junior can't be trusted. This could be a setup."

"I am fully armed." Really, I could take him with my eyes closed.

Dante parks on the side of the road and turns off the lights. "I don't like it." He turns to face me with a serious look on his face.

"I can't show up with a masked guard, let alone three of them." I look at Matteo. "Sorry Bear. I know I promised we'd torture him together." He looks disappointed but he nods.

"Will you wear the earpiece and keep the mic open?" Enzo shifts in his seat so he's facing me.

"Yeah, I can do that." Enzo reaches behind us to the back and grabs his bag. "I won't be gone long. As much as I want to make Franks scream and beg for his life, there's someone else I want to do that to more."

"I'll help with that one." Matteo perks up.

"I'd love that."

Matteo beams at me, excited. "What's your plan?"

"Junior is meeting me in the lobby. He told his father he had business to discuss. I'm going to take Junior's gun and shoot his father."

Enzo hands me an earpiece and I slide it into my ear. "Smart using his weapon so it can't be traced to you. What about fingerprints?"

I pull out two black gloves and slide them on. "No fingerprints." I look at the clock, seeing I need to meet Junior in a few minutes. "I need to go." I lean forward and give both Dante and Matteo a kiss. Sitting back, I look at Enzo as I press my earpiece. "We all good?" My voice rings out from Enzo's phone. He smiles, knowing he doesn't need to answer. I lean forward and give him a kiss as well before climbing out of the SUV. I can feel their eyes on me as I walk around the front of the truck and head to the main office building for Franks' business.

As I approach the building, the hairs on the back of my neck stand up because the windows are tinted and I can't see inside. What if this is a trap like Dante said? I pull my gun from my hip holster and hold it lightly in my hand as I push the door open. Everything in the lobby is still and silent as I step into the building, holding the door open and scanning the large open space. When I look over at the sitting area, I almost jump out of my skin, finding Junior sitting there in the dark. "You're lucky I didn't shoot you." I let the door close behind me, but I don't put away my gun.

Junior stands from the leather chair and buttons up his suit jacket. "I figured it would be best to stay quiet until you saw me and not spook you."

"Probably smart. Your dad here?"

"Yeah, on the top floor waiting for me." I nod and head toward the elevators.

"You coming to watch?" I look over my shoulder at him and he's already following.

"I wouldn't miss it."

We step into the elevator, and I nod to the security camera. "Off?"

"Looped. The whole building." Junior pulls out his phone and shows me a camera feed of an empty elevator.

The elevator numbers rise and I hold out my hand to Junior. "Gun?"

"What's wrong with yours?" He looks down at my open palm and back to my face.

"Nothing." I hold Junior's stare, telling him I'm not going to ask again. Reluctantly, Junior reaches behind him and pulls out his gun.

He holds it over my hand. "Don't use this on me."

I grab the gun and push mine into the holster. "Don't make me have to."

The elevator doors open and I nod for him to go ahead. I follow behind Junior as I scan the open space filled with a few empty desks. Junior stops outside a closed door and I step against the wall as he knocks.

Franks' voice comes through the door. "About time. Get in here."

Junior opens the door and Franks continues, "What the hell do you need to tell me at this hour?" Junior steps to the side and I step into the doorway. Franks is sitting behind his desk and his shocked expression is priceless.

"It's not something he needs to tell you." I raise my arm and aim Junior's gun at his father. "It's something he needs to take from you. I told you I'd kill you if you continued to deal in skin. I hope it was worth it." Before he can even speak, I squeeze the trigger rapidly, sending three bullets into his body. One in the head and two in the chest. Frank's body slumps back in his chair and I look at Junior. "Do you have someone to clean this up?" He nods and I unarm the gun, removing the bullets before handing the empty gun back to him. "This shouldn't need to be said but I'll say it anyway. My name shouldn't be mentioned at all when his death is recorded."

He smiles. "Riona who?"

I roll my eyes and leave Junior to handle his father's dead body. Instead of the elevator, I take the steps down just to make sure Junior's guys aren't waiting for the elevator to come down. Knowing the guys are listening, I talk into the empty stairwell. "I'm coming down. Meet me out front." I jog down the five flights of stairs and out the exit that opens to the front sidewalk. The guys pull up as I step out and I climb into the back. "Last stop, Mystique."

Chapter Twenty-Nine

Riona

Screams fill the elevator before we even reach the bottom floor and when the doors open, I find Bianca's ex hanging from the ceiling with his shirt removed and red welts all over his body. A pipe swinging into his ribs has me about to fuss out Colton and Tanner for starting without me but when I step out, it's Stella holding the pipe.

Tanner and Colton are standing far enough behind her to not get hit with the pipe when she swings back. "Go for the feet and ankles if you really want him to scream." Colton suggests. I guess they're giving pointers as well. Stella brings the pipe over her head and swings down with a groan as she puts her whole body into it. As Colton predicted, the asshole screams out as the pipe slams into his foot that's barely touching the ground.

I chuckle, walking further into the room. "You got started without me?"

Stella whips around with a guilty look as Tanner and Colton have victorious smiles. "I'm sorry, Ri. I talked them into letting me come."

Matteo chuckles behind me. "I'm sure they didn't need much convincing." He walks over to join Tanner and Colton, and his brothers follow.

"I just wanted to cause him pain. I made sure not to do anything to kill him."

"Do you want to kill him?" He's going to die tonight and it was her and Bianca he hurt, so if she wants to do it, I'd give her that.

She shakes her head. "Just pain. Can I take a few more swings?"

I wave my hand to the asshole. "Go for it. Knees and balls are good places to hear his screams too."

She gives me a wicked smile. "I went for his dick first."

"Smart woman." I leave her to let out her anger and join the guys over by the weapons table. "So did you resist at all when she asked?" I look at Tanner and Colton.

"Should we have told her no?" Tanner asks as he continues to watch Stella behind me.

I wait for him to look at me before I answer him. He briefly looks at me with a cocky expression because he knows the answer. "No." He shrugs his shoulders and looks back at Stella. "What's going on with you three?"

Colton smiles as he watches her too. "Nothing yet." I can almost hear what he's not saying. Hopefully soon. Arms wrap around my middle and I'm pulled up against Dante's chest so I'm facing Stella. I relax into Dante's arms and his lips run over my neck. "You're upset that they like Stella."

What? I look up at him, shocked. "No, of course not."

"Good. I don't like the idea of you being jealous of who they want." His eyes darken to a familiar shade that has my blood pumping.

"Would that make you jealous?" His hands run down my slides as he growls into my neck. I rub my thighs together as my body heats at the thought of Dante jealous.

Stella swings at the asshole again and a very selfish dirty thought pops into my head. Dante's hands go to my hips and he pulls me back so he can grind his erection against my ass. "What are you thinking about, Rose?"

"Oh. I think you know, but I'll be happy to show you." I grab his hand and pull him to the door that leads to the sex rooms. "We'll be right back." I type in the code and the door unlocks.

"Have fun," Tanner says.

"Don't do anything I wouldn't," Colton adds.

"Where are you going?" Matteo asks.

I look back at him as I open the door. "I'll show you later."

He must see the naughty promise in my eyes because his eyes roam over me. "I look forward to it."

Dante moves past me and into the hallway. As he passes me, he grabs my hand and starts pulling me through the door. My eyes lock with Enzo's before the door closes and I can see how turned on he is. Maybe he'll want to watch me and Matteo later.

That thought evaporates as Dante pulls me into the first room and pushes me against the wall next to the door. The room lights turn on as Dante's mouth smashes against mine and we tear at each other's clothes. Once my pants and underwear are off and Dante's pants are pushed down enough to release his erection, he picks me up and slams into me. A loud moan leaves me in pleasure and I wrap my legs and arms tightly around him so no distance is between us.

"You feel so good. I've missed this so much." Dante kisses down my throat and I whimper at his words.

"I missed you." I roll my hips against him trying to get him to move. "Dante, please."

"Please what?" Dante kisses across my shoulder.

I place my hands on either side of his face and pull him back up so he's looking at me. "Fuck me now." I pull him to me and kiss him with everything I have. Dante pulls back all the way to the tip and thrust back in and I moan in satisfaction. He continues to fuck me against the wall with no words passing between us, just the noises we make in pure pleasure as our skin slaps together.

Dante runs his hands from my hips up my sides and I arch into him. His hands cup my breasts and I break from our kiss, throwing my head back. "Ohh… yes...Dante." My body starts to shake as my orgasm comes rushing forward.

"Scream for me, Rose. Let the others know how much you love me inside you."

He picks up his pace as he rubs circles over my clit and I come screaming his name. Dante continues to fuck me as I ride out my pleasure until his whole body locks up and he comes, groaning. "Fuck... Ri."

My hands run over his shoulders as our foreheads rest together, and I breathe him in. I wasn't just saying I missed sex with him earlier. I missed everything about him. His touch. His voice. His eyes. His loving words. His want for control. My eyes hold his as I open myself up so he can see how much I want him. He closes the distance between us and kisses me slowly, expressing the feelings I was showing him. Dante pulls out of me, lowering me to my feet as he continues to place loving kisses down my body.

He kneels down in front of me, placing one last kiss to my stomach before grabbing my panties and helping me into them. Our release instantly dampens the inside of my upper thighs and my panties and I clench my thighs together, wanting to stay filled. He watches me with a knowing and satisfied smile and my core pulses, wanting more, as he runs his fingers up my thighs all the way to the edge of my panties. He pulls his fingers away from my skin, covered in our release, and brings them to his lips. He sinks his pointer finger in his mouth and hums in pleasure. "We taste so good together, Rose. Do you want a taste?"

I nod instantly as I bend forward and take his middle finger in my mouth, running my tongue over it before sucking it clean. "We taste wonderful." Dante gives me a heated, possessive smile before he slams his lips to mine. Before we can fall into round two, which I desperately want, Dante pulls back from our kiss and grabs my pants. I let out a disappointed huff and he chuckles as he helps me back into the rest of my clothes. Dante stands, running his eyes over my now clothed body as he shifts his hardening length back in his pants. When his eyes connect with mine, he pulls me against him and places a soft kiss on my lips. "Are you doing okay, Rose?"

Knowing he's making sure he didn't push too hard, I smile brightly up at him. "I'm perfect, Boss Man. I love you."

"I love you too." He kisses me again with more passion and I melt into him.

Chapter Thirty

Matteo

Riona and Dante walk back into the room looking flushed and very happy and I fight myself not to pull her back through that door. I don't know what's behind it, but I bet I could have her naked and bent over something in seconds. The only reason I don't is because torturing this douchecanoe is foreplay. Watching each other inflict pain gets both of our blood pumping and hearts racing.

I can imagine all the things we can do to him to make him scream. Does she want to bleed him? Finish what Stella started and break every bone? Have a little target practice? Traditional torture? My pants get tighter just thinking of all the possibilities and I shift myself to relieve the pressure. The sound of the pipe hitting the floor has my attention focusing back on what's in front me.

Stella looks exhausted as she breathes heavily and stands in front of the man that's the reason she was taken. The douchewiener whimpers in pain from where he hangs and I hope Stella feels powerful. She turns away from him quickly and walks toward us. "Okay I'm done. Take me home." The last part is directed only to Tanner and Colton.

They move instantly, heading toward the elevator as Stella gives Riona a hug. Those guys got it bad, and I know exactly how they feel. My eyes connect with Riona's, and she smiles at me over Stella's shoulder. She's just as excited as I am for what we're about to do.

I head over to the tables, looking over the different weapons, and my eyes focus on the sledgehammer. That could definitely shatter his bones. On the other end, there are small blades laid out and I know my princess would love to do some target practice with these. Two jumper cables catch my attention and I step back and look underneath the table. Oooh nice, a car battery. Electrocution could be fun. A hand rests on my lower back and I relax into her touch. "What are you thinking?"

"There are a lot of options here to inflict pain."

"Which way do you want?"

I smile at her, ready to spill his blood. "Do we need to pull information from him?" I nod toward the battery.

She shakes her head and scrunches up her nose. "No. Plus I don't want to deal with the smell."

"Then I think you should have a little target practice and then we can smash some bones." I point toward the sledgehammer.

She smiles at me, excited. "Will you throw with me? We can make a game of it."

"I like games. Are we playing strip darts?" She chuckles and shakes her head. "This asshole doesn't get to see me or you naked. I'm thinking whoever hits the bullseye the most gets to choose which room we use when we're done."

"Room?" I collect six knives and hand three to her.

"Six rooms with different kinks." She points to the door her and Dante went through and now I want to know which room they used. She twirls one of the knives around her finger as she walks toward the douchefart. "Let's make a real target."

Her knife cuts into his chest to carve different size circles and his screams ring out. I didn't even realize the guy was quiet because I had blocked out his annoying screams a while ago. "Please stop. I'm sorry, okay?"

She glares up at him. "I don't care if you're sorry. You should've never traded my girls to Lorcan. You'll die for that."

She sticks the tip of her knife into the center of the three circles and twirls it, creating the small bullseye.

The douchesack sobs as he continues to beg for his life. What a weak man. "Is his whining annoying you?" I stand next to Riona.

"Kind of." She shrugs.

"Oh good. Me too." I grab the duct tape on top of the table and pull off a small piece, long enough to cover his mouth. Stepping up to him, I quickly silence his cries.

"So much better." I walk backward until I'm standing next to her again. I look back to Dante and Enzo who have made themselves at home on the couch. "You want in on this game?"

They both shake their heads. "I'm good just watching." Enzo runs his eyes over Riona, who's still looking at the douchebaby while twirling a knife like she's mapping out her throws.

"You know you're going to lose, right?" Dante asks.

"Of course I am, but I'll be winning in whatever room she selects." I turn back to the doucheturd and look down at her. "Princesses first." I hold out my hand as I step back, letting her go first.

Riona chuckles as she moves to the imaginary line on the floor and smiles back at me. "One by one."

I nod and she turns forward, gripping the knife that already has his blood on it between her thumb and pointer finger. She brings the knife back over her shoulder with her other hand out in front of her for stability and throws it effortlessly. The knife spins, heading right toward the bullseye and lands dead center, impaling the doucheweenie. He screams against the tape so it only comes out as a muffled groan.

Ignoring him, I step to where Riona was. "So tell me, what rooms do I get to choose from?"

I bring my hand back holding the knife and throw it forward, releasing the knife at just the right angle to hit his chest. My knife lands just inside the second smallest ring.

"Round one: me." She smiles gleefully at me.

"I was close though." Watching her smile like that, I'll happily play this game all night and lose every round.

We shift and she bounces on her toes as she gets ready to throw. "We have voyeurism, exhibition, role-play, ropes and bondage, sex toy and edibles, and BDSM rooms." She releases the knife and, once again, it hits the center, right next to her other knife.

"Role-play? So, I can ask you to dress up as a naughty teacher?" I step up for my turn.

"Do you have a naughty teacher fantasy?" She looks over at me, shocked.

"No, not really." I throw my second knife and hit the center right below hers.

"Good, because I'm not a very good actress. I giggle a lot."

I pull her to me. "Everything about you turns me on. Even if you were a giggling Princess Leia."

She giggles in my arms and pushes at my chest playfully. "You're a Star Wars fan?"

"No, but Dante is." I nod to my brother who's listening to everything.

She turns in my arms and looks at Dante. "Do you want me dressed up like Princess Leia?"

He shakes his head. "I prefer you naked." Riona shifts, rubbing her ass against my erection and I take the moment to grind against her, showing just how hard I am.

"Stop that." She swats at my leg and steps away from me. "How about you, Enzo? You have any fantasies of me dressed up as someone else?"

He shakes his head. "No way, Beauty. I just want you."

"So, you guys don't want me to wear sexy little outfits for you?"

"You'll be breathtaking in anything." Enzo leans forward, resting his elbows on knees.

"We just want you." Dante adjusts himself in his jeans.

"You for you. Not someone else." I step up behind her again and wrap my arms around her waist.

"Well, that's good, because I have a surprise for you after the party." Her heated smile tells me we're going to love this surprise.

"Can we unwrap our surprise now?" I run my lips down her neck.

"No, because I don't have it with me." She turns around in my arms. "But you can unwrap me when we finish with him." She nods behind me and I look back at the douchedick who's watching us.

Shit, I forgot about him. Riona makes me have a one-track mind. "What are you looking at? Do you want me to rip out your eyes?"

He immediately looks away from us and I quietly chuckle. "Shall we finish up this game?"

"Yes, I'm ready to win." She skips over to the point we were throwing from and pulls out her last knife. Without missing a beat, she throws the knife and it lands perfectly in the center. The douchebag's whole body tenses but he doesn't make a sound or look at us. At least he's starting to listen; too bad he'll be dead soon.

"How set are you on smashing all his bones?" Riona looks at me with so much unspoken desire.

"I'm open to other ideas." Like removing every piece of her clothes instead.

"We kill him now and go to Room 2 and put on a show." I pull out my gun and hold it out for her to take as she briefly looks at Enzo.

She wraps her fingers around the gun and lifts it. Her body is still facing mine but she's looking toward the douchewagon with her arm raised. A shot rings out and the chains jingle as his body recoils. A bullet to the head will definitely kill you.

She looks at me with a victorious and lustful smile. "Looks like we're done here. Are you ready to show him what you want to do to me?"

Oh, I definitely am. If she wants Enzo watching, I'll make him wish he was me. "You do love when he's watching you."

Her smile is heated with anticipation as she walks toward them. She steps in front of Enzo and leans forward resting her hands on his thighs. "You should check out Room 1."

"What's in that room?" Enzo runs his hands up her arms.

"A large two-way mirror with a perfect view of Room 2."

Enzo's eyes burn with lust and I know exactly what he's thinking. Riona smiles at him, knowing he won't say no.

She moves over to Dante and he pulls her onto his lap. "You can watch too if you want."

He pulls her in for a kiss and she melts into him. "I love looking at you, but we already had our time." He kisses her again. "How about I clean this up?"

"Okay." She gives him a third kiss and climbs off his lap, beckoning us to follow her by hooking her finger and Enzo and I willingly step toward her. Our hands roam her body as she enters the code, opening the door. She takes each of our hands in hers and pulls us down the hall. Room 2 comes up on our left and she lets go of my hand to show Enzo Room 1.

She rises up on her toes and kisses Enzo. He pulls her to him and I lean against my door letting them have their moment.

"Wait until I come to you," Riona whispers before she pulls away and heads to me. I open my door and step aside for her to walk in first.

I look at Enzo as I follow behind her, finding him walking into his room as well, matching my heated smile. "Make it a good show."

I give him a cocky smile without answering because I plan to make her scream. The door closes behind me and Riona turns to me giving me a look that tells me how much she wants me.

"Do you want to unwrap me, Bear?"

"You know I do. Come here, Princess." She shakes her head at me and starts backing up toward the obvious two-way mirror as she hooks her finger, beckoning me to her. Like a string is attached between us, I step with her until she's up against the glass and then I quickly close the distance. I cradle her head in between my hands and lower my lips to hers until they brush against them. "I love you."

Her eyes sparkle as she looks up at me. "I love you too."

I press my lips to hers before she finishes saying the last word. Riona fists her hands into the sides of my shirt as she moans into my mouth. My hands slide down her neck, over her shoulders, and down her sides until I reach the end of her shirt. "How attached are you to this shirt?"

"I have extra clothes here."

"Perfect." I fist the front of her shirt, ripping it open. My palms touch her exposed waist, and a shiver runs through her. Worried that I'm pushing her, I look up from her beautiful body to her face to see desire burning in her eyes. That shiver was in pleasure. Following the direction my eyes just took, I skim my hands up her body and push her shirt off her shoulders. Her bra is the next thing to go as I press my lips to the smooth, warm skin at her collarbone.

I kiss down her chest and across the swell of her breasts as my hands cup them and rub my thumbs over her nipples. They harden to a point, begging for my lips to wrap around them and I answer to anything her and her body wants. I kneel down in front of her and my lips wrap around her nipple, making her moan and grip onto the sill of the mirror. I suck and flick my tongue over her nipple, matching the movements on her other nipples with my fingers. Switching breasts, I give her other nipple the same attention until they're glistening with my saliva. I pull back, looking at her rosy nipples as I circle them with my thumbs, and she bucks forwards.

"More, please." She places her hand on top of my head and pushes down. Knowing what she wants, I slide my hands back down her body and hook my fingers into the side of her pants. I pull them down with her panties until she stands above me naked. I start kissing up her thigh as my fingers brush over her ankle and up to her calf. Bringing her leg over my shoulder, she opens up for me, showing me how turned on she is. I kiss her wetness and I flick my tongue against her clit, tasting her.

She bucks against my tongue and grips my shoulder for support. "Fuck yes, please." Her head falls back against glass as a long moan comes out and I suck her clit between my lips and rhythmically flick my tongue to the pace I wish I was fucking her.

"Scream louder for us, Princess. Let Enzo know how good you feel." I push two fingers inside her and she tightens around them. "You love knowing he's watching you right now and getting himself off."

"Yes." She pants.

I thrust my fingers in and out of her, making sure to graze my fingers along her upper wall, and her knees wobble. I grip her hip, holding her up as I suck her clit again. Her whole body starts to shake as her orgasm hits and she moans out, "Oh God. Yes!" Watching her come is one of my favorite things, especially when I'm the one making her. Pulling back from her clit, I replace my mouth with my thumb and watch as she rides out her pleasure.

She fists my shirt, breathing heavily, and pulls me off my knees and to her. Her lips slam to mine as she rips off my shirt and without missing a beat, she undoes my pants as well. Her hand wraps around my erection and I groan out. She pumps me in quick short pulls, and I can feel myself getting close to the edge. "I need you to fuck me, Matteo."

She gives me a challenging, lustful smile and I match it before gripping her hips and turning to face the mirror. "Let him watch your pleasure, while we watch each other."

Her hands rest on the glass as she sticks her ass out and wiggles it at me. I want her ass, but I know she's not asking for that. I step up behind her as she looks back at me and I watch her as I run my hand over the curve of her full ass. No fear flashes in her eyes and I know she trusts me not to misstep. And I won't.

My hands go to her hips as I rub myself along her center and glide over her sensitive clit. "Are you ready for me, Princess?"

"Yes, please." She pushes back against me and I grip her hips harder.

"Look forward, Ri. Let him see how much you love my cock inside you." Her eyes connect with mine in the mirror and I thrust in, making us both groan in pleasure. "Fuck, you feel so good." I pull out and immediately thrust back into her. With each thrust they grow more powerful and her moans grow louder. "Yes, let me hear you."

She pushes back into me, making me go deeper as she squeezes me tighter. Her eyes droop closed in pleasure and I reach around to her clit and pinch. Her eyes spring open with a loud moan, "Fuck."

"Eyes open, Princess." I lean forward so my body is pressed fully against hers and move my hand from her hip to her hand to interlock our fingers. With my lips next to her ear, I whisper, "Can you see him wanting you, watching you, picturing you kneeling in front of him?"

She moans loudly again as she squeezes around me and I know she's close to coming again. "He's going to come all over his hand and it's all for you." I rub rough circles over her clit and she squeezes me tight. "Come for me, Princess. Scream for me as I come inside you." I press into her clit while I fuck her harder and she comes screaming my name with a fully body shiver that has me coming so loud that my ears ring. We don't move as we catch our breaths and I place soft kisses across her back. Riona looks back at me and I capture her lips with mine. "Are you okay?"

I look deep into her eyes to make sure there is no flicker of panic or fear as she says, "I'm amazing."

Relief washes over me when I don't see any, so I kiss her again deeply as I pull out of her. With a smack on the ass, I step back and she looks at me shocked. "Go see Enzo. He probably has some angry blue balls right now." Something hits the other side of the glass and I chuckle because I'm right.

Riona slowly moves to the door next to the mirror, but her eyes don't leave mine. She gives me a loving smile before she disappears into the other room and my heart feels like it's about to explode. I want her to smile at me like that for the rest of our lives.

Chapter Thirty-One

Riona

Safe. That's how I feel waking up this morning or, should I say, afternoon. With my cheek resting on a sleeping Enzo's chest, I look up at his handsome face, smiling. It feels good to be waking up to him again. All of them. I can't believe it was just yesterday morning that I found out they were alive. I roll over and look at Dante who's laying on the other side of the Alaskan King with a pillow wall between us.

When we came to bed, I was worried about freaking out in the middle of the night so I asked to only sleep with one of them. I wanted to sleep with Enzo since I hadn't had much alone time with him, but the others didn't want to leave me. Dante made the pillow wall so he wouldn't accidentally move in his sleep and scare me. Matteo... I sit up and look at the couch that's in the sitting area. Yes, this room is large enough for a sitting room. Matteo is awkwardly sprawled out over the couch that looks uncomfortable but he's deep asleep. Making sure to move carefully, I crawl to the end of bed and stand, leaving my guys to sleep as I head downstairs to make some coffee.

I take my time going to the kitchen, exploring each of the rooms I pass, taking in all the details and decor. After we dumped the asshole's body, I got a text from Aisling saying the estate was ready and that was where we were staying. Apparently, they finished the place while I was in Italy so I had a place to call home. I didn't have the energy last night to explore but now I'm amazed how everything is so me.

Walking into the kitchen, I find it empty but a pot of coffee is already made. Grabbing a cup from the hooks underneath the top cabinets, I pour my cup and take a seat at the bar. I bring the coffee up to my lips and inhale the wonderful smell before taking a sip. Footsteps sound behind me and I turn to watch Aisling and Killian walk in with smiles on their faces as they look at each other. Aisling sees me first. "Good morning. Did you sleep okay?"

I know she's asking about my nightmares. "I slept great. That big bed definitely makes it easier."

"It does come in handy with all the men sleeping with you." She comes over to me as Killian moves to the coffee machine.

"Thank you for getting this place ready for all of us." I pull her into a hug before she sits.

"You deserve a permanent home and we need a place to crash until we can take over Lorcan's place. Safe houses are getting old." She hugs me back.

Killian walks over with two cups of coffee and they sit down at the bar with me. We're quiet for a second as we drink and I think of all the stuff Lorenzo told me. We have so much to tell each other. Killian breaks the silence. "The meeting went as planned. Everyone has agreed to the power shift and tomorrow is when we'll show Lorcan how little power he has."

"The girls are all safe. The younger girls were kidnapped, so our friendly officer became a hero and got them safely home. The teenagers were best friends and homeless, taken from the streets. They're at the apartments. Miss Claus already knows she has two new girls when it's safe to come home. The college girls were reported missing and they're back on campus. They were drugged during a night out. Although their stories are identical, they were from different universities and were taken from different bars." Aisling finishes her run down of how last night ended.

I give them my updates from last night. "Franks and Bianca's ex are dead and Phoebe is safe with Leo and his family."

"It's a good thing how well last night went. We need that luck to extend to tomorrow. Lorcan can't get the drop on us. He'll be pissed we've foiled his plans twice now." Killian leans forward and he looks worried. "We need a plan for if he tries to retaliate.

Especially with the power play move with all the families." He's right. We all need to be on our toes until the party because an unstable Lorcan is a scary thing.

"Before we get into that, Mr. Russo told me something about Lorcan that I need to tell you guys." Their attention is fully on me as I tell them about Lorcan's involvement in our mother's and Aisling father's death and my kidnapping when I was a teen. Also, I tell them my theory of his involvement in Aisling's kidnapping as well.

They're both silent when I finish as they take in all the damning evidence of the man we all considered a parent. Aisling looks shocked but it's Killian that I'm watching as his face turns red and rage burns in his eyes. "That disgusting piece of shit."

"He's evil," Aisling breathes out.

"He's a monster. Only caring about himself and the power he can take," I add.

"We're ending this tomorrow. I don't care how, but he won't see another sunrise." Killian gets up and pulls out his phone as he walks out of the kitchen.

"Where is he going?" My eyes follow him, concerned.

Aisling looks at where he just walked out. "To call Tanner and Colton."

"They aren't here?"

She shakes her head. "They stayed with Stella at a safe house." I look at her, shocked and she shrugs her shoulders. "I have no idea what's going on there."

"Nothing right now. Stella will make them beg for it."

Aisling chuckles. "I'd like to see that. Maybe she'll want to come with us to pick out our dresses. We can force her to tell us."

"Oh, good idea." Maybe the planning can wait until later so we can have some much-needed girl time.

Chapter Thirty-Two

Dante

"I'm going to need a day off after all this to take Aisling away and only focus on her." Killian leans against the kitchen counter, bringing the whiskey to his lips. All us guys are here dressed in our black tuxes, waiting for Aisling and Ri to come down.

"Amen to that." Matteo raises his glass. "I could spend a day in bed with just Riona and I." I glare at him. He can't really think he'll get a full day without us.

"That's my sister." Killian looks disturbed.

"Don't think too much about it." Colton pats Killian's shoulder. "Matteo is delusional if he thinks he's getting her alone for a whole day. Look at the jealousy in Dante's eyes and..." He looks at Enzo who's stone-faced. "I have no idea what he's feeling but I bet he wants to be there too."

Tanner places his hand on Killian's other shoulder and smiles gleefully at him. "Really, it'll be more like a foursome all day. Does that make you feel better?"

Killian jerks his shoulder away, making Tanner's hand fall. "I hate you guys sometimes."

We laugh at Killian's mortification but the sounds of heels clicking against the hardwoods has us all quieting and turning toward the doorway. Both girls stand in front of us looking gorgeous. Aisling looks ready to rule the world in her glistening gold dress, but Riona takes my breath away. She's in a white dress that only covers the left side of her body and pulls to her right hip with a diamond sheer underlay covering her right side.

"We've shocked them silent." Aisling looks over to Ri. They chuckle and all of the guys seem to remember how to talk all at the same time.

"Holy shit," Leaves my lips.

"Queens," Tanner says.

"Beautiful," Enzo breathes.

"Fuck. Hot as hell, ladies," Colton adds.

"Stunning, Angel." Killian walks around the island and walks toward his girl. "You look ready to rule."

A huge smile breaks across her face but I don't hear her response because Matteo walks toward Ri and Enzo and I are close

612

behind him. He wraps his arms around her waist, pulling her to him. "Princess, you look like royalty. I'll kneel in front of you any day."

Ri smiles up at him with heated desire as she runs her hand up his biceps. "Maybe later I'll let you."

Her hands go to the back of his neck and she pulls him down to her. She only allows their lips to connect briefly before taking a small step back but Matteo obviously wants more because he tries to pull her back. "One more."

She chuckles and places her hands on his chest, stopping him. "Later."

Enzo steps up to her and they wrap their arms around each other's middle. Enzo leans down and softly kisses her. "This dress looks gorgeous on you. Definitely dressed to kill."

Her smile is beaming as she looks up at him. "I wanted to turn heads."

Getting tired of waiting for her to come to me, I move behind her and pull her away from Enzo. She smiles back with heat in her eyes and I slam my lips to hers, not letting her pull away until I'm ready. "You can turn heads all you want but no one is allowed to touch you or the party is going to be bloodier than expected."

"No bloodshed." Killian warns as I lean next to Ri's ear.

"No promises." She shifts, rubbing herself against me and I can almost hear her planning a way to let loose tonight. "You're gonna cause trouble, aren't you?"

"Maybe." She steps away and turns to me.

"Choose the sorry sucker carefully because Matteo and I won't let him live long afterward." We hold each other's stare and I can see fire burning in her eyes.

"Are you wanting blood on your dress tonight?" Matteo steps up next to her and runs his fingers down her back. "It would highlight really well against the white."

"Oookay. Let's get going. We can't be late." Killian links his arm with Aisling's and escorts her toward the front door. "Thank God we're riding in separate cars than them. I can't be traumatized by my sister and her sexcapades."

Tanner and Colton follow them out but it's Colton who's chuckling. "Sexcapades, Kill? Really? What are you, fifty? Orgy is more like it."

I smile at them. "Maybe we should all ride together. It could be fun traumatizing him."

"No." My attention goes back to Ri. "I want some alone time with you."

Who can say no to that? She links her arm with Enzo's and they walk toward the front door with Matteo and I behind them.

Killian's helping Aisling into the back of their SUV as Tanner and Colton climb into the front. We're in the second SUV, so I move around the front to climb into the driver's seat as Enzo helps Ri into the backseat behind me. Looking in the rearview mirror, my eyes connect with hers and she smirks at me. "I can't wait to walk in with you on my arm." Tanner drives away as Matteo and Enzo close their doors and I shift to drive to follow.

"We're going to be the talk of the party."

"Definitely in that dress. How about you give us a preview of what's under that skirt?" Matteo looks back at her with hunger in his eyes as he reaches back to run his hand up her thigh.

She slaps his hand away. "I meant with you guys coming back from the dead and me making my first appearance since the whole Maxim thing. Plus, the whole overthrowing my father." She reaches out and places her hand on Enzo's thigh. "You guys are looking very handsome as well. That's going to draw some attention, especially from the desperate wives and single daughters."

Enzo brings her hand to his mouth and he kisses the back of it. "We only want your attention."

"Oh, you definitely have it." I look away as she leans closer to him because I don't need to crash over being jealous of my brother.

We pull up to the Murphy mansion and two of Killian's guys that are still working for Lorcan secretly walk up to the driver doors. They volunteered to be the valets so they can make sure no one messes with our cars. Lorcan thinks they were sucking up to him, but they were just following Killian's order.

I open my door as Killian's guy grabs the handle, holding it open, waiting for me to exit. My feet touch the concrete and I move to Riona's door, opening it with my hand out to help her. Her hand slides into mine as she steps out of the SUV. She looks like an angel stepping out of the darkness. I step forward into her space, blocking her in between the car and car door. "I don't think I've said this out loud yet. You look beautiful." Closing the little space between us I give her a quick but deep kiss.

"You don't have to say it, I can see it in your eyes." She links her arm with mine when I take a step back and we walk around the back of the SUV to join everyone waiting on us.

"Who's ready to ruin Lorcan's big entrance?" Colton smiles gleefully at all of us like he can't wait to piss Lorcan off even more.

Killian looks down at his watch with Aisling on his other arm. "It's time. Let's go."

Every party Lorcan throws, he always enters right at 8pm. This time it'll be a little different. Riona and Killian will be entering at the same time as him but on the other side of the ballroom, taking everyone's attention.

As already determined, Killian and Aisling enter the mansion first with Tanner and Colton behind them, then Ri and I with my brothers behind us. Ri and I cross over the threshold and I shift back to the Italian leader I am and I know my brothers are doing the same. Our carefree personal lives we've been living the last couple of weeks are gone. It's time to hold our power as Russos. Feeling Ri's eyes on me as we walk down the hall, I look down at her with a stoic expression and she smiles up at me with a wicked glint in her eyes. "Hello, Dark God."

I can't stop the slight tilt up of my lips at her comment. She does like my darkness. "Watch yourself, Rose. You keep looking at me like that and we won't be making that entrance."

"You're tempting me with a good time."

I shake my head and lightly chuckle. "Trouble." She chuckles and squeezes my forearm as she leans closer to me. Through the doors in front of us, I can hear Lorcan starting his welcome speech and the sound of her father's voice has Ri's game face on.

The doors open, "I want to thank..." Lorcan's voice cuts out at the sound of the doors swinging open.

A hushed whisper starts to build as Killian, Aisling, Tanner, and Colton enter the ballroom but when myself, Ri, Matteo, and Enzo enter it turns into an outright roar.

The guests coming to the realization that we're alive doesn't hold my attention. It's Lorcan's look of shock that has me almost breaking my stone face so I can give him a gotcha smile. But I keep my look solid. He snaps out of his shock quickly and his rage has his face turning red.

Killian raises his hand in the air, silently commanding everyone's silence. "Thank you everyone for coming tonight. Tonight is a new beginning and I appreciate Lorcan for throwing this party. A great symbol of goodwill. Please enjoy the food, drinks, and music." The music starts when he's finished and all the guests start enjoying the party. Everyone except Lorcan.

He looks pissed as he charges through the crowd toward us. We stand strong together, unnerved by his rage. "How dare you walk into my home and act like you have my power, my position?"

Killian smirks. "I do have your power. I'm the Boss of the Murphy Clan. All the families agreed two nights ago."

"You little shit." Lorcan pulls out a gun and aims it right at Killian's head, but as he does that the twins, myself, and my brothers pull out our guns and aim them at Lorcan. Having five guns aiming at him keeps him from pulling the trigger but the crowd around us with their guns aimed at him as well has him lowering his gun. "You will regret this."

"Enjoy the party, Lorcan." Killian turns his back to him and walks through the parting crowd with his queen and his chiefs, leaving us with Lorcan.

"How does it feel, Father, to know you have lost everything because of your actions only?" Ri lets go of my arm and steps up in front of him. "You wanted me to be a killer. Well I'll take great joy in skinning you alive."

She walks by him, hitting her shoulder with his and I follow her, shoulder checking him as I go by. "We're harder to kill than we look." Based on the groan that comes from Lorcan, I'm guessing Matteo elbowed him in the side. Looking back, I see Enzo and Matteo walking side by side behind me and I give them a nod signaling them to spread out. We need to keep our eyes open to make sure we all leave here tonight safe. I scan around the room, seeing Tanner and Colton have already split up.

Ri slows ahead of me and I slide my hand around her waist. "Dance with me?"

She turns to me, so my arm is wrapped around her. "That's exactly what I wanted." I realize we're standing in the middle of the dance floor.

With my arm wrapped around her I pull her closer to me and take her hand with my free hand. Couples surround us as I move her across the floor and all I can think about as she smiles up at me is the first time I saw her in this very ballroom at the Murphy Gala. She shined from the moment she entered the ballroom on her father's arm with a bright, innocent smile on her face. I want to chuckle now at how I wished I could remove the innocence from her. How wrong I was about her.

She danced all night looking like the princess she was portraying. It was a perfect act. So perfect that even though my eyes never left her all night, I didn't notice her poisoning O'Brien. I never expected such a perfect good girl to kill.

"You're not planning to poison anyone tonight, are you?" I grab her hand on my shoulder and inspect her ring.

She chuckles. "Not tonight... unless you have someone in mind." Her thumb runs under the ring band and the stone opens revealing a needle. "I'm always prepared." I run my fingers up the back of her hand to her fingers, where I flip the stone back, hiding the needle, and place her hand back on my shoulder. "Only one person is dying tonight and it won't be by poison."

Chapter Thirty-Three

Riona

Happiness. It's a feeling I didn't think I'd ever feel again in this house, but Matteo has me beaming as he spins me out and pulls me back into him. I smile so big up at him that my cheeks hurt as I press up against him and he quickly places a kiss on my lips. I want to so badly get lost in his kiss but I'm too aware of Lorcan's eyes burning into the back of my head. They've been there for the last couple of hours as I've danced and chatted with people. He's pissed at me for everything, which isn't a surprise. Killian might be taking his throne from him but he's proud of him. Me, I started this by not listening to him. His rage is for me, which is why we're all spread out tonight, watching him. There's no way he's not going to try something.

Matteo slides his hands down my waist, over my hips, and to my ass where he takes a handful. "You're getting handsy for everyone to see."

He nestles into my neck where he places a kiss. "You know you love it." Goosebumps roll over my skin because I do love how they touch me, showing everyone I'm off limits.

"I prefer you do it in private. How would you like to see the room I grew up in?"

Matteo's smile turns cocky. "Do you want me to dirty up your pristine white sheets?" He hooks his arm over my shoulders and I bring my arm around his waist as we quickly escape the ballroom.

I grab his hand from around my shoulders and pull him through the halls and up the stairs. My father is so short-staffed we don't even pass anyone. "My sheets haven't been white in a long time."

Matteo growls into my ear as he stands behind me as I open my door. "You better hope they're brand-new sheets."

I chuckle as I swing open the door. "Of course they're new sheets."

Matteo presses his body against mine, looking at my room. "Pink sheets? Wow you had to play the pretty perfect princess even in here." I squeal out in joy as Matteo surprisingly picks me up and throws me on the bed. The door closes behind him as he stands over me next to the bed. His hand runs up my slit over my closed legs until he finds my knives strapped to my upper thigh. He releases one of them and skims it up my stomach as he climbs on the bed over me. "Maybe we can add a little red to this pink."

"Not tonight, Bear. I don't want to ruin this dress."

He places the knife next to me and leans down, pressing his body weight into me. "Maybe just a few wrinkles instead."

I wrap my legs around his hips as I run my hands down his chest toward his belt. "I can work with that."

Matteo smashes his lips to mine and it sets us both off, not wanting to tease anymore. I grip his belt, unhooking it and get his pants open as he pushes my skirt open, exposing my white thong. My hand wraps around his hard cock, angling it toward my entrance as Matteo exposes me, moving my thong to the side. I wrap my other hand around his hip, pushing him closer to me. The sound of a gun cocking has us both freezing. "Fuck. They couldn't let us finish first." Matteo grumbles against my lips and I can't help my smile.

"Get the fuck off of her."

With Matteo on top of me, I can't see who it is but I can see the gun pressed to his head. My heart rate picks up as I look at Matteo, who has the same expression as mine. Game time. He gives me a subtle nod and we both slowly start to move. I grip one of his guns in the back of his pants as he fixes my thong and dress before putting his dick away. Matteo raises on his knees with his hands out as I hold the gun out of view.

The man holding the gun comes into view and I raise the gun, aiming it at his head as I'm still laying on the bed. "Put the gun down, Steve." Fire burns through me seeing my old bodyguard hold a gun to Matteo's head. Steve's eyes connect with mine and instead of seeing anger or vengeance there, I see jealousy. What's he jealous of?

Before I can even think to say anything else, Matteo grips my thigh hard as a gun is pressed to my temple. "Put the gun down, Riona." Slowly I follow the other man's order because we weren't expecting two guys.

The guy I haven't seen yet grabs the gun from me as soon as I have it low enough not to hurt Steve and the gun on my temple leaves. I can see it out of the corner of my eye aimed at Matteo who looks ready to rage on this guy. "He said get off her."

Matteo climbs off of me and the bed with his hands up still and I quickly close my legs and cover them with my dress because they don't need to see any part of my body. "Now your turn, Riona." The guy behind me grips my shoulder and pushes me up. I glare back at him as I sit up, getting a good look at him for the first time and recognition hits. "You..."

A victorious smile spread across his face. "Me."

My hand hits the knife Matteo took out earlier as I push myself up to stand and I grip it, hiding it against my wrist. Standing in front of him, I take in his features. "You wrote the note at the bar."

This guy runs his eyes down my body and disgust fills me. "That I did."

I remember how guilty and disappointed in myself I felt when I read that note. Thinking that Aisling was hurting while I was having a night with my guys.

You've been missing for days.

You finally reappear and you're letting them touch you.

You're supposed to be looking for Aisling, not fucking your bodyguards.

She's screaming in pain and you're moaning in pleasure.

What would she say if she knew?

Now that I know it wasn't from one of Craig's guys, I can hear the jealousy along with anger in the words.

"Why? I don't know you."

"Oh you know me..." He steps closer to me and I can feel Matteo shift behind me ready to kill before this man touches me. But instead of touching me, he walks past so he's standing between me and Steve. "You just know me looking like this guy."

I look between the two and while Steve is clean shaven with a buzz cut and this other guy has a short beard with slightly longer hair with it combed back, you can't miss how identical they are. A weird feeling washes over me thinking that these two men have been watching over me for years, but I never knew they were two different guys.

"Your father always wanted eyes on you and we were trying to rise in his ranks. We were with you every minute for over a decade. Taking shifts, keeping you safe, watching you grow up, sparring with you, and falling for you." Steve holds my stare as he confesses something I never expected.

"But you didn't see us." Steve's twin glares at me. "Instead, you fell for the three Italian scum as soon as you were in their clutches." He reaches out and pulls me against him so my back is to his chest and his hands go to my stomach and throat, holding me there. "But you'll see us now." He runs his nose up my cheek and I try to move away from him. "They were supposed to be dead, but your father will make sure they actually are by the morning. Starting with this."

Fear runs through me as Steve grips the gun tighter at the back of Matteo's head. "NOOOO!"

Matteo swings his elbow back at Steve, connecting with the gun and it flies across the room. Steve tackles Matteo to the ground as he turns to throw a punch. The ground shakes as they hit the floor and I fight against the brother's hold. Throwing my elbow into his ribs, I bend forward trying to throw him off balance and break his hold but it's useless as he barely even flinches and starts to drag me out of the room.

"Matteo!" I yell out as I'm pulled through the doorway and he looks over to me, giving Steve a chance to land a punch to his face. Matteo looking dazed is the last thing I see before I'm pulled out of view. Worry courses through me as I continue to fight. I won't leave Matteo alone.

I kick back at the brother, right in his shin and he lets out a curse. "Stop fighting me. I'm taking you to your father."

"Go fuck yourself." I try to slam the back of my head into his face, but I miss, hitting his chin and it has me disoriented.

He takes advantage of my dizziness by throwing me around, flipping me over his shoulder, and starting down the stairs. I punch at his back, making sure to hit his kidney. "Put me down..." Two quick gunshots go off as we reach the bottom of the stairs and I freeze, looking up the stairs waiting to see Matteo running toward me. When I don't see him, dread fills me.

"MATTEO!" I lose it, pulling the knife I reserved for my father from my sleeve and stab his back with anger. He groans out in pain and the next thing I know he's turning and the wall is coming right at me. My head slams against it and pain shoots through my head as black fills my vision. I lose the grip on my knife as I grab my head trying to alleviate the pain. It feels like my brain is rolling around and banging into the sides of my skull.

Pain sears through me as my body is thrown around until my backside hits something hard and I groan out in pain. I curl in on myself and cradle my arms around my head as I rest it on my knees, taking slow breaths.

"Get the fuck out of here and clean yourself up." Lorcan's hateful voice makes my ears ring, but I know I can't be defenseless around him. I slide my hand into the slit of my dress and grab my last knife.

The click of the door has me trying to push aside the pounding in my head to listen for my father. I need to know where he is while I get this pain under control. Sneaking a peek in front of me, my eyes burn from the lights but it's the fact that I can't see my father that makes me panic. I lift my head further, fighting the pain to look behind me but I'm yanked back by my hair, letting out a scream in pain.

My back slams into the back of the chair I'm in and my neck is at an awkward angle bent as far back as it can. My father is there standing over me, looking disappointed and enraged. "You're such a disappointment. I gave you everything. Made you into who you are." With each statement, his grip on my hair tightens and I wince as I can feel hairs ripping from my scalp.

"I know everything you did to make me who I am and you'll never get a thank you for it. You disgust me. I can't wait to see your blood on my hands."

"But the thanks I get is you disobeying me, ruining a potential partnership, and my heir trying to overthrow me." He continues like I didn't say a thing. "But do you want to know a secret?" Lorcan leans forward and whispers next to my ear, "Your brother has two weaknesses."

He stands tall again. "One I couldn't get my hands on since she didn't leave his side all night. But you weren't protected." His fingers on his free hand run down my cheek. "He'll do anything to protect his little sister." He's quiet for a moment as he stares at me and for a second, I think I see the father I grew up with. "Now him being soft is my fault. I shouldn't have let him get attached to you and Aisling. I should have shipped you both off and forced him to my side, watching and learning everything. Maybe then he would've learned love and emotions are worthless."

"Ahhh." Lorcan jerks my head up and pulls me to my feet so I'm standing facing him.

"Now let's go dear daughter and show everyone how weak your brother is."

I trip over my feet as he pushes me toward the double doors we always enter through for his parties. I'm definitely not on his arm this time.

He pulls out a gun and bangs on the door with the side of his hand. The doors open out and he raises the gun to my head. The ballroom is quiet as we step out and the click of my heels sound like gunshots in the empty space. Only Killian, Aisling, Tanner, Colton, and Enzo stand in front of us.

Chapter Thirty-Four

Enzo

We all have our roles to play tonight but Riona is being very distracting. Even when I'm not dancing with her, I can't seem to keep my eyes off her for more than a few seconds. She's breathtaking and glowing and I know I'm not the only one who's noticed. I've had to scare a few men to look the other way a couple times tonight which is perfect. The fewer eyes on all of us the better.

A flash of red brings my attention back to Riona and Matteo who are dancing on the other side of the room as me. Riona is smiling brightly as Matteo spins her around and I can't help my smile. I look away from her and scan the crowd as I move along the wall. Just like all night, Lorcan is sitting in his special lounge area with his raging eyes on her. Not a single person has gone over to speak with him all night. The only time he opens his mouth is when he beckons one of his twenty men and silently gives an order. But not once has he looked away from Riona. He's obsessed. It's kind of creepy.

Lorcan's eyes start tracking across the room and I follow his line of sight. Matteo and Riona are leaving the ballroom, looking like lovesick teenagers, sneaking off to get into some dirty trouble. Matteo is a lucky bastard. I reach into my pants pocket, gripping one of the needles in my pocket. Uncapping the needle, I swiftly jab it into the thigh of the soldier I'm walking past. Discreetly I lower him to the floor and continue along the wall as I take out two other soldiers. Dante smiles down at me as I lower the last guy to the ground and I look over to where Lorcan has been all night and find his couch empty. "He left almost immediately after them but he didn't follow; he went to his office."

"Did any of his guys go after them?" I stand up and fix my jacket.

"Not that I saw." We look around the room and Killian, Aisling, Tanner, and Colton give us nods that we return, letting everyone know our guys are down. We didn't want to kill them, so they're just sleeping soundly until it's time for them to choose their fates. The only two soldiers left are the valets.

Killian goes to the stairs through which we entered and climbs up two steps with Aisling standing next to him. "Everyone..."

Silence falls on the ballroom as everyone turns to him. "I want to thank you for coming tonight and showing your support for this change in leadership. But I'm sad to say this party is over, so please allow myself and Aisling to escort you out." The valet soldiers disappear out the side door to start collecting cars of those who drove here as Killian and Aisling head up the stairs with their guests following.

Our group works as a barrier to make sure all the guests leave. Once all the guests are gone, we gravitate toward the bar while we wait for Killian and Aisling to return. "Alright, who needs a drink?" Colton twirls the bourbon bottle around the palm of his hand.

We all nod and he pours two fingers of bourbon for all of us. I down mine in one swallow and Dante chuckles next to me. "Stressed?"

"Worried. Not having eyes on her while she's in danger doesn't feel right."

He grabs my shoulder in support. "She'll be fine. No one can take our girl down. It's Matteo we need to worry about."

I chuckle and he grips my shoulder tighter before he releases and downs his drink. "Time for my part." He walks away and slides through the side door leading into the rest of the house.

The clang of glass hitting glass draws my attention from the door Dante went through to Colton, who's refilling my glass. "Take it slower this time. Red will kill you if she has to take care of your drunk ass instead of killing Lorcan."

I raise my glass and tilt it toward him. "I wouldn't want that." This time I just take a sip and we both head over to Lorcan's VIP lounge area, joining Tanner who has happily already taken over a whole couch.

"I've always wanted in this section growing up. Right here was where all the deals were made."

"You're telling me that over all the years you grew up with Killian and Riona you never sat up here?" I ask.

Tanner looks over at us. "Never. Only the Murphys and Lorcan's person of choice. Aisling has never been up here either."

"I can't believe Killian and Riona allowed that." That doesn't sound right.

Tanner sits up. "They didn't but couldn't change their father's mind."

Colton takes a drink as he leans forward, resting his elbows on his knees. "So instead they didn't step foot in here while we were at the parties. But as we got older and had jobs or school, us three sidekicks came to parties less and less. That's when Killian got in on the deals and Riona was a fly on the wall, collecting secrets."

"Wow. Lorcan is a dick. How's it that it's just coming to light?"

They both shrug their shoulders. "I guess our focus wasn't on him really. We were living our lives, following orders, never seeing a reason to question anything." Tanner leans forward with a look of regret on his face.

"Hey man, I didn't mean what I said as blame. Nobody goes through their lives questioning everybody's motives." I reach forward and slightly shake his shoulder.

"I know but I can't help but think if we watched Lorcan more, so much of the trouble we've been through and the trauma Aisling and Ri have endured could've been stopped."

"MATTEO!" Riona's screams in terror ring through the room, and I jump up out of my seat, dropping my glass as I sprint toward the door. A body slams into me and I'm knocked onto the floor.

Rolling over, I find Killian standing over me. "You cannot intervene."

I jump up and try to push past him. "Ri and Matteo are in trouble. I need to go."

He grabs my arm and slams me into the wall and holds me there. I fight against his hold and the twins step up on either side of him, holding me down as well.

Killian grips my jacket. "Listen to me." The order in his voice has me stop fighting against them and I push all my rage I'm feeling about them through my glare. "Dante is there. He's their backup. If something is wrong, he would've called. Plus, my father wouldn't hurt Riona in private."

But he would hurt her. I push off Tanner and Colton and straighten my suit. "You better be right. If anything has happened to my brothers or Ri and you stopping me from leaving is the cause, I don't care if you're Ri's brother, I'll kill you."

I shoulder check him as I move past him and pull out my phone.

Enzo: What the hell is going on?

I position myself on the dance floor right in front of the doors that lead to Lorcan's office. The two valets are back at the doors waiting and watching me closely. Riona better be walking through those doors within five minutes or those two soldiers won't be standing in my way. They'll be on the floor dead.

Chapter Thirty-Five

Riona

Lorcan is visibly shaking with rage as he presses the gun to my temple and pulls my hair with his other hand. I try to relieve some of the pain by tilting my head back, but I don't look away from Enzo. His eyes are laser-focused on me and I try to read them to see if Matteo is okay but all I see is a beast ready to be released.

"Where the fuck is everyone?" Lorcan pulls me in front of him as he realizes he's outnumbered.

Killian takes a step forward, drawing my attention for just a second. "It was time to end the party. Sorry you didn't get to say your goodbyes."

Enzo pulls out his gun slowly as his eyes connect with mine and I can see the silent promise that he's not going to let anything happen to me. I hope he's right because this isn't going to stop my father.

Lorcan growls in frustration and I know he's about to lose it. "I don't need an audience to get you to bow down. You want your sister to live, you'll concede. You'll kneel in front of me and pledge your allegiance."

I slide the knife I hid in my sleeve down my wrist and grip the handle at my side. I'm not going to let my father kill me without a fight.

"I don't think he's going to do that." Relief floods through me at the sound of Dante's voice. "You're going to remove that gun from Riona's head and let her go."

Lorcan doesn't move. "You think ..." The sound of a safety being flipped has my father shutting up.

"Don't make me take your death from Killian and Riona. I'll happily take it and feel their wrath for the rest of my life. Lower the gun and let her go." The authority in Dante's voice would have anyone following his order and Lorcan is no different.

The grip on my hair loosens slowly until his hand falls away and my scalp tingles like a thousand needles are poking me but I don't move because the gun is still pressed against my temple. Time freezes as I wait for the feeling on the gun to leave the side of my head. I don't know if it's seconds or minutes but as soon as the gun moves from my head, I spin around toward my father, swiping out at his wrist with my knife, cutting across it, making him drop the gun and then I jab my knife into his thigh. As he falls to his knees in front of me, I hold the knife to his throat.

"You going to kill me now?" Lorcan glares up at me.

"Not yet." I'm deviating from the plan. "First you'll learn that all of this is your fault." I look up to Dante and give him a nod. Dante swings his gun back quickly and brings it down on the side of Lorcan's head knocking him out.

"I thought you didn't want to get blood on your dress." Matteo steps out from behind Dante with a bruise already forming on the left side of his face and blood splattered on his white button up.

"Matteo." I step over Lorcan's unconscious body and Matteo envelopes me in his arms and I kiss him. "I heard the gunshots and I thought..."

Matteo kisses me again. "I'm okay." I look up at him in relief that he's okay and everything worked out. We're all safe.

Ringing starts in my ears as the pain I've been pushing aside floods forward and all of a sudden, I grip onto Matteo as black spots fill my vision. "Something's wrong."

"Ri?" Matteo tilts up my face toward him and his concerned face and the sound of him calling out my name is the last thing I remember before everything goes black.

Soft hands rubbing over the top of my head gently pulls me awake but the pain stops me from opening my eyes. I groan out and curl in on myself as my head pounds.

"Ri, I have some aspirin for you." Aisling runs her fingers through my hair. I peek up at her with one eye and the light burns so I curl further into whatever I'm lying on. "Can someone turn off some of the lights?"

"I got them." Enzo's voice gives me relief. I feel him stand from where he was sitting down at my feet and a few seconds later the light against my eyelids dims significantly.

Peeking my eyes open, the light isn't as searing so I roll over, looking up at Aisling. "Hi."

She smiles down at me. "Hi. You passed out."

I nod slowly, trying not to move my head too much. "Steve Number 2 slammed my head against the wall when I stabbed him."

She lightly runs her fingers over my hairline and I wince. "You do have a nasty bruise forming. Do you think you can sit up?"

Instead of answering her, I slowly start to sit up with my eyes closed. Aisling helps me with support on my head and someone grabs my arms, pulling me up. The pounding in my head intensifies as I move but I fight through it until my back is resting against the back of the couch. I wait to open my eyes until the pounding dims and when I do, I find Enzo sitting in front of me, holding both my hands.

"Hi Beauty. You scared us."

"I'm okay. My head is just pounding." Everything makes the pounding worse, even my own voice.

Enzo reaches behind him and picks up a bottle of aspirin. "How many do you want?"

"All of them."

He chuckles. "How about three?"

I nod and hold out my hand. He places three in it, and I bring them to my mouth. Aisling holds a cup of water in front of me and I take it, swallowing down the pills.

Looking behind Enzo, I realize we're still in the ballroom on Lorcan's special couches. "How's it feel being in Lorcan's special area?" I look at Aisling.

She chuckles. "The couches aren't as comfortable as I thought. They'll definitely be replaced once I get my hands on this place."

"Can't wait to see what you'll do with this house." I look around the ballroom. "Where is everyone?"

"Matteo and Dante are disposing of the two Steves. Which is weird to say." Aisling shakes her head like she's still trying to wrap her head around it. She can join the group.

"The second one too?" When did they get him?

"They met him outside your father's office and slit his throat." Enzo is stone-faced as he tells me this with no emotions.

Aisling continues, "Tanner and Colton are taking Lorcan back to the estate and Killian is addressing the soldiers here tonight. Giving the ultimatum." Join him or die.

"You should be there with him, Ash. He shouldn't do it alone."

She rests her hand on my arm. "You needed me more and he's not alone; his two soldiers from earlier are with him. Now let's get you home so you can rest."

Aisling and Enzo both stand and reach out to help me, but I hit their hands away. "We're not leaving. We have things to do."

"All of it can wait." Enzo tries to help again but I push his hand away.

"I'm fine."

"If you're fine then stand up." Aisling stares down at me in a challenge with her hands on her hips. I glare at her as I push myself up, using the couch. My head screams as I stand and I instantly get dizzy.

Before I can even try to stabilize myself, Enzo swoops me into his arms bridal style and I rest my head on his shoulder. "Let's just get some rest. There's no rush now to finish this. Lorcan isn't going anywhere."

"Fine. If you say so." Enzo smiles down at me as he walks through the ballroom.

"Wow. Enzo, I need you around every time I need her to do something." Aisling smiles at me as she walks with us.

"Shut up, Ash." I stick my tongue out at her so she knows I don't mean it and she does the same.

Instead of going through the front door, Enzo carries me into the garage. My smile is excited as I look over our family cars.

"The SUVs are being used so I thought we could make use of the family cars." Aisling smiles at them too. We've had a good time in most of the cars. The only one I don't have good memories of is Lorcan's Lincoln. I look over at the seven cars in the garage. "I want my Tesla, Range Rover, and the Bugatti."

"You'll have to fight Killian for the Bugatti." Aisling crosses her arm over her chest and stands defiantly.

I glare at her, letting her know I'm not backing down. "I'll happily take down the new king for that car."

"We're taking the Range Rover." Enzo steps in before a verbal argument starts.

He carries me over to the passenger side of the Rover and opens the door. Very carefully he sits me down and brings my seatbelt across me to buckle. I want to tell him that I can do that, but I keep quiet because I know he needs to take care of me.

Before he steps back, I grab his shirt and pull him into a kiss. Our kiss is gentle and quick but when he pulls back, I don't let go of his shirt.

"I love you, Beast."

"Not as much as I love you, Beauty." I smile up at him as I let go of his shirt. He's wrong about that. I might have all three of them to love but I love each of them with everything in me.

Enzo steps back and gently closes my door and I don't take my eyes off him. He rounds the front of the Rover and catches the keys, Aisling throws. Aisling heads back into the house as Enzo climbs into the driver's seat. "Aisling told me to tell you she's riding

with Killian and they might as well get one last ride in before
handing the keys of the Bugatti over to you."

A vicious smile grows across my face. "What is it about that
car?"

"Wait until you drive it, opening it up on the highway."

"Does that mean you'll let me drive it?"

I smile over at him. "Of course. We can make a date out of
it."

Enzo reaches over and squeezes my bare thigh. I can almost
picture us in the Bugatti sitting just like this as we escape to
somewhere. I can't wait.

Chapter Thirty-Six

Matteo

Looking down at the dickhead twin that hurt Ri, I want to kill him all over again and this time much slower with his tears running down his cheeks as he begs for his life. He shouldn't have been allowed to touch her. Why the fuck did I just slit his throat when he walked out of Lorcan's office?

The dead perv stares up at me and I wish I had my chainsaw or machete. I'd love cutting him into tiny pieces and scattering him all over the forest for the animals to eat. I twirl my knife around my hand. Maybe I have time to filet him.

"Would you start digging? This is going to take forever as it is." I glare over at Dante who has made a decent dent in the dirt.

"How about you dig and I get to make sure the creepy twins are never identified?"

"No one is going to find them. Pick up the damn shovel."

I know how to convince him into letting me do this. "Do you really want to take the chance? They were Riona's bodyguards."

"Fine, but they're both going in this hole." Dante turns his back to me and starts digging again. I can hear him grumbling to himself about doing all the work, but I ignore him and get to work. I won't be able to hear them scream for mercy but at least I get to peel their fingerprints off and fuck up their faces with the tire iron.

I start with the one that almost killed me. If Dante was just a second later, I would be dead from a shot between the eyes. My face still hurts from the punches that almost knocked me out and my shirt has spots of his blood on it from where Dante shot him above me.

With each slice into his skin, I curse him for not coming alone, for lusting after my girl, and for causing her to get hurt. His fingertips are red and raw when I put the knife away and grab the tire iron from the back of the truck. With my gloves on, I bring the bar over my head and bring it down with full force right across his mouth. I can hear the bones crunching as the bar hits his face over and over and it's music to my ears. He deserved this for ruining our plans. Ri would've killed him if his brother wasn't there. Speaking of his brother, I turn to the dickhead laying a few feet away. Now it's time to let this rage out.

I swing down hard on his face and it caves in the middle but it doesn't stop me. He tried to take her away. He thought she belonged to him. He touched her like he had the right to. And he hurt her so much that it made her pass out. Pass out in my arms. Riona would want me to obliterate him for touching her, causing her harm, and making her weak. My princess is never weak. She is always strong, even when she needs to be held or needs help. And definitely when she needs love. And she has all of my love. Huffing, I drop the iron to the ground and stare down at his concave face.

"He's definitely not recognizable anymore." Dante pops up next to me and looks over at him.

"He deserves worse."

"That he does." He pats my shoulder. "Finish up with him so we can get this over with." He turns, walking behind me and I hear the sound of a body being dragged across the ground.

Now it's time to remove his touch from Riona and steal the feeling of her skin from his memory. When I'm finished, I drag him over to the hole Dante dug and toss the sorry piece of shit into it. Dante sprays lighter fluid over their bodies and lights a match before throwing it in. They blaze immediately, like a bonfire, and we have to take a step back from the heat. We only let them burn for a few minutes because of the smell and we don't need to draw attention to ourselves in the middle of the dark forest. Shoveling dirt onto the flames, we bury the bodies until the ground is flat again and it looks like we were never here.

Dante throws the shovels into the back of the SUV as I wipe down the tire iron and put it back where I found it. "Enzo texted. Ri's awake and they're heading home soon." He closes up the back as he looks over me.

"Then let's get home."

We walk into the kitchen of the estate from the garage and I already know she's not back yet but it doesn't stop me from looking for her and being disappointed that she isn't here. I really need to get my eyes on her to truly believe she's okay.

"Hey guys. Come join us for a drink." Colton holds up the bottle him and Tanner have apparently been passing back and forth. Dante walks over to them and grabs the bottle but I just walk past all of them and head upstairs. I'm not ready to celebrate when I still have so much anger coursing through me. I can hear Tanner and Colton calling out for me to come back but instead I take the stairs two at a time. Walking into the master, I'm hit with all things Riona. Her smell. Her style. Her clothes are thrown around. Her makeup on the vanity. Her weapons chest is open in the corner. She could've not been coming home tonight. Things didn't go as planned. I couldn't protect her. Instead, I had to watch her be pulled away from me. I had to feel her go limp in my arms. I had to see the fear in her eyes.

Ripping off my jacket and shirt, I throw them on the ground next to her clothes and head into the bathroom. I turn the shower on to hot and walk over to the counter to let it heat up. The bruises across my body are darkening and they tell the story of how I let Steve beat me. How I couldn't kill one opponent. How I couldn't protect her. The memories of her screaming my name, needing me, haunt me. I push off the counter and remove the rest of my clothes before stepping into the scalding hot shower. The temperature has me hissing in pain as it hits my sensitive skin but I take it. I don't move from under the water, letting my skin turn red and numb.

"Bear?" I jump at the sound of her voice and quickly turn down the heat. Looking back behind me, I see her beautiful silhouette in the steam, and as she slowly walks forward, her body becomes more visible.

I reach out for her, needing to feel her skin under my palms to make sure she's really here. "Princess." Her skin feels cool against my heated body and I pull her to me and bury my face into her hair as I wrap my arms around her shoulders. "I'm sorry."

Her hands run up and down my back. "What for?"

"You should've never gotten hurt. I was supposed to protect you."

"Is that why you're so hot?" She pulls back from me so she can look at my face. "Are you punishing yourself?" She looks me over from head to toe, taking in everything and I don't say a word. When her eyes connect back to mine, worry and guilt floods from her. "Matteo..." She places a hand to my cheek that isn't bruised. "Nothing that happened to you or me is your fault. Yes, things didn't go as planned but we got what we wanted. There were just a few bumps along the way."

"I don't like that you're the one that got hurt." I run my fingers through her hair.

"I don't like that you got hurt either." She hovers her hand over my side as she looks at the bruises. "Thinking he shot you wrecked me. I felt like a part of me was ripped away. When I saw you standing behind Dante, okay, I was so relieved, but I didn't feel whole again until you were holding me. I needed you to put me back together." Her arms wrap around me, pressing her body against mine. "I'm here however you need me."

I'd love to take her offer in the dirtiest way possible, but I can see how exhausted she is and I can feel her hold on me, keeping herself steady. She's definitely not as okay as she's trying to be. That's okay though because what I need is to take care of her and make her feel better. "What I need is to take care of you and then hold you." She nods and I carefully move her so she's under the water. I let the water soak her from head to toe before grabbing her shampoo and softly massaging it into her hair. As I help her rinse the shampoo out of her hair, Ri reaches for my body wash and pours it into her hands. "I'm supposed to be taking care of you."

She places her soapy hands on my chest and looks up at me. "Don't fight me on this."

I shake my head, continuing what I was doing as Ri's hands slowly start to move across my skin. We both take our time washing each other and when we're done, I pick her up and carry her out of the shower. I softly set her in front of the counter so she can rest against it as I dry us both off. Hanging the damp towels up, I look back at her. "Do you want pajamas?"

She shakes her head slowly. "I just want to go to bed."

I'm not going to argue against that. I love feeling her naked body against mine. I carry her to the bed and curl in with her so my whole body is pressed to her back. I know she worried about us sleeping behind her, but I need to hold her tonight. "Is this okay?"

"Of course, Bear. Don't even think about letting go." She pulls my arm tighter around her and kisses my knuckles.

"I love you so much, Matteo." She looks back at me and I lean forward, kissing her.

"I love you too, Princess. You have no idea how much."

"I think I do because it matches mine." She pulls me into another kiss that lasts until we're both breathless. We settle back into the bed, and I listen to her breathing, waiting for her to fall asleep and when she does, I let myself follow behind her.

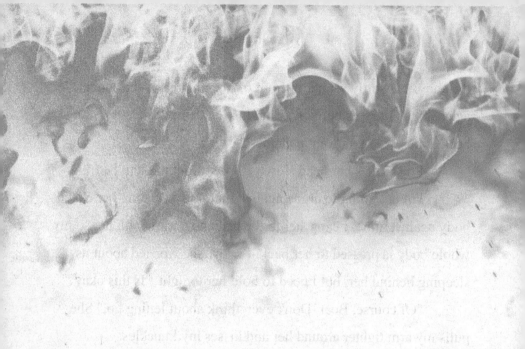

Chapter Thirty-Seven

Dante

Knowing word of us being alive was going to spread like wildfire, I had Zach call a meeting for this morning with all our people. There have been a lot of changes these last several weeks but I want to make sure they know the rumors are true, who's in charge, and how strong we are.

I pull on my suit jacket as I watch both my brothers place a kiss on Ri's sleeping head and walk out the room. She doesn't even stir from their kiss, telling me how exhausted she is. I know she'd want to come with us but it's more important that she rests and heals.

I walk over to the bed and carefully lean over it to her. Her bare shoulder is exposed from the sheets and I press my lips to her skin, kissing her lightly. As I pull back, she starts to stir and I freeze, hoping that she's just shifting in her sleep. She rolls over toward me as she wiggles into the sheets and hums. Her eyes start to flutter open and I sit down on the bed and gently stroke her hair. "Where are Matteo and Enzo?" Her sleepy eyes connect with mine and a soft smile pulls on her face.

"Downstairs. We need to head to the club and deal with the fallout of coming back to life."

"Oh." She sits up slowly, holding the sheet to her chest. "Why didn't you wake me? Give me 10 minutes."

I place a hand on her thigh, stopping her from getting up. "We didn't wake you because you need to sleep. Please go back to sleep; this won't take long."

Her eyes harden with determination. "I'm fine and I'm coming." My hand slips from her thigh as she scoots across the bed to the other side. Her beautiful body is on display for me as she stands. My eyes track her movements as she moves across the room and rummages through her closet, grabbing clothes. Her naked skin is covered with each piece of clothing she puts on but I'm not complaining. She's gorgeous in anything she's wearing, especially in the black leather leggings and black silk spaghetti strap tank she chose to wear.

She turns away from me to put on her shoes, giving me the best view of her ass. Her ass in these pants makes me think of all the places I want to bend her over. Who am I kidding, her ass in anything makes me want to bend her over any flat surface.

Realizing that she's facing me again with her hands on her hips, I look up at her face and she's smiling at me. "Get your head out of the gutter, Boss Man." She moves to the bathroom, and I reach into my jacket to pull out my phone, sending my brothers a text.

Dante: Ri's awake and coming with. Be down in a few.

Ri sticks her head out of the bathroom, and I put my phone back in my jacket pocket.

"Can you grab me some aspirin?" I stand from the bed and grab the medicine from the nightstand. Pouring three into my hand and grabbing her bottle of water, I follow her into the bathroom.

Ri is pulling her hair up into a ponytail and I walk up behind her and wrap an arm around her stomach. Holding out the pills and bottle with my other hand, she takes them and pops the pills in her mouth as I wrap my other arm around her. "If your head is still bothering you, maybe you should stay here."

She swallows down the pills and runs her hands over my arms across her stomach. "It's a dull headache. It'll be gone once these kick in. Plus, it's not like we're doing anything active."

"Fine. Just promise to take it easy." I place a kiss to the side of her neck.

"I promise." She looks back at me and taps her lips. I take the hint and close the distance between us and kiss her. Bringing one of my hands up to her chin, I hold her there as I deepen the kiss. When we pull back from each other, I place one more quick kiss on her lips. "I love you, Boss Man."

"Rose, you're my world. I don't think the words I love you can even cover a small portion of how I feel about you." She turns in my arms and pulls me back down into a passionate kiss.

"I told you they'd get distracted." I pull back from Ri and look over toward the bathroom door to find my brothers standing there with 'you got caught' grins.

Looking away from them, I lean down toward her again and skim my lips against hers, not really kissing her. "I should've closed the door."

She chuckles against my lips and presses her lips to mine in a quick kiss. The space between us increases as she pulls away with a cheeky smile and walks to my brothers.

Matteo pulls her to him and kisses her. "You coming with us, Princess?"

Her smile is excited. "I wouldn't miss it. I finally get to see all of you in front of your people. It's going to be such a turn on seeing you command the room and give orders." She strokes Matteo's chest, and I can see his resistance straining. Thankfully Enzo steps in and pulls her to him because none of us would be making it to this meeting if that started.

Enzo gently places his lips to hers, but the kiss gets deeper with each second until they pull back from each other. "How's your head this morning?"

"Better. I'm okay to go. I want to be there, to be a part of all aspects of your life." She looks at all of us with me last. I hold her stare but I'm not going to tell her no.

"Make sure you bring your gun." These are our people, but she needs to be armed just in case.

Her smile is victorious. "I'll grab it."

She moves past Enzo and Matteo, going to the room, and I walk toward them. "Let's go."

Ri meets us in the room as we head out and Matteo crouches in front of her. She giggles as she climbs on his back and Matteo looks like he won the lottery with how happy he is. I know exactly how he feels. Hearing her laugh and getting her smiles are the best things in the world and if she does either of those because of something you did, it feels like you're flying.

We arrive at the club a little bit behind schedule, but I don't give a shit. Zach is waiting outside the back door for us with a happy smile. He's ready for us to take back the power. Just because he's our second doesn't mean he ever wants to step into our shoes.

I open my door and go to the back door, opening it for Ri. She moves to get out but I'm not having her walk. Swooping her into my arms, she hits my chest. "Put me down. I can walk."

"You promised to take it easy."

"There is no way in hell I'm going to be introduced to your people by being carried in. Even if I had broken legs, I'd crutch myself into that club." She gives me a determined look, but I stare back at her, not budging. "You can either put me down or I'll get down myself."

She'll definitely fight me to get what she wants, and I don't want that. Slowly, I lower her to the ground, and she smiles up at me lovingly. "Come on, Dark God. Let's go rule the world."

She walks away toward the front of the car, and I follow after her. We might rule over our men but Riona Murphy rules over us. And I'm totally okay with that.

"Oh my God! You're alive!" Zach runs past Ri and throws himself at me, hugging me and acting hysterical. "My prayers have been answered!"

I can hear everyone's chuckles over Zach's fake crying, and I can't help but to join in.

"Get off me, you goof." He chuckles as he steps back. "It's good to see you. All of you." Zach turns around holding his arms out. "But I'm really excited to see this pretty lady." He wraps his arms around her middle. "Our love story can never bloom with these jokers back." He picks her up and spins her around.

"Whoa." I rush to them and so does Enzo and Matteo.

Zach stops abruptly, looking confused as he sets her down. "I was just kidding around."

Ri pats his chest and steps back. "It's not you." Annoyance shines in her eyes. "I'm fine. Stop babying me." She turns away from us and heads toward the back door.

Before she gets too far, Matteo hooks his arm around her shoulders, slowing her down. "Don't be mad, Princess. We're just worried." I move around them before they get to the door, opening it for her.

"I'm not weak. I don't need the three of you acting like I can break from one touch." She sounds upset but she doesn't pull away from him.

Enzo walks in after them. "Your head was smashed into a wall yesterday. You can't blame us for worrying."

"Shit, Ri. I'm sorry," Zach calls out, taking up the back as I follow in after Enzo.

"No apologizing." She gives him a sharp look.

Matteo pulls her to a stop, and Enzo and I stop with them as Zach continues. "No apologizing. You're a badass bitch that can handle anything."

Her smile brightens. "Damn straight." He waits for us at the end of the hall and we can hear the muffled voices on the other side of the door.

Enzo steps in front of her and lifts her chin so she's looking up at him. "We worry because we love you, care for you, and never want harm to come to you. That's never going to change."

She starts softening to him. "So, I just need to accept it?" Her attitude tries to be strong, but she's already accepted it and loves how we take care of her.

"Damn straight." Enzo mocks her, making her chuckle and he places a quick kiss to her lips.

Matteo places his finger under her chin and turns her to him so he can kiss her too. When she pulls away from Matteo, she looks at me and I wait where I am. She wants us to not be hesitant with her, fine. If she wants something right now, she's going to need to take it.

Riona walks out of Matteo's arms and over to me. Her hands run up my chest until she grips the lapels of my jacket. "Are you going to kiss me before you go out there to show all them who's..."

I slam my lips to her lips before she finishes in a brutal, passionate kiss. She gives me the control I need as I deepen our kiss. Pulling back from her, I'm breathing hard and fighting myself not to push this forward. "Let's get this meeting over with so we can finish this."

She smiles up at me suggestively. "Sounds like a plan to me."

We walk down the hall together with Enzo and Matteo behind us, and as we reach the door, Zach opens it and the entire room goes silent. You can hear a pin drop as we walk across the room and up on the stage the DJ stand is typically set up on. I stand out in front as Riona, Enzo, and Matteo stand just a step back but in full view and Zach stands further back by the steps we just walked up.

The club is filled with the men and women that work for my family in our various businesses and their faces all express different emotions. Relief, shock, anger, confusion, and happiness.

The ones that look angry I keep an eye on as I start my speech.

"We're here today to confirm the rumors that we're alive and to explain why we faked our deaths and how we're going to move forward." I pause, running my eyes over the crowd. "Lorcan Murphy tried to kill us by blowing up our house. So, in order to stay safe and keep others safe from any further attempts, we decided to be dead."

"Then why the fuck is she here?" one of my older officers asks as he glares at Riona.

"Riona is with us. She was before our house was attacked and is very much with us now."

"So what? You forgave the Murphys for a marriage?"

I can't see Riona, but I know she's not liking how he's talking about her. "You better not be calling us a sell-out." I cross my arms over my chest and glare down at him.

"Of course not, sir." He steps back and drops his head.

A hand touches my back and I know it's hers before even looking back. She smiles at me, but I don't smile back, making sure no one can see how much she softens me. "Can I?"

I nod, stepping to the side, giving her front and center and I can feel my brothers moving closer. To anyone with eyes, there's no denying we'll do anything to protect her. "I know you're skeptical of me because of who my father is but over the years my father has had me kidnapped, which resulted in rape, has sold me to the Russian heir who beat and raped me, and last night, my father planned to kill me. My loyalties lie with the Russos and my brother, who's now the head of the Murphy Clan. You can either accept that or not but I'm not going anywhere." She shrugs her shoulders, turning her back to everyone, dismissing them.

"I'll wait in the office." Her eyes connect with each of ours. "Come alone." And they're filled with wicked desire. The three of us watch her walk away and I take a deep breath, cooling myself. I need to finish this quickly.

Chapter Thirty-Eight

Riona

I'm not going to ever tell the guys, but I needed to get out of
the room because my head is pounding. I make my way up to the
office and head straight for the bathroom, hoping to find some
aspirin. Tylenol sits right in the middle of the medicine cabinet and I
quickly take a few. Keeping the lights off in the office, I walk over
to the tinted glass that looks over the club. They command
everyone's attention as they talk and I wish it wasn't soundproof.

Now, I love my men when they're loving and soft but I also
love when they're the mafia bosses they were born to be with their
serious and dangerous expressions. Dante has a take-no-shit look on

his face that gets my blood pumping and my defiant side wanting to come out. Matteo looks deadly, like he'll tear anyone apart for even breathing, which has my thighs clenching, waiting for his rough hands on my body. Enzo, my quiet one, has his classic stone expression, not showing what he's thinking while taking in everything. I just want to walk into his arms and run my hands over his face until the stone relaxes.

Wanting to give them a surprise when they come up, I head over to their closet. Pulling out one of Dante's shirts, Matteo's jackets, and Enzo's ties, I head to the back of the room just to be safe. No one is supposed to be able to see in here but I'm not taking any chances with so many people downstairs.

I let all of my clothes fall to the floor before I slide Dante's shirt over my arms and only button the middle button. Pulling Matteo's jacket on next, I roll up the shirt and jacket sleeves together and then flip the shirt and jacket open giving a wide, deep V over my chest. Lastly, I tie Enzo's tie around my neck so it's pulled tight at my throat. I really wish I had some heels with me.

As I walk across the office, I turn on a few lamps so there is a soft light. The meeting must be over because the majority of the men and women are gone, leaving a few working around the club or talking to my guys. Giddiness spreads through me for what they'll think when they walk in. As if they can feel me watching them, they look up from the man who spoke up earlier and somehow find me behind the tinted glass. I take a step back as they say their goodbyes to the final few people.

Pulling out Dante's chair, I take a seat and prop my feet up on the desk with my ankles crossed. I make sure the bottom opening of the shirt and jacket splits right over my left thigh and place my hands on my stomach, waiting for them to appear.

Matteo is the first one through the door with Enzo and Dante right behind him. They see me instantly and Dante reaches behind him, locking the door.

"How did the rest of the meeting go?"

"Who cares?" Matteo says eagerly.

"Fine," Enzo adds.

"You've won them over," Dante says as he moves around his brothers, scanning me from head to toe. "They loved your bluntness... And I love how great you look right now." His hand starts at my foot and runs all the way up my leg. "But..." He grabs my hips, lifting me onto the desk and he takes the seat. "This is how I've envisioned you at my desk."

He smiles up at me with heat in his eyes as his hands run up my inner thighs, opening me up for him. "You wouldn't get much done with me on your desk like this."

A chill runs through me as his thumbs run down my folds spreading me open for him to see. His eyes on me have me squirming in anticipation but his hands hold me still.

"Lay back, Rose, and let me show you how serious I take my work." I lay back on the desk and find Enzo and Matteo waiting for me.

"Let us worship you, Beauty." Enzo smiles down at me as his hand slides down between my breasts and unbuttons the one button. "I want to see all of you." The shirt falls open with the jacket and three mouths descend on me.

Matteo's mouth catches my moans in a deep passionate kiss as my back arches off the desk, pushing my breasts against Enzo's mouth and grinding my core against Dante's.

I wrap my hand around the back of Matteo's neck, bringing him somehow closer to me and my other goes into Enzo's hair, gripping tightly. My body feels like it's about to explode from the fireworks of pleasure.

Dante sucks my clit between his lips and grazes the bundle of nerves with his teeth as he pushes two fingers into me.

"Oh fuck." I rip away from Matteo's kiss as I squeeze my thighs around Dante's head.

"Scream for us, Princess. Let everyone here know you're our lady." Matteo kisses down to the breast that has been left untouched.

Matteo kisses all around it, getting closer to my nipple, but when I think he's going to finally touch my hard nipple, he starts licking away, teasing me. I want to groan at that, but on my other breast, Enzo bites down on my nipple at the same time so the sound that comes out of me is a mix between a gasp, groan, and scream.

"Are you going to come for us, Beauty?"

"I'm so close." I thrash my head back and forth as I hold all three of them to me. "Please."

"Is this what you need?" Matteo finally flicks his tongue against my nipple and I start falling. "Yes." All three of them bring my body into a screaming, intense orgasm from their three different touches. None of them remove their mouths from me until the orgasm rolls through me and I'm pushing them away.

With my eyes still closed from the orgasm, soft lips touch mine and I instantly know it's Enzo. Before I can take it further, he pulls away, making my eyes shoot open and Matteo is there taking his spot. But once again he pulls away before I'm ready.

Dante draws my attention as he places a kiss to my stomach. "How are you feeling?" I know he's asking about my head, but I answer his underlying question.

"Like I'm nowhere close to being done." I raise up on my elbows looking down at him, seeing his pants already open. Placing my heels on the edge of the desk, I spread my legs open more. "So, what are you going to do about it?"

Dante shoots from his chair as he slams his lips to mine and pulls me all the way to the edge. My center rubs against his open pants but that's not what I want. Reaching forward, I slide my hand into his boxers and wrap my hand around his dick. He helps me free his erection and I line him up with my entrance. Not waiting a second, Dante thrusts all the way in until our pelvises meet and we both let out pleasurable moans against each other's lips. I reach up to wrap my arms around Dante's neck, but the jacket and shirt stop me since they have fallen down to my elbows.

Hands touch my arms as I try pushing the jacket and shirt off and they pull them off. I squeeze their fingers as they pull the final bit off and then wrap my arms around Dante. He kisses down my neck as his thrusts pick up and I can't help but to cling to him. I bring my knees higher up his sides and use my heels against his ass so I can meet each of his thrusts and grind my clit against him.

Looking down, I watch where we're connected and my body sparks in pure pleasure. "You feel so good, Rose." He places his fingers under my chin, tilting my head up so I'm looking right in his blue eyes. "You're made for me." His hand drops from my chin and slowly skims down my neck, over my shoulder, and down until my breast sits in his hand. "Now scream for me."

With our eyes connected, he powers into me, taking my breath away with each thrust, and I lose myself as he rubs circles on my clit. I scream out his name just as he wanted as I tighten around him. He's right there with me as I feel him swelling inside me right before he comes with a groan as he slams his lips back to mine. We steal breath from each other as we come down from our highs.

A pair of lips pressed against my shoulders has me pulling back from my kiss with Dante and loosening my hold on him. I look back over my shoulder to find a naked Enzo smiling down at me and a naked Matteo standing a few steps back fisting his cock.

Enzo skims his lips up my neck. "You feeling good?" I nod my head, not able to talk.

"You want to come have some fun with us?" My heart beats faster as he says us because I love taking them at once. I nod again with a heated smile and his eyes blaze in desire.

Dante places a kiss to my cheek as he pulls out of me and I look back at him. Before he can pull away further, I grab his shirt and press my lips to his, not ready to break our connection. My connection with Dante is different, just like I have separate connections to each of them, but Dante's and I's always feels like it's fragile or toeing a line. I don't think it'll ever break, but when we're both this open, we need to reassure our feelings since we both are stubborn and like to push the other.

Arms wrapping around my back and under my thighs pull me away from him and the desk and I reluctantly let him go, but before our connection is broken, I mouth 'I love you'. His smile brightens as he mouths the same words, falling back into his seat. My body warms knowing he's not leaving.

I smile up at Enzo as I run my fingers through his blonde hair. "Where are you taking me?"

"Not far." A warm body presses against my other side and I smile over at Matteo. I reach out and touch Matteo's chest and run my hand up and around the back of his neck. "Now that you have me, what are you going to do with me?"

Enzo sets me down so my back is to his chest and my front is against Matteo's. Lips press along my neck from behind as Matteo pulls me into a passionate kiss. A pair of hands run up my sides as another glides over my shoulders and down my arms. I tighten my hold on Matteo pressing closer to him as I deepen our kiss and reach for Enzo, running my hand down his forearm. "We're going down memory lane, Beauty." Enzo pulls back from my neck and I break my kiss with Matteo and he gives me a wickedly heated grin.

"Just this time together."

Flashes of our second night together fill my mind. God, I want that and them so bad. Enzo reads my desire and quickly closes the distance between us, kissing me desperately.

"Oh, she definitely likes this idea." Matteo kisses across my collarbone as his hands grope my breasts, kneading them.

Running my hand down Matteo's chest to his hard erection, I shift my hold on Enzo so I'm holding him to our kiss and grinding my ass back against him. Enzo grips my hips tighter with one hand using my ass cheeks to rub himself off while the other goes to my clit. A flicker of fear tries to rise but I quickly push away because I'm loving that he's using me for his pleasure.

Matteo helps me wrap my hand around his erection and I slowly pull up his length until I reach his head and after a quick sweep of my thumb over the top, I slowly slide my hand down, teasing him. With each stroke, I go a little bit faster until I'm jerking him off just how he likes it with a strong grip and steady rhythm. They work me up quickly, switching off on kissing and touching me everywhere until I'm about to come. But right when I'm there and they're growing harder, ready to explode, they stop.

"Fuck, Princess. The plan is to come in your pretty mouth, not your hand."

I feel Enzo move behind me as he sits and he runs his hands up and over my ass cheeks. "Come sit on my cock, Ri." With his support, I climb backwards onto the couch so my knees are on either side of his thighs and I'm hovering right over his erection. With his chest pressed to my back and his hands on my hips, he slowly lowers me onto him. Being full of Enzo's cock is one of the best feelings, along with his brother's cocks, that I let out a hum and relax into him.

"Fucking perfect," Enzo whispers into my ear and he slowly thrusts into me as he holds my breast, pinching the nipple, and flicking my clit with his other hand. Pleasure shooting straight through me, ramping me back up, has me moaning out loud.

"Damn it. I love hearing all the noises you make but I'm feeling a little left out." Matteo steps in front of me with his erection at eye level and I shift forward so I have one hand on Enzo's knee for support and wrap my other hand around Matteo.

"No one is left out, Bear." I wrap my lips around Matteo's erection and pull him in all the way to the back of my throat before sucking him back out. I toy with him for a little bit as I slowly ride Enzo, licking him like a lollipop and getting used to the two of them together like this. Matteo runs his fingers through my hair, making sure not to touch the side I was hit on, before he takes a fist full. I wrap my lips around his erection again as Enzo grips my hips tighter and thrusts up into me. I moan around Matteo as Enzo hits just the right spot.

"Fuck," Matteo groans and I look up at him, finding him looking back at me with so much fiery lust that a shiver of pleasure rolls through me. I let them both take control of my body, setting the pace and taking what they need. I meet Enzo's thrusts, bouncing down on his cock, while sucking Matteo's large cock and flicking my tongue over his tip.

"You love having my brother's cock in your mouth as I fuck you, don't you?" Enzo's lips skim over my ear as he continues to fuck me. "No need to answer, Beauty. I can feel you squeezing around me." Enzo runs a finger down my spine but stops before getting to my ass. "One day, whenever you're ready, all three of us are going to fuck you. You will be filled up completely with us." A wave of pleasure rolls through at that image and I can't help to look sideways at Dante who has dark desire in his eyes as he strokes his hardened cock. My wanting moan is muffled but they all heard how much I want that.

"I want you to come thinking about riding me, with Matteo in your ass and Dante in your mouth." Enzo starts thrusting into me faster as he rubs my clit and Matteo grips my hair tighter, taking his release as wave after wave of pleasure courses through me, causing me to scream out. Matteo is the first to come, filling my mouth and I swallow it down quickly as Enzo comes shooting up inside me. Matteo's dick pops out of my mouth as I fall back on Enzo's chest, exhausted. Enzo holds me to him as he runs his hands over my body and places soft kisses along my hairline, comforting me.

This right here is my connection to Enzo. His loving, romantic touches where no words are needed. Like I'm the only one that can truly read him. I turn toward him, capturing his lips with mine, reciprocating his love through my kiss. Pulling away, I give him one last kiss before climbing off his lap and grabbing Matteo's hand, who's sitting on the other couch. "Come shower with me."

Matteo stands and quickly picks me up so I'm cuddled to his chest as he carries me into the bathroom. Matteo is my cuddler. He's my teddy bear. I want to be wrapped up in his big arms all the time and that's actually where he wants me to be. He sets me down to turn on the shower and I wrap my arms around his middle, resting my head on his chest. "I love you, Bear."

He wraps his arms around my shoulders, hugging me to him. "I love you too, Princess."

We shuffle into the shower without letting go and as we wash each other, there isn't a single point where we don't have at least one part of us touching the other.

Enzo and Dante are waiting for us fully dressed once we walk out of the bathroom, dressed as well. I give them each a kiss and without a word we head out of the office with Dante in front, Matteo with his arm around my shoulders, and Enzo holding my hand.

Chapter Thirty-Nine

Riona

Aisling rushes toward me with a huge smile on her face as we walk into the house. "Hi!" She grabs my hand and pulls me away from Matteo's hold around my shoulders. "Sorry guys, I get Ri tonight. We need a girl's night."

"We do?"

She beams back at me as she pulls me to the stairs. "Yeah, we do."

I shrug my shoulders as I look back at my guys, who are chuckling at Aisling's excited urgency. "I thought we were dealing with Lorcan tonight."

"Nah. He can suffer down there like I did. Right now, I'm really happy we didn't get rid of the sound system and blinding lights." A wicked smile pulls across her face and I love her vengeful ideas.

I follow her up the stairs and into her and Killian's room to find the bed covered in wedding magazines and *Say Yes to the Dress* playing on the TV. She turns toward me, bouncing excitedly. "We picked a date!"

"Finally!" I hug her tightly. "So, when are you walking down the aisle?" We release each other and crawl onto the bed.

"New Year's Eve. It's going to be an all-day affair. We want two ceremonies. A formal one with the families and then an intimate one at night with a party." Aisling picks up her tablet and looks through Pinterest as I pick up a magazine.

Wow, two weddings to plan in three months. "That's a lot and not a lot of time."

She smiles. "That's why I needed a girl's night."

"Well, where do we start?" One night isn't going to help. We need a month.

"Venue is set. Murphy mansion for the morning and here for the intimate evening."

I nod. "Perfect. We'll get that ballroom looking fantastic, no more dark wood, and we can use the back courtyard here."

"That's what I was thinking. I already called Helen Moore and she's clearing her schedule so she can get everything planned. So, we need to decide on flowers, color scheme, decorations, and where we're going to get our dresses." Okay maybe not a month with Helen as the planner.

Now dresses, I got that covered. "Let me call in some favors with a certain designer for the dresses."

"Simone Castle?" We smile at each other.

We live in New York City. Of course I'm calling the best wedding dress designer in the city. "Of course."

Aisling claps. "So exciting. So, I'm thinking of the Murphy crest color scheme for the first one and Gatsby-themed for the second one. I want our friends in tuxes and flapper dresses while they watch Killian and I say our vows and party into the New Year."

"Yes. Ideas are already coming to mind." We huddle together for the next couple of hours, snacking on the food the guys bring up, and figuring out everything for their meeting with Helen Moore, at least until Killian comes up.

"Alright, time to go to your own room. I need to celebrate with my fiancée." The heated look he has as he looks at Aisling has me hurrying out of the bed and out of the room.

That isn't something I want to witness. Aisling's giggling squeals as I'm closing the door has me making a fake barfing sound. "Gross."

Something hits the back of the door. "Get the fuck out of here. Go to your own side of the house." The sound of their giggles brings a smile to my face as I make my way to my room. Even though Killian is now the head of the Irish mafia, I know that Aisling will keep the light in his life so he never turns into our father.

My room is dark when I step inside, but I can see my guys asleep. I strip down to my panties as I move across the room until I'm standing over Enzo sleeping on the couch. Bending down, I run my fingers through his hair and place a kiss on his lips. He stirs and I smile down at him as his eyes open. "Come to bed."

I slide my hand down his arm to his hand and pull. He sits up and sleepily follows me to the bed. I let go of his hand as I climb into the middle of the bed between Matteo and Dante. Matteo is sleeping on the other side of the pillow barrier so I pull those away and hand them to Enzo who's now standing by the side of the bed, waiting for Matteo to move.

I place soft kisses across Matteo's cheek until I reach his ear. "Rollover Bear. Come snuggle with me so Enzo can lay down." Matteo follows me as I roll over into Dante's chest.

Dante's arm comes out from underneath me and wraps around my back, holding me to him, as Matteo's arm goes around my waist, wrapping his body to mine. I relax into their holds and start drifting to sleep. The last thing I remember before slipping into a beautiful dream is Dante's lips kissing the top of my head and Matteo's pressed to my shoulder.

Chapter Forty

Riona

Lorcan has been down in the basement for nine days, living through the torture Aisling did, living off only water and a few scraps of food. And while he's slowly losing his mind, we've spent the time dismantling everything of his. It's like old times. Killian is doing business. The twins run off to get our needs stocked. Aisling switches between Killian's sounding board, designing the Murphy mansion, and bringing Miss Claus back with the girls and helping set up the new girls. And I do what I do best. I track down the last of Lorcan's allies and permanently erase them. But what makes things so much better than old times is coming home to Matteo, Enzo, and

Dante after they have been out taking back the reins of their organization.

Tonight though, we're taking the night off to finally end everything with Lorcan. I follow Killian and Aisling down the stairs to the basement with Matteo, Enzo, and Dante behind me. As we enter the hallway outside the room, I can hear the screaming music through the concrete walls and a smile spreads across my face. I haven't seen my father since the night at the party and I can't wait to see how broken he is.

Killian pulls out the key and unlocks the door. The music turns from a low muffle to my ears ringing from screaming rock as the door opens and, within seconds, the music stops. Aisling has her phone out and I'm glad she had control on what happens in this room.

Killian steps back, letting Aisling and myself in first and the sight of my frustrated and dirty father is a shock. He's still in his clothes from the party but they're now dirty and torn and hang from his thinning body.

He looks up with rage in his eyes as we stand in a line in front of him tied to a chair. "My kids are such pussies that they have to tie me up to come see me." A wicked smile pulls across his face and I want to punch it away.

"The chair is for your comfort. But if you prefer, we can make you kneel as we kill you." Killian pulls out his phone like he's about to call someone to remove Lorcan from the chair and hold him on his knees.

"You're right, this chair is very comfortable." His smile turns fake, but I can tell it would mortify him to kneel in front of us. I'm tempted to have Killian still call his guys but I just want to get this over with.

I step forward. "Well now that you're comfortable, I have a burning question. You blame me for your downfall, but this all started with Aisling's kidnapping, which you orchestrated and gave our location to O'Brien. But what I can't understand is why? If you wanted the Russos dead and me married to Maxim, why send me with them? Why take Aisling?"

"O'Brien ruined everything. He was supposed to kill Aisling to get her out of the way. My deal with the Russians was for Killian and Kiera to get married." He glares at Aisling and Killian growls as he steps in front of her.

"I was going to honor my deal with the Russos for your hand in marriage, but O'Brien found out she was family. Plans had to change when you saved her. My deal with the Russians was too important."

I look back to Killian and Aisling and they both give me a nod. I pull out my knife from my back pocket and walk three steps until I'm right in front of my father.

"What are you going to do with that, Ri? You going to skin me alive? You going to slit my throat?" He taunts me. Or at least he tries.

"No." In a swift motion I stab the knife down into his left shoulder right above his collarbone. He groans in pain as he bites down on his lips, stopping his screams. I lean down so we're eye to eye as I pull out the blade. "That was for having me kidnapped by Tony." His eyes blaze but before he can say anything, I slam my knife in the same spot but on his right.

A groaned "fuck" slips through his lips as he glares at me.

"That was for everything that happened to me while I was with Maxim."

I pull the knife out, bringing it back close to my body ready to strike out again. "This is for Mom."

"Your mother deserved to die. You know my rules, Riona. She betrayed me. She betrayed us when she got into bed with my piece of shit best friend. They signed their death certificates when they tried to take Killian from me."

"You lost her and us because of the monster you are." I swing out and slice him across his stomach. As he groans out in pain, I stand up and reach out sideways with the knife and Aisling wraps her hand around mine, taking it. I step back until I feel my guys warming my back. I don't reach out for them, but knowing they're there settles me.

Aisling twirls the knife in her hand. "This shouldn't be a surprise." She slices deep down his right forearm from elbow to wrist. "This is for my father." She switches to his left arm and presses it deep into his skin. "And this is for having me kidnapped and trying to have me killed."

Lorcan's blood seeps from his wounds and drops to the floor and my guys walk around me. Aisling passes the knife to Dante and my guys swiftly stab Lorcan in the stomach only once, one after the other, without saying a word. Enzo drops the knife on the floor and the brothers walk away, heading toward the door, and I take one last look at my father, bleeding through his shirt, turning it red.

He's slumped over in pain, but he still has his angry glare that he shoots at each of us. Out of the corner of my eye, I see Killian pull out his gun and I turn, heading for the door giving both Aisling and Killian an encouraging smile. This is Killian and Aisling's time. Only they can take this shot and fully take the power.

"Do you have the balls to kill me, Killian?" My father's words try to cut into Killian, but I know they won't. I hear the gun cock back as I reach Dante, who's holding the door open for me. "You can't stomach watching your brother kill me, Ri? I trained you better than that. I want you to watch me die." Without looking back, I grab Dante's hand and we join Matteo and Enzo in the hall and head toward the stairs. "Riona, you better come back here...Riona!"

I flinch at the sound of the gunshot and Dante squeezes my hand tighter and a tear runs down my cheek. My father died screaming my name and our good times flash in my mind. All the dances we shared, all the games we used to play to see who had better skills, and our father-daughter days, where he would do whatever I wanted. Before these last couple of months, my connection with my father was strong where I relied a lot on him and wanted to spend time with him.

Tears pour out of me unexpectedly as we climb the stairs and as soon as we step onto the kitchen floor, Dante pulls me into his chest. I wrap my arms tightly around him as I let go and the warmth at my back tells me Matteo and Enzo are there too. Dante runs his fingers through my hair as he presses his lips to the top of my head and one of the other's hands runs up and down my back as the other kisses my shoulder.

"Let it out, Beauty. We've got you."

Through my sobs, I say, "I don't know why I'm so upset. I wanted him dead."

"Rose, you're allowed to mourn the side of your father that you loved."

"I just didn't think I'd be this upset." I look up resting my chin on Dante's chest.

He runs his thumbs across my cheeks, wiping away my tears and I can see the love in his eyes, telling me he's got me. That they got me.

"Riona." The sound of my brother's voice has me looking to my right and the second I see his red eyes, I slip out of my guy's arms and move over to my brother and Aisling. "I'm so sorry you had to do that."

Killian pulls me into a hug. "For what he did to you and Aisling, I'd do it over a million times."

"I love you, Kill."

"I love you too, Ri."

"Aww." Aisling steps up behind me and hugs me too. "I love you guys, too!"

"Bear hug," Matteo yells out before he joins in and a chuckle breaks out of me as he forces us all to sway a little bit.

Dante and Enzo pull him off of us, chuckling, but Matteo doesn't let me go, pulling me into his arms, which I happily go to.

"No more crying, Princess." He kisses the top of my head.

"He's right. Let's drink." Aisling holds her hands in the air with champagne bottles in each hand. Killian takes one and Dante takes the other and magically Enzo appears with glasses. The sound of the bottles popping makes me jump but I scream out in excitement with Aisling. We all take a glass, holding them together, waiting for them to be filled. A silence falls over us once our glasses are filled as we smile at each other.

"To our future," Killian calls out.

"May it be filled with happiness and new beginnings," Aisling adds.

"To love," I look at each of my guys.

"To family," Enzo adds.

"To the city," Matteo calls out.

"To us and our unbreakable bond," Dante finishes and we all clink our glasses together as we cheers, "To us."

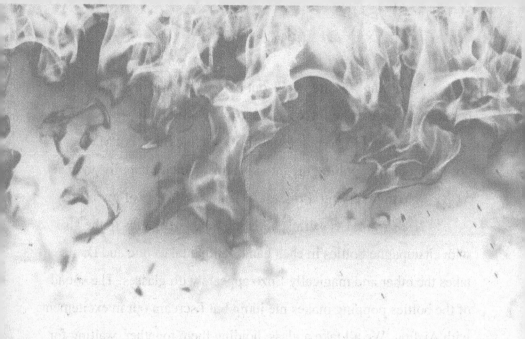

Epilogue

Riona

Two months later

"You better be done with whatever you're doing because we're sweeping you away for the weekend." A smile spreads across my face as I swivel my computer chair around to face a smiling Enzo who's leaning against the doorway to our combined offices.

"And where are you sweeping me away to?"

He pushes off the doorway and slowly walks toward me as I lean back in my chair and rest my hands over my stomach.

"You're going to have to lock up and come with me to find out." He leans down on the chair's armrests with his hands so he's face to face with me. "I think we should take that ride you promised me." He smirks at me and holds up the Bugatti keys. I pull him toward me and our lips crash together in a passionate, excited kiss.

` "Only two people fit in that car." I look up into his eyes that are only inches from mine.

"Yeah, you and me. Matteo and Dante are already on their way. I get some alone time with you." He picks me up out of the chair so I'm standing on my feet and turns me toward my computers. "Now lock-up." I bend over, locking everything up and Enzo takes the opportunity to run his hand over my ass and grab a handful.

I playfully slap his hand away. "I'm sure you'll get plenty of that this weekend. You don't need to get handsy now."

My computer screens go dark and I turn so I'm facing him but his hands never leave my ass. "I'll never get enough of you, Beauty." He squeezes my ass with both hands as he pulls me up against him. "Any part."

"You're not talking like you're wanting to leave right now." I run my hands up his arms and over his shoulders.

"You're very distracting." He runs his lips down my neck and then steps back out of reach. "But we have special plans for you tonight, so we can't be late."

He pulls me from our office and out toward the front door. The Bugatti is sitting in the driveway as we step outside and the front door closes and locks behind us. "Who's driving?" I look up at him and hold out my hand and he shakes his head no.

"I'm driving, as you promised." He opens the passenger door for me. "Plus, you don't know where we're going." I slide into the passenger seat, and he closes the door. I watch him walk around the front of the car and slide into the driver's seat.

The car purrs to life and he smiles over at me and shifts it into first. "Are you ready?" I nod excitedly and he floors it out of the driveway and onto the street. I let out an excited squeal and relax back into the seat.

It doesn't take me long to figure out we're heading toward the Hamptons as Enzo speeds down the highway, not giving a care about the speed limit. I enjoy the feeling of the engine's vibration as I reach over to Enzo's thigh and close my eyes. I only open up my eyes when the car finally slows and I'm greeted with beautiful sandy beaches and the town of East Hampton. Summer has already ended and fall is in full swing but the beaches still have people on them, soaking up the last of the warm weather.

"I haven't been to the Hamptons in years." I smile over at Enzo, and he smiles at me as he pulls into a driveway with a quaint beach cottage sitting directly on the beach. "Well get an eye-full now because I can't promise you'll get much of a look other than from our bedroom."

"You brought me all the way here to get me into bed?"

"We brought you here to get 48 hours of just you. No interruptions." Enzo parks behind the Range Rover. "Do you have any complaints about that?"

I shake my head no and he pulls me into a quick kiss. "Then let's get inside to see what my brothers have been up to." We separate from each other and get out of the car, and he meets me in front of the Bugatti.

I take his outreached hand and follow him up the stairs to the white two-story cottage with blue shutters. "Whose place is this?"

"Ours." He looks down at me with a happy smile.

I look back at the cottage with more scrutiny. It seems too homey for them. "It doesn't seem like your style."

"We bought it like this. Wanted the location and didn't care about the look. We rent the place out most of the summer and get some legit income from that. After the summer rush, we like to come up and spend time here."

"I like it. Looks very relaxing."

"Good. We can come up here whenever you want." He opens up the blue front door and I freeze in the doorway. With the sun setting behind Matteo and Dante, the room is glowing with candles. Enzo pulls me into the house so the door can close behind me and he lets go of my hand to stand next to his brothers.

"From the moment you stormed into our kitchen and threw knives at Enzo, I knew you were a perfect match for me. I asked you that night to marry me and while it took you a while to answer, you told me I needed to ask you for real. Well, here it is." I gasp as I cover my mouth and watch as he goes down on one knee and holds out his hand for me. Slowly, I walk toward him and place my hand in his. I look at Dante and Enzo, seeing love in their eyes before looking down at Matteo, who's smiling up at me.

"Princess, you're my everything. Your crazy fits perfectly with mine and you bring out this softness I never knew I had. I couldn't imagine not spending the rest of my life without you, sleeping next to me, stealing kisses from you, killing all the creeps together, and holding you in my arms. Please make sure that never happens. Marry me?"

I start nodding before he even asks the question. "Yes, of course, Bear." Matteo shoots up from his kneeling position and slams his lips to mine and I melt into him, showing him how much I love him.

When we pull apart, Enzo is standing to my right with a hand out. I didn't think it was possible to smile harder but somehow, I do as I take his hand and he kneels in front of me. "Beauty, the moment I first saw you I knew you were special. Your beauty is unmatched, but your smile makes you shine. Any man would kneel for you to just direct that smile at him. Please let me be one of your lucky men who gets to make you smile for the rest of your life. Will you marry me?"

He smiles up at me and I nod as I smile down at him. "Yeah, Beast. I'll marry you."

He stands in front of me and places his hands on either side of my face and wipes his thumbs across my cheeks. Tears I didn't even know I had shed start rolling down my cheeks, but I don't care. All I care about is Enzo and the love in his eyes. I reach out for him, and he closes the distance between us. Our kiss is slow but deep and I can feel him all the way to my toes. When we pull back from each other, I can feel Dante's eyes burning into the side of my face, but I don't look at him. I keep my eyes focused on Enzo who happily soaks up my attention, knowing I'm just riling Dante up.

Dante doesn't last long before a growl escapes him and I give Enzo a wink, making him chuckle as I turn to Dante. "So, you're last?"

Dante pulls me to him with fire in his eyes. "Riona, I love your fire. I love how you fight me at every turn and I love that you bring light to my darkness. Marry me, Rose, and drive me crazy for the rest of our lives."

I shrug my shoulders as I give him a teasing smile. "Yeah, I think I can work with that."

He pulls me tighter against him and tilts my chin up, so I'm forced to look up at him. "I need you to say yes."

"Are you not going to kneel?" I bite the inside of my cheek to stop my smile.

"Do you need me to kneel?"

"It wouldn't hurt." I smile down at him as he lowers himself to the ground. "Yes." I fall to my knees with him. "Yes, Boss Man."

He pulls me into a kiss that I lose myself in for a few seconds as we fight for control. He nips my bottom lip and I let go, letting him have all of me. Dante leans forward, pushing me to the ground as he climbs between my legs. "Now… now. You're missing a step." I wiggle my fingers on my left hand in between our faces. He reaches into his pocket as we both sit up and pulls out a three stone ring on a white gold band. "Are you referring to this?"

I smile and nod, loving that there are three rectangular diamonds. Two smaller ones on either side of the larger one. It's like I got a diamond from each of them. "It's beautiful." I hold my hand out and he slides it on my finger.

The weight of it feels like I'm finally complete. "I love you." I pull him into another kiss. Dante stands with me in his arms, and when my toes touch the ground, I pull back from our kiss and turn to Enzo. "I love you."

He pulls me to him, and we share a kiss until I'm pulled away and held in Matteo's arms. "Tell me too."

I look back at him, smiling. "I love you."

A possessive smile pulls on his face. "Good, because you're ours now. You'll never be free of us." He slams his lips to mine in a deep quick kiss.

"I'm okay with that. Now who's going to show me this bedroom I've been promised not to leave?"

"Oh, I've got you, Princess." He sweeps me off my feet just as my phone starts to ring.

"Wait. Put me down. I need to check that."

"Nope, no work." Matteo starts walking toward the stairs.

"Put me down, Matteo." He freezes mid-step and looks at me to see if I'm serious. After a second, he puts me down and I place a kiss on his cheek. "Thank you." I pull my phone from my back pocket and see Stella's name. I swipe my thumb across the screen to answer but I'm too late; the call disconnects. I try to call her back, but it goes straight to voicemail.

My phone vibrates in my hand and a voicemail alert pops up. I bring the phone to my ear expecting something about the club, but my veins turn cold when I hear her terrified voice. "He's back."

The only *he* she could be referring to is Nance Cunningham. Her stepbrother. Her captor. Her abuser. Her husband. He vanished the night we took down his high end brothel, saving her and several other women, and if he's back, it's for her.

I quickly try to call her again, but it goes straight to voicemail like before. I try her office phone next and it just rings and rings. "Shit." I can feel the guys' attention on me, but I don't look up from my phone as I pull up Tanner's contact.

It rings three times before he picks up. "Hey Ri..."

"Tanner, please tell me you're with Stella right now."

"No, she's at the club."

"Fuck." I run my fingers through my hair.

"What's wrong, Ri?" Panic fills his voice.

"I just got a voicemail from her. Her stepbrother is back."

The End

Thank you so much for reading the Set the World on Fire Duet. Stella's story is next so please follow me for any future updates. I would be honored if you had the time to write a brief review letting me know what you thought.

Acknowledgements

First, I want to thank my family and friends for their support while writing this duet. These are my first dark themed books I've written and when I needed some brightness to clear the dark world I was creating, they were always there.

Next, I want to thank my adorable dog, Mia. She has been my partner throughout the entire writing process either laying on my lap or demanding my attention when the words are just flowing out of me.

Finally, the readers. You're the reason I write the stories in my head down. It's great to know there are people out there that have the same reading preferences that I do.

About the Author

E. Molgaard was born and raised in North Carolina. She currently lives in Raleigh, NC with her dog Mia. When she isn't writing you can find her curled up with her dog watching her favorite shows or hanging out with her friends and family.

She became an avid reader after college, which inspired her to start writing down the stories she imagined.

Connect with E. Molgaard

Instagram
TikTok
Author Profile on Goodreads
Amazon Author Profile
Facebook Author Page

Also by E. Molgaard

Hockey Romances

Love on Ice Series

Checking for Love
Saving My Heart
Fighting Attraction

Skate With Me Series

Wake Me Up
Talk to Me
Return to Me

Police Officer Romances

Forever Us Series

Wanting Us
Secretly Us
Wonderfully Us

Reverse Harem Romances

Set the World on Fire Duet

Ignite the Fire
Watch it Burn

Stained with Ash

Printed in the USA
CPSIA information can be obtained
at www.ICGtesting.com
LVHW031649091123
763115LV00085B/703